The Galactic Mage Series

Book 1: The Galactic Mage
Book 2: Rift in the Races
Book 3: Hostiles
Book 4: Alien Arrivals (out mid-2014)

Prequels

Ilbei Spadebreaker and the Harpy's Wild
Ilbei Spadebreaker and the Zombie Apple Collapse
(in progress)

John Daulton
www.DaultonBooks.com

ILBEI SPADEBREAKER AND THE HARPY'S WILD

John Daulton

East Baton Rouge Parish Library
Baton Rouge, Louisiana

ILBEI SPADEBREAKER AND THE HARPY'S WILD
A Galactic Mage Series prequel

The phrase "The Galactic Mage" is the trademark of John Daulton.

ISBN-13: 978-0-9894787-2-4 (Paperback)

ISBN-13: 978-0-9894787-3-1(Kindle Ebook)

ISBN-13: 978-0-9894787-4-8 (Ebook)

Cover art by Cris Ortega

Interior layout by Fernando Soria

DEDICATION

In loving memory of Uncle Jim.

Chapter 1

Jasper's jump was terrible. Less than a pace and a half of water separated the riverbank from the weathered gray planks of the raft, and yet the misaligned mage missed that craft by as far as he would have had he been trying to jump the whole river. He'd given it a go, of course, and he flung himself forward headlong, fully committed, his frail body parallel to the water and already falling short before his feet left the mud. He soared—if such failure might be so described—for less than a moment, achieving an altitude so scant that his toes dragged the surface, arresting what little momentum he had and dooming his launch. He reached for the raft, head up, eyes wide, mouth wider. His face hit the planks with a thud, and his hands clapped two drumbeats on the wood. His skull rebounded, throwing him backward, where he slid into the water, the last things visible his pale palms, held up as if he'd surrendered to indignity. And, of course, Kaige and Meggins laughed.

Sergeant Ilbei Spadebreaker saw it happen and harrumphed, then bent at the waist to shrug off his chainmail. He was a muscular fellow, broad across the shoulders, extremely so, and, admittedly, broad across the belly—though that was a different sort of girth, which he

1

blamed on alehouses and eateries. But despite his bulk, the heavy rings came off easily, being a practiced exercise, and they slid over his head and down his powerful arms with a metallic hiss, pouring onto the riverbank like a slurry of silver coins. He straightened and quickly undid the brass buckle that held his weapons belt in place beneath his rounded middle. It fell to the grass, and a moment after, he was in the water, his dive timed neatly with Jasper's place in the current so that the scrawny sorcerer was just tumbling by.

The water was dark and gray, the silt stirred up and cloudy, churning with the confluence of two tributaries whose flow was only marginally diminished by the late summer sun. Ilbei dove under and looked around for the washed-away wizard. He saw the flash of a white leg, the angle of a foot flitting by. He reached for it, grasping the boney shin in a grip made powerful by a life of soldiering and toil. He hauled the young wizard to him, and then, with a few strokes and a few kicks, he got them both back to the riverbank.

The mud was slick and the grass slicker, but with some effort, Ilbei crawled up the bank, dragging his catch behind him like a wet sack of sticks. Once Jasper was out of the river, Ilbei turned back, shaking his head at what he saw. The exposed body of the mage was barely more than bones rattling beneath pale skin, as white as the belly of a frog. He wondered how a kid like that got through boot camp at all, knowing even as he thought it that it didn't matter how, since the mages always made it through. They had to. The Queen's law, and that was that. Every platoon got a wizard, whether they wanted one or not, and no matter what the magician could or couldn't do. So Jasper was Ilbei's new wizard.

Ilbei watched the sodden sorcerer lying there and let go a long breath. They hadn't even started the mission yet. But at least the skinny kid was still breathing. "Get up," Ilbei said. "Ya ain't dead yet."

Jasper sat up, the wet cloth of his robes clinging to him and revealing the wicker cage of his body beneath. His hood had somehow got up over his head, and it lay upon his face, looking as if molded from dark blue phyllo dough. Through it, Ilbei could see the movements of the magician's eyes as he blinked and tried to get his bearings. He expected young Jasper to cry out, but the wizard did not. Instead, he peeled the wet fabric away and stared up at Ilbei, bewilderment upon him like a pox. "I was certain I had planned that jump correctly. I hardly understand why it didn't work." His voice broke some as he spoke, a pubescent warble, though Ilbei knew he had to be in his late teens or early twenties. The army wouldn't take them any younger than that.

"Well," said Ilbei, reaching a hand down to help the fellow up, "from where I sat, didn't look like ya planned it at all. I seen box turtles jump farther'n that."

Jasper regarded Ilbei's hand suspended in the space above him, contemplation creasing his countenance as he considered what Ilbei had said. A moment after, he looked up and remarked, "Well that can't be true. Not even the Solbax-Ferrund box turtles in the southern marshes of Dae can jump that far, and they have the best skeletal structure for it. While it is possible that, in a state of agitation, they might manage some marginal degree of lift, it couldn't possibly be considered a ju—"

Ilbei cut him off by bending down and lifting him to his feet, gripping him by both shoulders and standing him up as easily as if he were a child. He did it so quickly, and with such easy strength, that the didactic spell caster simply blinked at him, his mouth still open but silent, the word he'd been shaping abandoned. "Listen, son," said Ilbei. "I don't need no stories about no jumpin turtles from Dae. What I need is fer ya to pay attention and do what you're told. I don't know why they keep sendin you magic fellers out here, when ya ain't fit fer campin out back a' yer parents' house—much less ridin down bandits in minin camps—but if'n ya got any ideas about goin home when yer time is done, ya better straighten up quick."

"I was only trying to point out—"

"Son, just plug up that there gob of yers and get on with another run at the raft."

Jasper swiveled his head and looked forlornly at the raft, upon which sat the rest of the squad amongst a few crates and bags of gear, all three of them bent by laughter. The largest of them, a giant of a man named Kaige, had fallen to the planks, struck down by the hilarity of Jasper's folly and at risk of rolling right off into the river. Their guffaws mixed with the giggling of the current, and Ilbei reckoned that in Jasper's ears it must have seemed as if the whole world laughed at him. The movement of the wizard's shoulders beneath the sagging drape of his robes set Ilbei's head to shaking once again.

"Them fellers ain't gonna take ya serious till ya straighten up," Ilbei said, low enough that only Jasper could hear, and not without a note of sympathy. The endless tendency of the army to send these young wizards out so unprepared, year after year, had given Ilbei some degree of empathy for the lads. Some of these fellows simply weren't cut out to be outdoors. Doting, proud mothers and coddled upbringings didn't prepare young mages for army life—or any life worth much, as Ilbei could figure it. "Now get over there and give yerself three or four steps to get goin first. And aim for the middle of the raft, not the edge."

"But they're in the middle of the raft," Jasper said. "I will collide with them."

"They'll keep ya from runnin off the other side when ya get there, so just do it. I ain't here to steer ya wrong."

The young wizard looked Ilbei in the eye, having to tip

his head down to do it, as Ilbei was a hand and a half shorter than the mage, but he nodded that he would try. He strode purposefully back up the bank to where the raft was tethered to a stake and once more contemplated the trajectory required.

Ilbei watched him evaluating the distance, the wizard's brows furrowed, his eyes narrow. The old sergeant had to resist the temptation to go haul the raft back to the shore and spare him the trouble. If he did it for him, the rest of the men would never give Jasper any respect, and worse, their teasing would make a tough road even tougher, at least for a while. "Go on," he said. "We ain't got forever to get this here mission done."

Jasper backed up the bank four long strides, then hoisted his soggy robes up above his knees and ran for it full tilt. He hit the edge of the water, made his leap, and out went his foot, sliding sideways in the mud. He piled left ear first into the water with a smack and rolled the rest of the way in like a corpse. Fortunately, he managed to grab onto a thick tuft of watergrass, preventing him from being carried out into the swifter currents, and Ilbei had time to get to him and drag him out and up the bank again.

The boys on the raft were, of course, aflame with hilarity, and this time Kaige's great muscled mass did roll off, right into the water with a splash.

"By Hestra, you're a sorry sort of athlete if'n I ever saw one," Ilbei said as he stared down at the flummoxed Jasper lying at his feet. "Worst ever, and I seen a few."

"Well I never said I was an athlete." Jasper made no move to regain his feet. He lay back in the grass, wearily content to stare up into the warm summer sky. "Frankly, I think it's ridiculous that I am forced to waste two years of my life in the service of barbarity anyway. I have no more interest in taming the wilds than I do in purging the kingdom of Her Majesty's enemies. Clearly, we both agree that I am not suited for this kind of activity."

"I expect the two of us won't never agree on anythin as much as that there," Ilbei said, once again hoisting the soggy sorcerer to his feet. "But you're here now, and ya do have to get on that damn raft. So get to it. I'm gonna give ya another crack at it on yer own before I'll sell ya out to them laughin devils there and let em figure how to get ya aboard as they please. Now, let her fly this time—that is, unless ya think ya can haul that thing to shore yerself, against the current and them boys a-layin there no less."

"You already saw that I could not."

It was true. Jasper had tried that first. "Well, maybe if'n ya put yer back into it this time. Use yer legs."

"I'll get him, Sarge," said the mountainous Kaige. He was coming up the riverbank, having made short work of extricating himself only a few spans downstream. He snatched up the spindly Jasper and lugged him under one arm like an ale keg to the water's edge, where he then cleared the distance to the raft in what was little more than an energetic stride. He dumped the dripping wizard at the feet of the other two already aboard, then turned back to Ilbei with a shrug. "See."

Ilbei looked downstream to where another raft was already tiny in the distance. He blew out a long breath that inflated his cheeks like white-whiskered balloons. It was going to be a long mission, he could tell.

"C'mon, Sarge," called Hams, the one man among the group near Ilbei's age. "The wizard is aboard well enough. If we let the others get too far ahead, they're gonna blame me for dinner being late."

As Ilbei donned his armor and weapons again, he watched his squad untangling themselves from the knot of their amusement, preparing to get underway. He wondered if they might be the rattiest batch of misfits he'd gotten in all his ninety-some years serving Her Majesty. It seemed like the most powerful woman on planet Prosperion ought to be able to conscript a sharper lot than this. With a grumble and a curse sent to Anvilwrath for what had to be a great heavenly joke, Ilbei pulled up the stake and leapt onto the raft.

Chapter 2

Ilbei let Hams work the rudder, as Hams knew the river and Ilbei did not. Ilbei had never been down the Desertborn River before. The army had brought him south because there was trouble in Three Tents. Three Tents was a small network of foothill mining camps near the Softwater River, a place where Ilbei Spadebreaker would be well suited to address problems that might arise. And they likely would, as a band of highway robbers led by a man known as Ergo the Skewer had found Three Tents and the strings of private claims along its local waterways. The bandits preyed on the miners for the copper they dug and the pittances of gold dust they occasionally came across—which by all reports would not even fill a teaspoon over the course of a year.

At first, the miners had come together and attempted to run the brigands off, but the Skewer was too clever to be caught, and worse, too brutal to be dealt with directly—the heads of three miners were found mounted on pikes a week after the vigilantes made their first, and only, brave head-on attempt. The locals had set traps after, but those failed as well and, worse, brought further violence. In fear for their lives and the meager livings they scraped out of those brush-covered hills, the miners had been forced to go to the garrison to ask for the army's help.

Ilbei was called down from the north to lead the mission because mining was in his blood. It was his past, his present (albeit reduced to a hobby when he got leave), and likely his future—when he decided to retire from the army someday. He'd grown up in a mining camp, and while he'd never been to Three Tents before, he knew it wouldn't be much different than the camps he'd grown up around. The fact that some gang of thieves would fall upon the kindly sorts that took up such simple, honest lives rankled him. So, when the assignment came up, Ilbei made no objections at all.

Besides, one job was as good as another in Her Majesty's army, as long as the pay came steady. If he could do a bit of good for good people, that was all the more reward, although, he was getting older now. Sometimes he felt like neither was enough to keep him at it much longer. At a hundred and fifteen years old, it might be time to retire from army life. Maybe go find a river or some nice ravine to mine on his own. Spend the last six decades of his life in peace. Maybe eight or nine decades if he dug up enough gold to pay them fancy magic doctors to keep his old carcass alive. Magickless folks like him, *blanks* as they were called, rarely made it past two centuries on Prosperion, but that was still a lot of time. It was also still a long way off, and he had work to do. He suspected the dragon's share of that work would be spent dealing with his new sorcerer.

As if to prove that very thing, Jasper sat upon a corner of the raft, naked as the day he was born, his wet robes set aside and not the least bit of modesty or embarrassment evident. He held a small hand mirror and moved it about with twitching motions, maneuvering it as best he could that he might see down his back and around his pasty pale backside. Ilbei thought the odd fellow might throw out his neck, he was contorting himself so urgently. And of course the rest of the lads, barely having caught their breath from laughing at Jasper's attempts to board, were now once more tortured with hilarity as the ghostly white wizard twisted and pried, peering anxiously about with his mirror as if looking for a spider crawling on him somewhere.

"There's one," goaded Ferster Meggins, a seasoned soldier in his early middle years, a man with a promising gift for both the bow and the small battle-axe, if Ilbei's glimpse of him practicing the other day was any evidence.

"Where?" Jasper shrieked as he said it, his eyes so wide Ilbei could see the whites all the way around the irises. The frantic wizard leapt up and spun in a circle like a dog chasing its tail, leading each revolution with the mirror hooked around and trying to catch a view of his entire backside. After two full circuits, Jasper looked back to Meggins pleadingly. "Where?"

"I think it's gone and run into your butt crack there," Meggins said. He pointed helpfully toward Jasper's rump and nodded with a most serious look upon his face. "Likely hiding under Jimmy and his traveling bags."

This gave poor Jasper pause, as he had to stop and work through the slang, his eyes once more flung wide. He reached down and lifted up his privates, horrified, his skinny legs bowed outward in a diamond shape as he bent and peered beneath, dreading what he might find.

This spectacle set the rest to new heights of hysteria, and even Hams had a hard time holding it back. Ilbei had to resist the urge to throw himself into the water and swim for shore. He could tell General Hanswicket that he'd fallen in and gotten tangled in some roots for a time, and by the time he got out, the rest of them were too far off to catch.

Instead, he asked, "Dragon's teeth, son, what are ya lookin fer?"

Jasper looked up at him as if he were missing the most obvious thing in the world. "Leeches, of course. What else would I be looking for?"

"Leeches?"

"Yes, leeches. Leeches frequent bodies of water in this part of Kurr, especially this time of year, and, in particular, the species known as the 'concubine's pin,' which, while small, can extract nearly a pint of blood in under an hour. They've got both heat and magical resistance, making surgery the only way to remove them."

"Oh no," Meggins said, sounding terribly concerned. "They don't have any surgeons down here. Sarge will have to carve them out with his old dagger. But he'll do it if you need him to. Won't you, Sarge?"

Jasper gasped, fixing Ilbei with a shame-on-you sort of look. "Do you have any idea how unsanitary that is?"

Well, the three of them, Kaige, Meggins, and Hams, got to laughing so hard they all might have tumbled off the raft had not Ilbei silenced them with the whip crack of his voice. Funny as it might be, they were too much on the poor young wizard already, even if he didn't recognize the joke at his expense.

"Listen here, Private," he said to Jasper once the others were down to rumbling snorts and sniggering. "There ain't no 'concubine's pins' in this here river. It's movin too fast fer that sort to make a home, so ya can stop watchin yer hammock swingin in that mirror of yers. Worst you'll get down here is the regular sorta leeches, and they're big enough to see and easy enough to set off with a hot stick. Moreover, ya ain't got none of em on ya neither, so suit up and quit yer worryin afore ya spin yerself right off the damn raft and set these others after ya fer laughin."

"Well, I beg to differ," the young mage pressed in a tutelary tone. "But there are two varieties of concubine's pin leeches that thrive perfectly well in fast-moving streams, the spotted blue concubine's pin and the ice knife variety. Surely you are familiar with those, and if you must know—"

"Well I don't must know, and there ain't no leeches. None

in there ...," Ilbei pointed to the water rushing by, "and none on yer shinin white behind." Again he pointed, this time at Jasper's posterior. There was something in that firm, no-nonsense jab that threatened violence if his orders weren't followed straight away. "Now get dressed. There ain't nobody wants to stare at ya standin around in yer all natural the whole way downstream."

"Well, why should they stare? The human physique is perfectly natural, and given that everyone on this raft is—" Ilbei's eyebrows dropped with the speed of a guillotine blade, and Jasper wisely cut himself off.

Ilbei turned and fixed the rest of them with the razor's edge of that glare, the slice of its authority beheading the body of their remnant laughter so quickly they seemed to choke on the very blood of it. "That's right," he said, seeing them fall to. "I got no patience fer the rest of ya, neither. Quit nippin this here feller's heels. Won't be one of ya what ain't ripe for pickin on somewhere down the line, and I can't be draggin a gaggle a' hyenas through the brush out there, gigglin our whereabouts to the Skewer like silly girls. So stow it and keep it stowed."

There were a few mumbles of acquiescence, to which the broad-shouldered sergeant shouted back for good measure, "What's that?"

"Yes, Sergeant Spadebreaker," came the chorus of replies.

The young magician was slow about getting his robes back on, picking through them and clearly still looking for leeches, but Ilbei let him do it so long as he was getting dressed. He felt sorry for the youngster. A real momma's boy that one, and it was going to be hard-going for him for a while. Ilbei had broken in more than a few raw young mages in his time, and the soft ones were far more common than not.

The nobles got their magic-gifted kids run through the War Academy in Crown City, so they came out officers most of the time. It was the same with the merchant class, though usually through lesser institutions. Only the poorer sorts and the blanks, the magickless commoners, sent their magician children through the enlisted ranks, like Jasper there. The worst of these were the first-generation sorcerers, kids born to blank parents and the first in the family line to have the gift of magic at all. Those families had no experience to draw on, and they were the worst at spoiling their young wizards, making them soft and whiny. It didn't even matter how strong—or weak—the young one's magic was. A family of blanks that birthed a child with magic for the first time in the bloodline, even with power as low as A- or B-rank, would pamper that child just the same as if they'd birthed a Z-ranked wizard into the highest class of nobility. By the time Ilbei got them, they were nearly worthless: full of expectations and demands, with no work ethic and no common sense. Ilbei sometimes felt like the army's higher-ups picked on him in that regard, because he could swear he got more momma's boys and daddy's girls than anyone else ever did.

He hadn't gotten round to asking this new one, poor skinny Jasper, what his magical rank or ranks were, much less how many of the eight schools of magic he might have access to. Jasper was essentially a total mystery. They'd all but dumped the lad on Ilbei at the last minute, as he and the others set out from the garrison. All Ilbei really knew about Jasper was that the magician spent nearly half his boot camp back and forth between the pillory and the stockade. And, frankly, after barely a half day with the lad, Ilbei could well imagine how the young wizard might set a drill sergeant off.

Some answers in regard to Jasper's magical abilities revealed themselves shortly after, however, as the young wizard opened a large trunk that had been put aboard the raft with his other gear. From a compartment within, he removed a scroll. He unfurled it and read it under his breath as he leaned over his wet robes, which he'd piled in his lap. There came a flash and a wisp of smoke that smelled like cinnamon, and then Jasper got up and pulled on the robes, which were now as dry as the day they'd been made. By this feat, Ilbei knew that Jasper was an enchanter at the very least.

Ilbei was glad of that fact, for enchanters could read scrolls from any magic school. Ilbei smiled privately behind the gray, tangled cover of his mustache. Even if the gangly Jasper wasn't a healer in his own right, he could still read healing scrolls, which was the next best thing—assuming he was strong enough to read the useful ones. Ilbei wanted to ask him, but if he couldn't, Ilbei didn't want to embarrass him in front of the others. The lad had had enough of that as it was. There'd be time to find out later. Hopefully, not under duress.

Chapter 3

The river ran smoothly all day and into the night, the few tributaries that emptied into it bringing little water this late in the season, but enough to keep the main channel deep and moving along. By the time the sun was rising on the second day of the voyage, Ilbei, at the tiller now, could see the woods that would swallow them up by noon.

"Get us some trout fer breakfast, Hams. Time enough fer salt pork and hardtack to come."

Old Hams was already fishing through his gear for his line and hooks before Ilbei had finished speaking.

Ilbei watched the tree line for a while, enjoying the quiet and the morning chill. The pleasant gurgling of the water beneath the raft reminded him of murmuring patrons in a gambling hall, just the right levels for a crowd that hasn't gotten too boozy to be fun anymore. Ilbei loved mornings like this. They gave his soul time to contemplate the day before his mind went to work and his mouth had to start barking out orders.

Ferster Meggins was up shortly after, and when he saw what Hams was about, he rustled in his pack and pulled out a ball of twine. He tied a length of it to the end of an arrow, and then, bow in hand, took a place near the front of the raft, intent on helping with breakfast. He had two fat trout flopping on the deck before Hams finally hauled in his first.

Ilbei let the rest of the squad sleep until Hams had twelve fish cleaned, two of them already breaded and frying in a pan. The old sergeant put on his sergeant face and gave the remaining dreamers a jab of his boot to the ribs. "Get up, ya lazy lot. Where do ya think ya are, some pamperin waterfront inn? Up, I say!" Jasper was right up, startled nearly out of his mind, but Kaige might have been a bag of bricks for all he responded to Ilbei's prod. Ilbei gave the big fellow a second tap with the toe of his boot, less gentle than the first, and when that failed, a third, which thudded loudly. Ilbei might as well have kicked an oak stump, so he resorted to dumping water on the big man's face. Gods help them if Kaige ever fell asleep on watch.

Soon enough, they were all up. After ablutions and other morning necessities, the lot of them sat about eating, spirits generally high as they often are at the beginning of an adventurous enterprise.

"A damn fine way to start a day," Ilbei observed over a cup of steaming Goblin Tea, the darkest, most potent form of coffee in all the land—and an unexpected surprise produced by the resourceful Hams. "Hams, weren't never nobody could throw down grub good as you."

Hams smiled over his cup. "I'd argue with you, Sergeant, but there weren't no grounds to make my case."

Nobody could, apparently, and for a time, most were silent but for the wet sounds of mastication and a few grunts from Kaige, who ate four trout in the time it took Jasper to half finish one.

"So where are we going, Sarge?" Meggins asked at length, as the rest were still finishing up their food. "I see Gallenwood coming up ahead. How far we going in? I heard stories about South Mark soldiers being dire territorial if you get too deep in there."

"South Mark soldiers are still Her Majesty's, no matter what they'd have ya believe." Ilbei paused to throw the skin and bones of his breakfast over the edge of the raft. "But we ain't headin far enough in to trifle with them fellers anyhow. Only goin as far as where the Softwater meets the Desertborn. Then we'll unload and head upriver a few days into the hills to an area General Hanswicket called Three Tents. It's a handful of little minin camps as I gathered it, somewhere near the base of the Gallspires."

"Why are we going there? Someone pull up a fat lot of gold and need an escort back to Hast?" Meggins poured himself a second cup of coffee and flashed Hams a madman's sort of smile, which Hams winked at in reply.

"Bandits troublin the miners," Ilbei said, breathing the last of the statement into the steam rising off his tin coffee cup. He grinned after he took a sip, not so enthusiastic as Meggins, but well satisfied. He closed his eyes and let the bitter joy of it settle in. Goblin Tea. It wasn't a luxury he could afford. Not often anyway. He was almost afraid to ask Hams how he'd come by it.

"Technically," Jasper said, upon seeing that Ilbei wasn't going to elaborate, "the Three Tents camps are in copper country, so it isn't likely they would have pulled a significant amount of gold. The most recent survey maps show Three Tents to be *barely* in copper country, as the main copper seam ends three hundred measures northwest. Whatever they're mining is an aberration at best. I saw the geology reports. That far east, I should think statistically those miners barely collect enough of anything to recoup living expense, whether from trace gold or from copper and lead combined—those last two being the most likely constituents to be had, again based on the survey, which was taken only a year ago. The prior survey, taken three years before, had promised a dispersion of gold, but subsequent investigations revealed that not to be the case. Therefore, while there may be copper to be had, I would think at this point those mining the area are surviving primarily on the sale of lead, given the growing demand for pipe in urban centers these days, and given that the camps themselves are populated by scofflaws who live there largely to avoid paying taxes to the Queen—which the copper, should they report it by weight, would incur. These people are ruffians to the last, the sort who'd choose a spartan living over one of comfort merely for the illusion of being free from the monarchy. I imagine they're practically animals."

Everyone on the raft was staring at the young wizard by the time he'd finished speaking, including Ilbei, whose lips had paused in the action of blowing across the top of his coffee when he began to realize just how long Jasper was going to carry on. It was in part surprise at the unexpected nature of the young man's dissertation, a sort of awe at its long-windedness, but it was also out of genuine interest. Ilbei had had no idea that Jasper knew anything about Three Tents or its mineral history—much less about the disposition of those men who chose to live on the edges of the empire rather than under its thumb—as neither were the sorts of things he would have thought the scrawny young mage would know of or think about.

"How come you know so much about the southern mining camps?" Meggins asked, saving Ilbei having to inquire himself. "You talk like a sissy northern boy—no offense of course—so I figured you for Leekant or Crown City, or one of the small high-north towns at least."

Jasper made an impatient face at him. "I'm from a little mining town on the western edge of Great Forest called Alumall, if you must know. But even had I been born on Duador, I would have read about Three Tents and its history. You see, I enjoy reading. You do know what that is, don't you? All those little marks on parchment that they stack up into books? Well, it turns out there's all sorts of information in those there things." The last bit was spoken in dialectical way, obviously intended as an insult. He was clearly still out of sorts over the treatment he'd gotten yesterday.

"My mum taught me to mark my name," Kaige put in happily. "And I learned myself to read most tavern signs. The ones that are serving has the same four marks every time: a 'O,' a 'P,' a 'E,' and a 'N.' Ones that aren't serving has some other ones. I don't recollect what they are called, but they count to six. I just look for them that I know, and it works fine."

Hams and Meggins laughed, and Meggins asked through his chuckles, "You figured all that out on your own, did you?"

"I did," replied Kaige. "There wasn't nobody inside whenever they hung up the six-letters sign. Plus you can tell if the door don't open. Didn't take me long to recognize."

Well, that was about as far as that conversation could go because even Ilbei had to laugh, and so they set about to cleaning up the dishes as the river carried them bodily downstream and laughter floated their spirits right along with it, at least for most of them. Once again, poor Jasper seemed to have missed the joke.

As Ilbei had anticipated, the sun was high above by the time their raft was carried into the first shadows of the woods. The sound of the river came back differently now, amplified in a way, its tone changed by the acoustic disposition of the leaves and so many overhanging boughs. He hadn't seen the other raft since yesterday morning, but he knew they weren't more than twenty minutes or so ahead. They'd find them by nightfall, hopefully, with a fire already started and a fat buck roasting above. Just in case, however, he'd had Hams set his hooks into the water again. And it was during the maintenance of those hooks near midafternoon that the old army cook drew in a reverent breath. "Blimey," he said, nearly a gasp.

Ilbei turned toward him, as did all the rest aboard, and saw him gaping down into the water with his mouth as wide as a trout's.

"Snag a fat one, Hams?" Meggins asked.

Hams, however, did not respond. He merely stared into the water and, truth be told, let forth a clear thread of drool, which began as a small round bubble, like a tear, at the lowest ledge of his drooping lip, but then went on to descend on a line of saliva like a legless crystal spider on a thread of web.

Meggins, being nearest to the cook, crawled the short distance to where Hams leaned down, adding volume to the river in his astonishment. The younger man glanced briefly up at the stupefied Hams, then peered over the edge as well.

Ilbei saw Meggins recoil as something struck him a surprise, and then Meggins seemed to freeze, staring motionless into the water, his mouth agape the same as Hams'.

"What is it?" Kaige asked, getting to his feet and clomping across the deck to see. He looked down into the water with his two companions and uttered a low "Whoa." He dove in before Ilbei could even ask.

The ensuing splash made the tannin-stained water difficult to see through, and the wave of its cold wetness knocked both Hams and Meggins back to their senses again. With a shake of his head to clear whatever had cottoned up his thoughts, Hams looked to Ilbei with eyes wide. "Naiad," he said. "And that idiot jumped right into her arms."

"Shite," Ilbei swore. "A water nymph? These gods-be-damned boys can't even control theirselves around regular females. Take the tiller, Hams, quick now."

Meggins, who wore an expression of shock, was only barely beginning to blink back to clarity. "She's so beautiful."

"I'm sure she is," Ilbei said, "and she's gonna drown that

big idiot fer sure." Even as he said it, Ilbei snatched up a rope with a grapple on it and heaved it up the bank, snagging it in a thick tangle of roots. With brute force, he hauled the raft back up against the current as Hams at the rudder guided them toward the bank. "Secure the raft," Ilbei ordered as he leapt to the bank. His boots splashed in the shallow water at the edge, and the mud forced him to scramble up the embankment, using his hands as well.

He ran back to where Kaige had gone in, hoping all the while that the young man could hold his breath long enough to be saved. He hoped as well that the fool would come to his senses in time to at least try to fight. There was no telling how spellbound the lad would be.

Fortunately for them both, Ilbei could see the shadowy figures of Kaige and his captor down near the bottom of the opposite bank, and from the thrashing about, it was clear the brawny soldier had realized the danger he was in. He might not be the brightest candle on the altar, but at least he wasn't the willing sacrifice.

"I need rope," Ilbei called as he ran back. "Rope, quick. And someone get upstream and pour in a gift of wine. Meggins, get the gray wineskin out of my pack, not the black. Hurry, boys, hurry."

Hams threw Ilbei a length of rope, which he snatched out of the air and ran back, going another ten paces upstream. He set to work tying it to a thick root that arced out of the bank. He stooped, dumped off his helmet and chainmail, then tied the other end of the rope around his waist.

"Pull us out," he called to his men with a glance downstream. Hams was already running toward him, and Meggins had just pulled the gray wineskin free. He held it aloft as he ran across the raft and leapt up the bank. He passed Jasper in doing so, the mage motionless as he regarded the scant half pace that separated him from land as if he were charged with leaping over the Great Sandfalls.

Ilbei had no time for the mage's hesitation. Any delay could mean Kaige's life, so in he dove and down he swam, grateful to discover there were no terrible rocks down there against which he might be bashed.

The current wasn't swift, but there was a solid thirty spans from bank to bank. The water was clearer this far downriver, away from the convergence of the many creeks and lesser rivers that formed the Desertborn, and at least he could see through its hazy green transparency. By the time he was halfway across, he'd come even with where he'd seen Kaige grappling with the naiad. As the current carried him past, he could see the hole into which the naiad was dragging the youngster. Kaige was still putting up some fight, but not much. He'd been alert enough to hook his boots into some roots, preventing the water nymph from dragging him all the way in, but that seemed to be all he could maintain. He couldn't possibly hold his breath much longer.

Ilbei swam for all his might toward the opposite bank. The rope around his waist went taut and threatened to swing him back to the bank to which it was tied. He dove down and grabbed roots jutting out from the opposite side. They were slick as a snot-covered ice lance and extremely hard to hold, but desperation gave him claws. He pulled his way back upstream, one root at a time as if they were the twisting rungs of a submerged ladder. Finally, he got to where Kaige's boots were. He came close enough to grab the soldier's ankle. Planting his feet against the edge of the hole, Ilbei hauled with all his strength, drawing the soldier out like a great arrow from a muddy wound. Through the water, he could hear Kaige trying desperately not to breathe the river in, the anvil thumps of stifled gasps, his lungs pounding against his will with an insistent reflex. Ilbei grabbed him by the front of his pants and an ankle and lifted him upward, thrusting with short, powerful legs, driving for the surface and shoving him into the air.

He saw the furious face of the naiad coming out at him as he did. She was beautiful beyond anything he'd ever seen, a pale blue figure of statuesque femininity with a face nearly divine. Her nose was narrow and dainty between two sea-green eyes. Her lips, though twisted into a silent snarl, promised a kiss that would finish a man on the spot. And yet, despite that promise, that lure, Ilbei did not lose his head. He blinked and turned away.

He'd left his pickaxe, his weapon of choice, on the raft, but he had a sharp knife, which he drew and held poised to strike. His own breath was growing short, but he knew better than to rise up and offer the creature his feet while he breathed. Who would pull *him* out?

"Back, shrew!" he called, but the words, submerged as they were, were drowned by the water coursing by.

She did draw back—and stopped. He glanced over his shoulder and saw it. He also saw that her rage was gone, as if knocked loose by his threatening command and carried off by the currents. She looked as if she might cry.

He watched the melting away of her anger, the softening of that beautiful face, her succulent mouth turned down at the corners and quivering a bit. It was heartbreaking. She was so sad. So beautiful. So tempting. Light dappled her soft blue skin, her breasts gently buoyant, all torment, taunt and promise. Ilbei wanted to apologize. To explain. He started toward her, his knife hand lowering, his free hand reaching out, but he was just old enough to realize his mistake. He caught her watching him. His own eyes narrowed, his lips curled in. With a quickness that belied the bowed nature of his legs, he pushed off from the bank, not up toward breath—where she had expected him to go, where she darted in anticipation—but downstream, low and away.

He straightened his body like a dart and shot out into the current where it was swifter, then bent himself against the current as the rope went taut again. This time, he angled his body like a rudder and steered himself upward and toward the opposite bank.

It worked well, and quickly, and he came right up, gasping for air, grasping into the mud for the purchase by which he might haul himself free. He shouted at his companions as soon as he could breathe well enough to do so. "Pour the gods-be-damned wine! Pour it into the water!"

He got hold of a thick clump of weeds and clambered up onto the bank, still gasping as he wriggled clear of the water. He spun round and crabbed backwards, his knife in his fist, ready to fight. He watched the churning current for signs of her, for where she would rise up and once more set the full force of temptation upon him, the will-draining power of a magical allure, but she did not. She did not chase him at all.

She was moving toward the others instead, swimming against the current as easily as if she were in a quiet little pond, raised to her waist above the waters and having mesmerized them all to statues, their round mouths as hollow and vacant as their minds.

"Give her the wine, for Mercy's sake, ya fools. The wine!" He shouted it as he ran back up the bank.

Jasper was the first to look up, Ilbei's voice jarring him free of the stupefying loveliness for a time. He blinked rapidly and made a point of looking up and away.

"I love you," the water creature said, looking directly into Meggins' eyes instead.

"I love you too," Meggins replied. He stepped toward her, reaching out with the wine he'd brought at Ilbei's command.

"Meggins, ya sod, pour the wine into the water," Ilbei called, still closing the distance between them as fast as his bowed legs could run.

Meggins turned, dazed, the addled remnants of his mind staring through the orifices of his pupils like a prisoner through his cage.

Ilbei snatched the wineskin from his hand and yanked the stopper off, but Jasper grabbed his wrist and yanked it back as Ilbei began to squeeze. The jet of red liquid shot uselessly into the grass.

"Jasper, by the gods!" Ilbei began to swear, but Jasper, for once, cut him off.

"Potameide," the young wizard said, his head shaking steadily side to side. "She won't like the wine."

Ilbei scowled at him, blinking, confused. Meggins took another step toward the beautiful figure in the water beckoning him, her soft eyes batting, lips pouting at his delay. The water running from her body shaped her figure with a sheen. "Be with me," she said to him.

Ilbei jerked his hand free from Jasper's grasp, but Jasper snatched at it again, spastically, his grip on Ilbei's wrist weak, but his purpose urgent and clear. "You'll only anger her with that. You need mead. Give her mead if you must give her alcohol, or better still, just honey. Even milk will do. But not wine. She'll kill us all if you poison her water with that wine."

Ilbei glared at the scrawny magician, deciding whether to break his fingers or heed what he had to say. "They taught us wine up north. Everyone knows wine will suit a nymph, satyr-lovin whores they are."

"Some northern varieties, yes. The nymphs of Great Forest and the Daggerspines are known to favor wine, but not this one. She's a potameide of the old-world kind. Just look." He pointed with a movement of his face, unwilling to let go of Ilbei's wrist.

Meggins stepped into the water. Ilbei heard the splash and grabbed him by the waist with his free hand, scooping him into the crook of his arm and flinging him up the bank as if he were some great fish Ilbei had caught. He spun back to face Jasper right after, his hand twitching to pour the wine. But there was such conviction in Jasper's eyes.

Jasper saw the hesitation and pointed. "Look," he said again. "Count her ribs. There are only three pairs visible below the line of her breast. Potameides have only twenty ribs. You can see the missing floating pairs are conspicuously absent. There can be no doubt." He jerked his scrawny arm forward as if feinting with a short, pale spear. "Just look."

Ilbei turned back, glanced at the breathtaking beauty approaching and looked quickly away. He didn't want to fall under the spell.

"I can see your future," she promised Meggins, who was on his feet and heading for the water again. "Can you imagine our happiness together?"

"I can! I can!" Meggins replied.

Ilbei backhanded the bewitched private, belting him so hard he was knocked clean out, crumpling as if his body had lost all its bones. "Sorry, son," Ilbei said, even as he turned back to Jasper—who had made the mistake of looking the nymph in the eyes again. "Son of a jackal," he swore. He slapped the gangly wizard, more gently than he had Meggins. Jasper blinked back at him, thoughts returning once again. "Go get it then," Ilbei commanded him.

"Get what?"

"The honey. In Hams' crates."

Jasper had to blink a few more times to figure out what Ilbei was talking about, but a glance toward the potameide reminded him. He paused briefly, regarding Meggins lying there motionless, but he went straight off down to the raft after. He jumped aboard, stumbling upon landing, but he managed to catch himself before falling off over the far side.

Ilbei turned and threatened the nymph with his dagger, taking care to stare at her stomach, which was hardly less compelling than her face, but not so pleasant as to cost him his ability to think. "Stay off my lads, sister," he said. "They got troubles enough without the likes of you gettin yer hooks into em."

"I love them," she said. "They shine with the beauty of youth."

"That they do, and I'm fixin to make sure they rot it off slow, same as I done. Now stay where ya are, or I'll carve ya up so as ya ain't so fine to look on no more. Blimey, I will."

"I can make them happy," she promised.

"Happy for a half minute, then dead. Young fellers like these don't weigh them both the same—least not once the first is done. But I got the measure of it fine." He stepped forward with the knife. "Save us both the trouble and swim on along."

He looked down to the raft and saw Jasper rifling through Hams' supplies. He glanced back to his left where Hams stood, still mesmerized. At least she had no interest in the older man. Stunned stupid though he was, he was not easing himself into a drowning death by her attentions. There was some advantage to the invisibility of old age.

She glided nearer to the shore and put one long, slender leg up onto the bank, the water running down it like a skin of glass.

"By the gods, woman," Ilbei gasped. "Climb back into that water afore I have to do somethin will haunt me all my years." His heart yammered in his chest, his pulse pounding.

Jasper was running up the bank, his skinny legs visible, as he'd drawn up his robes like a lady saving her skirts from a muddy road. "I have it. I have it," he called.

He was panting by the time he'd covered the distance between the raft and Ilbei's position on the bank. He paused when he saw the long, water-slicked limb of the potameide, and traced the line of Ilbei's seeming hypnotism from the shapely flesh back to Ilbei's glazing eyes.

"Oh dear," he said. He turned to the idyllic vision of feminine allure and, careful not to look her in the eyes, held out the honey he'd found, twisting off the lid of the jar. "A gift," he said, staring carefully at the water's edge. He poured the honey down, the line of it, like Hams' first line of drool had, lowering itself lazily into the water, a golden thread that thinned as it stretched toward the river flowing by.

The moment it touched the water, they could all breathe easier. It was as if, in that instant, some smothering cloud had lifted, a numbing fog blown off by a honey-flavored wind.

Ilbei staggered backward, stumbling as if he'd been in the midst of a tug-of-war when the rope broke. He landed on his backside at the top of the riverbank and sat watching as the naiad, Jasper's potameide, knelt at the water's edge, winding the honey around her finger as the current stretched it like a rivulet of molten gold. She pulled her hand out and slipped a slender digit into her mouth, sucking on it slowly—sumptuously by Ilbei's account. Her breast swelled with contentment, also sumptuous by Ilbei's account, and she smiled at Jasper and reached for the jar. He handed it to her, and then she slipped away, melting back into the water as if she were made of the stuff.

Jasper watched after her for a moment more, then turned back to Ilbei, who was still staring into the place where she had disappeared. "You see," Jasper said. "A potameide."

Four full minutes would pass in silence before Ilbei nodded, acknowledging that Jasper had been right.

Chapter 4

With Kaige collected from the opposite shore and Meggins revived with a splash of cold water, Ilbei's squad made their way downriver to the landing point. They found the other raft hauled out of the water at a place just above where the Softwater River joined the Desertborn. As expected, Ilbei and his raft mates were late enough that the occupants of the first raft were not only out of the water, they were well underway setting up camp. Someone had a fire ablaze, so Ilbei sent Hams scurrying to do his part in preparing the evening's meal for the platoon, near two dozen fresh-caught trout flopping on a line over his shoulder as he ran.

Ilbei helped Kaige pull the raft up the bank, and then the two of them made their way to the camp being erected on a modest rise a few hundred spans from the river.

Soldiers worked in pairs to put up small two-man tents, and Ilbei had paired Kaige with Jasper despite the obvious intellectual conflicts. He was fairly sure Ferster Meggins would have tormented either of them to no end, and if the wiry warrior angered the giant one, Ilbei suspected Meggins would be mangled straight away. And perhaps worse, if Meggins upset Jasper, well, it was hard to tell what the magician might do. Despite over a day on the river, Ilbei still hadn't found out what the wizard was capable of.

He'd thought about asking, but there wasn't a polite way to do it—not that Ilbei bothered with that sort of thing when it came to his men. The truth was, magicians always left Ilbei a little unsettled, no matter how many years he'd worked with them. Most times they were useful enough when need arose, but that was, being completely honest, relatively rare. There just wasn't that much fighting anywhere these days. It had been a long time since the Orc Wars were won, centuries, and the occasional flare-ups that did happen were always just that: flare-ups. Some clan of orcs or another, emboldened by an imbecile chieftain, would come pouring out of a mountainous pass somewhere, hack into a farming village, fishing town or mining camp, and then kill everyone, eat some of them and burn the rest. Shortly after, the savages would be annihilated by the overwhelming forces of Her Majesty's army, which she could get teleported into the area on nearly a moment's notice upon receiving word of the attack. And that was pretty much it. The simple truth was that only in small seams along the edges of the duchies and marks—where boundaries were gray and enthusiasm for authority meant not spitting when someone spoke a noble family's name— was there much cause for regular army work: situations like the mission they were on. If Ilbei could have had his way, he'd have come without a mage. Without *any* mage, not just without Jasper. He hardly needed a wizard to deal with simple highway robbery.

But Ilbei didn't get his way, because they hadn't asked him. So here he was. And there was Jasper, buried by the onslaught of a dingy white army tent, the poorly planted pole having collapsed, leaving him to thrash about beneath the canvas. Ilbei sighed as he watched. It looked like a ghost having a seizure. Jasper's tent mate stood silently by, the brawny Kaige seemingly torn between assistance and laughter. Ilbei wondered if his decision to pair them had been a terrible one. He'd hoped between the two of them they'd make one functioning soldier, but perhaps he'd missed his bet.

He stomped over to the moaning heap and set himself to liberating his mage, hauling folds of canvas free and snapping at Jasper to "be still" while he untangled the rope from the wizard's neck and left arm. "How can ya come from a place like Alumall and not know how to pitch a tent?" he marveled as he worked. "Ya said ya weren't present fer most a' yer boot camp, but surely yer people back home took ya out of the cabin from time to time?"

"Why would they?" Jasper asked upon being freed. He sat back on his heels and smoothed his robes over his knees.

Ilbei started to answer, but the expectant look on Jasper's face suggested that whatever the answer was, it should be obvious. It wasn't, but Ilbei didn't care what it was. He was sure it would be ridiculous, so instead he set himself to teaching Jasper how to pitch the tent, hoping that somehow the process would stick.

An hour later, the platoon, minus two sentries, sat around the fire devouring the evening's meal. For a time, all that could be heard was the *tink-tink* of tin spoons and steel knives on the metal trays, the men and women ravenous as a locust swarm.

Not long after, wineskins were passed around, and a soldier from Corporal Trapfast's squad, a young woman whose name Ilbei had only recently learned was Auria, began to sing. She was accompanied on a fiddle by another woman, who Ilbei had also recently learned was the singer's sister, Decia. The song was a melancholy one, a story of a garden and long-dead mother's house. Mournful as it was, Auria's voice was beautiful. The longing notes and homesick lyrics lay upon Ilbei like the gray clouds of a rainy day, the sort where one can sit on a porch and watch out across the landscape as silvery drops stir up the sweetest scents, wet soil and peat. Home smells.

The boys back home used to call him Hound Dog for his sense of smell, and it was true he had a gift, albeit a reluctant and temperamental one. He could smell a polecat over a mile away, where most folks needed to be within at least a few hundred spans. He could smell ants the moment they crawled into a room. The first time he'd announced that, all the boys had laughed—until he led them straight to a line of the insects just forming through a crack in the floor. They figured Ilbei had set to fool them with that, however, claiming he'd known the ants were there all along. To prove it, they'd blindfolded him and taken him out into the woods. "Find us some ants now," they challenged.

So he did. He led them to six colonies within a hundred paces of where they stood and told them that somewhere on the other side of a fennel patch there was a blackberry cluster and beyond it a big termite mound.

Several of them tried to find where Ilbei was peeking through his blindfold—which they couldn't, as he wasn't— then they ran off together to verify the termite mound was there. Which it was. And thus he was dubbed Hound Dog, and he bore that brand for nearly twenty years. Until his young wife died.

The song ended, but Ilbei stared into the fire, thinking back over all the decades since that time. He couldn't quite shape her young, pretty face anymore, but he could feel how pretty she had been inside. Such stark contrast to that potameide. It was the difference of a moment and a century.

"Decia, you're sucking the light right outta Luria with that depressing shite," someone called from the other side of the fire. "Like enough we'll be feeling sorry for our feet come end of the week. Save that sap for the blisters we'll get climbing up and down these hills."

"Yeah," someone else said. "Play something merry."

The two sisters turned to each other and shared a brief exchange, and soon the fiddle was set ablaze nearly as bright as the fire itself, sparks of music rising up out of the forest into the black river of the night, which flowed around the treetops like salted ink. A few of the lads were struck to dance by the song as others tried to accompany it, and soon after the woods were filled with the howling, off-key bawdiness of their revelry.

Ilbei, less inclined to song than the rest, having been disinclined to wine that night, sat on his log, tapping his toe and measuring with a practiced eye all that he could glean about the men and women of his company. And it was as he made his mental notes that he heard the sentry's shrill whistle, coming from down by the river.

The whistle came again, the note rising high and short, followed by a longer warbling one, signaling that a lone boat approached from downstream. Ilbei called for Kaige, Meggins and a young soldier sitting nearby stringing a bow. "Come," was all he said, and the four of them ran toward the river.

They found the sentry crouched in a low fork of an alder. He pointed at orange spots of light issuing from lanterns that hung at the stem and stern of a riverboat. The oars dipping in the water splashed audibly, an even sequence of splash and silence, stroke after stroke.

The light of the moon, pink Luria above, was little use in a fight here, given the forest overhang, but since the boat made no attempts to conceal its approach, Ilbei allowed himself to be somewhat at ease. "Run fer camp if they make any move, Meggins," Ilbei said in a low voice. "But I expect these here are harmless enough."

They waited patiently, the man with the bow jumping down from his place in the tree and moving back to a tree a little farther up the bank, where he sank into the shadows and was gone from sight. Eventually the longboat came close enough that its lamps revealed its crew: twelve men at the oars, a coxswain at the back and one man in the center, astride a horse so black that for a time it looked as if the rider were levitating a span and a half above the deck.

"Run fer a torch," Ilbei ordered, and Meggins was off like a rabbit. By the time the boat was drawing parallel to Ilbei's position on the bank, Meggins was back, his breathing hardly up despite the sprint.

"Hallo," Ilbei called. "A fine night fer a row then, is it?"

"Sergeant Spadebreaker, I presume?" came the reply from the mounted man.

Ilbei took the torch from Meggins and held it aloft, squinting in the light. He saw in it that the man was an officer, a major by the crossed lances on his sleeves, though a young one by the lack of lines upon his face. There was a cleanliness to him that bespoke wealth, and a rigidity of spine that promised noble blood. Ilbei had seen enough of them in his time. A black cloak was fastened by a golden clasp at his throat, the rich fabric draped like a sable waterfall, flowing off him and cascading over his horse's flanks and rump. "Right, sar. That'll be me."

"I am Lord Cavendis, major in Her Majesty's Eleventh Cavalry. I am now in command of this expedition."

The helmsman tossed Ilbei a mooring line, which he caught reflexively in his free hand. He pushed the torch out over the water, amplifying its light by the reflection. He passed the line off to Kaige, continuing to stare up at the officer as the burly soldier hauled the vessel to shore. The coxswain threw another line to Meggins, who did as Kaige had done, and soon the boat was moored and joined to the bank by a stretch of sturdy plank pushed out by the crew. The young Lord Cavendis, upon his black horse, eschewed such conventions. Rather than clatter down the ramp, he chose to leap free of the vessel in a great bound of equestrian finesse that left the oarsmen groping the gunwales lest they be dumped out by the recoil of the boat. It was a large boat, but not that large.

Ilbei kept his thoughts on the display to himself and instead pointed the smooth-faced officer toward the bawdy songs being sung several hundred paces through the trees. "Camp'd be that way, sar," he said. "We'll see to yer gear, and to yer men. Get y'all fed up good."

"They've provisions enough to get them back to the garrison at Twee. Just get my things."

"Twee, sar? Have ya been rowin up so far as that?"

"Spadebreaker, let us get off on a good foot, shall we?"

"I should like that just fine, sar," Ilbei said.

"Good news, then. So we'll start by you not questioning me as if we were long-lost chums."

"Right, sar. I just thought yer boys might like a hot meal afore headin back, fer to see to their strength and all. There's more fish cooked up there than our boys can eat, and more than a few spits of fine, greasy quail too. They're everywhere out here."

"And there goes our good footing already, Sergeant. But then, what should I have expected from the man who's been knocked back down to strip sergeant how many times now? Eleven? Or was it twelve?"

Actually it was only six times, and all six for insubordination—all six incited by baby-faced lordlings blowing out bad orders on breath that stank of mother's milk as the ink on their commissions dried—but Ilbei wasn't going to tell him that either. "Right, sar. My apologies, sar. Shall I cut em loose now or give em long enough to clear their bowels if'n they need to?"

It was a bit of good fortune for Ilbei that the officer's eyes were not crossbows, for that might have been the end of him on the spot. But rather than rebuke Ilbei, the young lord turned back and gave the order himself. "Hand over my gear and off with you. If I get word that you were longer back than two days, I'll have your pay docked the missing time, all of you."

Ilbei's eyes narrowed dangerously, but he kept his head low enough that shadows concealed it. The men on the boat made similar angles of their own faces, but they saw well enough to hand off the major's crates and to catch the ropes that Meggins and Kaige tossed back to them. Understanding flashed between them as Meggins shot the coxswain an apologetic glance, but that was all.

When the boat had slipped back into the main channel, Ilbei turned back toward camp. "This way, sar," he said, wondering privately why nobody in Hast had told him there was an officer coming up from South Mark. General Hanswicket's last words on the problem of the highway robberies had simply been: "See to it, Spadebreaker. Make it go away."

Meggins had apparently been having the same thoughts, and he asked about it as they were heading for their tents. "Why didn't anybody say they were sending an officer from Twee?" His breath blew misty in the chill night air, the plume of it turned pale pink by the moonlight. Ilbei hissed at him to keep his voice down. The man shrugged in the shadows. "I'm just asking, is all," he said, his voice lower but still audible enough to make Ilbei uncomfortable. "I thought we was just after bandits. What do we need a Twee major for? A cavalryman, no less?"

"Our job is to do what we're told and not ask questions," Ilbei said. "If'n blokes like us get to needin whys and wherefores every time a command comes down, the whole army'd lock up and fall in on itself."

"South Mark officers got no call in Valenride."

"Them two silver lances on his lapels says different, so just mind yer yap and do as you're told."

"Of course I will. But I don't see why this mission needs

some damned major come along. 'Specially one fresh off his mother's dugs."

"Listen up, son. I reckon I done waxed his back as it is, and there ain't no room fer sass from the likes of you. So stow that bile and keep to what they pay ya fer, which ain't fer thinkin. Hear?"

"I hear."

"I hear, *Sergeant*," Ilbei said.

"Yes, Sergeant," Meggins said. He turned and went off to find his dreams.

Ilbei would have found his own dreams if he could, but the day's events prevented him from sleeping straight away. Ilbei was a man of order. He didn't like chaos, and he didn't like surprise. This mission was supposed to be simple: get to the hills, ask a few questions, track down the bad guys, and bring them in. In, out, easy. He figured a short skirmish was the worst there would be. And yet, here he was, his boot socks hanging above him, drying from his encounter with a potameide—he'd never even heard of a damned *potameide* before today—and now they had a nobleman from Twee taking over before they'd even had breakfast on dry land. So much for simplicity. By the time Ilbei finally fell asleep, he'd concluded that the two of them, the river nymph and the major, counted up to bad luck.

Chapter 5

It turned out that "bad luck" was not an entirely accurate description of Major Cavendis, which, in its particulars, came as something of a surprise to Ilbei. On the third day of marching, as the foothills grew steep enough that they might be deemed mountainous, the platoon arrived at Cedar Wood. It was the closest of the mining camps that made up Three Tents and hardly more than a cluster of plank buildings and log cabins. And it was on that first evening in Cedar Wood that Ilbei discovered that Major Cavendis—the very young and very noble Major Cavendis—had quite a gift for cards.

Miners, like sailors and soldiers, were famously fond of games of chance, and premier among them was *ruffs*. Ruffs was a game of luck and bluffing, and the better a man was at bluffing, the better his luck turned out to be. For the most part, the game was simple. The deck was made up of sixty-five cards with five suits of thirteen cards each, the suits being: orcs, elves, harpies, dwarves and men.

When Ilbei was a boy, he'd played it with the other mining camp kids. Unlike their parents, the boys usually played for acorns or trinkets, learning the skills required to one day compete with the adults. However, there had been

41

one especially memorable game, very high-stakes in the minds of boys, in which he and his mates wagered real money against a peek in on Gervon Gravelstack's sister when she was having a bath. Ilbei, a natural at the game, had won that pot gleefully. In payment, he was shown the location of a knothole in the Gravelstack family abode, done so on the promise that he would never tell another living soul.

Oh, such a victory that had been! And as adolescent Ilbei settled in for a second night enjoying the profits of his fine play, old man Gravelstack caught him looking in. Seldom had Ilbei encountered such rage as that, and the broad-backed miner beat poor Ilbei black and blue, so badly he lost a tooth, a permanent one, which had to be replaced in gold— gold that his own father took out of him in toil that went far beyond the value of Ilbei's original bet. Despite the net loss, however, Ilbei never regretted his win, and his skills at ruffs had only improved in the century since. But ruffs was a commoners' game. It was a game for blanks and ruffians. Firstly, because a player with magic most likely had telepathy, and where there were telepaths, poker-style games were fraught with cheating of the worst kind; and secondly, where there was ruffs, there was fighting. The game got its name from the tacit understanding that it sometimes became violent, and as far as anyone could tell, it had always been that way. Which is why the arrival of Major Cavendis asking for a game caught Ilbei entirely off guard.

Ilbei himself had come to Cedar Wood's dilapidated tavern to question the locals about the highway robberies. He'd found himself with a pair of them and, using money the army had provided for just such a thing, plied them with Her Majesty's generosity, learning what he could about the bandits' activities. He'd just begun getting details of heists along a track the locals called Deer Trail Road when in came

Major Cavendis in all his silver lances and golden clasps.

"I was informed there is a game here," the major said simply to the tavern keeper. The arrival of the young lord and officer set nervousness dripping from the barman like ale foam down an overfilled mug. He dabbed at the pineboard counter before him, wiping away nothing with a filthy cloth as he stammered something unintelligible.

The major swung his gaze around the room and spotted the ruffs game right away, five miners seated around a table made from rough-hewn planks set atop four flat-cut logs. To the last of them, they were doing their best to cover their cards with dusty sleeves, or set mugs down as obstacles to the major's line of sight. The two nearest to the bar stared into the wood, pretending they hadn't noticed the resplendent officer enter. The major called their bluff, saying, "Ah, there it is," which set them to shifting in their seats.

"At ease, gentlemen," the major said as he approached. His silver spurs jingled at his boot heels with each long stride. "I've not come to stop you. I've come to play."

Eyes darted from man to man, lips pursed, then the group together gaped as the young lord pulled a chair from a nearby table and inserted himself into their game.

There followed a period of sputtering and stammering, a few *milord*s interspersed with dissembling and unintelligible remarks, clearly protests, though muffled to indecipherability for fear and duty to noble blood. Fear and duty were things not much to the taste of men who've gone to the trouble of choosing a life so far from anything "civilized."

The major shocked them a second time—shocking Ilbei as well—as he explained that he was a lover of the game. "I simply can't find a good round of ruffs back home," he said. "The stuffy sorts who haunt the manor or would curry favor with my family are simply incapable of putting up a proper game." He explained that he had to travel pretty far to indulge himself in a game with men of real skill, and finished by saying, "And I have it on good authority that there were none so gifted in the art of ruffs than those who dig their wagers out of the very flesh of the world."

This compliment put half the game into a state of ridiculous vanity, and as easily as that, most of them were exacting promises on his oath that there would be no penalties upon them should they "bleed His Lordship dry." This was met with a broad smile and a happy clap on the back for the nearest of them, and it was Ilbei's turn to gape.

"There weren't suppose to be no magicks at ruffs, Milord," said one dusty old miner whose seat was in the corner, the one player who'd not been so quick to grin and extract oaths from the nobleman. "And if'n ya are the ruffsman ya say, then ya know it true."

"I do know it," the major said. He glanced once over his right shoulder, then his left—the good fortune of that sequence giving Ilbei time to turn his face toward the wall. The major then leaned in and told them in a low voice that filled the room, "On your honor, boys, this can't get out, but, sadly, I am as magickless as you."

The revelation brought a breath of collective surprise from the men. Many commoners—mainly the uneducated and the blank—believed the nobility could not be born without magic of at least some kind. Ilbei knew better, having encountered enough nobles in his time, and he'd heard plenty of stories about bitter nobles born blank and doomed to ridicule among that high class. While Ilbei had no experience living in high society or being peer to those folks with the blood in them, he could still imagine what it might be like to be a blank among them.

"It's true, gentlemen. A sad fact. But one that has put me on my own road, and today that road has led me to you, the truest men of chance, carving your very existence out of rock. I came to test my game against yours, straight and fair." He poured out a small purse filled with gleaming new coppers, the commonest coin in the realm, and beside the stack he placed one gold coin, a royal crown, as the coins were called. It was imprinted on one side with the likeness of the Queen, which he turned, orienting it so that Her Majesty might be said to watch them.

"Weren't likely you'll see game for that, Milord," muttered one of the gamblers. The bobbing heads around the table agreed.

"So you say, my good man, so you say. And yet, I expect when time comes, one of you might surprise the rest, as is usually the case with men of chance. We're all beggars, the lot of us, until the moment comes round. Then we wield our own sort of magic in procuring our next and our biggest bets."

"Be that as it may, Lordship, I'm letting ya know straight off. So as ya won't be disappointed after, and, ya know ...." The implication was left unsaid, but Ilbei knew they expected trouble from the major if the game didn't go the way he wanted.

"Not at all," the major said gaily, "not at all. On my honor, gentlemen, my coppers to you if you can take them. My gold as well. Nothing for you if you can't, and no reprisals either way. The game is the game. That and, of course, you must promise never to say a word of my little secret to anyone."

"Bugger me with Her Majesty's broadsword if'n I say a word of it," said the man who'd been apologetic just before.

"Right so," said another. "Same fer me, twice."

They were all in agreement and for the most part appeared eager to tap the coins of the rich officer, who they all quietly knew fancied himself a better player than they. Obsequiousness was a mask the lowly learned to wear early and well, but it's not the countenance of truth. Ilbei watched them smiling and genuflecting with their eyes when the major spoke to them, but he saw them look differently to each other when the major's eyes were away.

Only the old man in the corner remained reluctant about having the major in the game. "Now far be it for one such as myself to speak some impropriety, Milord," he began, and from where Ilbei sat, he could see the man's fingers twitching in his lap. "And I sure mean no dispute to your highborn assurances about, well, that secret you gone and shared, but as a rule of this here game—which I bank myself, mind you, and have steady and fair for the last twelve months—we always get the last say-so on the magic powers of newcomers through my old Abigail."

The major's eyes narrowed, and there was no way that the old man didn't notice. Card-playing sports made their living watching people's eyes. Still, Major Cavendis leaned back and waved his hand in the air, a "go on, then" gesture of acquiescence. He even smiled. "By all means, bring the lady in that I might win her over with my honest eyes."

The men at the table laughed a little at that, as if they'd been crossing a deep ravine on a rickety bridge and finally made it to the other side. The old man waved to the barkeep, who came around from behind the bar and left through the tavern's front door. The gaps in the plank walls were wide enough that Ilbei could see the man passing along the front and side, and for a long time after he'd gone out of sight, they all sat in silence, a nervous pall settling on the room like mist in a hollow.

That's when Major Cavendis saw Ilbei sitting there. They locked gazes for a moment, and then the major's sweep of the room passed on. The awkwardness that followed lingered for two full swigs of his ale before Ilbei turned back to his two companions and resumed his questions, pressing them for more information about Ergo the Skewer and his activities on Deer Trail Road.

"There was three muggins a month or so back," a rugged fellow in his middle years went on. He scratched at a week's worth of stubble growing dark like coal dust along his jaw.

"We wasn't there fer none of it, mind, but heard the stories enough times to know. First time caught us all off guard, what with the killins. But they just been mean since. Was eight of em jumped out of the woods and took aim on old Mitty and his boy Juke. Told him hand over all his dust and any nuggets that he got. Juke tried to tell em there weren't no gold around here, that we dig copper and lead mostly, but they wasn't havin it, so they bust poor Juke in the head. A big feller done it to him, near nineteen hands, tall as a tree and arms like anvils. Well, he bust Juke between the eyes with the arse end of a crossbow and down he went, and his old daddy to his knees beside him, snivelin ladylike and beggin they let em alone.

"The feller what struck him turned the crossbow round and pushed the bolt agin' Juke's eye and told Mitty he had count of three before Juke was done fer. So Mitty dumped out his wallet and sure enough gave em twice an ounce. Juke had nothin after Mitty turned his pockets out, so they clubbed old Mitty like they did his boy, and then all of em went off.

"That was the worst of it, but fer that first time. Word went round after, and when them villains showed up again a week or so later and waylaid Corbin Daiker and his brother Toes, well, they got to handin over what they had quick as wyvern strikes. Same for Zoe Spotrotter and his partner five or so weeks back. That was the last we seen of em round Cedar Wood." He finished his narrative and turned back to his companion to confirm what he had said.

The younger man nodded. "Yep. That's how it happened as I heard it too. Word is they went upstream and hassled the boys at Fall Pools fer a week or so, then headed over and set in on Camp Chaparral. I haven't heard anythin since, so it's been maybe a month since we got news."

Ilbei pulled out a pipe and set himself to tamping in a bit of tobacco as he thought about their report. When he got the pipe lit, he drew on it for a moment, preparing to ask his next question. The door swung open and in came the tavern keeper again. Padding along behind him was a lanky hound dog with ears dangling down the sides of its head like long brown tongues. It was a lean creature but well fed, its coat dusty but otherwise clean. Ilbei knew a well-kept creature when he saw one.

The tavern keeper walked across the room, threading between the few shabby tables until he stood beside Major Cavendis. He looked nervous standing within reach of the young lord and all his gleaming weaponry. He glanced across the table to the old man in the corner, who nodded.

"That there is Abigail," the old man said. "If it pleases Your Lordship, give her leave to sniff one of your hands, so we can be on with it, on with lightening you of that there gold crown and what others might be rattling in your pockets besides." He made a point of pushing as much levity into the remark as possible, but the miners found themselves once more upon that rickety bridge, swinging in the winds above the gorge of noble privilege.

Cavendis, however, let go a great laugh, one from the chest, and Ilbei knew instinctively that the officer was genuinely amused. "By my sword, she is a dog, then? And here I'd prepared my most charming set of lines." He pulled off his glove and reached out a hand to the dog, who raised her head and gave his outstretched fingers a sniff. She leaned forward a moment after, tilting her head a little so that her left ear swung pendulously, clearly in hopes of a friendly scratch, which she got. The major gave her skull a vigorous rubbing and the velvet of her ears a good-natured fluff. "Sweet thing," he said. "A fine specimen, and well maintained. You people must do fairly enough if you can pamper a creature so much as this."

Once more the miners were on sturdy ground, the gorge now well behind them, and all the smiles were genuine.

"She's a peach," the old man said. "Can track raccoons in a rainstorm, and even led us straight to Doonger Wagonright's boy after he turned werewolf a half year back. Found him curled up naked as a harpy, lying in the bone pile of the lamb he ate. Was a sore thing having to do him like we did, but least we got him before he got somebody other'n a lamb. Abigail is a blessing from Mercy round here."

"Well, on the subject of harpies," Major Cavendis said, "how about we deal some around and get this game aloft, now that I have met with the approval of your good Abigail here."

"Fair enough," the old man agreed. "Coppers only to start, no limit, and for the first hand, the harpy's wild. Just the lady, of course."

"A wild card? Are we children?" the major said. For the first time since Cavendis had come in, Ilbei saw a flash of the man he'd come to know these last three days.

"Round here folks start the first hand with the lady bird wild. You'll find it the same any game in the camps. It's for ... well ...," he paused and glanced up at the tavern keeper, whose gaze dropped to the floor. No help there. "Well, it's on account of staving off bad luck is all. Harpy ghosts and that sort of rot."

"And I suppose next we'll have our nannies trimming our bread crusts? Maybe stir some honey into our Goblin Tea?"

"Miners is superstitious folks, Milord, and in these parts, it's only prudent. There's been deaths, you know. And it is but one hand. Only the first."

"Well, get on with it, then. I didn't come all this way for children's games." He tossed a lone copper into the pot. "You can be sure that's the last of mine this hand."

Ilbei cringed inwardly, though there was little he could do for it. The major could afford to insult those men, for, as a nobleman, he had no care for their opinions anyway. Ilbei, on the other hand, needed to be polite. Beyond it being his nature to be so, he also needed to learn everything he could, which the major's behavior could put in jeopardy if Ilbei didn't get on with it straight away. So, hiding his irritation, he turned his attention fully back to the men he was talking to and got back to work.

By the time he'd learned everything he could from the two miners he was speaking to, from the tavern keeper, and from another man who entered as Ilbei was about to leave, Ilbei had a general notion of what they were up against in terms of the highway robberies. A quick glance to the ruffs table as he was leaving, however, showed that those poor miners hadn't had a clue what they were up against playing with the young nobleman. Rich as he was, polished as he was, decked in the finest clothing and weaponry as he was, there the man sat anyway, raking in and heaping the grubby copper coins of the men before him, hand after hand and grinning all the while like some petty miser selling candies to kiddies at a carnival. It was one of the most curious sights Ilbei had ever seen.

Chapter 6

The following morning, shortly after the golden sun began backlighting the treetops to the east, Ilbei went to the major's tent. He was intent on procuring permission to take some men to the other two mining camps, Fall Pools and Camp Chaparral, and he was careful to conceal his irritation at having to seek that permission as he called through the canvas flap. "Major, sar. May I have a word, sar?"

"If you must, Sergeant," came the reply. "Enter."

Ilbei stooped and went in, and didn't quite check the rise of his bushy gray brows upon observing the musical Decia, sleeping soundly in the major's bed. Her sandy brown tresses webbed his pillow, and her face was turned away, pressed awkwardly against the tent, though she remained oblivious. The canvas glowed like an old lampshade as sunlight filtered through, casting her features in soft light. Ilbei witnessed her lying there, one bare arm flung out as if she'd been reaching for the major as he rose. Ilbei noted it silently, then glanced back to wait for the major to finish pulling his trousers on.

The major saw his expression and seemed amused. "It's been awhile then, Sergeant?"

Ilbei spent a moment catching his meaning, then shook his head. "No, sar. It hasn't. Though I make a point of not engagin with the troops. Her Majesty's strict policies and all." He made a point of keeping his tone level as he said it.

"Well, I trust a man of your experience has long since learned how that all plays out in a vertical structure such as we have in the Queen's army." There was no malice in the man's voice, but there was a threat in it all the same.

"Yes, sar." Ilbei turned so that only the major was in his field of view, out of respect for the young soldier still lying there in her indispose.

"So get on with it then, Spadebreaker. What is it that brings you in before breakfast?"

"Breakfast is bein kept warm fer ya, sar," he said. "But I come to request yer nod fer me and a few of the men to check the other two camps fer news of Ergo the Skewer, sar. Wouldn't have bothered ya fer such a thing, but with yer bein here, seems proper I clear it afore I get to the work the general hisself gave us to do."

"Are you a gambler, Sergeant?"

Something of a mudslide began upon Ilbei's brow. "Sar?"

"With cards. Have you any experience at cards?"

"I reckon I can hold my own against most, sar. Cards and dice the same. Can't hardly go ninety-some years in Her Majesty's army without pickin up a thing or two, much less an upbringin in lands not so different as all of this." He tilted his head toward the tent wall to indicate where they were upon the world.

"Yes, I'd heard that about you. They went to a good deal of trouble to gather you and that emaciated excuse for a magician you have."

Ilbei was enough of a card player to keep his expression blank. He waited for the major to make whatever his point would be.

"I'd like to get a game going with the boys when you get

back."

"A game, sar?"

"Of course a game. You've been standing here for the last fifteen seconds, surely you aren't so old that you can't remember what we are talking about."

Ilbei cocked an eyebrow at the remark, but kept his mouth shut.

"Can you get to both camps and be back by nightfall?"

"I don't expect so, sar. If'n ya check the maps, you'll see Camp Chaparral is near eight measures as the ravens fly, west-northwest, back down into the foothills some. Fall Pools is closer, only four measures upriver, but steep the last to make it slow."

"Then I'll go to Fall Pools myself. I'll take Decia and her sister with me. You can take whom you will so long as you leave enough behind to secure the camp."

"Sar, all due respect, word last night says there's eight men at least what's jumped the roads. Might be best if'n ya take a few more along. Corporal Trapfast is a fine sword and a keen shot, and we got more than a few sharp archers like him in the company. There's plenty to guard the camp and make a decent company fer yerself goin up Softwater."

"I appreciate your concern, Sergeant," the major said as he buttoned up his coat. "But what I can't parlay out of, I can whip handily enough. And ...." He paused and looked down at the woman lying beneath his blankets. He grinned. "I happen to know she can handle herself perfectly well in a fight, if the vigor of her affection is any evidence. So she with her sister, both hearty farm girls as I understand, ought to be enough force to handle business in the company of my sword."

"Well, I'm sure they are, sar, but fer the sake of showin more force than ya need, perhaps consider takin the corporal at least. If'n ya got some beef with him, then take one of my regulars, Meggins or that big feller Kaige."

"Spadebreaker, that's enough. If I need more of your opinion, I'll whistle for it. We've had this conversation before. So get your people going. You've got a long march through rough territory, and I want you back within an hour after sunset."

"Yes, sar."

"And your man, Meggins. He's got a touch of the weasel in him. I can see it in his eyes. Does he, by any chance, possess any spirit for sport?"

"Aye, sar. Meggins can hold his own at cards, so long as he goes easy on the wine. Learned that fact just two nights back."

"Good. Inform him that he is also invited to our game."

Ilbei's lips squirmed like hostages caught in the trap of his tatty gray mustache. He knew he ought to stay still, but what he had to say needed an escape, so he set the words free. "Sar, it ain't right to take their pay at cards. The men, I mean. Fine enough if'n I play with ya, but the boys, well, they ain't got their minds trained up the way high folks such as yerself do. And even them what Mercy gave the gift of natural wit is inclined to mistakes when come to sittin across from a nobleman. It's bad fer morale, sar."

"You act as if they are incapable of beating me. And besides, I'm more than fair about that sort of thing. You were there last night."

"Aye, sar. I seen ya there. But, if'n I may inquire, so which of them fellers took that gold crown home with him?"

"I did." He said it simply and matter of fact, as if it were obvious and quite out of keeping with the point he'd been trying to make. Ilbei, of course, noticed and commented in kind.

"Right, sar. That's the nugget I'm tryin to dig out, sar."

The major turned away and began combing his hair, using a silver comb produced from a pocket inside his coat. "Bring Meggers to the game, Spadebreaker. And don't be late."

"It's *Meggins*, sar."

"Meggins, then. Off with you now. I need to prepare for my trip up the hill."

Ilbei started to say something but realized he didn't know exactly what he wanted to say or how he wanted to say it, so he shut his mouth again. He glanced down at Decia and prevented himself from shaking his head. It wasn't right for a major to bed down with enlisted folk, much less game with them at cards, taking the pittance they earned for the hardships they endured. He didn't expect the major brought the lass in here with an eye for making her the lady of the manor one day—and quite despite whatever enthusiasm she might have had for the roll. Ilbei realized he was lingering, so he left.

Not long after, he was leading his men through the narrow trails, up and down hills that were steep and arduous. While the journey was only a matter of eight measures, and technically downhill, it was rough going all the way. By the time they were within a measure of Camp Chaparral, they knew precisely how the camp had gotten its name, and Ilbei's voice was hoarse for the steady stream of profanity that had poured from his mouth like summer snowmelt. Some of the oaths he swore were so colorful they set Kaige and Meggins into fits of laughter, which in turn brought forth more profanity.

Adding to the wear and tear of the journey, Ilbei found that by the last measure of it, his shoulder had grown sore. It was worn from swinging a shortsword into the dense, woody brush, hacking out space through the endless scrub that clogged the winding deer trail the miners ironically called a road. Ilbei could certainly understand why the locals got so little news from the other camps if this was how traveling had to go, squeezing through, under and between manzanita limbs as thick as Ilbei's wrists while dodging poison oak tangles and barbed berry brambles at every turn. The only redeeming features of the torturous terrain were the occasional wild apple trees, whose large, sour fruit had provided them with the occasional treat and, when squeezed, with liquid that hadn't gone completely hot in the heat of the day. But even the lukewarm juice of a few sour apples was hardly enough to sustain him past noon, so when Meggins suggested Kaige "lend the old man a breather," Ilbei was more than happy to oblige.

They stopped long enough for Ilbei to gulp down half a jug of water, hot as it was, and he dumped the other half over his head. "Forge of Anvilwrath, but it's shapin up a hot one," he said. "Heat's drippin out of the desert like acid off a dragon's jaw." He picked up his kettle helm from the ground where he'd set it, touching its wide metal brim gingerly. It would have raised a blister had he left his finger on it. "No use fer heat like this," he grumbled. "None at all."

"It will be better when we get to ...," Meggins rolled out the map he carried for them and glanced at it briefly before finishing, "... Harpy Creek. Shouldn't be a whole lot more."

Kaige's eyes went wide at that, and he tilted his face upward and scanned the skies through the gaps in the trees, of which there were plenty, being that they had come down nearly a thousand feet as they traveled. Most of the pines had given way to scraggly oaks that were half-strangled by the heat of the sun most of the year, living mainly on the memory of sparse winter and springtime rains and gleaning whatever moisture was squeezed up from the depths by the weight of the mountains sitting so heavily upon the land higher up. Kaige's head moved back and forth as he warily tried to sight through and around the sporadic growth.

"Why do you suppose they named it that?" Jasper asked.

Ilbei shook his head, blinking water out of his eyes. "Named *what* what?"

"The creek. Why would they name it that?"

"Why wouldn't they?" Ilbei said. "You know the minin sorts well as I do. They don't reach too far fer highbrow ideas when it comes to namin things. We're standin on Deer Trail Road, fer Hestra's sake. There's damned straight more *deer trail* to it than *road*."

"Precisely as I feared," the young mage said. "Such nomenclature suggests a similar justification behind the name of a creek designated *Harpy* Creek."

That was when Ilbei realized that Kaige was still scanning the skies, nervous as a priestess in a prison camp. He looked back at Jasper. "What's yer point, son?"

"If the creek is named for them, then there will likely be harpies somewhere in the vicinity."

Ilbei glanced skyward, thought about what he'd heard, which was nothing on the matter, then shook his head. "Weren't likely to be no harpies this close to human settlements. Folks'd have run em off long ago. No reason fer em to come down this far with humans about."

"Well," said Jasper. "They do tend to follow roosting patterns, and they have great range. If there's a harpy wild within a hundred measures, they might come around."

"There ain't no harpy wilds around here. There ain't one on the map, and this here is a brand new-made map what weren't like to ignore a thing like that. So ya can all just quit with the harpy whinin. It's a damned creek what got a name off some story someone heard or some shape some miner's kid saw in the clouds."

"I don't want to be dinner for no damn harpy," Kaige said. "We should have brought the rest of them bowmen out here with us."

"Oh fer dungeon's sake, lad. You're too damn thick to carry off," Ilbei said. "And they got to get *to* ya first, so ya can just carve em with that giant sword ya got there on yer back. Quit actin the helpless child, and quit yankin yer head out of joint fer fearin skyward." He turned on Jasper and set his shoulders squarely. "And you. Don't be throwin oil on my haystack, ya hear me, boy? There weren't no harpies about, and if'n there were, they wouldn't be meddlin with the likes of us."

"It's the diseases that are the most troubling," Jasper said. "Carving them up is not the problem. I don't have scrolls for the specific diseases borne upon harpy spit or excrement, not if it gets set in. I could possibly prevent one, and I'm being optimistic here, but I don't think I could cure it if it took hold. That could be very bad."

Kaige heard this and his eyes bulged. He stopped and stared, horrified. "Scrolls? Like paper magic?"

"Yes," Jasper replied. He didn't look as if he appreciated the implications in Kaige's tone.

"You mean you can't heal for real? Like a real wizard?"

Indignation pushed Jasper's eyebrows upward, and he clearly restrained his initial response. Instead, he said, "Since you are a simpleton, I will explain it to you—not that I expect you'll understand, but I will try. I am an enchanter. That is my only school of the eight, so, doing the math for you, yes, that makes me a One. Enchanters make scrolls, and we read scrolls. And what happens when we read them is *magic*—magic just like all other magic that's ever been cast by any human in history. My gift, the enchanter's gift, is the gift of sigils and signs. It is the gift of permanence." He straightened to his full height upon finishing, the hauteur in his bearing suggesting that he expected Kaige to appreciate the information he'd just been given and maybe even offer an apology. He did not.

"Yeah, but if we get harpy spat, you can't just lay on hands like a real healer. We'll all die."

Jasper rolled his eyes, rolling his head along with them. He looked back to Kaige. "I will 'lay on' parchment, and it's all the same."

"But you just said you don't got the scrolls."

"That is true. But my point is that a healer who doesn't know the correct spell can't help you any more than I can without the right scroll. So you see, your objection is groundless."

"What about, say, spider bites or copperheads? Or a bad fall? Or a patch of death weed? What about dragon's fire, or even if someone just gets a hole poked in them with a sword?"

"That's enough," Ilbei said. "It's gonna be me what puts a hole in ya with my pickaxe if'n ya don't quit with all that. All of ya. Now Kaige, if'n you're gonna spell me fer clearin the road, then take yer damned sword back and get to it." He nodded toward the shortsword he'd borrowed from the big man to cut their path, droplets of water shaking loose and falling from his beard as he did. "Go on now. We need to get to that camp, gather what word we can, and get back by nightfall. So move it."

Kaige looked warily from Ilbei to the skies, then to Jasper, then back to the skies. Ilbei took a step toward him, menacing him with the promise of violence far more immediate than anything an imaginary harpy could contrive. Kaige saw it and stepped away, taking up his sword and setting himself to work, hacking here and there at the crooked, red-barked limbs of the manzanita brambles that reached across the trail to block their way. Such was his worry over the possibility of harpy diseases that he made quick work of it, hacking through thick limbs as easily as cheese. In little more than an hour, they'd made it to Camp Chaparral.

Chapter 7

Camp Chaparral, like Cedar Wood, surprised Ilbei by its small size. Neither camp could have supported the needs of more than fifty or so miners and their families—those that might be inclined to drag a family so far away from the rest of humanity anyway. The camp consisted of five wooden buildings. Two were barely more than shanties, but three of them were built well enough to have the look of civility. One sent up a plume of smoke from a mud-brick chimney despite the scorching heat of the day, suggesting the preparation of a hot meal underway. Harpy Creek ran at a pretty good clip forty or so paces beyond the buildings, and the sight of the water and the promise of food set the soldiers' spirits on high as they gazed out over the last hundred spans of brush that separated them from the tiny little town. That is, until they heard the wail.

The sound rose from the buildings below, at first barely on the edge of hearing but rising, sharp and high, slicing through the promise of the tranquil scene below them. It stopped abruptly, and once more the day's mounting heat was the only thing in the air.

"What was that?" Jasper asked, eyes darting between the camp and his brawny sergeant. He shifted closer to Ilbei.

Meggins glanced sideways at the nervous mage and stifled a grin. "A banshee, most likely," he said. "That nymph didn't get us, but there's an angry curse upon these hills, a female spirit gone bitter with all them miners abusing the ground all these years. And she can see a man coming long before he sees her. Likely smelled *you* when you poured that honey into the water, trying to trick her, and sent the banshee to finish us off." He winked at Kaige while Jasper looked frantically to Ilbei.

"Oh dear," said Jasper. "Do you really think so?"

"No doubt—" Meggins began, but Ilbei silenced him with a hiss.

They waited, looking down into the clearing where the camp was, watching and expecting another wail. A few chickens ran out from the unseen side of one of the smaller buildings, clucking and fluttering in fright. Jasper tensed, prepared to run, and Ilbei, without looking at the mage, reached out and clamped a manacle's grip around his arm, holding him in place.

An old woman came out after the chickens, cloaked in rags of graying homespun, her long hair as filthy and ragged as her raiment. She stooped and ran with her arms outstretched, her hands like claws as she shambled after the chickens ineffectually. One of the chickens got close enough that she dove for it. She missed, and the chicken skittered away, once again clucking its indignity.

Again came the wail. The woman, upon sliding to a dusty stop in the wake of the renegade chicken, got to her knees and, seated upon her heels, let forth another of the piercing cries. She sounded it with every ounce of her breath, her head cocked back, her mouth wide, howling with the full-bodied passion of a wolf.

"A banshee!" Jasper cried. "It's true!" He turned and bolted back the way they had come, but he only got as far as the length of Ilbei's arm, at which point he was jerked to a halt like a dog hitting the end of the rope that tethers it to a tree.

Meggins had all he could do to keep from laughing aloud and giving their position away, although for once Kaige wasn't sharing in Meggins' levity. Meggins' ruse had been too well crafted for one wink to dissipate. The big man, like Jasper, looked nervously to Ilbei for a cue.

Ilbei remained vigilant, looking down the hill into the clearing. The woman stopped her wail and once again chased after the chickens. She dove headlong after another, and, after failing to grab it, once more loosed a long, agonized wail.

A second woman appeared after a third episode of chicken chasing. This one was much younger than the first, and she walked rather than ran despite the ruckus that had summoned her. She came out of the building from which the smoke rose and went to the bedraggled woman, helping her up gently. The younger led the elder into one of the small buildings, all the while patting her gently on the back of the hand and speaking to her in a voice too low to be heard from where Ilbei and his men were concealed.

When the two women were out of sight, Ilbei nodded and straightened himself. "Weren't no banshee, that. Come on, then. Let's get down there and see what we can learn. Jasper, you stay with me. Meggins, you and Kaige wait outside while we go in."

"Right, Sergeant," Meggins said.

A few moments later, Ilbei and Jasper entered the largest building, where the smoking chimney was. They let themselves inside on account of there being a "welcome" sign on the door.

Inside were several tables, no better made than those at Cedar Wood but twice their number all around, and there was a big mud-brick fireplace on one wall. A fire burned inside it, above which hung a large black stew pot, filling the air with promising smells of meat. Near the far wall, a long, narrow plank lay across a row of fat pine stumps cut flat on each end and long enough to prop the plank up to serve as a bar. A door stood open behind it, allowing Ilbei to look into a room beyond: shelves on all four walls, amply supplied, and a door leading into another room. Nobody was about.

"Halloo," Ilbei called anyway, "anyone here?"

Nobody answered, so Ilbei went to the fireplace and checked the pot, in which various roots and hunks of dark and light meats simmered in savory brown gravy.

"Halloo," Ilbei called again, this time loud enough so that the woman across the way could hear him easily.

Again no answer came, so Ilbei motioned with his head for Jasper to come along. They exited the building and went to the one across the way, to the shanty into which the young woman had gone with the not-quite banshee.

A flimsy door fit into the frame with large gaps above and below. Ilbei peeked through a gap at the left side. "'Scuse me, mistress, but is everythin as it should be? Might we lend a hand?"

"It's as good as it's likely to be," replied a strained female voice. "And yes, come in and help me, please."

Ilbei entered, Jasper still at his heels, and the two of them beheld the speaker seated upon the chicken chaser's chest, the young woman's knees pinning the older woman down on a bed of rags upon the floor. The squirming hag upon whom she sat—and 'hag' was a fair description, for she was filthy and wild to look upon—rolled her head from side to side, her eyes closed and her mouth clamped tight as a priestess of Mercy's knees. Her stiff-lipped security served in the cause of avoiding whatever the younger woman was trying to dose her with, a clear liquid that sloshed about in a bulbous ladle made from a dried gourd.

"Can you hold her head for me?" the gourd-wielding

woman asked. She rose and fell with the bucking of her patient, who thrashed upon the heap of rags. "I swear, the crazier she gets, the stronger she gets right along."

Ilbei guessed by the ease with which the younger woman rode the spasms that this wasn't the first time at this for either of them. "What's wrong with her?" Ilbei asked as he moved toward the pair.

"She's got the craze," the woman replied. "Please, hold her before I waste the medicine."

Ilbei cleared the remaining distance between them and knelt on the floor, taking the twisting woman's head in his strong hands and holding her still, as gentle as he might a babe but firm as a vice.

"Can you get her arm too?"

Ilbei looked to Jasper and directed him to the patient's arm with his gaze. "Grab her," he said.

Jasper looked as if he'd rather eat bees, and he actually stepped away, backing into the wall behind him and then sidling along it until he was nearly hidden in the dark shadows at the corner of the small room. He might have stayed there too, had he not moved into a tangle of spiderwebs that set him to spasms not unlike those of the woman writhing on the mound of rags. He spat and swatted desperately, wiping at his face and mouth.

"Worthless wizard!" Ilbei spat. "Get over here and hold this woman's arm. She needs yer help, ya craven fool."

Jasper, slapping at his face, neck and hair, protested frantically. "But she's got 'the craze'! And I've got spiders all over me!"

"Jasper, if I have to get up, I swear to sweet Mercy herself I will break every bone in yer body and pour ya into a chamber pot. Now get over here. Now!" He spoke this last so loudly it shook dust from the thatch above and startled the young wizard into motion. He came shrugging and tiptoeing hesitantly across the room, his fear of Ilbei only slightly

65

greater than his fear of spiders and whatever it was wracking the poor woman lying there. He paused when he got close enough to see the spittle running down the side of the patient's face, and once more Ilbei snapped at him.

"Tidalwrath's teeth, son, ya got one more second, and then I *am* gonna hurt ya." He meant it.

Jasper heard the danger in Ilbei's voice. He swallowed hard, his Adam's apple bobbing visibly up and down his pale, skinny neck as he crept the rest of the distance across the room. Staying as far back as he could possibly arrange, he stooped down and, with two fingers, took the supine and twisting woman's arm by the wrist. He held onto it with his thumb and forefinger, the barest pinch, as if her arm were the stem of a fragile—and poisoned—wine glass, even his pinky upthrust as if manners held some present supremacy.

Stricken by the wizard's abject delicacy, Ilbei roared at him. "Jasper! By the gods, take hold!" Ilbei's hand darted out like a snake strike and snatched hold of Jasper's wrist, the force of his grip cosmically opposite Jasper's in both will and strength. With a yank, he jerked Jasper to his knees and dragged him up against the makeshift bed. "Use two hands like ya mean it, and if she gets loose of ya, I'll snap that pinky finger off and eat it right before yer eyes."

That was enough convincing for Jasper, and at last he set himself to holding the woman down in earnest, freeing the other woman to pry the patient's mouth open and pour some of the concoction in. The younger woman had to hold the elder's nose pinched tight, and she forced her gnashing mouth shut, pressing the palm of her hand upon the patient's chin. She held on, riding the waves of fury until finally the dose was delivered and everyone could relax. Well, all but the woman with the craze, of course. She lay there, still thrashing for a time, well after everyone had released her and stepped away. She tossed and spasmed, scattering what little comfort the bedraggled bed could offer her and swearing foul enough to raise even the veteran Ilbei's worldly eyebrows.

"Thank you," said the young woman, who was still holding the gourd. She held it up and said, "There's not much of this left. I don't know how long I'll be able to keep her going now."

"What is it?" Ilbei asked.

"Sarrowroot extract, but the Healers Guild mages in Hast do something to it as well. It helps calm victims down and keeps them from hurting themselves before their time comes."

Ilbei looked back to the raggedy woman on the bed and saw that already she had gone to sleep. Just like that, as if someone had blown out the candle of her suffering.

"What's 'the craze'?" Ilbei asked. "Obvious symptoms aside."

"Nobody knows. People started showing signs of it ten months ago or so, but it began getting worse in the last few. By the time we realized it was a real problem, it was already too late. At first, miners started coming down complaining of headaches and nausea, maybe feeling weak. I'm no doctor, so all I could do was give them some powders I had lying around. We sent for a doctor from Hast, but nobody ever came. By the time we sent again, people were starting to die."

Ilbei turned to Jasper. "Got anythin fer it in yer box of scrolls?"

"Of course I don't. There's no such disease as 'the craze.'"

"I'm thinkin this here woman divin on chickens and screamin her fool head off signifies otherwise."

"Well, if there's a real name for it, I've never seen 'craze' listed as an alternative."

"How about ya tell us what ya can do rather'n what ya can't do and ya don't know. I know ya got some mendin papers in that there satchel of yers. Ya ain't the first enchanter I ever had along." Ilbei had had enchanters serving alongside him frequently, but truth be told, Jasper was the first who was singularly an enchanter, a One, with only one school of magic out of the eight. Perhaps it was just chance that had made it so, but Ilbei thought there might be some degree of oddity in that. He figured Jasper must be pretty high level to have been sent out here if that was all the magic that he had. But then again, who knew? The army did what it did, and it was for the likes of Ilbei and Jasper both to do what they were told.

"I do," Jasper agreed. "And I've brought along five of them for this trip. However, I don't believe there is anything that needs to be knit together here, and a venom spell is the only other type I have. You don't suppose she's been bitten by an insect or a snake, do you?" He looked to the young woman, who shook her head. "Well, then all the rest are light healing spells—knit spells, we call them—suitable for broken limbs and cuts, minor internal wounds. I didn't anticipate we'd be stricken in the course of one day's travels with instantaneous diseases or onset lunacy."

"Have ya anythin at camp, then?"

"I have some that might work. I am not promising anything, because I didn't get to pick most of my spells, much less get to write them all. The quartermaster practically threw my trunk together before we left. I know, because I watched him, and when I tried to protest, he told me to, and I quote, 'get stuffed.' Honestly, I think all you military people are desperately in need of a course in common courtesy." He looked down at the haggard figure sleeping amongst the rags and watched her for a time. At least her breathing came easily now, no more panting like a rabid animal. "I will look when we get back. In truth, I've been avoiding taking a total inventory as a form of protest."

Ilbei looked back to the woman who was hanging the gourd up on a nail pounded into the doorframe. "How long she got, miss?"

"Who knows?" She seemed suddenly tired, as if fatigue had been hiding in the energy that animated the work of treating the woman lying at her feet. Ilbei saw the weariness in the deep lines beneath her eyes, lines too deep for a woman of her apparent age. He didn't think she could be much past twenty-five, if at all. She pushed a strand of hair back behind her ear as she drew in a long breath and then let it go. "She could linger for another week or two, or she could be dead tomorrow. It's hard to say. She doesn't know me anymore, so her memory is gone. That's usually not a good sign. But she hasn't got the seizures like some of them do. They don't all get them, though. Sometimes they just drop dead."

"We'll bring back Jasper's trunk of magic tomorrow to help her out," Ilbei said. "He's got some fancy magic scrolls in there; somethin might fix her right up." Jasper frowned at that, started to protest, but Ilbei squelched it with the single finger he held up the wizard's way.

The woman nodded and smiled, though it didn't move her lips very far. "Thank you. We appreciate your help. I'm Magda, by the way, but everyone calls me Mags. That's Candalin there." She pointed to the woman at their feet.

Introductions followed round, and then Ilbei looked out the door to where Meggins and Kaige were standing in the street, watching the area around the camp sometimes, other times trying to peer inside the shanty.

"So where is everyone else?" Ilbei asked. "Word at Cedar Wood is that you folks had a bigger camp than them, or used to but fer some incursions by highway robbers not so long ago."

She smiled, a wry thing accompanied by laughter that sounded as if it were being murdered in her chest. "The robberies didn't last long. They hit a few of the boys on the trails coming down from the excavation sites, and they ran a few others off. But most of the rest were killed or run off by the disease before the bandits showed up, leaving hardly anyone for them to prey on. I haven't heard of anyone seeing them in a month. They probably got bored. Pretty thin pickings robbing men so poor they turned to digging for copper in Harpy Creek. This is the leanest side of Three Tents. Always was."

"So they're all gone off Harpy Creek here? The miners, I mean?"

"Not all. There's still a few at it, at least as far as I know. The camp here has been desolate for well over a month, and I may just be an optimist in hoping the bandits are gone. The last of the boys to come by was Gad Pander, although he's actually from up at Fall Pools."

"Had he heard anythin of bandits up there?"

"Not that he mentioned. He was heading to Hast with three loaded-down packhorses. Said he had a nice strike and was going to deposit what he'd dug at Gevender's Bank."

"He came through alone?"

"He did. But he always does. He runs supplies for the miners up there from time to time. I asked him if he'd inquire about the doctor that was supposed to come by, but I haven't seen him since. That was two weeks ago."

"Maybe he stayed in town to enjoy his take awhile?"

"I never took Gad Pander for the festive type, but I suppose he might have. Or the bandits got him."

"Could he have gone back to Fall Pools by a different route? Comin this way seems a bit roundabout if'n a man's got money fer a boat."

"He might have. We didn't ask him to bring us anything, only to inquire about a healer while he was there. I suppose he had no reason to come back this way. And it was a wet winter, so the rivers are still running high enough for a boat to carry horses and gear."

Ilbei spent a few moments digesting what she'd said,

chewing on a stray length of his mustache that had managed to get into the corner of his mouth. After a time, he changed the subject some. "So, I suppose this here will seem a bit uncomfortable, but would ya mind if'n I have a look around before I head up the creek and see if any of them fellers what might still be up there have seen any bandits recently?"

Her smile was polite, if obvious artifice, and her chin dropped some. "Be my guest. I've nothing to keep from the reaching arms of Her Majesty."

Ilbei winced but didn't say anything. He understood well enough what sort of folks chose a life of such scarcity, and why.

He turned full circle around the small room they were in, but saw nothing of significance. "Jasper, have a look in them other two shacks, I'll check the rest across the way."

"A look for what?"

"Just make sure there ain't no brigands lurkin under a dust cover or beneath the sheets."

Jasper's horror was obvious even before he spoke. "And what am I supposed to do if there are some?"

"Holler quick before they slit ya open and gut ya like a fish. Now get movin."

Chapter 8

The sun was high and bloated above them as they made their way up the creek. Jasper was still in a mood about having been put in "unspeakable peril," which kept him quiet, sparing Ilbei and the rest further lectures about local fauna, flora and folklore. Traveling along the creek made for easier going. The banks were, for the most part, wide and gently sloping, a few paces on either side carpeted by a low ground cover. The narrow swaths of growth made the creek seem a crooked green line painted upon the browns and yellows of the rest of the countryside. In a few places, brush grew down to the water. In others, long curves of the creek had high walls carved into the foot of a low hill, making cut banks that were impassable without wading across to the other side or going up and around the creek where the water was too deep to cross comfortably, especially given all their gear. But even that was hardly a chore, and travel might have been pleasant were it not for the still-rising temperature.

Eventually, as the heat was approaching unbearable, they came across a hut built atop one of the cut banks. It looked down on a bend of the creek, a wide turn in which they saw a man pounding on a great boulder with a sledgehammer. The hammer was huge, the steel head as long and fat as a loaf of bread. Each blow he smashed down upon the rock sent sparks flying like shooting stars and clanged like a stuffed iron bell. The man saw that he was being observed and stopped his work, setting the end of his hammer down in the gravel of the creek bed, which was only a little more than ankle deep where he stood. He looked up at them, one hand on the haft of his hammer, the other raised up to shield his eyes.

"If you come to rob me," he said, "then you'll want to take up hammers and help me at this rock, as whatever's under it is all I got, be it nothing or a hundred stone-weight of gold."

"We're here in Her Majesty's service, sar," Ilbei said. "My name is Sergeant Spadebreaker, and we come to dispatch the robbers what been plaguin the minin roads. Have ya seen such in recent times?"

"Since when did Her Majesty care who picked our pockets?" the miner asked. "Surely she doesn't worry much over losing a few coppers from out here."

"A few coppers, no," Ilbei said, growing impatient with the constant disrespect for the monarchy. "But all her subjects have her protection equal-wise, and she don't abide brigands at all."

"Well, they haven't been through here in a month," the man said, confirming what Mags had told them back at Camp Chaparral. "I'm hoping them harpies got them and ate them all up."

"Harpies?"

Kaige and Jasper began shifting nervously behind Ilbei, at which Meggins could be heard laughing behind his teeth.

"Yeah, seen three of them circling a week or so ago." He let the handle of his hammer lean against his thigh and pulled a tattered bit of sackcloth out of his belt, dabbing at his forehead.

"There ain't much chance of harpies down this low," Ilbei said. "And they wouldn't show theirselves to ya if'n they were. They can fly higher'n a man can see and still keep watch down below."

"Well, if that helps you sleep at night, Sergeant. A man needs his rest." He turned and went back to work on the stone.

Ilbei looked to Jasper, then back at the man in the water, pounding on the rock. "How did ya know they was harpies and not just buzzards up there? I expect harpy wings at a thousand spans look the same as buzzards at eight hundred, same as gryphons and eagles do."

The miner stopped and looked up at Ilbei again. "Because I saw them, that's how. Males, all three of them." He paused and wiped his brow once more. "Listen, I been out here every day for near two years. I've seen more buzzards than I can count. Even ate one once last fall when times was lean. If those three weren't harpies, then you ain't standing there."

Ilbei turned to Jasper. "Is it possible?"

Jasper, looking pale, nodded that it was. "It could explain the disease back there as well."

"Mags didn't see any harpies," Ilbei said. "I think she would have mentioned that."

"You didn't ask," Jasper said. "But the larger point is that she wouldn't have to see them. They could be fouling the water anywhere upstream."

Ilbei nodded. That was a grim but well-reasoned possibility. "Where's this here creek originate?" Ilbei asked.

"Comes out of the rocks some four measures up," he said. "Hole in the side of the mountain."

"Ya noticed any difference in the water recently? Clarity or taste?"

"Nothing that doesn't measure with having men mining upstream. You get used to strange tastes and odors over time. Best to draw your drinking water well after dark or well before sunrise."

Ilbei asked the man a few more questions, digging for anything unusual he might have seen beyond the harpies he claimed he'd seen, but that was the main of it: a month since the last sign of robbers and three alleged vulture-men. With that, he thanked the miner for his time, and the troop set off up the creek again.

They hadn't gotten very far when Jasper broke his traveling silence finally, asking, "I know you people amuse yourselves by teasing me, but if a serious answer is even remotely possible, do you believe it likely that harpies might have come down to roost? It's obviously more than just theoretically possible, as I have pointed out, but you seem very confident, Sergeant. "

"Well, I didn't figure it reasonable at first, but now I reckon it's damned likely," Ilbei said. "Ya done pointed some of it out at first, where ya got a creek named for them filthy things, and that feller back there swears he seen three of em. Ya count in that them other miners back at Cedar Wood thinks harpy curses are so likely that they play their first hand at ruffs with the harpy queen wild, well, then it seems these folks up here got harpies on the mind. Ya know as well as I do that these sorts of folks is superstitious, but ya also know most of them stories don't grow that big a bramble without no roots."

Jasper shuddered. "I knew it. I should have brought more scrolls for disease."

"You're the most nervous little man I ever saw," Meggins said, and the way he said it sounded as if he'd wanted to say it for some time now. "You're like that yappy little ankle-biter dog my aunt in Crown City has got. Eyes bugging out in fright at anything at all, shaking like a palsy and pissing itself for fear of everything."

Jasper seemed unfazed by the analogy. "A reasonable

degree of trepidation is to be expected from one who reads. Fear is the logical outcome of having an abundance of information and the intelligence to make connections between that information and potential realities."

Meggins laughed. "You've got a better chance of getting eaten by sand dragons out here than you do getting sickened by harpy spit."

Kaige turned to Meggins at that comment with the question rising in radiant wrinkles upon his brow. "Sand dragons?" he asked. "Up here, this far off the desert?"

Meggins gave a twisting sort of grin to Jasper and turned back toward the big man in front of him. "Oh, yeah," he said. "We're not that far off, and sand dragons love it up here. It's still plenty hot enough for them, and they can scratch their bellies on all this scrub." He rustled the blue-green leaves of a nearby manzanita bush to prove it. "Plus, they love eating all these wild apples everywhere. Cleans their teeth and gives them a place to hide. That's why these apple trees are so dangerous to be among. A man can get scooped up and eaten just as quick as a whip. Never see it coming."

The question wrinkling Kaige's forehead squirmed toward doubt. He looked about, all around them, back down the slope in particular, where he could see over the brush and trees. The manzanita and scrub oak didn't grow much more than man high, and even the oldest of the apple trees weren't more than three or four spans tall at most, and only a few of those in sight. "But where would they hide?" he finally asked.

Jasper started to say something, but Meggins spun back and silenced him with a glare, pointing at him menacingly. He turned back to Kaige and said, "They hide in the apple trees."

Kaige's face might have caved entirely in on itself in his confusion had not the skull bones beneath kept it all in place. Clearly, the prospect of an enormous sand dragon hiding out here in the apple trees was simply beyond believing. "But that doesn't make no sense."

"Their testicles are red," Meggins said, putting on a professorial tone like the one Jasper used almost constantly.

"Their what?"

"Their berries, the boys in the bag. All red like apples. So are their toenails. It all gets mixed in amongst the apple boughs and they blend right in."

Kaige's face was absolute vacancy, his expression contorting as he marveled the unspoken question: "Could it possibly be true?"

"Look here, Kaige," Meggins said. "Have you ever seen a sand dragon in an apple tree?"

Kaige shook his head that he had not.

"So you see, it works."

"But that's not even reasona—" Jasper cut in, but once more Meggins spun and silenced him. This time he twitched his finger back and forth a little bit. *No, no*, it clearly said.

Kaige, on the other hand, looked as if he'd just discovered something incredible and new. And dangerous. He turned back around and swept his eyes across the undergrowth, up the hill and down. "And here I wasn't even looking for them," he said. "Sergeant Spadebreaker, sir, you ought to tell a man before you put him on point."

Ilbei gave Meggins a scouring look. "Now look what ya done."

Meggins laughed for almost a full half hour as Jasper went through a long and painfully detailed explanation of the nature of dragons, habitat and simple scale. By the time Meggins was done laughing, and Jasper had finally convinced Kaige that Meggins was "perpetrating inaccuracies for the clear purpose of mean humor," they'd come to another hut.

This one, better built than the last, if barely, occupied a

low rise between Harpy Creek and a narrow little rivulet barely a half pace across. The smaller flow ran down out of the hills from the southwest, though it did not appear on the map. There was no one to be seen in the immediate vicinity, and by the silence, it seemed as if the hut was unoccupied. Ilbei called out anyway. "Halloo. Anybody home up there?"

Nobody answered.

Ilbei moved up the gentle slope to the hut, and, cresting it, saw the remains of two people on the other side, their skeletons picked clean but for hair and a few of the tougher ligaments, and both lying out in the open by the remnants of a long-dead campfire.

"Stay back," Ilbei warned. The three men behind him froze. Kaige and Meggins drew their weapons as Ilbei approached the camp with his pickaxe in hand. He pulled back the door of the small plank cabin and looked inside, but soon determined it was clear. He went around back and looked under a tarp that covered a stack of firewood and a few barrels filled with native copper and green chunks of malachite. Most of the barrels were full.

He came back around to the front of the cabin. "Check the trees," he ordered, sending Kaige and Meggins into the brush on either side. Their movements could be heard as they poked into the brush with weapons and called for anyone hiding to "come out or die."

Ilbei, in the meantime, looked around the bodies and saw what he'd dreaded he might see: large vulture tracks, three-toed impressions like a trident, each of the thick toes as long as his dagger. The tracks were everywhere, all around the fire and crossing over each other around the skeletons. He went back and checked the cabin to see if there were any inside, dusty prints to match those around the bodies. There were none. Nor were there any near the barrels and the firewood.

Kaige and Meggins returned, declaring the area clear.

Meggins saw the harpy tracks straight away. "Damn," was all he said.

"Damn is right," Ilbei said.

"Damn what?" Jasper looked more than a little worried as he asked.

"Seems they really do have harpies *and* bandits to worry about," Meggins replied.

"Weren't no bandits what done it," Ilbei said. "Barrels back there are full of ore. If there was bandits here, they'd have taken some."

"It doesn't seem reasonable that anyone would steal copper anyway," Jasper said. "Why would anyone risk, well, us, sent by the Queen, for what little profit there is to be had? It doesn't make economic sense, even for a criminal, not this far from anywhere."

Ilbei nodded. "I expect you're more right than wrong with that, but weren't no way to tell. Whoever done these fellers weren't after it, that's sure. Makin this a feedin opportunity."

"How many do you think there were?" Meggins asked, stooping near the fire and looking at the tracks as Ilbei had done before him. "I'm thinking there were maybe three."

"I'd guess the same," Ilbei said. "Makin that feller downstream spot on."

"So what do we do now, Sarge?" Kaige asked. "Jasper already said he don't have nothing for harpy disease."

"We'll check the rest of the miners up the creek to the source, if'n there are any, then head back and see what Major says. Hopefully it will be somethin what makes sense."

Kaige grimaced. "But what about the craze? I don't want no craze."

"You've had it since birth," Meggins said, attempting levity. It failed. Even he didn't laugh.

"You won't contract anything from them straight away,"

Jasper said. "It's not a magical affliction, you know. There's no instant onset of symptoms. You simply run the risk of exposure to all the standard diseases expected around unwashed bodies, offal, human excrement, decaying flesh and those sorts of ailments that perpetuate themselves in brothels, particularly in those found along the Decline in Murdoc Bay, Blanks Quarter in Leekant and some of the darker parts of Crown City where especially nasty varieties abound."

"Well, I feel much better about it now," Meggins said, making no attempt to disguise the sarcasm in his voice. "Don't you, Kaige? Sarge?"

Ilbei ignored it, studying Jasper for a moment instead. The young magician looked back at him steadily, with such open innocence, such unaffected surety, that Ilbei decided the lad likely knew what he was talking about. Ilbei had never heard anything about harpies using magic either, though the truth was, he'd never had reason to ask. Harpies, like yetis, ettins and giant scorpions, were known to exist in mountainous regions and high foothills. They were seen often enough, killed often enough or found dead often enough to keep their existence from becoming myth, but just often enough and not one bit more. They were more the stuff of campfire stories to frighten city folks and small children than realities for grown men to worry over much. Much.

However, Ilbei was not the sort to throw caution into the campfire based on long odds, and given what they'd found, it didn't seem the odds were so long as he'd thought they were only a few hours before. It was only with the assurance of the young mage, who seemed so well read on the nature of the threat, that he decided to keep his people moving upstream. Onward they went, though this time with grim hearts and a quiet sobriety uncharacteristic of the first part of the day—excepting Jasper, who, having been somewhat pouty earlier, now seemed to appreciate being taken seriously for once. He, in the absence of that dark mood, once again began to pronounce the names of certain flora as they came across them, extolling the various properties therein: what made this weed useful as a reagent, this bit of moss perfect for a poultice and a healing salve, or this little leaf ground up in a recipe for bitter or for sweet.

Over the course of the next two hours, they found five more small camps, all of them abandoned. Given the skeletal condition of the last miners they'd found, the vacancies were either a blessing or just more bad news. There were no more harpy tracks, however, nor were there bodies to be found, so there was some hope that the miners had simply grown weary of such a dismal, scarce existence and moved on.

Another half hour beyond the last of the individual camps, the climb had begun to grow steeper, and the flanking slopes that shaped the path of the creek began to become pinched and steep themselves, carving out a long, wide gully. At this point, the grass and scrub oaks that had been growing along the edges of the high-water line for most of the trip gave way to scraggly pines that seemed to cling to the gravelly soil in desperation. More than a few thrust out from nearly vertical inclines, and in places nothing grew at all. The creek was much louder there.

They found the source of the creek, just as the miner had told them it would be, or nearly so, as he'd failed to mention it originated from an opening some twenty feet up a nearly sheer incline, spewing out of a hole that looked as if someone had come along and tried to tap the ridgeline halfway up like an ale keg. Judging from the loose shale that banked and heaped itself along the lower parts, where the scrappy pines took on a horizontal growing strategy, ascent would be a nightmare of shifting rock with edges that would cut like dull, nasty razors. And that was only to get started going up.

Ilbei glanced around again, suspecting that the area had once been the bottom of a large pool. Looking up to where the incline pinched into the mountain itself, a cliff face marking the easternmost portion of the lowest of several steppes, it seemed likely that once, long ago, there would have been a good fifty-span waterfall. Harpy Creek was all that remained of a once significant waterway.

"It smells like vinegar," he said, upon assessing the area. He tilted his head back and looked up into the hole from which the water spat. "But I damn sure don't smell anythin like vulture filth blowin out of there."

Meggins and Kaige took the comment in stride, having been told back in Hast of Ilbei's olfactory gifts. But Jasper turned a querulous look upon the gray-bearded sergeant with a tilt of his head. "I don't smell anything."

"Smellin is my sort of magic, son."

"So what do you suppose the vinegar is, Sarge?" Meggins made a point of sniffing carefully at the air, which Kaige emulated right after.

"I don't know. We'll get up there and have a look right quick." He swiveled his head and saw Jasper staring up at the hole, sniffing the air as Meggins and Kaige were. "Jasper, since you're the skinniest of the lot, see if'n ya can get up there and have a look inside. Careful now, that shale will slide on ya and slice ya up like a heap of dragon's teeth."

"Me?"

"Yeah, you. It'd be the work of half a day to open that wide enough fer me or Kaige to get through, and we might even have to grease Meggins up to make him fit, even if'n there was one of them potameides inside, flirtin and makin sweet promises. That means it's you what goes. So get along now."

"Get along and what?" Jasper gasped.

"Get on up there and see what's in there makin that

smell."

"But I don't smell anything. And frankly, I think your assessment of the diameter of that opening is rather stingy. Granted, it's difficult to gauge from down here, but by the volume of water issuing from it, I'd sa—"

Ilbei grabbed Jasper by his arms and turned him physically around, facing him toward the hole. "Ya done heard me already, lad, so up ya go."

"That's right, lad," Meggins echoed, doing a fair impression of Ilbei's voice. "Up ya go." Both he and Kaige were snorting and making sounds that bordered on giggling.

Jasper started to protest again, but the firm hand of Sergeant Spadebreaker on his back was enough to set him in motion. He looked up toward the opening and sighed, withering in the heat. "Fine," he said. "But if I die, let it be on your conscience."

"I can live with that," Ilbei said. "Now get to it."

Chapter 9

Just as it had appeared it would be, climbing the slope under his own power was impossible. Though not vertical, the slope was so steep that, try as he might, Jasper could not get more than three or four spans up it before the loose rocks slipped and slid beneath his feet, his balance gave way and down he'd come, sliding amongst a small, sharp-edged avalanche. Needless to say, the first few times quite amused Meggins and Kaige, but on the fourth attempt, Kaige stopped laughing when Jasper slid to the bottom again, this time protesting and showing several cuts on his hands and along his shins where the slate had sliced him. The long red lines of blood that ran freely into the slender wizard's shoes apparently touched the big man's sensibilities. Kaige turned to Ilbei at that point and shook his head. "He is sort of scrawny for it, Sarge. Maybe I should go and set him up a rope."

Ilbei had just been thinking the same thing and nodded, despite Meggins protesting, "Now where's the fun in that?"

Kaige helped Jasper up, the young magician's hand vanishing in the great mitt of Kaige's giant one, and then the burly warrior set himself to the task. If it could be said that Meggins was amused by Jasper's failed attempts moments before, well, the sight of mighty Kaige rolling back down the slope put him into seizures. Kaige took a second run at it, his long legs speeding him up the slope, and he managed nearly half the distance before his feet slipped out yet again. Down he came, this time tumbling all the way down and bowling into Meggins, the two of them rolling into a tangled heap. Meggins was in tears, he laughed so hard, and even Ilbei was grinning some, but only until Kaige unwound himself, drew the bastard sword off his back and strode up the slope again, this time plunging the weapon into the hillside to use as an anchor. At that point, Ilbei had to call him off.

"That's enough," he said. "Don't do that. We'll find another way."

"I'll get it, Sergeant," Meggins said. "You can't send a ninny or an oaf to do a man's job." And with that, Meggins launched himself up the hill, scrambling on all fours like an ape in leather armor.

He didn't fare any better than the others had, and when his feet slid out from under him and he rolled back down, not only was Ilbei laughing, even Jasper was. Meggins lay on his back near Kaige's feet, looking up at his comrades, the dust of his descent still swirling around him, as Ilbei asked, "So which one are ya, oaf or ninny?"

"Both," he said, grinning.

Jasper took his satchel off his back and began rummaging through it, until eventually he pulled out a scroll with a ring of orange ribbon binding it. A length of ribbon dangled from the knot, which he stretched out so that he might read what was written there. He nodded, confirming something to himself, then held the scroll up for the rest of them to see. "This will work," he said, "if one of you wants to attach a rope up there."

"What is it?" Ilbei asked.

"It's a levitation spell. I can get myself up there, of course, but once I go inside, I'll have to cancel it. So I'll have no way down. I am abundantly familiar with knots, of course, but if there is nothing to tie to inside, my bringing a rope with me will still be meaningless. I don't believe I am physically qualified to safely drive a piton into the rock." He inclined his head toward Meggins in an indicative sort of way, then stared at Ilbei patiently.

Meggins narrowed his eyes at that, but there was still laughter lingering in them. "You sneaky bastard," he said. "I should have known you had it set for me all along."

"It's only reasonable to send up the person most suited to the task," Jasper replied. "A few moments ago, when the only obstacle appeared to be an issue of size, I was that candidate in your minds. But now that there is an element of strength required, you, being the next order of leanness from me, are the obvious choice."

"Enough," Ilbei said. "Read yer scroll. Meggins, get yer climbin gear. We need to be on with this and head back. We're already goin to be pushin our time as it is."

"I still don't know why we have to hurry back to sit in on a game of ruffs," Meggins said. "What's he think, we came out here for the camping and recreating, like we're on our leave?"

"I ain't even tried to figure it," Ilbei said. "Speculatin on such a thing puts me too close to insubordination if'n I speak it, and there's been often enough in my time where I couldn't see the landscape fer the spot a' land I was standin on. If'n he's got a bigger idea than I can reckon, so be it. If'n he don't, well, I don't expect he's gonna win anythin from me that will set me back much. He may fancy hisself a fine sport at ruffs, but there ain't a trick I haven't seen a thousand times."

"Well, I'm not too proud to admit I can be beaten—or cheated," Meggins admitted as he hauled out a length of rope, a hammer and a rolled leather packet of steel spikes.

"Been both enough times to know it." He pulled out one of the spikes and threaded the end of the rope through an eye punched in it near its blunt end.

"Well don't ya go accusin no nobleman of cheatin tonight. Even if he is. Just come in with whatever ya think ya can turn, and if'n ya can't turn it, make sure it ain't more than ya can walk away from without hurtin ya none. I'll try to get it back fer ya, by cards or by protest, if'n ya do. And if'n I can't, when we get back to Hast, I'll put in a request fer reimbursement, bein as ya been ordered to play."

Meggins looked up from his work, watching Ilbei, who looked him straight back in the eye and nodded that it was true. "You will?"

"I will, if'n ya don't play the fool about it," Ilbei said. "I ain't got no say-so over a major, but I know the system well enough to make it right when we come round."

Meggins smiled, nodded and went back to work. "Then maybe I'll enjoy the game."

"Just keep to what I said. I can't promise to get yer stake back."

"I understand," Meggins said. He slipped the coiled rope over his head, around his neck and shoulder, and tucked a few extra pitons and the hammer into his belt. Turning to Jasper, he said, "You ready there, wizard?"

"I am," Jasper said. "Just tell me up or down, closer or farther, softer or harder."

Meggins frowned. "Softer or harder?"

"Yes. I can adjust it so you are standing on solid ground or something that gives like mud or sand, and even lateral movement as if you are standing on ice."

"Ah, I got you," Meggins said. "Okay, well, let's go, then. And don't drop me."

"I won't."

Jasper stretched the scroll to its full length and began reading in a language none of them understood. Ilbei watched him, waiting, and eventually wondering how many damned words could possibly be written on a single scroll. And then Meggins was floating in the air.

The wiry warrior rose up smoothly, straight up, until he was standing in the air at chest height to the rest of them, at which point he gave out a whoop. "Holy Hestra and her seven-headed son! Kaige, you seeing me?" He turned, as if fearing somehow he might fall off, and grinned down at everyone.

"I see you, Ferster. I see you." Kaige looked absolutely delighted, and he turned to the chanting wizard, buoyed by giddiness. "Jasper, Jasper, can I go next?"

"Don't interrupt him, you fool," Meggins snapped. "He'll drop me like a burning rat."

Kaige looked horrified and apologized.

"All right, get me up there, Jasper," Meggins said. "Easy now."

Jasper did not acknowledge the request, but up Meggins went, angling toward the hole midway up the unassailable slope. He flew straight for it as if on a line, and when he got to it, Jasper's cadence as he read slowed and became a mumbling repetition of a singular set of lines.

Meggins leaned toward the hole where the water spat out, and he peered into the darkness. "I think I can get through," he called down, "but I'm going to need a light. I should have brought a light. Can you bring me back down for one?"

Just like that, he was descending again, a broad grin on his face. Kaige could hardly contain his jealousy, and he ticked and hawed like an eight-year-old in line for a gryphon ride at the Crown City Royal Faire.

Ilbei lit a torch and handed it to him with two extras, just in case. "Ya can toss em in if'n ya need to."

"Good idea," he said. "Okay, up again."

Once more Jasper's chant altered a little as he read, and a few moments later, Meggins was peering into the hole with his torch. "Not much room in there," he said. "A crawlspace in the water. I think it opens up a few spans in."

"Ya smell carrion or shite?" Ilbei called up to him. "Anythin that might be harpy stink?"

"No, Sarge. Don't smell anything. Not even your vinegar."

"Can ya get in there far enough to see?"

"Yeah, I think so. Give me a sec." Meggins shifted the rope on his shoulder and leaned into the hole, bracing against the bottom of the flow with one hand, reaching in deeper with the torch. "Move me up about three hands," he called back, his voice amplified as it washed out of the hole.

Jasper altered his reading slightly, for the barest few seconds, and Meggins' feet moved up to where his knees had been.

"That's good," Meggins shouted. Then he hunched down and crawled into the hole, his knees as wide apart as the opening would allow, sort of hopping on his one hand while raising the other as high as possible to keep the torch from getting wet. The water splashed all around him, and he spat and swore as the current, disturbed by his blocking it, nearly snuffed the torch anyway.

"Are ya all right in there?" Ilbei shouted up at him.

"Yeah, fine," Meggins called back. "Just give me a few."

For a time there was silence as Ilbei and the rest of them craned their necks, watching the hole and waiting for Meggins to reappear. Jasper stopped chanting as soon as Meggins' boots vanished into the darkness. He blinked a few times, shook his head as if to clear a daze, and began waving the parchment in the air at arm's length, trying to stay clear of the blue smoke that had begun issuing from it the moment he stopped reading.

Ilbei and Kaige stepped away from the smoke as well, as there was no telling what it might contain, and they watched for a few moments until it finally stopped. Jasper held the parchment taut, and Ilbei saw that it was now blank. All that magic writing was gone. Jasper stretched it and tilted it away from himself, then blew off a dust of purplish ash. Apparently satisfied that it was as he wished, he rolled it back up again, sliding the ring of ribbon around it and adding a small knot at the dangling tip to mark the scroll as spent. Without even glancing to Ilbei or Kaige, he simply resumed watching the hole from which the water came.

Shortly after, they could hear the sound of hammer on steel, suggesting Meggins was pounding a piton into the rock somewhere inside. A few moments later, out came the rope, a black stripe that shot out with the flow of the water and waggled in the current, being carried downstream until the line passed over their heads and its full length was achieved. It went taut, then slack, and it dropped out of the bottom of the gushing spray, most of it anyway, all but a length of half a span, which bounced and fished about in the mild torrent just outside the hole. The rest of it slid out of the stream, and some four spans of its length fell flat against the slope with a wet slap, lying against the warm stone like a fresh-washed serpent that's hung itself out to dry.

"Ya see there, boys, it's just waitin fer to be climbed," Ilbei said. "Let's have a look. Kaige, you stay down here, watch that nobody comes in after us, what with ya not likely to fit in there anyways." He wasn't so sure he was going to fit either, given how tight it had been for Meggins going in, but he was bent on having a look anyway.

Kaige nodded, and with that, Ilbei motioned for Jasper to come along. Ilbei took up the rope and began his ascent, angling himself against the incline and moving slowly, checking each placement of a boot carefully before trusting it.

Shortly after, he was at the opening, studying it dubiously. He didn't much care for the prospect of stuffing himself into it, not once he was right up to it and could see how narrow it was. It was smaller than it had seemed, and he wasn't too sure his broad shoulders would fit, even with the aid of lubricant and a flirting potameide. There definitely was no possibility of Kaige getting in there without time spent on the edges with pickaxe or hammer. He turned back to check on Jasper's progress behind him and saw that the young wizard was clinging to the rope for dear life. He'd managed to slip and had rolled sideways into the stream where it hit the rocks, where he was now caught by the weight of the current. He clung to the rope desperately, his head peeled back and his mouth gasping for air as the water choked his cries and he battled to keep from being swept away. He was losing that battle half a hand's length at a time.

"By the gods, I've seen newborns stronger than that," Ilbei muttered, but he shouted down to Kaige. "Can ya help him? Get him up to me, and I'll push him through. I can't get inside."

Kaige shouted back that he could, and he waded into the creek. He caught Jasper and the rope and dragged the mage onto the shale. Jasper was still sputtering and wheezing as the big warrior picked him up and set him on his feet again. "I'll help you this time," Kaige said. "You go on and try again. I'll come up behind. You can lean back on me, sort of sit in my lap."

Jasper started to protest, but Ilbei's shout came down upon them both like thunder. "Come on, girls, we haven't got all day."

"Go on," Kaige said again. He gave Jasper a gentle push toward the rope. "Just lean back like you seen Sarge do, and make sure to set your feet. Put your weight on me."

Jasper did as he'd seen Ilbei do, and before he could protest that he didn't have the arm strength to hold himself like that for long, Kaige pressed in behind him and reached around Jasper on both sides for the rope. He gripped it firmly, with his elbows outward enough that Jasper still had room to move a little from side to side, but the big man now supported both their weights. The curve of Kaige's steel cuirass pressed solidly against Jasper's back, which set the sorcerer to complaining some, as did the hilt of Kaige's dagger jabbing into the back of Jasper's thigh. But, Jasper's discomfort aside, soon Kaige was half walking, half hoisting Jasper up the shifting slope. Shortly thereafter, Kaige got the wizard to where Ilbei waited impatiently, at which point Ilbei grabbed the mage by a fistful of robes and hauled him up and shoved him into the hole as if he were stuffing a pillow.

"Sorry," was all Ilbei said as he did so, but there was little else to do, and he didn't have time for more whining. He jammed the scrawny sorcerer into the current as far as possible, keeping a hand on his foot so he wouldn't be washed out. Just when he was satisfied that Jasper could get through on his own, they heard Meggins shout.

"Curses, I'm diseased!" Meggins cried. That was followed immediately by a yelp and a splash. Ilbei looked past Jasper, blinking, trying to see through the spray. Meggins was sliding toward them at speed, flat on his back, washed out by the current and coming with enough momentum to blow through Jasper and Ilbei both. Meggins shot a full pace into the air and fell, landing hard in a natural chute formed by centuries of erosion. Jasper, blown out by the impact, landed right behind him. The slope was steep enough and the rock smooth enough to prevent major injuries, but they bounced together, grunting in unison, and then shot down the wash, sliding around the waterworn bend with enough current behind them to carry them thirty paces downstream.

Ilbei had it somewhat better than the other two, as he'd been holding onto the rope. The impact with Jasper and Meggins had swung him away from the hole, but he was strong enough to maintain his grip, saving himself being flung down into a cascade of miserably sharp stone. As it was, he slammed into the rocks two spans beneath the hole, where he spent some moments scrabbling in the shifting shale, trying to get his bowed legs underneath him for his descent.

By the time he managed it, Meggins and Jasper were straggling back, both of them panting as if they'd just run the Queen's marathon. Ilbei didn't have to ask what had gone wrong, for Meggins was yammering on about it like a city girl who's had a mouse run up her skirt.

"I seen it," he said, his eyes wide and his face pale. "A harpy all right. And me crawling in that water, choking my way through that hole with my mouth open half the time. I'll get the craze for sure!"

Kaige looked horrified. "There's a harpy in there?"

"Damn straight there is. Dead as dust and seeping disease into everything. I'm sure to die of something terrible." He turned and grabbed Jasper by the front of his robes. "You've got to save me. Don't let me die in some horrible wasting way. I need something bad. I don't want to rot or bloat up or get all scrofulous like they say, not even dead before I'm all filled with maggots and decay. Please, Jasper, I'll give you all my share the rest of the year, the rest of my career even. Don't let me get the craze."

Jasper's eyes were nearly as wide as Meggins' were. He'd never seen the soldier discomposed, and for once, he didn't think a litany of statistics or probabilities was what he was supposed to say. He glanced beyond Meggins to Ilbei, who nodded at him, the suggestion that Jasper should give some assurances. So he did. "I won't let you get it," he promised. "Surely that quartermaster will have provided us with scrolls that will help. They have policies for that sort of thing, don't they?" He tossed the issue back to Ilbei with a glance.

"I reckon they do," Ilbei said, though he had no idea how army policy went when it came to the procurement or issuing of magic scrolls. "So let's get movin. It's a long way back."

Nobody spoke much along the way, only what was necessary. It turned out that one dead harpy was enough to kill humor entirely.

JOHN DAULTON

Chapter 10

Upon their return, Ilbei saw to it that Jasper did in fact have a scroll suited to preventing any onset disease: a spell called, simply, "Purge Disease." Jasper looked the spell over and explained that it was suited for most common varieties of ailments—colds, influenzas and minor infections—but he confessed he could not be sure it would meet for whatever the craze was. He also reported that it was his only copy of the spell. Ilbei told him to read the scroll on Meggins anyway. The young wizard shrugged and set to work, Meggins seated on a rock beside him, twitching his leg nervously.

Leaving them to it, Ilbei set off for Major Cavendis' tent, bringing with him one small pouch half filled with coppers and not one silver slug more. He stopped on his way only long enough to stab a thick slab of venison on his knife, a generous portion that Hams carved from a deer haunch sizzling above the fire as fat dripped into the coals, hissing and spitting and filling the air with its savory smell. With a grateful nod to Hams, Ilbei was on his way to ruffs.

"Spadebreaker," the major said when Ilbei finally appeared, "you're an hour late." Seated next to him at a table that had been set up for the game was a man Ilbei did not recognize, a lean fellow of middle years, well dressed, well groomed, and with a long blond mustache that drooped well past his lips on each side. Despite his polished and even urbane appearance, he had a weathered look about him that belied a life in leisure. A glance behind the man revealed a fancy black longbow and a quiver with green-fletched arrows to match, leaning in the corner of the tent. It hadn't been there that morning before Ilbei left.

"We had a run-in with a dead harpy," Ilbei said. "And our wizard, young Jasper, is seein to one of the lads so as he don't come down diseased."

"Right, then," was the major's response. "And where is your man Meggles, so we can get the game underway?"

The lack of interest in the soldier's condition made Ilbei's cheek twitch. "It's *Meggins*, sar, and he'll be along shortly. He was the feller what had the run-in I spoke of."

"Ah, I see. Well, we'll give him a few moments, then. In the meantime, I'd like you to meet Locke Verity. He's the local huntsman extraordinaire. He provides most of the meat the locals eat. You can thank him for that fine meal you've got speared there on your knife."

Ilbei inclined his head politely. "A pleasure, Master Verity." To show his gratitude, he took another bite. He was famished beyond manners from the rigors of the trek.

"So you found a harpy, you say? That's an odd discovery. Where was it, and were there signs of others around?" The major caressed a stack of silver coins on the table before him, lifting the top half of the stack a few hairsbreadths and then letting the coins slip through his fingers onto the rest again with a *clink, clink, clink*.

Ilbei saw it and his cheek twitched again. He didn't bring silver, and he wouldn't be fetching any either. "We did find some tracks near a couple of dead fellers, their bones was picked clean as gleanin. And the dead harpy itself, we found that in a cave where the creek come out. Meggins seen it. He figured it had been dead a long time, maybe six months or more, rot hadn't got it all ate up yet fer the water bein so cold."

"Birds in general are nasty creatures," the hunter said. "Harpies worst of all. I found signs that they were what killed a woman from Cedar Wood a year and a half ago. I tried to track them down, but, well, it's difficult to track creatures that fly. So I never found anything. Then I spotted a pair of them a few months ago. Filthy things. Not sure if they were the same ones, and I would have shot at least one of them, but there is no telling what kind of trouble that would have caused. There are no harpy wilds around here anymore, not for a hundred measures at least, but who knows how far they'll fly for revenge, so best to let them be. The fact that they saw me, saw that I had spotted them, was enough to run them off. I haven't seen them before or since, so I imagine they were passing through. It's not entirely unexpected to have a run-in every few years, way out here like this, I suppose."

"Where'd ya see them two a few months back?" Ilbei asked.

"They were watering at the river, way up in the rocks, about a measure above Fall Pools where the waterfalls are worst and a man can't really get around much. I could smell them even through the mist blowing off the waterfall. Worst sort of bird there is, worst of man and vulture. But birds are birds, like I said, and vultures aren't all that much worse than turkeys and even chickens in the end. That's why I stick mainly to deer, goats and pigs. I'll go after pheasant and quail, even turkey if I have to—money's money, after all—but give me a choice, and I'm going with four-legged meat. It pays better, and it's a lot less likely to kill you after it's dead."

Major Cavendis smiled, but it was clearly strained. His stack of coins continued to clink. Ilbei couldn't tell if he was irritated or simply bored, or just impatient for the game.

The major let go his coins and took up a goblet and a pitcher of wine, which he raised toward Ilbei invitingly. "So what did you find out about the bandits on your foray down the hill?" he asked.

"I'll surely have some of that, thank ya, sar," Ilbei said as he took the cup in his free hand. He let the major pour as he answered the question. "We didn't find much else about them bandits. Seems they struck the lower camp just like the boys at Cedar Wood said they did, but after a month ago, they never come back. Neither has any of the folks what used to frequent that camp come back neither, though. That struck me odd, as they sent more'n a few off toward Hast fer help. Seems curious so many locals disappeared and no help come fer em."

"I should say help arrived when you did, Sergeant. Or do you think your being here was some bit of chance?" He followed it with a patronizing sort of hum, which Ilbei ignored in favor of the contents in his cup, which he drained before answering.

"Well, that camp is only four days out of Hast if'n we'd gone direct, two if they'd sent us ahorse. Seems to me, someone might have been there a long time sooner than us here. Tangled-slow as things are sometimes, orders don't take as long as all that to filter through, sar, beggin yer pardon and no disrespect to the methods of Her Majesty's service, of course."

"Of course." He motioned for Ilbei to hand over his cup for a refill, which Ilbei gladly did. When he handed it back, it was filled so full that Ilbei had to be careful lest he spill on the white linen spread upon the major's table. "Drink up, Spadebreaker. You've earned it. A long day, certainly."

"And a hot one, sar," Ilbei said. "Straight outta the gutters in the lowest parts of hell. Fry a man's bacon just sittin in the shade—not that we had time fer sittin as such, given this here game and all." He made a point of looking into the wine as he drank it rather than looking the major in the eye.

The major noticed, of course. "I take it you aren't eager to play?"

"Not that I ain't keen, sar, but I expect I don't understand what the purpose is."

"Sport, Sergeant. For the fun of it."

"Well, seems a long way to come fer a game of ruffs, sar, but I'm in fer a few coppers before I hit the wool, maybe just to shave yer purse down some." He put up a greedy grin, but it was all for show.

Just then Meggins could be heard outside, calling for permission to enter the officer's tent.

"Yes, yes, come in, Megger—Meggins."

Meggins entered and looked around. He was obviously uncomfortable, but seeing Ilbei gulping down the major's wine relaxed him considerably.

"Have a seat, soldier," the major said, directing him to an upright log to his left meant to serve as a chair. "Have you gotten yourself something to eat, as the sergeant has?"

"I did, sir. Hams set me up, and I wolfed it down quick as I could. Mostly why I was delayed in coming. I apologize." He took note of Locke Verity and paused, a fleeting frown, then looked past him to the fancy bow leaning against the tent. "Have we played before?"

Verity looked Meggins up and down, pursing his lips for a few moments, then shook his head. "I don't believe so. I never forget a man who has taken my money. I make a point of it, so that I know to avoid him. And if I've taken his, I make a sharper point of remembering that, in case I should find him following me one day. It's not a game for carrying off a draw now, is it?"

Meggins laughed. "No, it's not, at least as it depends on the stakes. My mistake then." He sat down as directed by the major, nodding in deference to the hospitality. "Thank you, sir."

"Not at all," said the major. "I was just telling Sergeant Spadebreaker how much I respect your hard work today. That was a long trip, and there you had an incident with a harpy, I hear."

"I did, sir. A foul moment in my personal history, I can tell you. But Jasper fixed me up, and I'm good and ready for what comes again."

"A foul moment, you say?" said the major. "*Fowl!*" He glanced back and forth between them, then to Verity, and began laughing uproariously at his joke. The hunter followed suit. Ilbei put on a show of amusement as well, which Meggins had the sense to emulate.

"All right then, it's settled, we're to have a game," said the major. "Sit down, Sergeant, and let's get it underway."

Ilbei sat down and dumped his small pile of coppers onto the table before him. The major's eyes flicked toward it and counted it in the time it took for the lamplight to glint off the dingy coins.

Meggins did likewise, his own stack only a little bigger than Ilbei's, and the major could be observed working his jaw, the movement visible in the line along his cheek where the lamplight shadowed some. "You boys didn't come for the long haul, did you?"

"Like I said, sar, it's been a long day. If'n my luck is good, I'll turn this copper to gold from yer pile there, the winnin of which will keep me awake and as giddy as a spanked milkmaid. But if'n ya fellers pull my pockets to rabbit ears, well, then I'm fer a pillow and fine with that too."

The major smiled, a wide, generous thing, nodding as he shuffled the cards. "Well said, Spadebreaker. I suspect there may be more to your game than you let on."

"Weren't my maiden voyage we're playin here, sar, I won't lie."

The major dealt the cards amongst the four of them with

movements too quick for the eye to see, his hand nearly a hummingbird's wing. Ilbei knew in that moment that the major took the game far more seriously than he did. Far more. Nobody handled cards like that who wasn't a disciple of the game, and one who wanted that fact known. Still, it was impressive to see.

Flick, flick, flick and the hands were dealt, so quickly that everyone besides the major seemed to share in Ilbei's awe. There was a stunned pause. The major had already lifted his cards and looked at them by the time Locke Verity gasped, "Wait!" He was too late, however, for the major was sorting his cards.

"What is it, man?" the major asked, his eyes narrowed and his tone marginally annoyed.

"You didn't say the lady harpy's wild."

"Why in the name of Crown would I do that? You can't possibly buy into this superstitious local claptrap too."

"I am one of the locals, as you'll recall," Verity replied. "In a manner of speaking, anyway. And it is bad luck in this part of the world, my friend. Bad, bad luck. Especially with what befell Private Meggins there. Bad, bad luck." He stared at his hand, head down, making a point of not looking the major in the eyes.

"Oh for Mercy's sake," said the major. "You make a fortune feeding these idiots up here, and your wealth is the product of capitalizing on the same backwoods idiocy that conjures up such ridiculous beliefs. Have you gone native on me or just soft in the head?"

"Things like that don't come about on their own, Major, and you know it better than most." He let his gaze linger on the major, then turned to Ilbei and Meggins. "Besides, there's no sense tempting Lady Fate, is there?"

A shadow passed over the major's face, his eyes narrowing again, but it flew off right after. He laughed. "And you call yourself a gambler. What gambler lasts a week believing in luck, curses or Lady Fate?"

"Just because I'm not so sure there's an Anvilwrath or a Mercy up there in the heavens, waiting to come back and smite me or come down and save my soul, doesn't mean I don't still drop a silver piece on the altars from time to time. Only the arrogant won't pay the ante on that pot every now and again."

"Then you're a fool and a silver piece poorer for it. I should hope you are able to rise above such things when it matters."

The hunter glared over his cards at the major, which Ilbei observed but didn't know what to make of. Verity reached into his stack of coins, then tossed out five coppers with the carelessness of a child throwing breadcrumbs to ducks on a pond. "Just play," he said.

Ilbei and Meggins were broke in a quarter of an hour.

Chapter 11

Ilbei lay staring into the dark angle of his tent, the sun still an hour from setting another day aflame. He'd been staring up there for the last hour. He couldn't stop thinking about that damned game of ruffs the night before. It wasn't for the loss of a few coppers—though it had been the worth of a few days' pay. What rung him so strange was how the major and that hunter had worked Ilbei and Meggins like they had. There was simply no point in it that Ilbei could see.

Ilbei had been cheated at cards plenty of times in his hundred and fifteen years, and he was sport enough to spot the tricks most crooked gamblers used. But those two, Major Cavendis and that Locke Verity, with his fancy black-and-green bow, were in a league of deception like he'd never seen. They'd send false signals early on, the type they likely expected a veteran player like Ilbei to see, things like glancing at their chips to bluff they had a good hand, or rubbing a forearm comfortingly, as if they had a bad one even though their cards were great. They sent false tells and then sent no tells, and then sent true tells that Ilbei ignored. By the time they'd gobbled up all his money, Ilbei was down to playing his cards without even looking up. There was no point trying to read either of them, and when he stopped trying and simply played solid ruffs, base mathematical strategy, they still won every hand. Every one. He'd left feeling pretty embarrassed, embarrassed for having had Meggins witness how poorly he'd done and embarrassed for knowing that he'd been the mark.

And the real question was: why? He wondered what the point of that game was. He wondered it more now than he had before going in. There was simply no reason for a lord like Major Cavendis to care one jot about a handful of coppers from two grunts like Ilbei and Meggins. It was the same for the coins collected from those poor sots up at Cedar Wood. Likely as not, the major had taken money from the miners up at Fall Pools too, though Ilbei hadn't had time to ask given how easily he'd been dispatched last night. But he could fix that. It seemed important to him, so he made up his mind to ask when he asked the major what he'd learned about the bandit raids—another thing he'd not gotten around to.

So stirred was he by the emotions of being sorely whipped that he finally gave up on the sun ever rising and got up just for the sake of having something to do but think. He found old Hams working up the cook fire for the morning meal, and he spent some time helping him prepare it, lugging wood and water and toting flour and potato sacks. The work helped him clear his head. He was shoveling the last few coals onto the lid of the castiron roaster he'd buried for Hams when he saw Decia leave the major's tent and skulk back to her own. His first instinct was to go grab her by the ear and drag her out of hearing range of the camp, wanting to give her an earful on camp morale and the consequences of sleeping within the company, but he snuffed the impulse.

He was no longer in command here. He decided it might be better if he took it up with the major instead, though he knew how that would go as well. Cavendis was too young for his position. Too damn young. Ilbei couldn't figure how a man like that could get a commission, much less as major. He should know better than to act that way. It was out of keeping with reality. Sure, some of the young lords weren't as prudent or wise as the career officers were, but for the most part, they still had honor to uphold and reputations to make. A record of malfeasance and issues amongst the troops would not set well within the workings of high-blooded families. It just didn't make sense. And this major couldn't be figured for either competence or idiocy. He seemed to swing between both extremes, convincing Ilbei the man wasn't what he seemed.

Ilbei watched the young soldier slip back into her tent and shook his head. He didn't know her or her sister very well, but he hoped she was the tough type and wouldn't be too let down when Cavendis was done with her. The way her sister, Auria, had sung the first night off the rafts suggested that one had a gentle soul. He could only hope Decia was the hardier of the two.

Ilbei turned toward the cook fire and had hardly made five steps toward it when Cavendis called him by name. He turned back. "Yes, sar?"

"A word, Spadebreaker."

Ilbei set the coal shovel down and went to where the major stood outside his tent. Cavendis stretched as he stared down through a gap in the trees, out over the misty green pines sloping off toward the northern spur of distant Gallenwood. The sun outlined the brushstroke limbs of the nearer treetops and trimmed them with golden light that gleamed like the edges of newly sharpened knives.

"Spadebreaker, you've done good work," the major began. "And I've made a point of commending you and your men in my report."

There was a note of finality in the remark, which struck

Ilbei as curious despite his soldierly reflex ejecting a tactical "Thank ya, sar."

"Have your men pack up camp and head back to Hast. Your job is done here, so there's no point lingering any longer, burning up the local hospitality. I'm sure the presence of Her Majesty's army is felt as an imposition out here."

The lines upon Ilbei's forehead told the story of his confusion, but his mouth shaped an acceptable response. "Yes, sar. I'm sure it is, sar."

"Very well, then," said the major. He turned to reenter his tent.

"Major, sar, if I might ...," Ilbei began. He waited for the major to turn around, which the man did, making no effort to hide his irritation at having to do so.

"Yes, what is it?"

"Sar, I'm not sure as we've put the issue of the highway robbers quite to rest. I'll be asked fer my report upon our return, and, frankly, sar, I don't have much to tell the general but that there's been a pause in the criminality. I was told I was to find and apprehend said villains or bring back heads to prove the banditry was done."

"Well, it's done, Sergeant. I sent the pigeon yesterday. The boats will be here tomorrow morning to take your people back."

"But, sar—"

"I won't argue with you, Sergeant. Her Majesty hardly needs to spend a fortune paying her soldiers to fish, hike and go off exploring caves after a problem has been solved. If you need some time off for recreation, put in a leave requisition like everyone else. If there are no more robberies, then the mission is finished. Chasing the perpetrators across the continent of Kurr is a job for the constabulary, not the Queen's regulars."

"But, sar—" he began again. The major cut him off a second time.

"You heard me, Spadebreaker. No highway banditry, no mission. You have your orders. Don't make me rewrite my report. I'd hate to see you lose another stripe."

"Yes, sar. As ya say, sar."

The major spun back and vanished into the shadowy confines of his tent, and Ilbei went back and checked the coals on the small oven he'd buried near the fire. He shoveled a few more coals over the top and then stared down at them for a while, not seeing the red glow or the ash of their edges so much as what he saw in his mind: a panoply of contradictions whipping by. Hams saw him doing it and ventured over after a time, concerned that Ilbei might be having trouble with the roaster somehow.

"It ain't right," Ilbei said as he saw Hams' feet move into his field of view.

"What ain't right?" the old cook asked.

"The major done ordered us back to Hast."

Surprise lifted Hams' wiry eyebrows like rising bread. "They catch the bandits somehow? Bounty hunters, maybe? The local boys?"

"No. Nobody caught em, near as I can tell."

"Well, how we going to go back to Hast and tell the general that? He'll just march us straight back and dock us the tug fees."

Ilbei tugged absently at his beard. "I wish Hanswicket had said somethin about this Cavendis showin up. There's somethin squirrely about him that I can't make out. But he's ordered us back, and there ain't much I can do. I can't hardly order him to show me his orders so as I can check the seal."

Hams laughed. "No, you damn sure can't." He shrugged and went back to the other side of the fire, where he began laying strips of salt pork into an enormous rectangular pan that he had set on rocks above the coals. "So what are we going to do?"

"Go back," Ilbei said. "Major already sent fer the boats.

I'll talk to the lieutenant, and he'll push it up the chain to the general if'n it matters to em I suppose. I sure hate leavin these folks up here with no help if'n that Ergo the Skewer feller comes back, though. That one feller is up that creek all by hisself, and them two women are in that Camp Chaparral with nobody to watch over em at all, and one of em sick with some kind of dead harpy disease. We told em we'd come back with helpful magic if'n we could."

"Well, didn't Jasper have some scrolls for that? He did something to Meggins last night as I heard."

"He did. But he made it sound like he ain't too sure what was wrote on it will do any good. He's got some others he can try, but I expect he don't figure they'll do fer much neither. Worst is, we said we'd come back, and that's a hard piece fer me to chew on, leavin off without so much as sendin word."

"Well then, why don't you take a few of the boys back and at least offer to bring that one feller and them two women back to Hast, where they can treat the sick one right. We can have the boats wait for you where that creek runs in."

"Ain't any faster goin down the creek to meet up than us just cuttin straight across to Hast," Ilbei said. "But other than that, I was thinkin just the same. Them bandits may have run off, and they may not have, but we ought to at least make the offer of escort. Plus, that water ain't no good fer em to be drinkin. If nothing more, we have to tell em that much, so as they don't all die off. Question is clearin it through the major there."

"Don't clear it unless you want to be told you can't. He already ordered us back. But did he say *how* you had to go?"

"He sent fer the boats." Ilbei liked where Hams was steering the plan, but Ilbei was a firm believer in the essential nature of the chain of command.

"Aye, he did. But did he order you onto them? Way you

told it, he ordered you back to Hast. Sending for the boats was more for convenience."

The corners of Ilbei's mouth twitched, first one, then the other, then both together, rising into a grin that cut through the tangle of his mustache and beard like ground beneath a plow. "Hams, you're a genius as sure as you're ugly as a bucket a' guts. And right is right."

"Aye, it is. Such is the good cut of a technicality."

"Better than the bad ones, that's sure. Suits conscience and duty the same. I'll send most of em back with ya, though. Them boats leavin empty won't do fer appearances."

"You gonna take them boys you brung yesterday, then?"

"Yeah, they'll do fine. Kaige will make fer a fine pack mule, and Meggins is a good sort in a fight, and a thinker too."

"How 'bout young Jasper? Seems a bit jumpy to me."

"He is, but he's got his usefulness. Unless ya figure you'll need him more on the way back. There was that ratty water nymph down there what near got us all killed."

"We'll have a whole boat crew with us, and we know about her now. You take the wizard. He needs the outdoor time anyway, shake the book dust off of him and grow himself a pair."

Ilbei laughed and clapped Hams on the shoulder. "You're not off the mark with that. Not by a hair."

Chapter 12

For the sake of appearances, Ilbei and his little troop went through the motions with the rest of the camp, packing it up and heading downstream as if they were all on their way to meet the boats that would row them back to Hast. Once beyond the range of the major's eyes and ears—the major having stayed behind with assurances that Locke Verity would be his companion until a boat returned to take him back to Twee—Ilbei and his squad were free to turn toward Camp Chaparral. The plan was simple and just as Ilbei and Hams planned it: check in on the sick woman and her kind keeper, Mags; put the patient in Jasper's care; and then head up Harpy Creek to where the one miner was. They would offer him their protection, then head for Hast in compliance with the major's command. Ilbei bade Hams goodbye a measure down the Softwater, promising they'd only be two days at most behind him. With that, they were underway.

The day brewing was to be as hot as the one before, and the journey was only made marginally easier by the fact that they'd been there before. Despite the heat, they made decent time, and as they came over the ridge that looked down on the five buildings of the camp, the sun was barely blazing noon.

"I wish their water wasn't full of harpy rot," Meggins said after a draught of warm water from his waterskin. "If mine gets any hotter, it will just be steam."

"They got company down there," Ilbei observed as he, like Meggins and the rest, caught his breath after cresting the ridgeline. He sat on his heels, leaning against a rock and watching as a man came out of Mags' modest business and began tying down the leather covers on a pair of panniers weighing down one of three packhorses. It was impossible to make out much detail about him given that he had his hood pulled up against the heat and that the heat itself rippled the air as it rose from the ground beneath his feet. "I bet that's that feller what Mags was worried about, fearin he might be dead."

"Well, that's good news," Jasper said. "Perhaps he's brought back a doctor to help the sick woman. If we can discover what the disease is actually called, my next set of scrolls will be more useful to anyone else who might suffer similarly. I realize it is customary for the uneducated to slap whatever word they want onto whatever set of symptoms comes along, but healing is a discipline. In fact, forty years ago, there was an epidemic that swept through Pompost and Norvingtown that the locals were calling black-eyed fever, but it turned out not to be that at all, and instead they discovered it really was a malady called—"

"Jasper, by the gods, ya make more noise than a dragged bag of pans. If'n I have to hear a whole 'nother sermon on black-eyed fever—and after just survivin that hour-long racket on extract of prickly pear—I fear I may have to kill one of us, me or you. Not sure which yet, but I'm thinkin it's most like to be you."

"Please make it him, Sarge," Meggins said. "I'll carry your gear to Hast if you do it now."

"Sermon? What sermon?" Jasper asked, ignoring

Meggins entirely. "A sermon requires a topic of religious nature, or at very least a moral one. I certainly made no claims about prickly pear in the context of morality or faith. Not even as academic discourse pertaining to religion, morality or deities, why, I—"

Meggins came up behind Jasper and placed his hand over his mouth, gently, but firmly, silencing him. "Sarge is right. You talk too much. Put a cork in that yawning saucebox of yours before I hold you down and Sarge beats the wind out of you. Maybe Kaige can pull your head off after."

Jasper looked indignant, sending a silent plea to Kaige with his eyes. Kaige shrugged. "I don't mind listening to you so much," he said. "I won't pull your head off, neither. Though, Sarge got the final say-so."

Jasper rolled his eyes. "Fine," he said. Although given that he spoke it through the filter of Meggins' filthy hand, it sounded more like *airee aw*, which suited Ilbei fine.

They climbed down the slope, weaving through the manzanita brush, and once again made their way into the tiny imposter of a town. "Miss Mags," Ilbei called as they came even with the first of the shacks, the very same in which the madwoman with the craze had been anesthetized. "It's Sergeant Spadebreaker come back to speak with ya, if'n ya happen to be around."

The man with the packhorses checked the cinch on the saddle of his lead horse but didn't look up at them when Ilbei called. Ilbei saw his head move enough to allow a sideways glance from beneath his cowl, but the fellow made no motion to acknowledge them.

"Sergeant," said Mags, coming out of the building that served as tavern and supply depot. "I'm glad you came. Though it's a sad reason that I'm happiest to see you, I confess."

"Why's that?" Ilbei asked.

"Candalin didn't make it through the night. The medicine wore off in the evening, after you left. It burned off really quickly this time. I dosed her twice more overnight, but when I woke up late this morning, she was gone into Mercy's arms. More's the better for it, I suppose."

"I'd hoped she'd hold up long enough fer Jasper here." Ilbei shrugged backward, a gesture intended toward the mage.

"Yes. I did too. But her time came."

"I'm sorry to hear it."

"Well, that was kind of you to come back, Sergeant. You and your men." She looked to them, each in turn, the four of them standing there covered in dust, foxtails and cockleburs, the latter of which stuck to them nearly everywhere. "Thank you all," she said. "You have good hearts. The world needs more of them."

"So, bein as we're too late for Candalin," Ilbei said, meaning to draw the conversation into an arena of action for which he and his men were better suited, "what was that 'sad reason' you was speakin of? Whatever it is, just say the word. We'll see to it if'n we can."

"The soil here is hard and rocky," she replied. "And I don't want to see her ... well, you know, picked at by the scavengers. I know it's an imposition, but if you and your men could help me get her buried properly, it would likely save me two or three days' work."

"It's no imposition at all. It's only right to see to that sort of thing. Mercy don't take kindly to leavin good folks fer jackals, coyotes and buzzards." He was careful not to mention the two skeletons they'd found up the creek only just the day before.

"No, she doesn't." She said this loudly, pointedly, and she turned toward the man down the lane from them, who was swinging into his saddle as she spoke. "She finds it to be the most offensive thing a *man* could do." Her emphasis on the word *man* made Ilbei cringe, like watching some poor fellow take a swift kick to the crotch. Still, Ilbei reckoned if Mags hadn't been as well mannered as she was, she might have said worse. Frankly, he was surprised she didn't spit right after she'd said her piece, as it seemed by her expression that she wanted to.

The man glanced back over his shoulder, keeping his hood pulled low enough to shield his face, but he didn't look long before heeling his horse and getting underway.

"Ya mean to say that feller refused to help ya give yer friend a proper send-off?"

"He did."

"And ya asked him to? Direct, so as he understood?"

"I did."

Ilbei growled low in his throat. "I'll be dipped in frostberry sauce and fed to fire ants before I'll suffer a man like that to go on without a proper talkin to." He threw down the pack he'd been carrying and tossed his steel hat with its sergeant stripes on top of it. He set off down the dusty lane between the buildings, his bowlegs stomping and his elbows out as he went, rolling up his sleeves. "You there, feller on the horse, come on back here, as I'll have a word with ya."

The man made no move to stop, nor did he turn back to look. Instead, he kicked his horse into a trot. Immediate speed, however, was impeded by reluctance on the part of the three pack animals he had in tow.

Ilbei saw that the man's intent was to flee, so he set off running after him, swearing for all his worth. "I said ya need to come on back here, son, as I have need to speak to ya." Speed was not Ilbei's strong suit, but his bowed legs pumped for all they were worth, eating up ground. The man yanked at the lead rope, trying to work the packhorses into at least a trot.

Ilbei caught up to the rearmost packhorse right away, and he got past the lead one a few strides after, near enough that he almost could have touched the rump of the rider's animal. But his approach startled the packhorses, and they sidled and leapt sideways and away. Ilbei pressed on after, reaching for the mounted man.

"Stop this instant, ya whoreson dog," Ilbei spat, but the rider whipped his mount furiously and yanked violently on the lead rope, shouting them all to speed. The pack string was drawn back toward Ilbei, and the lead animal knocked him a step sideways. The rider's horse bolted out of Ilbei's reach.

Ilbei knew he couldn't catch up, that he was going to lose them all, so he veered toward the pack string and leapt between the second packhorse and the third, throwing his shoulder bodily into the animal's chest and driving it to a stop. It reared up, terrified, yanking the lead rope out of the retreating man's hand. Ilbei ducked beneath the churning, iron-shod hooves and snatched the rope for himself as it slid across the dirt. "Easy now," he soothed. "Sorry there, girl. I didn't mean nothin fer ya personal in that."

A span of moments passed as Ilbei worked to quiet the mare, but soon enough she settled and warmed to Ilbei's practiced hand. He stroked her on the neck, and when he was confident he had her under control, he turned, expecting to see the rider coming back for her. But he was not. In fact, the dust cloud the man churned up as he got away suggested he'd gotten his remaining pack animals up to speed and never once considered turning them around to retrieve the third. Ilbei wondered if he even knew he'd lost a horse. It was hard to imagine that he did not.

Nonetheless, Ilbei watched him go, his head tilted in the way of the curious and the pink patch of his bald spot slowly heating in the sun. "Didn't see that comin," he admitted to the mare. "And here ya seem like such a sweet girl." He patted the horse on her wide, soft jaw and led her back to where his men and Mags were. Kaige, having unloaded his burden and started off to help, met Ilbei halfway with a wide grin.

"I told you Sarge could handle himself," Meggins said, as Kaige and Ilbei rejoined the rest in the middle of what served as Camp Chaparral's only street. Both soldiers were grinning at Ilbei unabashedly, their eyes beaming with admiration. Jasper had yet to close his mouth, but for once there were no words coming out. It was clear he'd never seen such a thing.

Ilbei handed the rope to Kaige and directed him to take the horse around to the shade side of the tavern and relieve it of its packs. "I expect that feller will be back once he figures out a third of his load is gone."

"He knows," Mags said. "I watched him look back."

"Then why didn't he stop? Do ya know who he is?"

"I know him. It's Gad Pander. He's the one I told you about."

"I thought he might be. He really that much a coward as to drop his load and leave behind a fine animal just fer fear of a whippin?"

"Apparently. To be honest, I've only seen him three times, so I hardly know him. He showed up the first time about a year ago and came through two or three times more, each time saying he was off fetching supplies for the lads at Fall Pools, as I think I mentioned yesterday. Last time was the first time he ever brought anything down that he'd dug out for himself, and even with a proud haul, he was hardly any friendlier than what you just saw."

Ilbei ran his hand down the short length of his dirt-encrusted beard. He knew plenty enough of hill folks to know they often didn't take to outsiders too well, so the man might have run off out of some kind of hermitting instinct. But that's not all Ilbei understood about remote living. He was well familiar with how sparse the life these folks lived could be, and leaving behind a packload of supplies, not to mention the horse itself, was absolutely beyond reckoning. There wasn't any way a man in his right mind would do such a thing, recluse or not. Which meant that, once again, something didn't smell right out here.

Chapter 13

The work of digging Candalin's grave was arduous, especially given the morning's trek, and made worse by the heat that pounded down on them, so hot it seemed that the sun must be angry at them for something they had or hadn't done. The stony soil made the first half span of the digging miserable, and after, when they hit bedrock beneath, well, then the chore was little short of agony. But they split the work between the five of them, Mags too, who turned out to be tougher than her lean frame would suggest. She was certainly tougher than poor Jasper, who, when his turn came, cursed and whined the entire time, pecking at the hole with Ilbei's pickaxe with all the determination of a wet hankie. Meggins and Kaige teased him about it of course, prancing about with their wrists bobbing limply in the air, but he didn't care. All he could do was lament the pick's "ridiculous weight" and curse "the simian absurdity of its barbaric design." Occasionally he would bemoan the fact that he'd not brought an excavation spell, which would then turn to vitriol launched against the quartermaster back at the garrison, but only for short spans, and then he'd fall back to bemoaning the pickaxe again.

Nonetheless, between them, they did get the hole dug

and eventually laid the departed within. When they'd covered her up and Mags had found some pretty orange poppies to lay upon the grave, first Mags and then Ilbei said a few words over her.

By the time they were done, it was nightfall, and the five of them nearly collapsed into chairs inside Mags' little store and tavern. Too tired to cook, they made a meal of deer jerky and goat cheese, which Mags supplied, and they drank a fine apple wine, which it turned out Mags made herself, a treat for which she'd become, or had been in the process of becoming, rather famous around Three Tents prior to the arrival of Ergo the Skewer.

After dinner, Ilbei took the low-burning stub of a candle off the table and went outside to check on the horse and have a few pulls off his pipe. He led the mare out to the edge of the cleared space around the buildings and tethered her to a twisting manzanita limb, where she could at least graze on the dry brown grass. He patted her on the rump as she probed for choicer morsels, but, finding none, she settled in to eat.

Mags was waiting at the back of the building as Ilbei returned, a washbasin filled with water still sloshing at her feet. "She'll want this more than anything," she said. Ilbei nodded and took up one side of the basin. Together, they carried it to the horse.

"This come out of the creek?" Ilbei asked as they set it down.

"It did," she said. "I keep a few barrelsful inside."

Ilbei grimaced. "I feel bad givin it to her. Knowin what we know."

Mags tilted her head a little, and even in the faint pink light of a half moon, he could see curiosity flash in her eyes. "What do you know?"

"I'll be. I reckon we didn't tell ya about that harpy corpse we seen, did we?"

"No. Nobody said a thing."

"Well, we did. Meggins in there seen a dead one up at the head of the stream, hung up in some rocks just inside the cave where the creek comes out. I expect that's what done yer friend Candalin in. I'm sorry to have to give the news." He let his gaze wander to the horse, who was indeed more interested in the water than the weeds around her hooves. "I suppose before we leave, we ought to go on up there again and pull that nasty thing out so as nobody else gets sick. Come to think of it, I wish I'd done it while we was still there. It had been a long day, though, and we had a stroke a' bad luck gettin in and out, so I suppose the idea slipped past me at the time. We'll get it, though."

Mags nodded. "That would be the best thing. But, that's not what made her sick."

"I thought you folks didn't know what made her sick."

"We don't, but it wasn't water demons."

"Water demons?"

"Yes, that's how a harpy in the water might kill someone. They've got tiny demons like they've got mites and fleas."

Ilbei twitched his jaw side to side a little at that, but tried not to let the odd statement run him off course. "Ya figure, now? I don't know much about no demons, but that harpy up there's been dead in that hole a long while, at least long enough to explain the crazy sickness ya said been creepin up on folks out here. Everyone knows them things is cursed with everythin foul there is, and I wouldn't put it past em havin some kind of crazy disease."

"Right. But the curse is the tiny demons. Which is why I purify our water," she said. "I've got an alchemist's system inside. We stir in alum powder and run it all through that big wine cask you saw inside. That cask is full of sand and gravel that cleans the water up well. Then we boil it for drinking, just to be sure no tiny water demons are in it still. They may be too small to see, but they aren't too small to die."

Ilbei looked at her as if she'd just started speaking the language of the elves. "Why would ya go and do all that fer? I ain't never heard of no tiny water demons, and I been walkin Prosperion fer creepin up on a hundred and twenty years."

"It's just as I said: the process cleans and purges the water. It's a trick I learned from a young magician I met when I first came out here. He was a clever man with more than a passing interest in alchemy, and he taught me how to do it. He said the healer priests at the big university in Crown City divined the nature of water sickness. They learned that there are tiny demons living in all sorts of things, and that sometimes they will make you sick to amuse themselves. He said water has them living in it much of the time, dead harpies or not. He said you can never be sure if they are there, especially out of doors."

Ilbei nodded, thinking it did ring at least marginally true to his experience, at least in a sense. "We seen somethin of the sort comin downriver from Hast," he said. "Though what we seen sure weren't tiny and invisible. Jasper says they call that type a potameide. He's keen on books and readin like them fellers at the fancy school, so I suppose it's likely true."

"Well, there are demons that are big, too, at least so I've heard, but I've never seen one. I can only speak to the tiny types for my cask inside. I can tell you that since we started running water through it, folks stopped getting the squeezy bowels and hurling sickness like they used to. I suppose that's why we never could attract a healer out here to stay. Nothing to do but patch up a broken leg or stitch up cuts from time to time. Somehow I ended up serving as camp nurse afterwards, not that I have any qualifications for it outside of that cask."

"Well, seems ya got the kind heart fer it, least as I seen

yesterday. There's a great deal to be said fer that alone." He drew a long pull on his pipe, the red glow brightening in its bowl for a time. He blew the smoke out slowly, watching it smear the stars for a time as it drifted away. "Sounds like that alchemist mage of yers did ya a fair turn teachin ya all that. He must have been a fine feller to take the time."

She turned away from him as he said it, and her posture grew stiff.

"I take it that feller vexed ya then?"

"I was dumb and gullible. And he was bored. And mean." She didn't dwell on it overlong, however, and looked up, smiling. "As you say, I did learn a neat trick for making water pure, so it wasn't an experience without value."

"What was a Crown City–educated wizard and alchemist doin out here anyway? Not to say that yer company weren't enough to bring a man across great distances, mind ya."

"Sergeant Spadebreaker, you are sweet, but no, that wasn't what brought him. He was inspecting the mines for an employer. He said he was looking for reagents, minerals, dusts and powders for use in alchemy. He said he'd been sent to arrange contracts for things like, well, alum for example. Honestly, I think he was really just looking for gold like all the rest."

"Did he find any?"

She sighed and looked to the north, out across the scrub brush toward the stars clinging to the darkness above the Sandsea Desert. "No, not really. You've seen what comes out of these hills if you've been here more than a day: lead, copper, a little alum maybe—not much of any of it, mind you—and maybe an ounce of gold in a year for the man who stays at it long enough. Everybody thought they'd find a big strike, the mother lode, but never did. What few decent deposits there were got taken straight off, and then most everyone moved on—the smart ones, anyway, leaving just a few copper-scraping loners to peck out an existence as they could. My ... temporary suitor ... stayed in the hills for a month or so, coming down to see me almost every night. He seemed genuinely interested in me at first, but he kept getting meaner and meaner as the days turned into weeks. I tried to understand at first—I knew many of the others were growing frustrated by the lack of gold. Many had given up everything to come out here. So I put up with more than I should have, made excuses for him. And he was ... well, pretty rough, and I was starting to get really afraid of him. But then, by the grace of sweet Mercy, one day he stopped coming anymore. I found out later he'd gone home."

"Why didn't ya cut his throat, or have some of the boys around here do it fer ya?" Ilbei asked.

"He was a magician. What could any of the locals do, scant few as there even were back then? Most of them worked the Softwater claims. And I wouldn't have wanted to put any of them in danger anyway. Besides, no permanent harm came of it. But I sure didn't miss him when he was gone." She sighed and looked out over the landscape, a quiet blanket of star-spotted darkness drawn up and tucked round the sleeping hills.

There wasn't much Ilbei could say to something like that, so he stared out with her into the night. After a time, he relit his pipe and sent puffs of smoke climbing ambitiously toward the firmament again. He watched it rise and scatter in the warm breeze that had finally begun to blow down from the mountain, touched with a hint of pine despite having traveled all that way.

He offered her his pipe, which made her laugh, then shake her head no. After a time, she went inside.

In her absence, Ilbei looked for a place to sit and enjoy the night. He spotted the panniers Kaige had pulled off the packhorse and set against the wall. He went to the nearest and sat down, puffing pleasantly on his pipe for a while until the candle finally burned out and he couldn't relight it anymore.

For a time, he simply contemplated the sky and the pleasant cooling off of the hillside in the absence of the brutal sun, and with the help of the breeze, but after a while he got to wondering about the man who'd been in such a hurry to run off that he'd leave a horse behind. That was an oddity beyond reason. The man was gone to town for two weeks, finally came back, and then left a third of what he brought behind. That didn't fit with anything like sense. And it stacked up with lots of other things that didn't make sense. The whole mission didn't make sense.

They sent him and his men out to find bandits who hadn't committed a robbery in well over a month, if not longer, yet long after the bandits had started in on the people there—and long after the people had sent to the army for help. And when help finally did come, in the form of Ilbei and company, Ilbei barely got two days to ask around before he and his men were sent home again—well before they'd caught the least whiff of the bandits, much less a trail leading to them. And if that wasn't odd enough, the officer who sent them home was a South Mark major that nobody at the garrison in Hast had mentioned would be there, and he was the sort of man who came onshore and sent his rowers back without so much as a half hour to eat or even rest a spell. And that was the same major who had an obsession for gambling well beneath his station, much less his presumable wealth as a nobleman, and who had elected to stay in the hills after the platoon's departure with only a civilian hunter for protection—a hunter who claimed to hunt for the camps yet dressed like a well-trimmed city man. Together they were going to wait for the boat to return from Twee, which would take at least three days, if not four, from the time the rowers got word they were supposed to come back, word they would receive only a day at most after having returned to Twee from having dropped the major off to begin. Those men, assuming it was the same boat crew, would have spent at least three days rowing upstream, two days going back down, and now three or four more returning again.

Who would do that? None of that made sense.

Ilbei knew well enough that sometimes orders came that didn't make sense. It was true that some of those orders came from petty-minded men for personal reasons he couldn't fathom, and others from poorly designed plans. But the truth was, the largest number of nonsensical orders he'd been given over his career usually made sense eventually. His initial confusion often turned out to be a matter of his not knowing what the bigger pattern was at the time—he couldn't see the tapestry for being part of the weave, so to speak. All of that he accepted as army reality. But in all his years, he'd never come across something that set as sideways in his mind as this whole episode around the Three Tents robberies.

As he contemplated the crooked stack of facts around Major Cavendis, he found that the actual stack of goods piled into the pannier upon which he sat was jabbing him painfully in his backside. He shifted back and forth, hoping to wiggle whatever it was out of the way, but it wouldn't budge, digging into him as firm and hard as steel. Then curiosity took hold.

He knew it wasn't right to go sorting through another man's things, but as he shifted his weight trying to get comfortable, he kept thinking of all the heaped-up mysteries, including the man that had run off and left the panniers behind. Ilbei figured a man like that, running off without so much as doing his duty to Mercy and to the dead—much less to Mags out of simple courtesy—didn't deserve any courtesy himself. The more Ilbei thought about it, the more he was sure a man like that didn't deserve any respect at all, including the type that would have kept Ilbei from sifting through his packs. Or at least taking a quick peek inside.

The gods wouldn't mind.

So he did. Partly for the right of it, but mainly to see what it was poking his behind, as he told himself.

What was poking him so sorely turned out to be the handle of a castiron skillet. It stuck up between several packets of fine flour and cornmeal. Ilbei tried to push it down deeper into the pannier so as to make sitting comfortable, with just the soft stuffs on top, but no matter how hard he pushed, the pan wouldn't budge a finger's width further into the pack despite its obviously not being far enough in to have hit the bottom. It was as if there were bricks at the bottom of the pack, or something hard as stone.

Now, there wasn't any reason why a man would bring bricks or stone back out into the countryside, at least not by the pannier as this was. Ilbei wondered what was so dense as to be worth carrying back all that way. So he set himself to unloading it.

He pulled out the baking supplies, slowly exhuming the castiron skillet layer by layer until at last he could pull it out and set it atop the pile that he'd made on the ground. At the bottom of the pannier was a flat bundle of something wrapped in homespun, and a rap of the knuckles proved that it was indeed as hard as the skillet was, hard like a brick.

He tried to lift it out with a handful of the homespun, but the cloth tore, the burden within too heavy to be lifted so. Ilbei tore the rent open more and took a rectangular object out, pulling it off the top of what appeared to be a stack of others like it. The one he held was as long as his hand and not quite as wide, and only a few finger-widths thick. It didn't look like any brick he'd seen, as it was too thin and far too smooth, like ceramic tile or a plate of glass. Rolling it over, and holding it at an angle so he could see across its surface better in the moonlight, he saw that there were four circular depressions on the underside.

He pulled out a few more of the objects, and saw that they were all the same. There were ten of them, each with the same four depressions, all lined in a row, and all perfectly circular. He wondered what sort of oddity they might be. He would have put them back and resigned himself to not knowing, feeling a little guilty for snooping as he was, but then it struck him what they might be.

He took the first brick and two others and went round to the front of the tavern. He stepped inside, and saw Meggins and Kaige throwing dice against a wall. Jasper was reading in the lamplight near the bar. Seeing the mage, Ilbei headed straight for him, or more specifically, for his light.

He held one of the bricks beneath the lamp, ignoring Jasper's protests about shadows on his pages. Looking down into the bottom of each of the round depressions revealed four perfect likenesses of Her Majesty, the royal profile clear and obvious, her name spelled out around the curve beneath her image and easily recognizable despite the letters being in reverse. There was more writing above her image, but he couldn't make it out, in part for the letters being smaller and still backwards, but mainly because the language itself was unfamiliar. But he didn't have to read it to know what he was holding. His hunch had been right: these were coin molds.

He switched out that one for another to confirm it. It took only moments to see that the second was the same as the first: the War Queen in perfect profile. He put the third brick under the light and saw that it too was identical.

He turned and handed Jasper the plate, then took the lamp and brought it down close enough so there were no shadows in the bottom of the mold. "What's it say there along the top? That some kind of elf or dwarf speak?"

Jasper looked for a moment as if he might continue to protest over Ilbei's usurpation of his reading light, but Ilbei's having called upon him for his expertise stopped him from further sniveling. He took the proffered bit of ceramic in both hands and shifted it in the light until he could see into it clearly. He read the inscriptions impressed there carefully—though it only took him the span of a half second at most—then he sat back, almost slumping. "It's just a gold crown mold from Her Majesty's mint," he said, sounding disappointed and looking bored. "Everyone knows what it says."

"Well I don't," Ilbei replied. "Ain't never had one. And even if I had, I wouldn't have known how to read the foreign part."

"Well, it's dwarven for 'May it please the gods.'" He looked back up at Ilbei, who had picked up one of the other molds and was looking into it, captivated by the idea of lettering from a long-dead race. "And why do you have one of those, anyway?" Jasper asked. "They are illegal to own, you know. They're all the property of Her Majesty's mint in Crown City, and if you get caught with that, they'll cut off your head. Turn it, and you'll see that it says as much along the lower edge. They all do." He didn't bother to look at the one he held to verify it, as it was clear he already knew it would be true.

Ilbei looked, however, and he turned the one he was holding over in his hands. There was nothing on the edge he looked at, so he flipped it and checked the other side. He checked the back and then both the ends. He checked the other plate, then took the one Jasper hadn't bothered looking at. "There ain't nothin on any of these what says that," he said.

"Then they must be counterfeits. Frankly, that's worse than having real ones. If I were you, I'd bury them as deep as you can and then forget where you dug the hole. If the authorities find you with them, you'll be tortured for a month until you give up where you got them, and after you confess, you'll be decapitated by a headsman with a dull axe."

"We *are* the authorities, Jasper. What do ya think them red moons sewed into yer sleeves mean?"

Jasper looked at the lonesome crimson arc, the moon, Luria, in its crescent phase, embroidered upon each shoulder of his robes, the demarcation of the lowest military rank possible for a mage. "Oh, yes, I suppose I forgot." He made this odd little laugh, a faint sort of snorting thing, and for the first time since Ilbei had met him, he thought Jasper was genuinely amused.

"Well, we will get these turned over when we get back to Hast," Ilbei said. He spent a few minutes looking into the molds, shaking his head. "Knowin what these are makes a different sort of mess of the same heap of questions, don't it?"

Jasper's colliding brows knit the nature of his confusion. He had not been privy to what had been going on in Ilbei's head since the sergeant lay staring up into the shadows of his tent two nights before.

"Well, it's like this," Ilbei said, setting the lamp back in its place upon the bar. "I was out there wonderin why that feller took off out of here like he did, thinkin he might be ashamed of what he done, runnin off without helpin Mags and all. But that didn't make enough sense to set with me, and now we got reason to see why. One way ya look at it, him runnin makes sense if'n he thought he was gonna get caught with these. Except now I have to wonder what kind of sense it makes to take off like that and leave this here stuff behind. Seems more likely a man thinkin straight would see to just playin it calm and regular, takin a moment to greet us before easin on outta here normal like. All he had to do was not act the part of a criminal, and he'd have gone off without us thinkin a thing of it, and with all his packhorses in tow. Even a boy plays a better hand a' ruffs than that."

"Well, maybe he's not a good liar," Jasper said. "I know I'm terrible at it, and my mother always caught me every time I tried. She says I include too many details, which is how she always knows. It does seem to be the case that when people lie, they want to include as much detail as possible to add authenticity to their falsehood. But even knowing this, I find that I will still do it anyway. I'm not sure what that is, but there was a priest of Tidalwrath some years back who wrote about how sometimes when people are—"

"By the gods, son, ya add too damned many details when you're tellin the truth. Now pipe down and let me think."

"Well, I was only trying to explain—" Ilbei silenced him by walking away, taking the plates outside with him as he returned to the packs at the back of the house. He unloaded the second pannier and found that it too had ten plates, just like those in the first. They too were tucked carefully down at the very bottom of the pack, buried beneath items that were in keeping with a typical trip to town, expected items like flour, salt, beans, and even a small sack of Goblin Tea. While that last might be seen as an unexpected extravagance for the sorts mining these bare hills, nothing was out of the ordinary but those plates. But the plates were an abnormality that had to be dealt with. It was his duty to the Queen.

So now Ilbei had to decide how best to carry that duty out. Should he take the plates and head down to Hast, come back with a bigger troop of men, or go back and tell the major what they had found? Or maybe he ought to take the lads up to that Fall Pools and have a look himself. Speaking to the major was surely the worst idea, and going back to Hast meant losing a lot of time. If that coward Gad Pander figured Ilbei would discover those plates at some point, there was a good chance he'd pack up and hide for a time. He hadn't come back to ask for his gear, and he hadn't come back to take it by force. So, unless he showed up over the course of the night, Ilbei expected he didn't care to tangle with the army at all. That made hiding seem a more likely course. And he had time for it, as he'd seen Ilbei and company come into Camp Chaparral on foot, which would have told him they had no teleporter as much as it told him they had no mounts. That also told him that they were several days from Hast, which was time he could use to make an escape. Assuming that was his intent. He might just as easily be setting traps around his operation, in anticipation of Ilbei and his men coming up looking for him.

If Ilbei took his crew up the hill and did find that there was an operation underway, there was no telling how many men they would come across. Ilbei didn't figure it would be less than three, as the work of mining, smelting, melting and molding was a lot for one man to do, and there were likely extra steps for counterfeiting that Ilbei couldn't even account for. For all he knew, there was a whole troop of them up there; although, if the amount of supplies in the panniers was any evidence, there couldn't be more than a few—the nature of greed makes men stingy about sharing ill-begotten rewards. Which meant Ilbei needed to decide what he was going to do. Should he go after Pander or just do as they'd started out to do: get Mags, go up and get that other miner if he cared to come, and then get them all to Hast? Whatever he decided would shape what he did with the plates as well, and, frankly, what he did with Mags. If she didn't want to come with them, he wasn't too keen on leaving her at Camp Chaparral alone either. It was a lot to think about.

He decided to put himself on watch, since he wasn't going to sleep anyway. He poked his head inside the tavern long enough to tell Kaige to come spell him a few hours after midnight. He simply needed more time to work through what to do. He'd never been one of those sorts who could just blink and have the right idea. Nonetheless, by the time Kaige came to relieve him, he'd figured out what to do.

Chapter 14

Ilbei and his crew, which now included Mags, set out early in the morning, making their way up Harpy Creek toward the shack of the lone miner still working up there. They were just approaching the little bluff on which his shack was built when they saw the dust rising up over the line of brush before them. They saw it just before they heard the cries. By the time they'd run up the slope, ducking and weaving through the snagging, slashing scrub, they were too late to save the man. The miner they'd spoken to only two days before lay facedown in the creek, his blood painting a foggy red line down the center of the flow.

Ilbei and his men dropped to their bellies. Ilbei twisted so he could look back down the hill. He motioned for Mags to stay where she was. She saw and nodded, leaning closer to the packhorse, whose lead rope she held. The four of them snaked their way to the top of the cut bank and peered through the weeds, watching and listening.

Eight men surrounded the body, talking casually as the miner's life poured away. The largest among them was a monster of a man whose height and bulk rivaled Kaige's for size. He carried a huge crossbow, which he motioned with toward the center of the creek, where Ilbei noticed that the great boulder the miner had been beating on with his giant sledge was now broken in two. Part of it had splashed down straight across the waterway, partially damming it up on that side, and the other part had fallen onto the gravel closer to the bank. It was a lot of work to break such a thing, and now all of it for naught. At least for the man who'd been at the labor of it for so long.

"Get in there with that shovel and see if he was chasing his tail," the man with the giant crossbow said. He jerked his chin toward two of the men on the bank closest to where Ilbei and company lay. "You two go through his place and see if he didn't dig up something we haven't heard about. Check for false bottoms and loose boards, and any dirt that looks softer than the rest. Feel through the seams of his clothes."

The two men, one a short, lean fellow and the other a medium-sized brute missing half of his right hand, turned and climbed the bank, moving upstream and around the base of the bluff at the start of its curve. They were bound to see Ilbei and his men where they were.

Ilbei nodded for Meggins to come with him, signing with his hand for Jasper and Kaige to keep watch and call out if trouble came. He mouthed down the hill for Mags not to make a sound. She looked nervous as she nodded, her right hand hooking under and around the mare's neck protectively while the knuckles on her other hand turned white around the quarterstaff she'd been using as a walking stick.

Ilbei pulled his pickaxe off his back while Meggins drew a long dagger from his boot. They slunk up behind the miner's small shack and peered inside through a crack. They waited for the two men to go inside. Soon after, they saw shadowy movements between the boards and heard grunts along with the sounds of the dead man's few belongings being carelessly tossed about.

Ilbei and Meggins went around to the front door, pausing

long enough on either side for Ilbei to nod to the left, indicating Meggins to take the smaller man. The younger soldier nodded back, and in they went, two steps each, then wrapped a hand around the face of their respective targets, simultaneously silencing them. Ilbei gripped the haft of his pickaxe right near the head, and with one powerful thrust he shoved a long steel fang right through the back of the half-handed man's neck. Meggins cut a long line straight across the scraggly week-old beard that stubbled his victim's neck. They muffled the mouths of their marks until the thrashing stopped. Then together they quietly set the bodies down.

They left the shack as silently as they had come, and in moments they once again lay prone beside Kaige and Jasper in the weeds. Kaige didn't even look up from watching the men working in the creek, but Jasper's face was pale as he stared at the blood on Ilbei's face and on Meggins' hands. It was as if he had just realized what was happening. He had the sense to keep quiet, though.

After a few moments' more watching, with most of the group they were observing standing aside while two of the men worked with shovels digging up the gravel beneath where the boulder had been, Meggins made the sign for his bow, his eyebrow rising with the inquiry. Ilbei nodded that he agreed. Meggins crawled back down the embankment until he could get to his feet unseen. He went to the horse and pulled his bow from where he'd tied it to one of the packs, giving Mags a reassuring wink while he did. He made quick work of stringing it, got the quiver down, then returned to the top of the rise.

He raised both eyebrows at Ilbei upon his return, clearly asking when he should begin.

Ilbei mouthed to him, "How many can ya get fast?" To which Meggins held fingers counting three.

Ilbei nodded, adding silently with mouth and gesture,

"Get the big one."

Meggins gave a grin and a sloppy salute, then pulled five arrows from the quiver and laid four of them neatly spaced in front of him. With a glance at Ilbei, who gave him the go-ahead, he raised up on one knee and fired the first shot. The distance wasn't great, twenty-five paces tops, and the arrow found its mark squarely in the big man's back, causing him to call out and fall to his knees in the water, his arms angled awkwardly as he tried to grab it and pull it out.

The other men all shouted and looked around, and by the time they spotted Meggins atop the embankment, another man had an arrow through his open mouth. A third took one through the shoulder as he turned and looked for somewhere to run.

They scattered after that. Two of them ran back the way the men originally sent to search the shack had gone, and one drew a longsword and came running straight toward Ilbei and his men, ducking down and using the cut bank to hide from Meggins' line of sight. They could hear him breathing, right below them, pressed against the overhang.

"Shite," snapped Meggins as his fourth shot glanced off a studded leather pauldron of a retreating man.

Ilbei, pickaxe still in hand, jumped over the edge, landing in the gravel below with a heavy crunch. The man who had run there was already halfway along the dirt face of the bluff, moving to come around them from behind, where he would have found Mags straight away. Fortunately, he heard Ilbei and spun back before sighting her. He crouched, ready for the fight, his longsword held comfortably in his hand.

"Come on, you rusty army git," he taunted as he approached Ilbei confidently. He drew a long serpentine dagger from his belt. "The army don't train a fat bastard like you for what you're about to get."

In a rush, he came at Ilbei, his longsword flashing in the morning sun, licking out like lightning bent on opening

Ilbei's admittedly pronounced gut. Ilbei knocked the sword aside with the flat of his pickaxe blades and stepped into the man as he brought the dagger down. Ilbei caught the man's wrist in his hand and gave it a twist, then kneed him in the groin.

The bandit guffawed, and Ilbei heard the splash of the dagger landing in the water behind him. The groin shot had bent the man at the waist, and Ilbei brought his knee up again, this time into his face, breaking his nose and busting loose a rivulet of blood.

His attacker fell away, staggering as he brought his sword up in defense. Ilbei switched his pickaxe from his right hand to his left as he moved warily around, getting the cut bank at his back and trying to work himself between access to Mags and his assailant. He could see the man blinking and knew the pain from the broken nose was distracting him, so he stepped forward and feinted a blunt strike with the curved head of his pick. The man fell back a step. Ilbei feinted twice more the same way, rapid fire, each time causing the man to shuffle back. Then he stepped in and thrust for real, striking a hammer blow with the end of the pickaxe straight into the poor bastard's already bloody face.

Blood sprayed like the spokes of a wagon wheel as the man gasped and staggered back. Belatedly, he swung his sword around to parry the blow he'd already received. He then leveled it at Ilbei, shaking his head, trying to clear the spots dancing before his eyes. Ilbei dropped the flat of his pickaxe down on the sword blade, batting the point down toward the water. The man tried to turn the strike away, but Ilbei let the pickaxe shaft spin in his hand, causing the man to jerk his sword up too easily, opening himself up for an instant. He saw it and jumped back, lowering his sword again. Ilbei stepped forward and once again set the flat of his pickaxe blades on the sword. Metal ground against metal as he pushed the pickaxe down the sword a bit. The man glared at him, waiting until the pickaxe slid past halfway, then he quickly raised his weapon up, intent on trapping Ilbei's pick and tearing it away. Rather than resist, Ilbei stepped into him again, turned sideways, and with a swift and powerful hammering motion, he punched down with his palm on the pickaxe haft. He did it so suddenly the head drove down upon the man's hands and knocked the sword right out of his grip. His mouth opened in the first portion of a shout as he stared down at the falling sword and then at his empty hand. Though it was all in the space of a second, Ilbei could see the man's total disbelief as the weapon clattered against the stone.

Fortunately, right after observing that, he also saw the man's eyes widen, relief forming at something he could see over Ilbei's left shoulder. Ilbei didn't wait to find out what it was. Pure instinct set him diving forward, and he flew past the man he'd disarmed just in time to avoid a long crossbow bolt, a bolt easily as long as his arm, as it sailed through the space where his head had been only an instant before. He heard the steel shaft whistle past and saw it vanish nearly to its fletching as it sank into the riverbank.

The bandit dove to retrieve his sword as Ilbei rolled to his feet. Ilbei spun and threw the pickaxe with both hands. The distance wasn't great, and by the time the bandit had snatched up his blade and spun back to face Ilbei, the long curving tine of that deadly odd weapon bit through his chest and tore open his lung.

He spat blood to match that running from his nose, his face a wet, red mess. He coughed up a full pint of it as he stumbled forward. He looked down at his chest, at Ilbei's weapon there, and looked up again, as if surprised. He staggered drunkenly across the rocks toward Ilbei, reaching out for him with his sword, as if wanting Ilbei to have it before he died. Ilbei took it as the man fell, plucking it from his dying grip as the bandit pitched forward and landed face first with a gravelly crunch.

Ilbei had no time to linger, however, so with the longsword held high, he ran at the great brute still standing in the creek reloading that enormous crossbow. He swung the sword in a long arc, hoping to cut into the man's shoulder right where it joined the arm, a severing blow, but the big man was quicker than Ilbei thought, and quite despite the arrow in his back. He spun away and, in a bit of good luck on his part, managed to swipe Ilbei in the eye with the end of Meggins' arrow as he turned. The sting, and the delicate location, cost Ilbei a moment's pause.

In the time that bought, the big man finished his spin and used the momentum to launch a whirling swing of the giant crossbow. Ilbei saw it coming, but he was too close to get away. He deflected some of the force with the sword but still took a shot to the ribs hard enough that he dropped the sword. Worse, he found himself hooked in an arc of the crossbow, at which point the big brute began hauling him toward a great punch that was already underway.

Fortunately, it was the same sort of tactic Ilbei often used with his pickaxe, and he was able to move his head enough to avoid having his own nose broken. The blow glanced off the side of his head as he leaned back against the man's pull, digging his boots into the creek bed and driving with his legs. He blocked another punch aimed at his face, then dropped to his hands and knees. He did it so quickly he slid out from the trap of the crossbow, landing in the water with a splash.

The big man staggered back a step with the release of Ilbei's weight, but by the time Ilbei could grab the hilt of the longsword again, the burly bandit was standing on the blade. Ilbei threw himself backward, out of the way of another swing of that huge crossbow, and rolled onto his feet again. He ran to fetch his pickaxe from the dead man a few paces downstream. He'd barely got his hand on it when he heard Mags cry out.

"Shite," Ilbei muttered as he wrenched his pick free of the corpse. He turned back and had exactly enough time to drop to his back as another arm's-length crossbow bolt whistled past, so close it rustled the bristles of his beard.

"Tidalwrath's teeth," he swore, but he leapt right back up and ran along the embankment, following its slope to where he could jump on top of it, into the grass and weeds. As soon as he did, he saw the reason for Mags' alarm: one of the bandits he'd thought had run off had circled through the brush and come up from behind instead. His presence put Ilbei in fear for what might have become of Meggins and Kaige, neither of whom was in sight. Jasper was there with her, but he lay facedown in the weeds, his hand motionless, fingers still shaped for clutching the thin yellow tube of a scroll he'd apparently been going for prior to being knocked out, clearly struck from behind. Other scrolls lay in the dirt, thrown out of the satchel when he fell.

Mags' quarterstaff lay near him, and the bandit who'd disarmed her held her captive, her hands already bound and the point of his sword pressed against her side. His whole body tensed as Ilbei approached, one thrust away from puncturing her lungs.

"Come another step and she's a fountain," he said.

Ilbei glanced back over his shoulder, down the embankment, and saw the monstrous brigand with the equally monstrous crossbow loading yet another bolt—though it might more accurately have been called a short spear. Ilbei turned back to the man menacing Mags. "Easy there," he said, sidling away from the edge of the cut bank, hoping to get his head below the big fellow's line of sight. "No need to let things get to unravelin so fast. And there ain't no reason ya need to die here today."

"Won't be me dying," he said. "Now you just stop talking and set that pick down before the lady springs a leak."

"Well, thing is, if'n ya hurt her, you're dead anyway, which you and me both already know is true. Meanin, ya ain't gonna do it. So why not just step off and save yerself some trouble here."

The villain made a show of pushing the sword deeper into Mags' ribs, causing her to gasp. "That's right, squeak, little miss, let him know I mean it."

Mags slammed the side of her head into his ear and batted the blade away with her arm, opening up a long cut in her flesh in doing so. She spun and leapt on him with astonishing speed, wailing at the top of her lungs as if she'd suddenly got the craze. She scratched and clawed at his face, hammering at him with her bound fists and becoming the very manifestation of ferocity.

In the three or four seconds it took her would-be captor to catch her by the arm and throw her off, Ilbei was on him, one boot planted on his throat and his pickaxe raised and ready to spike him through the head.

A shout came from behind him. "Don't do it. Put it down!" It sounded like Meggins, of all people.

Ilbei swiveled his head and saw the big man with the giant crossbow leveled at him. It must have been him that said it, or so Ilbei thought at first. But it wasn't. Meggins was up the slope ten paces to his left, just coming out of a thicket. His bow was drawn back, an arrow pointed at the crossbowman's head. "Lower that spear launcher, you git bastard, or I'll put one right through your ear."

The big man's eyes narrowed at Ilbei, and Ilbei knew he'd just escaped a skewer through the back. As he considered the weapon still directed at him, he realized exactly how the man had gotten his name: that had to be Ergo the Skewer.

"Put it down," Meggins demanded again. "I won't say it a third time."

"You put it down," came a new voice from atop the hill.

"Drop it, or the giant gets it."

They all turned to see the last man that had run off from the creek now prodding Kaige ahead of him with the point of Kaige's own broadsword.

"That's right. Both of you drop your weapons, or I'll carve your friend here into steaks and shanks."

Meggins slid back into the brush a bit, enough to make seeing him harder to do, while the man beneath Ilbei's feet tried to make a move, twitching his hand down toward his boot, which he had slowly begun to slide up toward his hand. Ilbei mashed down hard against his throat, the heavy sole of his army-issue boot nearly crushing the man's windpipe, so nearly that the man gagged and sputtered, eyes wide and terrified.

"I'll snuff ya, son," Ilbei warned through gritted teeth. "Now ain't the time fer bein stupid." He looked back to the bandit with the crossbow. "Look here. There's no need everyone dyin on account of this here misunderstandin we got goin on." He glanced back at Mags, who was still on her knees, staring transfixed at the bulging eyes of the man Ilbei was nearly strangulating. In her peripheral vision, she saw him looking at her and turned to him. He looked down at Jasper, pointing at him with his eyes, urgency widening them, suggesting what he hoped she would do. She nodded just enough for him to see.

"What we got here," the bandit who had to be Ergo the Skewer said, "is a good old dwarven standoff." He actually laughed.

"I don't know, boss," said the man holding Kaige hostage. "I'm doing the math here, and I think we lose one, and they lose two, worst-case scenario."

"Yes, you idiot, and our loss is me."

"Well ..., yeah, I didn't mean it like that," the man said. "I was just, you know, ciphering the odds."

"Which is why we don't have you doing the ciphering

around here, isn't it?"

The man with Kaige's broadsword fell silent then.

"Hard to find good help, ain't it?" Ilbei said.

"You have no idea," the Skewer replied.

"So what do ya suppose we ought to do now?" Ilbei asked. "I ain't too keen on takin one of them steel spears of yers through the back, and ya just made it pretty clear ya ain't so keen on my man there openin up yer head fer the vultures and coyotes to feed on neither."

"I owe you a shot in the back," the Skewer said, a backward movement of his head indicating Meggins' arrow, still protruding from below his left shoulder blade.

"No, I reckon that was in kind fer that poor bastard lyin in the river over there. Looks to me like he was struck down blindside, the way he's lyin, face first and head hollowed out from behind and all."

"You've a sharp eye, Sergeant."

"It's what they pay me fer." Ilbei glanced back to Mags, who was trying to revive Jasper without drawing attention to herself, employing a technique that involved using her left hand, hidden behind her thigh, to pinch him at the base of the calf where his leg had flopped close to her. Ilbei turned back to the bandit leader with a smile. "So, seein as ya ain't dead, and that there feller in the creek has already been sent along to sing Mercy's song, I reckon ya got off with the best hand of the two. Why not take what ya won and move along, leave some years to all the rest."

"You've killed three of my men for certain, and I suspect the whole count is five," the Skewer said. "How am I supposed to walk away from that?"

"All five of em died with weapons in their hands. Can ya say the same fer the man ya murdered down there?"

"I can see you are a man of honor, Sergeant. A rare commodity."

"That last is true. Thieves and cowards is common as

147

dirt."

"Ouch. You wound me, sir." His words were not echoed in his smiling eyes.

"So, what say everyone just backs off now? You go on yer way, and we'll go on ours. Slow and easy as ya please. I'll let this one up, and our man up there can come on down, and we'll settle this peaceful and nice."

"I hardly think that's possible. We won't be gone long enough for a cockatrice to crow before you're after us again. I don't think I want Her Majesty's army chasing me around the rest of my days."

"Well, ya already got Her Majesty's army after ya. Ya had it before all this here began. And I ain't goin to promise I won't come fer ya after, neither, because we both know I will. Straight as that iron stick ya got pulled back there, I will. But if'n ya go and kill us, even one, you'll have more to worry about than me and a few of my boys. I'm only gonna drag ya in fer words with the general at Hast. If'n ya make em send out the cavs, well, them horse fellers ain't so nice as me, and there's a fair share more of em. Lot of em noble boys, too. Got less to reckon fer if'n they ain't so kind. They'll drag ya round through the brush up here, maybe tamp yer backside full of poison oak fer a laugh, then draw and quarter ya till ya scream. Rip ya in pieces fer all four corners of the world."

Jasper began to stir at Ilbei's feet, and Ilbei heard Mags let out a breath that sounded like relief. He would have let out his own, excepting for the fact he had no idea what, if anything, the skittish young wizard would do.

"I see your man there is waking up," the Skewer said, dashing Ilbei's plans for a long-winded attempt to buy them time. "And while that is a truly frightening story you tell about your cavalry friends, I think your caster there might tip the balance of power more immediately, don't you?"

"I don't expect I know," Ilbei said. "But he's a damn fine

wizard, so I'm likin our chances better knowin he ain't dead."

The Skewer glanced at Meggins for a moment, then back to Ilbei. He looked like a card player who knew he couldn't beat his opponent's hand. "Your word you won't pursue us if I agree to your proposal that we all back away?"

"I never said I won't pursue ya," Ilbei said. "I told ya right out, I'm gonna come and drag ya straight back to Her Majesty's justice where ya belong. There's a price fer bein a no-good murderin thief, killin folks what ain't done nothin to nobody 'cept try to hammer a livin out from under a rock."

Ergo the Skewer looked up at his man behind Kaige and signaled something with his eyes, but from his angle on it, Ilbei couldn't make out what. He looked up at Kaige, hoping for a sign, but the big fellow looked like he was only barely on his feet, his eyes crossing and uncrossing. The man holding his sword was nodding when Ilbei looked.

"Now don't try nothin stupid," Ilbei said. "I can smell the stupid comin right off the both of ya."

"Sergeant, please. You insult me. We both know—" He fired his crossbow and, in the same movement, dove back behind the embankment. Fortunately, Ilbei heard the catch in his voice and jerked to the side in time to watch the long projectile whistle past like silver lightning. It only just missed hitting the horse. In the next instant, less time than it took to blink, Meggins' arrow slid through the weeds and deflected high and out into the brush on the other side of the creek, the Skewer's trick affording him the protection of the bank, if only by half a moment.

Kaige cried out right after and came rolling down the hill, his own sword stuck half a hand deep into his lower back for the first flop before being knocked out as he rolled. The man who'd done it ran back over the crest of the hill toward the shack. The man who'd been under Ilbei's boot scrambled to his feet.

Ilbei nailed the man's legs together with one swing of his pickaxe, the blade entering through the left knee from the outside, exiting the inside, and then arcing in the other knee from the back. The curve of the pickaxe blade tore the right kneecap loose and pushed it through the skin. The small bone dangled against his shin, hanging on a bit of tissue like a cork tied to a bit of leather cord. The man screamed in agony as he fell, and Ilbei left him to leak and wail. He ran up the hill for Kaige.

Kaige rolled to a stop halfway down the hill, collecting dirt and weeds in his wound, which had started to bleed. Meggins ran past him over the hill and disappeared.

Ilbei rolled Kaige onto his back and looked into his eyes, fearing it was already too late, but Kaige was actually revived some by the pain and the fall.

"I think I let them get away, Sarge," Kaige told him. "Two of them boys jumped right out and whomped me in the head."

"Ya got bigger problems than yer thick head, boy," Ilbei said. "They done stuck ya in the back."

"Oh," he said, reaching back to feel for the wound. "Is that what that is?"

Ilbei looked down the hill to where Mags had cut herself loose on the screaming man's longsword and was now shaking Jasper fully back to consciousness.

"Hurry," Ilbei called down to her. "Hurry, hurry."

"He's coming around," Mags called up. "Just keep pressure on the wound."

"I'm keepin damn pressure on it. What do ya think I'm doin over here, pickin daisies?" He looked back up to where Meggins had disappeared, but there was no sign of the soldier yet. "Damn him if he gets hisself killed," he spat.

"Oh, I ain't killed, Sarge," Kaige said, smiling up at him as if he were lying at the bottom of a keg of ale. "I had worse than this before."

"I know ya have, son. So just pipe down, and we'll have Jasper over here to fix ya up."

"Where's Meggins? They didn't get him after they rung my gong, did they? He back yet?"

"No, they didn't get him," Ilbei said, taking advantage of the gap in Kaige's memory.

"Where's he at, then? You need to tell him next time to wait up for me. He's too damned fast. He ran right past them hiding in the brush. When I finally come through, *whack*, they ambushed me in the skull."

"Well, ya can tell him yerself," Ilbei said, looking back and forth between the rising Jasper and the last-known location of the still-missing Meggins. "Soon as he gets here."

"Where'd he go to?"

"He's off bein a gods-be-damned hero," Ilbei said, feeling as he did that he'd sort of let that slip. But he let the thought go as he saw that Jasper was finally up, collecting his scrolls. Mags helped him, and a moment later, they came up the slope, with Mags supporting the mage sturdily.

Jasper knelt down beside Kaige, whose blood was now running in a stream several finger-widths wide in the dirt between Ilbei's knees, and looked him over. He fished through his satchel and pulled out a scroll.

"Can ya read them things proper, what with yer brain been rattled recently?" Ilbei asked. "Hard to say which of ya got struck the worse."

"I can read it," Jasper said. Then he turned and vomited in the weeds. "I think."

Ilbei shook his head, and guilt filled him. He'd nearly led his men to disaster taking on the Skewer. And Meggins was still up there chasing them.

"Keep an eye on em both," Ilbei said, directing the statement to Mags, as Jasper was more firmly settled and unfurling a scroll. "I'll be right back." And with that he ran off in pursuit of Meggins.

By the time he returned, Meggins in tow, the bandits had gotten away. The one Ilbei had pickaxed through the legs was dead, and Mags and Kaige were pulling the miner out of the water respectfully. Kaige appeared to be as healthy as an ox. It seemed stab wounds and blunt head blows were just the sorts of things Jasper's army-issue healing scrolls were intended for. With Kaige up and as merry as a man just risen from a nap, Jasper had gone to where the miner had finally split open his boulder, his last act before being murdered. There was a hole where the bandits had been digging in the gravel there, and the wizard sat waist deep in the water, scooping out gravel with his hands.

"What in the name of wet idiots is he doin?" Ilbei asked as he stepped in to help Kaige and Mags carry the miner up to higher ground.

Before anyone could answer, Jasper called out, "I've got it. He was right!" He held up his hand triumphantly. In it, a bright chunk of gold, as big as his fist, gleamed wetly in the sun.

Chapter 15

Jasper ran the chunk of gold over to Ilbei, breathless as a boy who's caught his first fish. Though the distance was short, he was panting by the time he got there. "Placer gold, just like I knew it would be. He was right to think it was down there."

"Makes his murder all the worse. Her Majesty's laws are hard on men what kill fer greed. Won't go well fer Ergo the Skewer and those what got off with him."

"All the more reason to get after them," Meggins said.

Kaige straightened and put both hands in the small of his own back, stretching it, as if still trying to confirm that his wound was healed. He looked down at the man lying at their feet. "He needs to be buried. We can't leave him here."

Ilbei nodded. "We'll see it done. It's only right. And after, we'll get back to Hast and fetch some more men. With only us, and havin Mags along, it ain't prudent to keep goin up there. They know the country, and we don't, and that gives em more advantage than they need. We'll have the whole mountainside brimmin with folks what want to do fer us."

"Mags knows the country," Meggins said. "Don't you?"

Mags looked to Ilbei, who scowled, his tatty mustache bristling around his mouth. "I do," she said anyway. Honesty

153

required she admit that it was true.

"Well, we still ain't goin, fer all them other reasons I gave. We come close enough to gettin both Jasper and Kaige brained—not that either make much use of em—so I'm sayin we go back."

"Since when did you go all soft and motherly, Sarge?" Meggins asked. "We already cut the Skewer's numbers to less than half. You told us the miners said there were only eight. Well, now there are three. And they know we're not to be messed with."

"We ain't goin on without orders. The mission's changed, and that's the end of it." He looked briefly to Jasper, who was still holding the gold reverently, then to Mags. "Mags, this dead feller got any folks anywhere what we could send that to?"

"I believe he's got a sister who lives in Norvingtown or somewhere nearby on the gulf of Dae. I don't know her name, but his was Scaver, and his father was a tanner out there. We can find her."

Ilbei nodded, as relieved that she had that information as she appeared to be that he had asked. He turned back to Jasper. "I expect ya got somethin in that bag of tricks of yers to get word to Major Cavendis about the murderous nature of them criminals movin that way. He ought not to take so lightly to the woods alone knowin what we know. Them criminals is just as happy to cut down Her Majesty's men as butcher a man workin hisself a stretch of stream, and an officer covered with gold and silver baubles would make a nice prize." He shook his head ruefully as he said it, lamenting what had become of humanity, a race that supposed itself to be the most civilized on Prosperion.

"I do have a scroll for it," Jasper said. "It's actually one I did the enchantment for myself." He looked pleased. "What should I tell him?"

"What I just told ya. Tell him Ergo the Skewer and at least

two more are headin his way with a taste fer murder and gold. Make sure he knows the uniform of Her Majesty's army don't mean a heap of dragon dung to them fellers, and they'll likely gut a major as easy as they would have done any one of us, and like they done that poor feller lyin there."

"What if he asks why we are here at all?"

A portion of Ilbei's beard and mustache slid up toward his right eye at that. "Don't ya have some way of communicatin what ain't two-way? Like a magic messenger pigeon or letter carrier, so as we don't have to get no reply?"

"The army would only pay for me to make two-way message scrolls. It's what I was doing right before they dragged me off down here. The cost to make them is only marginally higher than making one-way reporting spells, so there's really no reason not to, given that carrying both only takes more space. The mitigating reagent is silver, actually, and it amounts to only a seventeen percent difference, purely for that, not counting the others. Although I read once tha—"

Ilbei cut him off before he could ramble off on a lengthy technical, magical and bureaucratic dissertation on the processes required for enchanting magic onto parchment. "Just get to it, son. We got half a day's march ahead, and you'll be a week in that story there."

Meggins made no attempt to hide his disappointment at the finality of Ilbei's decision to go home. "But what about that old, nasty harpy in the stream? Aren't we at least going to yank it out of there like you said? For the sake of the water supply?"

"The whole point of makin the water better is so that nobody gets sick or killed," Ilbei said. "I'm thinkin gettin one of them span-long crossbow bolts through the head will kill ya deader than any creek-born harpy craze. And quicker too."

"He will kill miners up at Fall Pools and Cedar Wood,"

Meggins said, which made Ilbei frown. Meggins raised his eyebrows optimistically. "I'm just saying, leaving has its own set of risks. It's not just the major we have to worry about."

"If we didn't have this here woman along—" Ilbei turned back to her, "no offense—I'd be all right with pressin on. But we do, and I ain't draggin her into another fight, as the last one might have done fer her as well as the rest of us."

Mags actually did look offended, and she thumped the butt of her reclaimed quarterstaff on the ground as if she were about to protest, but Meggins beat her to it by a blink. Or at least he tried to. "But they're going to—"

Ilbei silenced him with a glare, tipping his weight forward, his squat, burly body swelling with the familiar sort of breath that famously preceded a tirade or, worse, a straight-up beat down.

"By Mercy's light, the lot of ya. I said we're gods-be-damned goin back, and that's the end of it. Meggins, if'n ya make one more snivelin squeak, I'll bust yer head so lumpy yer phrenologist will still be tellin the stories ten years from now. Ya hear?"

"Yes, Sergeant," Meggins said. "I didn't mean anything by it. Just hungry for payback was all."

"Hey," called Jasper from over by the horse. "There's something wrong."

They turned as one to face him.

"What's wrong?" Ilbei asked. He moved to where he could glance down at the scroll the young magician held unfurled in his hands, as if somehow he, rather than Jasper, might be able to spot a problem with it.

"The spell. It's not working. The first line keeps dissolving back when I get to his name."

"Son, I don't know what that means."

"The locus line, where I fix the object of the spell as written on the page to the image in my mind. They have to

156

match for the smoke writing to work."

"Still meanin nothin, Jasper," Ilbei said. "Pretend I don't know nothin about magic and start again."

Jasper's eyes rolled heavenward, the mind behind them seeking a way to properly simplify. "It's not letting me start the spell because the object of the spell isn't working. Like aiming a crossbow at a target that isn't there."

"Like who isn't there, the major?"

"Yes. There's no object to stick the spell to. It's as if he does not exist."

"Well, that's the most fool thing I heard come out of ya yet. 'Course he exists. We just spent a fair miserable stretch of days in his company."

"That is precisely my point, Sergeant. We did. The spell should work. But it doesn't. Here, watch what happens to this first paragraph as I read. Do you see here, where I've filled in his name, this whole set of lines starting at the top?" He tilted the scroll so Ilbei could see, pointing to where he had written the major's name in a space near the end of the third line. Beyond those two words, Ilbei didn't recognize another one on the page. The whole thing was one great wall of indecipherability, the sort of thing that made him very glad he was a man who made his way in the world with his hands. He had no patience for all that chicken-scratch nonsense. "Now, just watch," Jasper said. "These words at the top will disappear as I read, and then, when I get to his name, the whole thing comes back again—I wrote it that way because, well, if I am permitted a bit of vanity, because I can. This is the army after all, and death is quite possible, so I included that circular enchantment in the locus lines so as not to lose a valuable scroll in the event of this person or that person's death, which of course makes targeting them impossible. Otherwise, this scroll, which cost Her Majesty a full half-crown, would already be used up. It's really a very clever piece of magic, if I do say so myself. I found the return magic in an enchantment the dwarves used on their catapults, believe it or not. Such is the value of a little research, I should say. It seems they had the ability to—"

"Jasper, sweet Mercy! I'd rather the gorgon turned my giblets to gravel than hear another word. Just show me what you're meanin to show before my retirement years pass me by."

The insult set one of Jasper's eyes to squinting, but, being outranked as he was, he began to read the scroll anyway, mumbling in the low, singsong voice of magic underway. Ilbei focused on the lines as directed, marveling at the words as they really did disappear, making it easy to follow, one word, then another, then the whole first line, as if it were all being slowly erased by an invisible finger pointing as Jasper read along. Ilbei had never seen a spell being read before. He'd seen scrolls used, of course, but never actually looked at the page as the enchanted magicks were being released. First went the top line, and then the second. The third line began to disappear as well, fading away toward where the major's name was written in. And then the page was full again.

Jasper looked up at him right after, his expression the sort seen most often upon the faces of hungover men. "You see," he said, grimacing, and rubbing the side of his head.

"Well, as you're intent on makin a fuss about it, seems clear it ain't supposed to be that way. So what's it mean?"

"I think it means he's dead."

"How can ya be sure? Maybe he's just gone back to Twee."

"I can't be sure," Jasper said. "But the spell has no limits to range. That means, if the spell won't go to him, then he's not there for it to get to."

"So that's it, then. He's already done fer? Ain't nothin else it could be?"

"Well, since I haven't spelled his name wrong, the only other thing would be if he wasn't who he says he is."

"Like an imposter?"

"Yes."

Ilbei scratched his head, his mouth wiggling beneath his mustache. "But wouldn't there still be a Major Cavendis somewhere, if'n the man we know as him weren't him? The *what* the spell ought to get to by rights?"

"Well ...." Jasper had to think about that for a moment or two. "No, I shouldn't think that would work. For one, he might have made the name up. But even if he hadn't, it still wouldn't work that way because the man I know as the major wouldn't be the same man as the one attached to the name I wrote down. It's the bringing together of language along with an idea. So, if he were an imposter, neither of them would suffice as the proper object of the spell."

"So then, ya either spelled it wrong or he's dead?"

"Well, he still might be an imposter, although he's rather highborn to bother with such a thing. And he is a lord of South Mark, where Cavendis is a well-known family name. Meaning the most likely answer is that he is dead. Maybe the man who ran off yesterday got to him."

Ilbei harrumphed. "Or that odd rip of a hunter, Locke Verity." Ilbei leaned forward to glance at the scroll again, which Jasper tipped for him to see. In truth, Ilbei knew he wouldn't know any better than Jasper would how to spell the major's name, if there were any irregularities as to how it ought to be done, but it looked right to him as it was. As much as he hadn't liked the young lord, he'd hate to think he'd gone off and left the man to be butchered all alone. That could come with ramifications all its own. Still—and gods knew Cavendis had behaved oddly enough for a man acting the imposter of some kind—there was an ironic sort of hope that he wasn't dead, despite the fact that Jasper sure looked confident that he was.

Ilbei let go a long, tired breath as he straightened and stared out across the top of the scrub, the endless-seeming bramble sloping gently away into the north. Manzanita gave the landscape a blue-green tint, and all the crooked trunks showed their color like the dried blood of old hemorrhages. He let his vision slide out over it all, moving northwest toward the edge of the Sandsea and beyond it to where the garrison and Hast lay unseen in the distance. Three days at least. Maybe four, depending on the heat.

"We should go back and check on him," Meggins said. "He wasn't much as an officer, but we ought to go look." Eagerness glimmered in the soldier's eye, an underlying desire for adventure poorly hidden behind the premise of his stated intent.

"That's borderin on insubordination, soldier. Keep yer opinions on the qualities of yer betters inside that pointy head."

"Yes, Sergeant." Meggins was grinning, though, because he knew his shot had scored.

Chapter 16

By the time they reached the spot below Cedar Wood where they'd last seen the major, the sun was already lost behind the mountain peaks to the west, pulling the draperies of the evening across the foothills a full hour earlier than in the flatlands. Ilbei ordered silence as the small company crept through the trees, listening for sounds of Ergo the Skewer and his two remaining men or for Gad Pander and whatever he might think to do. When the old campsite came into view, nobody was there. The major's tent had been packed up and taken away. Only the log Meggins had sat upon the night they'd played ruffs marked that it had ever been there.

After skirting the perimeter to verify that the space was indeed vacant and safe, they came out from the pines and looked around for signs of a fight. There were none, no smear of boot heels or patterned placements of feet to indicate swordplay, no blood or body parts, no sign that predators had come along and eaten anything.

Ilbei straightened and put his hands on his hips, harrumphing loud enough for everyone to hear, though he had eyes for Jasper alone. "Well, he ain't dead here."

"I never said he died here." Jasper turned to Kaige, who

was standing at his side. "I never said that. You were there. Tell him I never said that."

Kaige smiled weakly back at him and shrugged apologetically. "I don't pay so close attention to when you talk. Don't mean no offense by it, though."

"Well, I didn't say it was here." Jasper put his hands on his hips, prepared to defend himself as he looked back to Ilbei.

"He's probably down where the Softwater meets the Desertborn," Meggins said. "His people were a good three days away. Maybe he's down there waiting for them to show up tomorrow sometime."

That did seem likely, and it aligned with Ilbei's thoughts. "I expect you're right. If'n he's dead, could be that he fell in and drowned."

"Or the potameide got him," Jasper said.

"Damn. You're right about that," Ilbei said. "Forgot about her. Not sure we'd know if'n that's the case, but we ought to go down and check all the same."

The trip down the banks of the Softwater was easier than it had been coming up, taking only a day and a half. There were less of them traveling, and the slope was in their favor. They looked for signs of recent activity, but there were none—though Ilbei could admit it was hard to tell, given they'd only come through a matter of days before. When they got to their original landing spot, there was still no sign of the major anywhere. Both the rafts were gone, no longer tied to the trees where they'd left them, and recent marks showed where they'd been dragged back into the water for the return trip. Other than that, however, there were no signs that anyone else had come along in all that time. There certainly were no fresh hoofprints, no crescent-shaped marks from horseshoes turned in the direction of the river rather than away to suggest the major had come back.

"Well if this don't bite my hide more than a basketful of bedbugs," Ilbei proclaimed after a thorough inspection of the riverbank for several hundred paces upstream and down. "Wasn't much fonder of that feller than a case of crotch warts, but I ain't keen to leave him behind neither. That ain't proper. I reckon we ought to have gone up to Cedar Wood before we come down this way. Maybe even on up to that other camp at Fall Pools." Ilbei silently cursed himself for having not done so, even though he understood how hindsight worked.

"So we go back," Meggins said, his smile easy, his voice merry. "It's okay by me. I'd rather go up than head back to Hast. If we go back, we get rotated into desert patrols again, maybe stuck digging latrines in the heat. Pretty much everything that makes Hast the sewer of Kurr. I'd rather be here, even if it means climbing these damn hills. At least it gets cooler the higher we go."

Kaige nodded that it was true.

"What do ya think, Jasper?" Ilbei asked. "You're the one with the spell what brung us here lookin, and I admit we're pushin pretty far past orders now."

That seemed to shock the entire company, and both Kaige and Meggins looked as surprised as Jasper did. Jasper touched himself on the chest. "Me? You're soliciting my advice?"

"Yes, you, unless ya figure there's someone else here goin by Jasper now. Command put ya in the platoon fer a reason, same as me. What's yer gut tell ya we ought to do?"

Jasper considered the question for a long time, so long that Ilbei began to regret having asked, but finally Jasper pulled his fingers from his narrow chin and spoke. "I think what you said about leaving anyone behind is likely the primary operating principle here, as much as I am loath to continue back into the hills. I can't help but ask myself what I would want you to do if I were missing and presumed dead, and I am afraid, coward that I am, I would be hoping for rescue—of course assuming I am not dead already, at which point, if I knew that, I would not want you to come because, being dead, I wouldn't want to put you through the inconvenience and expense. Traveling does not come without some degree of inherent dange—"

"Jasper! By the gods!"

The candid, oratory expression that shaped Jasper's features when he launched into one of his speeches was replaced by a pinched mouth and raised nose, affecting his indignation at having once again been cut off. He made a point of studying the trees rather than looking at Ilbei. "You did ask, you know."

Ilbei sighed. "I did, lad. I did." To the rest he said, "So there we have it, then. Let's make a few hours of it back before nightfall, then see to a meal and a bit of rest before mornin."

The next day, they continued upstream, threading through the thickening trees, staying near the river but far enough away that they didn't have to pick their way over boulders and wade through ankle-deep pools. When they stopped for lunch, Meggins swore he saw a pair of harpies circling overhead, but by the time he'd decided they were harpies and not vultures, the air currents had already carried them off.

"Ya got harpies on the brain," Ilbei said. "Ever since we come across that dead one, you're seein em like illusionist magic: they ain't there but in yer head."

Of course, Meggins insisted he'd seen what he'd seen, but as no further instances of harpies showed themselves—and because Jasper explained in tedious detail the improbable odds of seeing a harpy this far east of the nearest, and last, recorded location of a harpy wild—the subject was dropped, especially by Meggins, who, by the end of Jasper's lecture, was nearly begging to be forgiven for having brought it up.

They arrived at Cedar Wood shortly before dark on the second full day of travel, having made excellent time up the hill. The smell of pork fat and baked bread wafted out of the little tavern welcomingly. They tied the packhorse to a tree, near enough to the river that it could enjoy the greenery growing there, and then went inside. Ilbei's stomach growled almost as loudly as the door hinges creaked upon entering.

The tavern keeper looked up from the rough planks of the bar and sneered at him. "You red-stripes ain't welcome here no more, so just get out. Don't need no more trouble from you lot."

Ilbei walked into the remark as if it were a stone wall, and he took a step back on impact. He looked to the table where the men had gambled with Major Cavendis the night Ilbei asked about the highway robberies. No one sat there now. Only one other patron occupied the establishment at all, and he made a studious effort not to look up from his meal.

"I don't recollect that kind of incivility a few nights back," Ilbei said. "Mind if I ask what's got yer feathers all afluff?"

"Just get out. Nobody's got anything left. You people are as bad as that damnable Skewer in the end. He only picked a few pockets before he went away. Sure, there were a few murders and a beat down for good measure, but at least he left. He never pretended he was other than a villain. But not you. You people are going to steal it all. Keep coming back until what? Till all the boys give up and go like the rest? Or just till they starve and die?" Contempt warped his features as he spoke. "You were supposed to come and help us."

Ilbei's mouth moved side to side beneath the bramble of his mustache. "Well, I ain't stole nothin from nobody, so I reckon ya might consider slowin down and tellin me what this here hostility is about. Weren't nobody tryin to starve ya out."

The tavern keeper's eyes narrowed as he studied Ilbei and the rest of them. That's when he noticed Mags. "Magda? How they'd get their hooks into you? Are you okay?"

"I'm fine, Topper. What's going on? I've never seen you like this. You know Bessy wouldn't have approved of you turning folks away out here."

"Well, Bessy's dead, ain't she?"

"You know what I meant."

"They come in here night before last and cleaned out the boys again. Sent em all home before they had time to pay their tabs. Couple of the lads are pretty riled, but most are just fed up. Old Mitty and Juke was down, and they said they're done. First the Skewer, now that major of theirs." He pointed at Ilbei as if it had been Ilbei that spawned the major out of his own womb, birthing him out of pure malice no less. "He took all they had and then some. Even followed em home to get em to pay up. Baited them boys so bad they were betting out of their heads. Gamers the both of em, that major and his old friend Locke Verity, and they completely wiped em out. Mitty and Juke left for Hast in the morning. Gave up their stake to Zoe, didn't even ask him for a speck of lead to pay. Just walked away."

"Over a gamblin debt?" Ilbei had heard of poor losers before, and he knew well enough how people could get if they'd been cheated at cards, or even if they simply thought they'd been cheated, but walking away from everything they owned simply because they lost one game? "How much did they owe?"

"Came near a crown, as I heard it. Maybe more. And them two had nothing near that much in all they owned. And that major of yours wasn't laughing or even seeming to enjoy winning much. He was as serious as a man pulling arrows out of his mother, he was. He told Mitty, and I heard it clear, 'If you got a crown buried up there and I find it before you do, it's not going to go well for you.' That's what he said, and he said it mean, like a threat."

Ilbei glanced over his shoulder at Meggins, who shrugged, his expression suggesting he was as perplexed as Ilbei.

"Well, I'll grant that's a peculiar way fer an officer of Her Majesty's army to behave," Ilbei said. "And I'll take it up with him when I see him next. I can't promise much, but I'll see if'n I can't get him to let ya folks alone at cards. Fellers what grow up with money like he done don't figure the value of coins same as you and I, so they don't reckon the damage they do."

The man Mags had called Topper studied Ilbei for a while, considering whether to believe Ilbei was as he presented himself to be. The barkeep seemed to conclude that the grizzled sergeant was, and shortly after, the rigidity in his posture dissipated. "Well, you give him an earful from me, too. They went upriver, as I heard them say, so you go on and tell him. And if he don't listen, which he won't, then you take it back to the garrison at Hast and tell someone over him what he's done." He turned away from the bar and rummaged through the shelves behind him, muttering mainly to himself. "A man like that comes in here, fancy blades hanging from him, each one worth more than most will earn in all their lives, and yet fleecing common folks for sport." He put a bottle of wine on the counter and poured himself a glass. "There's bacon, stewed taters and biscuits for you all, and it's on me on account of my lousy hospitality." He glanced at Mags. "You're right about Bessy. That was a poor showing on my part."

Mags forgave him with her smile, and the four of them took seats at the nearest table while Topper brought the food around. Ilbei invited him to join them if he hadn't eaten, and said he'd like to pay for Topper's meal, to which the tavern keeper agreed.

Over the course of that meal, Ilbei fished for more bits of information about the major's game, wherein Cavendis and the hunter Locke Verity had wiped out the tavern's patrons two nights before.

"I noticed ya called that hunter an old friend of the major's. Was that just figurin speech, or do ya know that as fact? And if so, do ya know how they come to meet?"

"I know exactly how they met," Topper said. "Verity was the ranger sent up from the garrison at Hast a year and a half ago when Bessy died. He's the one that told us that the harpies got her, way up near Fall Pools. He was up there looking for her when he met Lord Cavendis and that magician he used to come around with. That was before Cavendis took the colors of Her Majesty's army, of course."

Ilbei turned to Meggins and asked, "You've been stationed at the garrison over a year. Ya never saw Verity?"

He said it at the very same time Meggins slapped his forehead and proclaimed, "That's where I know him from."

Ilbei cocked a gray eyebrow. "Go on."

"Verity was at the garrison when I transferred in. He didn't have the long, fancy mustache or the expensive clothes, but I knew I'd seen that bow of his before. In fact, he got his discharge same day I showed up. I saw him leaving as I was processing in. That's why I barely recognized him, and I wouldn't have if it hadn't been for that bow. You don't forget an exquisite weapon like that once you've seen it. Funny thing was, I actually wondered if I might get one too. Dumb me thought they might be standard issue."

Topper nodded. "Well, that would be about the time when he showed up here and started hunting for the camps regularly. Said his time was up with the army and there was money to be made. True enough for that. He makes more selling the boys meat than they make digging, that's sure."

"Can't fault a man fer seein the smart angle to pay his way," Ilbei said.

"No, I don't suppose you can."

Chapter 17

The trek to Fall Pools the following day was steep and arduous. The trees grew farther apart and gave way more easily than the low hills, but the slope was merciless. Here and there along the way, they would come to the small domiciles miners had built. Most were abandoned, with trenches left half-dug into the sides of the riverbanks and wooden rockers left rotting in the moist air. In a few places, they did find men still at it, and in particular, one old man who looked to Ilbei to be at least three hundred years old—though when Kaige tactlessly asked him how old he was, it turned out he was only one hundred and fifty-three. Most common folks in the modern era could make a hundred and seventy-five, even crack two hundred if they could afford a doctor mage from time to time, but life out in the wilderness had taken its toll on the old man, that was sure.

They sat a spell with the old man and fed him lunch out of their own supplies, even brewing up a pot of Goblin Tea, which Ilbei brought out from one of the panniers—Ilbei felt doing so was not exactly theft, given he'd had to take on responsibility for the animal and all. They chatted for a while about the man's luck digging up precious metals, of which he said he'd had little to none in the six months since he'd come here to try. They asked him about the major, whom he'd never seen, and about Ergo the Skewer, whom he'd never seen either. Meggins asked him if he'd had any encounters with harpies, at which he'd laughed, as if Meggins were a child asking after pink mammoths. Jasper responded to that, of course, with a lecture on the migration patterns of harpies and the close family unit cohesion that could easily explain why some locals saw harpies and others did not. The old man, in turn, told Jasper he'd once served on a merchant ship with a man who had similar "squeezy bowels of the mouth," as he'd put it. He explained how one day the crew had had enough and "threw the blabbering lubber overboard to run with the sharks, as sharks was the only creatures in nature as ready to work their jaws as that windy sailor was." That, of course, precipitated a round of riotous mockery from Kaige and Meggins, which ultimately ended up in Ilbei yelling at them and getting them moving up the river again.

In places, they might have saved time by climbing the boulders and slick, root-entangled lower steppes, which were often little more than vertical shifts of two to ten spans and down which the river poured in a sequence of waterfalls like a rug over stairs. However, quicker as that direct assault on the climb might have been for men on foot, having the horse with them required that they go out and around the steppes, sticking mainly to the supply road. As it had been with Deer Trail Road, this one was little more than a path rubbed into the ground, and even that lost itself entirely from time to time, sending them back toward the river lest they lose their way. If they'd all had mounts, working their way back and forth up what the miners called the Lower Switchbacks would have been easy enough, but doing so was slow on foot, and it turned a half-day's journey into a full one.

The shadow of the mountain was once again upon them

as the sun hid behind the peaks. By the time they could smell the smoke from the fires at Fall Pools, the bats were already dipping their toes into the pools near the river's edge, and the occasional hoot of an owl could be heard from the treetops.

The crash of a waterfall ahead filled the air with a low thunder, the weight of the river falling from a great height thrumming beneath their feet. The wind stirred up by the falling water was misty and wet, and it made its own sound, as if an audience cheered the magnificence of the falls in the distance somewhere. The air grew cooler with every step up the trail.

Lights shone through the trees a short time after they'd rounded a projection of stone and angled up a natural ramp made by the last of the short lower steppes. The whole mountain was a great stairwell of sorts, the stone broken and forced into tiers during some ancient continental shift. Fall Pools sat atop the last of the easily assailable ones, at the base of the first of the mighty ones, walls of stone that thrust in places over a hundred spans high, like a great stairwell climbing to the sky.

When the ground finally leveled out, or at least the slope gentled some, they picked their way through the trees, heading toward the lights. Soon enough, Fall Pools was in sight. Ilbei noted Major Cavendis' glistening black warhorse tethered along with three lesser animals to a goat pen near the center of the assembled buildings.

He raised his hand that they should stop. "Well, maybe he ain't dead after all," he said, upon seeing the animal.

"Or someone got themselves a nice new horse," Meggins put in.

Ilbei turned on them and looked very grave. "Now listen here, the lot of ya. I don't much care for the sense I got of all of this what's goin on up here. If'n I'm right, the major ain't goin to be as pleased to see us as he ought to be, despite us comin up here to look after him. So, if'n it turns out true, well, ya need to keep yer heads."

Kaige looked nervous. "So what do we say, Sarge? What if he asks why we came up here, or why we went to Camp Chaparral at all?"

Ilbei knew the soldier wouldn't do well trying to lie to an officer and nobleman. "You just tell him the truth, son. We come back because of Ergo the Skewer and worryin on the major bein dead and all. It ain't no lie. And Jasper tried to speak to him through that paper spell of his, and he didn't get no reply, neither. We was worried, and here we are. Ain't that how ya remember it?"

Kaige nodded, looking relieved. "It is."

"Good. Just stick to that." He looked to the others. "And don't add nothin else, especially you, Jasper."

Jasper seemed to have no idea what that could possibly imply, but Ilbei raised a hand and quieted him before he could inquire.

"Enough on that," he said. "What I really want is fer you three to stay outside. Me and Mags will go in and see if'n we can't get all the talkin done anyway. You all split up and keep yer eyes open so that ballista-boltin bandit don't sneak up behind us and bury one of them long shafts a half pace up my arse."

Kaige and Meggins both nodded and moved off into the trees, one of them on either side of the trail. That left Jasper looking startled as he realized that he was going to be left alone. Ilbei patted him on the arm and directed him to a tree a few paces closer to the camp and only a few spans off the trail. "Go on and hide behind that crooked one, there. Crouch down so ya get some cover from the little bush beside it." Jasper nodded, but still didn't look pleased.

Ilbei and Mags went up the trail, Ilbei leading the horse while Mags tied her hair into a loose braid. He caught glimpses of Kaige moving forward from tree to tree, a swift, dark shadow. Meggins he couldn't see, but a pinecone fell to the ground as they neared the clearing around the camp, revealing where the agile fellow had scrambled up a tree.

Ilbei glanced back at Mags, who smiled confidently. "You don't have to tell me to keep my eyes open," she said in a soft voice. He winked, and they moved together out of the trees.

The camp consisted of eleven buildings. Like the other two camps, most of them were crudely made; although the main building, which, if patterns held, would serve as tavern and general supply, was a sturdy-looking structure built from pine logs that had been slotted at the ends and tightly stacked. Several windows were cut into it, though all of them were shuttered to keep out the advancing chill of the night. Still, light shone from around their edges and between the shutter slats, and Ilbei could see shadows passing over the bands of light, indicating that there was activity within.

He would have known without seeing the movement, however, for stray notes of music wafted in the misty air, dancing in and around the roar of the waterfall. The falls were a constant presence, a rumble in the near distance, just left of the tavern from where Ilbei stood and some forty spans behind. They fell from high above, plummeting fifty spans from the top of a wide steppe, a sheer cliff that dominated the view and marked the first of the upper steppes, or as the locals called them, Anvilwrath's Climb. At the top, at the very edge where the river rushed over and began its descent, the curve of the water shimmered pink and violet in the moonlight.

"It's pretty up here," Ilbei observed as he led the horse toward the goat pen. "I can see why fellers would stay content to live on copper and lead."

"It is," Mags agreed. "But don't let the setting fool you. The men up here are the worst of the bunch. Mean and greedy. These are the ones that are left. The ones that spent the first year up here diverting water any way they wanted, doing anything to get at the gold everyone was so damned sure was here. They did what they felt like doing without a thought for how it affected anyone else's operation downstream. Anyone that came up to complain came down with their mouths shut."

"So there *was* gold up here. I thought they didn't find any, or not much."

"No, they didn't find much. But they found some at first, and that's why everyone thought it was going to be a big haul. They spent it like drunken mariners, blowing it all on whores and gambling down in Hast or over in Murdoc Bay, all of them assuming there would be a whole lot more when they finally found 'the big lode.' But the big lode never surfaced. When what gold was there had been dug up and gambled away that first year—the first six months, really— most of them moved on. The ones that stayed only got worse. That's how Camp Chaparral got started, decent folks trying to get away from these."

Ilbei thought back to some of the deep trenches they'd seen, the abandoned gear, and nodded that he understood. He tied the horse to the goat pen, noting that there were no goats inside.

"Well, ya ready?" he asked.

She drew in a deep breath, then checked her braid. She nodded. "Let's get it over with."

Ilbei went in just ahead of her to give the place a quick once-over before she came in: fifteen tables, a big fireplace, the best-made bar in all three camps by far, and a whole roomful of rowdy-looking miners, who all stopped laughing and talking the moment he came in. There followed in the intervening stillness the dull thud of tin pints and pewter goblets being set down on tabletops, one after the next, and after that, absolute silence but for the crackle of the fire.

Ilbei took the opportunity to scan the room, looking for any faces he might recognize. There were none, though some concealed themselves in the shadows around the edges of the room, or shadows beneath the droop of dusty cowls and the downward tip of soggy hat brims. When the silence lingered beyond a few beats more, Ilbei twitched the corner of his mouth into a halfhearted smile. "Ain't someone supposed to yell 'surprise' or somethin? Ya make a feller feel like he walked in all pus-covered and spotted with the droppin pox." Nobody laughed. Mags stepped out from behind him and took his arm.

Seeing her, several of the men went back to their drinks and their card games, but the noise level did not return to where it had been, nor did all eyes turn away. A tall figure stood up from a table in the farthest corner and, upon stepping out of the shadows, revealed himself—by face if not by uniform—to be Major Cavendis. His regimentals had been exchanged for the finery of his status as a son of the House of South Mark, right down to the white ruffles at both collar and sleeves. He seemed to glide through the room as he came toward them, touching this man's shoulder or nodding reassuringly into that man's eyes as he passed by. He advanced on Ilbei and Mags and, with a flat smile, placed his hand on Ilbei's arm, opposite the one Mags held, and gave a part push and part pull, clearly meant to turn Ilbei around and propel him in a seemingly friendly way outside.

Ilbei, however—built, as an officer in Crown City had once put it, "like four cords of good firewood"—was not so easily spun and shoved about as that. He glanced down at the major's hand on his thick bicep and took a moment to consider what came next before looking up into the major's eyes. "Sar, I expect ya don't understand it ain't regulation fer an officer outta uniform to lay hands on an enlisted man, so I'm goin to let off snappin that there off on account of ya bein young and highborn."

The major removed his hand, his smile waxing saccharine. "I'm sorry. Of course you are right. Please, Sergeant, if I may have a word with you and ...," his eyes slid briefly to Mags, "... the lady, outside?"

Ilbei watched the removal of the major's hand before turning and, intending to send a wink at Mags, noticed that her face had paled. Her hand trembled on his arm as well. He frowned and glanced back at the major, who pushed past him and went out. Ilbei followed, tugging Mags along. He wasn't sure what the major had said that would have rattled her, but whatever else the man had to say, Ilbei would feel more comfortable hearing it outside, under the watchful eyes of Kaige, Meggins and Jasper rather than the frowning eyes still on him within. He'd gotten warmer welcomes stumbling into wolf dens and goblin camps.

No sooner had the door closed behind them, the young nobleman lit into him. "You had orders to go back to Hast. Why are you up here? I'll have you stripped and lashed!"

"Well, ya can strip and lash all ya want, but you'll want to make sure ya ain't been killed first, otherwise givin that order is gonna be hard to do."

"I let that little show back there go because this is the Queen's Age, and she does love her army and its policies. But I won't tolerate a death threat from the likes of a common turnip like you, Spadebreaker. We aren't so far in the woods as that. You're lucky I don't cut you down now, do you understand?"

"Yes, sar, I understand just fine. But it weren't me threatenin yer life. It's that murderin Ergo the Skewer is what I'm gettin at. He killed a man down by Harpy Creek, coldhearted as a fistful of frostberries, and he would have done yers truly were it not fer some luck and the fine work of my men and young Mags here." He turned and gave Mags a wink and a flickering smile. "He run off this way right after, and, if'n I'm bein honest, we more than half expected to find ya dead. So now ya been warned. If'n ya still want to lash me, ya go right on ahead, bein as that's yer privilege and all. I'll even take the orders fer it on back to Hast if'n ya want to spare yerself the strain of doin it."

The young nobleman rumbled in his chest, half growl, half groan, but it passed quickly. "How many men did he have?"

"They was eight all told, but we pruned em back to three. Meggins put an arrow in the Skewer's back, but seems he's a tough old knot, so he's one of em what got away."

Again came the rumbling from the major's chest. His jaw moved as he thought for a moment, the moonlight painting soft pink lines along the clean-shaven angles of his face.

"All right, Spadebreaker, here's what you're going to do. You and your men stay in Cedar Wood and protect the people down there. I'll send word to Twee and get more men up here straight away."

"Twee, sar? Hast is a full day sooner at least."

"We're in a hurry, Sergeant. We'll have the teleporters send them out. And by the gods, man, on my word, if you question another order from me, I will whip you myself. Do you understand?"

"Yes, sar. I hear ya clear, sar. I forgot myself what with ya in all them fluffs and frills."

"I have a job to do, just like you, Sergeant, and you'll do well to remember that you aren't privy to everything that goes on."

"That I do appreciate, sar."

"Then get down the damned mountain, and wait until you have orders to move. Do you understand?"

"I do, sar."

"Then, off with you."

"Yes, sar."

When Ilbei didn't turn around immediately and walk

away, the major had to ask, "Well, what are you waiting for?"

"I'm not sure whether or not I ought to salute now, sar. Are ya undercover or havin a night off?"

"You know what you need to know. Just go."

Chapter 18

Ilbei could not remember having been run off so readily by a commander in all his ninety-odd years in the military, at least never as repeatedly as Cavendis did it, and never in ways and situations that made so little sense. They'd been given a mission to ferret out the whereabouts of the bandits, and yet, after finding out nearly nothing in barely two days' looking, the major had sent him and his men away. They hadn't even been at it long enough to run out of the fish Hams had caught on the trip down the Desertborn before they'd been told to cut bait and go home. And now, after discovering that the purpose of their mission, Ergo the Skewer, *was* in fact still lurking around the mining camps— and confirming that he was both bandit and coldhearted murderer—the major, upon learning of it, could not get Ilbei away from him fast enough yet again.

The oddity of it left Ilbei muttering beneath his bristly mustache as Mags untied the horse and the two of them set off down the trail. They made a show of walking casually, but Ilbei's mind was churning furiously. What kind of a man sends two people down the mountain an hour after dark? He fiddled with his beard as he walked, his lips twisted sideways and his jaw clenched. He wanted desperately to ask Mags what the major had said that had affected her so, but he knew he needed to wait until they were out of earshot.

Mags, still silent beside him, reached up with her free hand and began working loose the braid she'd made in her hair. He saw the motion, and having been thinking about her just then, realized what she was trying to do. "Here," he said, reaching for the rope, "I'll take that." She'd already unraveled the braid, but that's when a realization struck him. "The horse!" he said. "I forgot to tell him about the damn horse and the coin-stampin plates."

Mags nodded. "Yes, you did."

"I ought to go back and tell him."

"Gad Pander is in there," she said, her voice strangely flat.

"He is?" Ilbei looked startled that he'd not noticed the man. He resisted the urge to ask her why she hadn't said anything. "Where was he?"

"Standing at the bar, staring right at you from under his hood."

"I never seen him, though I confess, like as not, I could have looked right at him and never known it was him. Never got a good look at the man."

"He was trying not to be seen. But I saw him, mainly because I was trying not to look at ... someone else."

"Someone else?"

Anger narrowed her eyes for a moment, and her lips tightened in a line, but then she looked down, as if ashamed.

Ilbei bent down enough that he could tilt his head and twist his face to where he could see hers. "Mags?"

"It's nothing. I should be past it by now."

"Past what?"

"Him. I saw *him*. The man I told you about before. The magician. He was in there."

"The one what done ya so ... the one what treated ya poor?"

She nodded.

Ilbei growled, deep and menacing, a temblor welling up from the very soul within. "Well, that's somethin I'll go on back fer. We'll see how well he takes to a measure of his own makin. Which one is he?" He was already marching back toward the building when Mags caught up to him and pulled him back.

"No, Sergeant. Please. It's in the past. Let it go. He just startled me being there. I thought he was gone."

"Well he ain't gone, so time's right fer a man like that to get what he's got comin."

"No, Sergeant, really. It was a lesson learned, and I've moved on. Literally. In fact, that's how I ended up at Camp Chaparral, where I met you and your men. Where I met Candalin and so many others before ... well, before that too went wrong. I don't want to drag it all back up. Let the dead rest. Please." She tried to smile, but the memories hung like deadweight at the corners of her mouth.

Ilbei studied her closely, their gazes locked. His anger slowly gave way to reason, and with it, to her request. "Ya can't be more than a pair of decades at most," Ilbei said after a time. "Was he yer first love?"

"I'm not. And yes, he was. Great way to start, eh? I was so enamored of him. Imagine, a magician showing that much attention to silly, blank me. I was a fool."

"First love is like that, I suppose. Sorta like yer first time playin ruffs. Ya go all in on the first good hand ya think ya got, don't even know who you're playin or what you're playin fer. Then it all goes bust. Goes like that fer us all, near as I've seen."

She actually laughed at that, a sweet note that flew from a real smile, one that even glimmered in her eyes. "It's true. Entirely true." She touched him on the arm again, giving him a fleeting, sober look that spoke a silent "thank you" before she was smiling again. "I wish I'd met a man more like you."

"Oh sweet Mercy, no ya don't," he said, serious as a stroke. "The last thing a pretty young thing like you needs is a bloat-bellied old soldier stinkin of alehouses and four days' sweat."

She laughed aloud. "Well, I did say *more* like you, not precisely like you."

It was his turn to laugh, and he patted the back of her hand where it still rested on his arm. "You go on down there where Jasper is, and I'll be right back. I'll see if'n I can't get the major to come out and speak to me again without that counterfeiter gettin wind of what we know." He turned to go back, but stopped.

Someone had slipped out of the tavern behind them and was in the process of mounting one of the horses tethered to the goat pen. With the darkness and the distance, Ilbei couldn't make out who it was, but the conspicuous timing of the man's exit coincided with the intake of breath that came from Mags. That had to be Gad Pander. This time, Ilbei recognized the horse and the shape of the man's hood.

Ilbei quickened his strides, hoping to catch the man before he got away, but he couldn't get there in time, not even at a run. He would have called out, but he didn't want to draw the attention of anyone inside. Soon the man was gone, galloping into the darkness beneath the trees, headed somewhere along the steppe to the northeast.

The curious timing of the man's getaway made Ilbei rub his beard, wondering once again and slowing his pace. He debated now whether he wanted to go back in at all. Surely the major would have noticed the man leaving too, wouldn't he? It might have struck him odd. But then again, the major was at his hand in gambling, so no telling what he was paying attention to beyond the game. Although, a man couldn't shark an old sport like Ilbei as fast as the major had without seeing everything—or without cheating, of course.

Ilbei waited several minutes to see if the major, or anyone else for that matter, came out, but no one did. When the thumps of the retreating hoofbeats were gone, there was once more only the dull roar of the waterfall and the muted notes of a lute and fiddle squeezing through the shutters.

Ilbei made his decision. He turned back and walked briskly down the trail, gathering up Mags as he went. He took the lead rope from her, gripping it where it was affixed to the halter just below the horse's jaw, and he tugged both Mags and the mare along. "Come on," he said. "Quick now."

He hissed for Jasper to join him, signing for Kaige and Meggins to shadow them for a time in the trees, keeping an eye out for anyone following. He and Mags waited for Jasper to join them, and then the three of them moved down at a steady clip for several hundred yards. When he was satisfied he and Mags were beyond hearing of Fall Pools, he stopped and waited for Kaige and Meggins to catch up and emerge from the darkness.

"Kaige, you and Jasper take Mags back to Cedar Wood. Meggins, you're with me. We're goin to follow that Gad Pander feller best we can and see where he's run off to hide. If'n me and Meggins ain't back at Cedar Wood before breakfast after next, you three get on back to Hast as quick as ya can. Tell the lieutenant what we seen with the Skewer, and make sure to tell him to get word to the general that the major is actin strange, gamblin up folks' money, and that there's a counterfeit operation afoot. If'n ya can, ya tell that to the general direct. Just make sure they understand this here neck of the woods needs a whole company to sort it out, and I don't expect that green lordlin of a major up there has anythin in hand but cheatin at cards. Out here, and with these sorts of folks, well, when they get wind of that, there's nothin to keep Cavendis from disappearin fer good. They'll find him a year from now floatin dead in some backwoods waterway like that old harpy was, and they'll have had that horse of his in the stew."

Jasper looked to Kaige, then back to Ilbei, a horrified expression tugging outward at his face.

"Oh, now I was just sayin so about the horse," Ilbei said in response to Jasper's apparent shock. "My gods, but you young folks is so particular about yer critters anymore. Try to take my meanin, son."

"It's not the horse that concerns me, Sergeant. It's just that ... well, I don't think we should separate." He made no attempt to conceal the fact that he was terrified. "What if Ergo the Skewer comes along?"

Mags slid her quarterstaff out from where she'd tucked it behind the pannier and said, "I can hold my own if I have to, Sergeant. I lived with the Sisters of Mercy until I was sixteen."

Ilbei grinned. "That's the spirit, Mags." He looked back to Jasper. "See there, Jasper? Now if'n you're that worried fer it, ya can dig through yer satchel there and get one of them paper spells ready just in case. Bein as Kaige can whip most any three men if'n he's got half a chance, and between the lot of ya, well, you'll be all right so long as ya stay to the trail. You'll be at Cedar Wood before daylight."

"I wasn't volunteering to go down to Cedar Wood, Sergeant," Mags said. "I was agreeing with Jasper that we shouldn't split up. And if we're being honest, I'm in no mood to run away from the fight, either." She glanced up the mountain, squinting a little, as if she were looking at something, or someone. "Frankly, my dander is up, if you want the truth. And it is my home these people are ruining, you know."

Ilbei blinked a few times, jerking back at that response in the way people do when large flying insects have just bounced off their foreheads. Jasper's obvious glee proved he was happy to have an ally on that front. Ilbei glanced at him, then at Mags with her quarterstaff planted firmly on the ground. His left eye nearly closed under the weight of that scrutiny.

"Well I didn't put it up fer a vote," he said. "This here is my outfit, and I say you're goin back, and that's the end of it."

"Well, I'm not in your outfit, and I don't want to go back. And for that matter, what am I going to do in Hast? Start over? Again? I'm tired of it. I'm tired of feeling afraid, I'm tired of being walked on, and I'm tired of feeling weak. The whole way down here just now, I kept thinking about that man up there, that idiot Ivan Gangue. I felt so stupid and pathetic, shaking there like some frightened child. And I didn't like how it felt to have my hands tied up the other day, either. Waiting to be saved. I'm sick of waiting to be saved, sick of having my hands tied. And while I mean you no disrespect, Sergeant—you are the kindest, sweetest, bravest man I know—I'll not be ordered around or pushed around again."

"Well, I ...," Ilbei began, but his voice died when he realized he didn't have any idea what to say. His mustache and beard twitched around on his face for a time, as if together they were a ratty old blanket and something was crawling around underneath. He tried again. "Thing is, Mags, it ain't a question of whether ya are brave enough, mad enough or even good enough with that there staff. It's a matter of speed. Me and Meggins can move along pretty quick after that feller, even with him on a horse. And we need to get to it, not pick our way cautious like. If we can find out where they's hid, and maybe how big the outfit is, we can figure what next to do."

"He's going to the old ettin cave east of the scissor switchback."

"The what?" Ilbei had heard what she said, but he needed a moment to process the surprise.

"The ettin cave."

"How do ya know that?"

"It's the only place near water other than the big caves where the Softwater comes out and the little one where Harpy Creek flows from. He didn't get on the switchbacks because they start behind Fall Pools, and that's not how his horse would have sounded as he ran up the trail. So, if he didn't go up, then there's nothing else that way but woods till you come to Harpy Creek."

Ilbei's cheek twitched some, making his beard seem to crawl in the dim moonlight. "He could have a place anywhere out there, then. Hid in the trees. Or he could work down the mountain some. Get around behind us and stay in one of them abandoned camps. Hells, he could just hide under a rock."

"He could, but those huts were all long vacant, as you'll recall. And as he only came to Camp Chaparral three times all year, he's obviously staying closer to here than there, or we'd have seen him more often for sundries like I sell. But he doesn't. He only comes by on his way to Hast."

"I know folks what can live years without passin within a hundred measures of a big city, much less any of the Three Tents camps. The sort of people what can do without no help or nobody and do it just fine."

"Perhaps, but he won't do well without water, and since everything up the river was abandoned, and you and your men were all the way to where Harpy Creek comes out, then that ettin den is the only other place the water runs year round."

"Well, why didn't ya tell me that before?"

"Because you didn't ask, and we weren't going after him. We were going back to Hast to talk to your general."

"Aye, we were. And ya were fine with goin then, too. Even seemed fine maybe stayin gone while we was at it."

"And I might still be fine staying gone, but if I leave, I'm leaving on my terms, not ... theirs."

"So I see." Ilbei looked in turn to each of his men. Kaige was clearly content to go anywhere. Jasper was clearly not going to be content anywhere they went. And when he got to Meggins, he saw a smirk on the wily soldier's face that made him look as if he held the winning hand of cards, which, this time, Ilbei supposed he did. "Ya can wipe that damn grin right off yer whore-born face," Ilbei said, but Meggins' smile did not abate.

He turned back to Mags, who continued to stand her ground, her quarterstaff planted like the flagpole of resolute femininity. Ilbei never could account for the ways of women.

"Fine. But if'n ya get killed real long and awful, just remember I tried to tell ya that ya shoulda gone back to Cedar Wood. All of ya."

"We'll remember," Meggins said. "Now can we go? He's already way ahead."

Ilbei paused long enough to fix Mags with a frown, but she stepped out from under it and took Meggins by the arm instead. "This way, Mr. Meggins. He'll be up this way."

Ilbei's frown lingered awhile longer, but in a benign sort of way, like the gray clouds that trail the worst part of a storm. The woman had spirit, he'd give her that. And, if he allowed for the truth of it, this was her home. He'd have stayed too.

Chapter 19

They made their way up the mountain, cutting directly through the woods on an angle Mags assured them would get them to the old ettin cave. Meggins stepped into a spring snare forty minutes up the hill, and after they'd finally cut him down, they'd been forced to go even slower than before.

An hour more passed. They crept through the darkness, blind but for rare patches of dim moonlight and a small radiant circle of their torch, which sent long shadows out from the trees around them like the black spokes of a wheel turned inside out. Finally Mags bade them stop. "It should be very close. We might be able to see their fire, if they have one."

"Wait," Jasper said. "You said this cave we're going to is an ettin cave. Twice, you called it that, the first time referring to it as an *old* ettin cave, the second as simply *an* ettin cave. So is it an old ettin cave, in that the cave is old and an ettin lives there, or is it just a cave in which ettins used to live in days of old, but live there no longer? And I suppose as a third option, I should ask if you meant that it is a cave of indeterminate age but in which lives an old ettin—that option being only slightly better than the first,

189

and markedly worse than the second. So which is it?"

Exasperation escaped from Ilbei in a short grunt. "Jasper, I swear, son, if'n ya don't grow a spine soon, you're like to collapse in on yerself. There ain't no damned ettin, or folks would have said so long before, and a pack of highway robbers wouldn't be the first time they called the army up here." He looked to Mags for confirmation.

"I've never actually been in it," she admitted. "But this close to Fall Pools, someone would have said something by now."

"Well, that's not very reassuring," Jasper said.

"What's a ettin?" Kaige asked.

"It's nothin, that's what," said Ilbei. "Now let's go. Meggins, put that torch out so our eyes can adjust."

Meggins extinguished the torch, and for a time they all stood in the silent darkness.

"Ettins are two-headed giants," Jasper said. "But that's all right. We'll just pretend that isn't important and stand here in the darkness trying not to smell like meat."

"How big of giants?" Kaige asked.

"Jasper, if'n ya answer that, I'll tie that flappin tongue of yers in a knot and cork yer pipe with it. Not one more word. Same fer you, Kaige."

"There," came Meggins' hiss through the darkness some distance up the slope. "I see it. West a spell. We've come back up and found the cliff again."

Ilbei and the rest followed the sound of Meggins' voice, and soon they too could see the sheer wall of the steppe rising suddenly out of the trees, gently curving in either direction, though in the darkness, none of them could see its upper edge. Ilbei found Meggins and put his hand on the man's shoulder. He looked around the tree behind which Meggins had placed himself, and sure enough, some two hundred paces along the base of the rock face there was a flickering glow, a panting tongue of golden light licking out into the trees.

"Well, they didn't bother to hide from us," Meggins said in a low whisper. "So they either didn't think we'd come or don't care if we do."

"Or else there's an ettin in there preparing the cook fires for the meal we've come delivering," Jasper put in.

"Hush, you," Ilbei said. "Now, all of ya stay here a spell. Meggins, you and me, let's go have a look. Swing wide."

They went downhill a ways and crept from tree to tree, keeping to the absolute darkest parts of the woods. When they came close enough to look inside, they saw a large opening, twice as tall as it was wide, big enough for four mounted men abreast to ride through. A small stream of water, hardly a half span across, ran out from the middle of it and disappeared into the woods, heading northeast. Inside was a large chamber in which sat two men before a large fire built in a pit. Both men had cloth tied around the lower half of their faces, over nose and mouth, and both appeared to watch something in the fire reverently. Ilbei realized that the man on the left was working something with his foot, though whatever it was lay out of sight behind the stones banked around the fire. The man's knee moved as it might have were it working the pedal of a spinning wheel.

Ilbei dared to creep up the hill, darting from tree to tree, to get a better look. Meggins shadowed him. They knelt and watched silently.

The men inside mumbled to one another as they stared into the fire, too far away to be heard clearly, and not speaking loudly enough to project. At length, first one then the other pulled what initially looked to be long black rods from the fire. They raised them up, then turned at the waist, without standing, and swung the hot ends around, revealing crucibles at the end of each rod, not very large, but glowing red hot from the flames. They tipped the contents out and, from Ilbei's perspective, appeared to pour it onto the rocks around the fire. When that was done, they leaned down and each pulled something from a wooden box that sat between them on the ground. Whatever they took out, they then dropped into the still-glowing crucibles. In the smooth movements of a practiced activity, they turned back and plunged the ends of the long black rods into the fire. The man on the left began working his foot again.

"What do you suppose that's all about?" Meggins asked, his voice so low it was hardly audible.

"They're meltin somethin," Ilbei said. "And I don't expect it's anythin other than part of that counterfeitin enterprise we're onto. We'll need to get inside fer a better look."

"Want me to get closer?"

"No, let's get back to the others. I don't like leavin them two fools together too long alone, lest they work up a disaster of some kind. I doubt poor Mags could keep em from it."

Meggins nodded that he agreed.

When the group was reunited, Ilbei laid out his plan. It was simple, relying on numerical superiority: there were two men and five of them. Meggins and Ilbei would go in first, Meggins with his bow at the ready, and move around toward the back of the cave. Kaige and Jasper would come in, Jasper with an offensive spell in hand. Ilbei would bind both men hand and foot, while Mags would stay at the cave entrance, just inside but well behind the rest, her role to make sure nobody came in from behind. Ilbei expected her to protest, to insist on a more frontline role, given her newly acquired bellicose attitude, but she did not.

"Ya stay where we can see ya, Mags," he said. "Don't go out lookin around."

She nodded that she understood, content to have a part.

They crept together to the edge of the cave, weapons out and Ilbei with four short lengths of cord tucked into the back of his pants to bind the men as prisoners. When they were near enough, Jasper drew out his small hand mirror and angled it so that it caught the reddish firelight bouncing off the inside of the cave entrance. He used the light to illuminate the inside of his satchel of scrolls. He rummaged in it for a while, the rustling of the parchment tubes making Ilbei cringe, certain the men would come charging out at any time.

Jasper extracted a scroll, slid its ribbon off, then reshouldered the satchel. He dropped the small mirror into a front pocket on the bag and nodded to Ilbei that he was ready.

Ilbei looked to each of the others in turn, and all nodded likewise. He straightened, for he'd been crouching, and then he and Meggins went in.

They could hear the breathing of a small bellows as they rounded the nearest edge of the entrance, and upon stepping into the bright orange firelight, a wave of heat washed over them. The man at the bellows, for that's what the movement of the man's foot had been, gassed the fire twice more before he realized that Ilbei and Meggins had come in. He grunted, which prompted the other man to look up, though slowly, as if waking from a daydream, the sort brought about by hours of monotonous work in a very warm place. It took him a moment to realize what was happening, and his eyes widened as his companion's had. He opened his mouth to say something, but Ilbei stopped him.

"Don't say a word," Ilbei said. "Not one peep." He and Meggins moved apart and slid along the walls on either side of the cave, Meggins keeping the men pinned in place with the back and forth of his bow, an arrow drawn back and ready to puncture either of them.

The chamber was widest where the men sat at the fire, and it bent slightly as it cut farther into the stone of the steppe. The water ran roughly through the center of the space, nearest the man on Ilbei's side of the fire. As he moved along its edge, Ilbei discovered that it came out from a high, narrow passage that angled back to the left, too sharp to see beyond. Something of a pocket had eroded at the rear of the chamber to the right, and when he was in deep enough to look, Ilbei found three horses tethered there. Three was a promising count, for Ilbei had been afraid there might be a lot more cave complex beyond what they could initially see. The existence of only three horses suggested that, with any luck, there would only be one other adversary.

The crunch of dirt and rock turned his attention, and he glanced back to see Kaige and Jasper coming in. The forge fire glinted wickedly up and down the man-high length of Kaige's broadsword blade and gleamed off his steel cuirass. Jasper unfurled a scroll as he came in, not even looking at the men near the fire, his eyes on the words before him and his mouth moving silently. Ilbei's exasperation was audible as he exhaled, and he could only hope the young mage wasn't going to cast anything. He hadn't told him to cast anything.

A glance across the fire at Meggins suggested Meggins was thinking the same.

"You there," Ilbei said, thrusting his pick toward the man who'd been daydreaming only seconds before, "stand up slow and come this way. Back toward me with yer hands in the air. Make a move fer that hot iron there, and you'll have this pick in ya elbows deep."

The two men exchanged glances, and Ilbei thought neither of them looked like Gad Pander—though he realized that in the absence of the familiar hood, and with most of their faces wrapped, either one could have been. He watched back and forth between the man and the opening at the back of the cave.

"Go on, get movin," he said. "Nothin stupid now."

The man stood as instructed, his arms out and hands high.

"That's good, nice and slow. Don't make no noise, just come on back. This don't have to go bad." He thought about how, not so long ago, Ergo the Skewer had had much the same advantage on Ilbei, just before Meggins had arrived. Again his gaze darted to the passage leading deeper into the mountainside.

"Kaige, come around here and watch that," he said, gesturing toward the passage with a movement of his head.

Kaige did as instructed, quickly and quietly. Ilbei took a step toward the man that was backing toward him. "On yer knees."

The man started to look back, but Ilbei placed the point of his pickaxe against his neck, right between two vertebrae. "You'll be a pissin doormat if'n ya try it, so don't do it, son. Ain't worth it."

The man looked back into the fire and dropped to his knees. Ilbei looped cord around his wrists and, with a few jerks, knotted it tightly. He quickly bound the captive, wrists to ankles and elbow to elbow behind his back, leaving the man's spine arced short of painfully, though not so short that it wouldn't become so if he thrashed about too much.

"Now you," Ilbei said to the other one, sidling around the wall and stepping past Kaige. "Come on back to me like yer friend there did." The man, like the first one, chose to comply, and soon he was trussed up as uncomfortably as the first. "Keep still, and don't do nothin reckless, and you'll get on out of here just fine come the end of this. Understand?"

The man nodded and remained silent.

Ilbei went to where Jasper was still silently mouthing whatever words were on the scroll, or at least mouthing something while staring at the document steadily. Ilbei slipped past him to where Mags could hear him ask, "Either of these two fellers Gad Pander? I can't tell."

Mags came far enough inside to look at them both. She shook her head no.

"Buzzard pus," Ilbei swore. "Okay, go on back and keep an eye out." She nodded and went out.

Ilbei went back to the fire and looked down at the rocks where the men had poured out the contents of their long-handled crucibles. Several of the rocks around the outer edge had round indentations, flat on the bottom, much like the impressions in the plates Ilbei had found. Most of them were filled with hardening lead.

He turned back to the nearest captive. "So what's these disks you're makin fer?" He already knew, but he wanted them to say it aloud.

"Slugs," said the man.

"Fer what?"

He nodded toward a stack of boxes near the cave wall, small, sturdy crates roughly three hands square, identical to the one that was sitting between him and his companion when Ilbei first came in. "For trade. Craftsmen in Murdoc Bay pound em out to make crystal ware."

"They what?"

"They pound em out real flat in molds to make bowls, beat em like a silversmith does."

"That ain't how they do it."

"Yes, it is."

"No, it ain't. Don't lie to me, son, or I'll melt ya into one of them slots and then pound ya into crystal ware myself."

"I swear it's true. Sure to Mercy it is."

"Don't drag her name into this here skullduggery. Ya already have the Queen's wrath to answer fer that. Save somethin fer after Her Majesty's done with ya, somethin fer yer eternal soul."

The man looked so frustrated by Ilbei's threat that Ilbei had to wonder if maybe he was wrong after all. Sometimes a man can be certain of knowing a thing, and yet it turns out he doesn't know what he thinks he knows half as well as he thought he did. Nonetheless, one thing Ilbei did know for certain was that neither of these two was Gad Pander.

What if Mags had been wrong?

"Ssst," Kaige hissed. Ilbei barely heard it over the wheezing of the man's breathing by his side. Kaige pointed down the passage and held up two fingers, then changed it to three, the shrug of his shoulders and retreat of his mouth making it evident he could only guess.

With a jerk of his head, Ilbei moved Meggins around to where he could get a clear shot down the passage with his bow. Meggins pulled three arrows from his quiver as he obeyed, placing one in his teeth and the others point first into the dirt floor of the cave, just deep enough they could stand on their own.

Kaige moved to the other side of the opening, giving himself an angle for surprise. Ilbei came up beside him, his pickaxe held ready in both hands.

Gad Pander was the first to emerge, and he was two steps into the chamber before he saw Meggins kneeling there. "Hey!" he called out. He repeated it right after, much louder, adding, "We've got visitors!"

Another man came out right behind him, his hand going for a knife in his belt as he crouched and glared at Meggins, then Jasper, and back.

One blow from the huge round counterbalance on the pommel of Kaige's sword sent the man to the dirt like a meat avalanche.

More shouts came from down the passage. Several more. Many more than Ilbei would have liked, disproving his three-horse theory entirely. He moved in front of Gad Pander with his pickaxe ready to strike him down. "Listen up, Pander. I never meant ya no trouble, but ya brung this on yerself. Now call them other fellers off; tell em stay where they are fer now. Then ya come on out here and take a knee beside yer boys, so as nobody has to get hurt."

"You don't have enough men for this ...," he paused,

glancing up and noting the markings on Ilbei's wide-brimmed metal helm, "... Sergeant. I think you've probably got just enough time to run."

"Well, there won't be no runnin. I'm takin ya in as a counterfeiter of Her Majesty's currency. That there is a crime most likely punishable by death, but if'n ya come along peaceful, there's a chance ya might get out of it with yer life."

Two men ran around the bend of the dark passage, one with a torch, both with wood axes in hand. Ilbei actually felt sorry for them as they, like the last man through, went down instantly, *bam, bam*, felled by a pair of rapid blows from the base of Kaige's big sword.

"Well, I expect this can go all day," Ilbei said. "How high we gonna pile em up before ya turn around and take a knee there by that feller over there?"

Gad Pander looked back at the three men lying at Kaige's feet. "Get the ettin," he shouted. "And there's one of them right outside the—" The butt of Ilbei's pickaxe took Pander right between the eyes, and he fell backward onto the growing heap of men behind him.

Kaige looked to Ilbei warily. "You don't think there's really an ettin in there, do you?"

"Look at that passage, son. How ya gonna squeeze an ettin in there? He's tryin to scare us off."

Kaige tilted his head to the side and looked down the corridor. When he turned back, he looked relieved. "You're right," he said. "Least not a big one anyway."

"Anythin what can fit through there, I reckon ya can handle easy enough," Ilbei said. "Just watch out they don't come round with somethin ranged."

"It won't go well for them if they do, Sarge," Meggins reminded him.

"Good, lad," Ilbei said. He looked to Jasper for similar confidence, but Jasper was exactly as he had been since coming in, chanting beneath his breath, unwaveringly. Ilbei would have said something to him, but he was afraid of interrupting whatever the young mage might have in progress, fearing that an interrupted spell was the only thing that could be more disastrous than the spell itself. He should have told the damn magician exactly what to do. He'd been too vague. That's why they weren't supposed to put magicians in infantry units like his. He hadn't been properly trained for commanding a caster like Jasper in all his army days—he wasn't sure there was any training for commanding a caster like him.

"There's more coming," Kaige said.

"Just add em to the pile."

"Someone's coming," Mags called in from the front of the cave.

"Okay, now that's a problem." Ilbei knelt down and scooped Pander up, throwing him over one shoulder like a sack of wheat. "Let's get outta here." He paused long enough to apologize to the nearest of the bound men near the fire, and then he whomped him on the head, knocking him out and guiding him toward the wall with a foot to be sure he didn't fall into the fire. "Kaige, do that one likewise, and let's go."

Kaige issued a short hammer blow with his fist to the bound fellow nearest him, collapsing him like a tent with broken poles, and then they made their way to the cave opening.

"Jasper," Ilbei hissed. "That's enough." He didn't know if the mage would be able to hear him, but shortly after, the wizard was moving back outside, still chanting all the while and seemingly the same phrase over and over again. At least he came. "Meggins, let's go."

Meggins picked up his two arrows and backed quickly toward the entrance.

Mags shrieked as a thunderous impact struck the stone

above their heads. A spew of gravel and sand blasted down at them, explosive and blinding, tiny bits like shrapnel, sharp enough to bite into their flesh. Bigger rock fragments fell right after, landing heavily onto the ground around their feet, one a glancing bell-strike off of Kaige's cuirass. Ilbei, like the rest but for Jasper, looked up and dodged as a few more large pieces broke loose and fell. Kaige punched one just before it could strike Jasper atop the head, a quick strike with the flat of his hand that knocked the rock far enough off course to prevent catastrophic injury. It thudded heavily into the dirt, like someone had dropped an anvil there.

Ilbei pushed everyone back inside, glancing left and right along the cliff as he did. Small flames slid down the rock face like burning tears on either side: two, three, then four on the left; three, four, five on the right.

"Shite," Ilbei pronounced, "where'd they all come from?"

"Should we make for the trees, Sarge?" Meggins asked.

The fires, which Ilbei knew had to be torches, bobbed in the darkness, encircling the area beyond the entrance to the cave, the movement indicative of men running to cut off any chance of escape. "Too late fer that. Back, back! Get inside. We'll make em earn it if'n we have to."

They retreated back into the cave, Meggins firing twice at movement rushing toward them as they did. Two men, one with a bow and the other with a sledgehammer, fell dead a few steps short of the entrance.

Gad Pander began to wriggle on Ilbei's shoulder, stirred from his stupor by being jostled and bounced. Ilbei threw him down and quickly drew out another length of cord, working furiously to get him bound like the others. When he was done, he ran over and did the same for the three men Kaige had knocked out. "Don't give em a shot at ya through that openin," he called out as he worked. "Get in behind the wall. We got no advantage on em out there with us in here in the light."

Mags and Jasper moved together to do as instructed, Mags looking frightened and Jasper, surprisingly, still reading the scroll. Ilbei wondered if he'd somehow gotten magically stuck reading it. He'd heard of such things before.

"Oh sweet mother of Mercy," Kaige muttered then. "Would you look at that!"

Unable to help himself, Ilbei glanced up from tying up the last man. Through the narrow passage from which the little creek ran came a man of extraordinary size, nearing some twenty-four hands high. A mountain in boots and chainmail. He carried with him a pair of crude spiked clubs, huge lengths of sawed-off oak limbs into which a whole lot of horseshoe nails had been pounded. It was hard to imagine more primitive weaponry, but the man himself fit the weapons perfectly. He was so large he had to come through the passage sideways, sucking in his stomach to squeeze through. The metal point of his iron-cap helmet scraped against the ceiling at its lowest point as he forced himself through, the sound drawing Ilbei's eye up, as if to remind him just how enormous this fellow was.

Meggins put an arrow in the brute's shoulder and another in his calf. He'd have gotten a third into him, but the big man hefted one of his oaken cudgels and blocked it rather than being shot in the face. He howled with each arrow's impact and once more as Ilbei rushed to intercept him before he could get out of the passage. He slammed the massive club back down, intent on hammering Ilbei into the ground like one of those horseshoe nails, but Ilbei raised his pickaxe above his head, the curve of its blade like an iron parasol, to deflect the brutal oaken storm. Ilbei thrust up with all his might to meet the blow as it came down, intent on mitigating the impact, but still it struck so hard it drove the pickaxe haft through his hands as if sliding it into a sheath. Ilbei had to drop to one knee to avoid being brained.

Having blunted most of the force of the blow, Ilbei thought to punch his enemy in the side of the knee, but realized he was too far away. As he came to that conclusion, he saw an enormous foot swinging up at him, ready to kick his head right off his neck. He had to roll backward, out of the way.

Kaige stepped in around him as he tumbled back out of the passage, and the brave soldier lunged at their attacker's throat, aiming to end the fight right there with the big brute's corpse as a cork to staunch the flow of any further reinforcements from within. But the oak-wielding warrior was quicker than he looked and knocked Kaige's sword thrust away.

Then he was out into the open room, no longer stymied by the narrow passage walls.

Ilbei saw by the way the man's eyes boggled, and by the shape of his jaw, the slanted angle of it as it thrust out to one side, that he'd been born an oddity. There was a wild vacancy in the way he looked at them, and he articulated no words at all. His anger sounded much like his joy likely would have: a garbled, throaty mess of noise.

Ilbei and Kaige menaced him warily. The thrum of Meggins' bowstring drew a glance from Ilbei, revealing that Meggins was shooting at torchlights outside of the cave. The archer danced back and forth, in and out of the line of sight. Every shot he took brought arrows clattering off the stone all around him, which in turn brought rounds of profanity from Meggins. Mags looked as if she wanted to help somehow.

"Stay back, Mags," Ilbei said. "And make sure Jasper don't wander into view neither. And Jasper, by the hells, if ya got somethin besides yawnin silence in that there paper, get it done."

Jasper's voice changed at the moment of Ilbei's command, and as Ilbei and Kaige ducked and dodged and feinted and parried the crashing mash of the big man's double-oak blows, Ilbei hoped that Jasper's magic would bring some form of remedy and not just make things worse.

But nothing happened. Despite several long moments of fighting defensively, waiting for an effect, the only thing that changed were the words Jasper spoke. His tone perhaps became a little more pronounced, though Ilbei couldn't spare the attention required to be sure. But no magic ensued. No fireballs or ice lances or lightning spears to burst the giant man apart. Jasper simply seemed to give different voice to the same sort of murmuring from before.

After three more dives to avoid decapitation, and a duck to avoid the same, a successful cut on Kaige's part had the towering assailant bleeding down one leg. Ilbei tried to get in close enough to finish him, but their towering assailant had too great a reach to get easily inside. Ilbei glanced back at Jasper, but the wizard still hadn't done a thing. Ilbei added his profanities to the stream Meggins had underway, and once again Ilbei gave up on magic and set to the work of finishing the big man off himself—although he had no strategy yet for how to get close without being crushed.

And getting close was not a simple thing, for despite the dullard look of him, their adversary's reach was astonishing. With all that size, his arms were more than half of him in length, fifteen hands, long as a horse was tall. And that just the start. Add in the length of those two great clubs, and the monstrous fellow could hold both his opponents easily at bay. Other than missing a second head, he might as well have been the ettin that long ago occupied this old cave.

An arrow *tinked* off of Kaige's armor and deflected toward the back of the cave, where it embedded itself in the flank of one of the horses tethered there. The horse added its frightened whinnies to the racket of the fight, the clang of steel, the thud of wood, bowstrings twanging and men cursing for all their worth. The not-quite ettin roared loudest of them all.

"Watch yer angle," Ilbei called to Kaige, who had just turned aside a blow that would have pulped him. Ilbei moved himself closer to the wall. He circled and tried to get in behind his enemy, but despite the vacant look in the man's eyes, he wasn't so vacant as that. Whoever had trained him to fight had trained him well.

A cry and a grunt from Meggins showed that the infernal Gad Pander had worked himself loose from Ilbei's too-hastily tied knots and had thrown himself on the archer. The two of them lay grappling.

In his distraction, Ilbei wasn't fast enough, and a sweep of a great oak club came at him like a hardwood hurricane. He got his pickaxe up in time to attenuate the blow on the haft some, but the force still threw him the two spans between himself and the cave wall, where he struck with a breath-blasting thud.

Two men ran in from the outside, and Mags, hidden from their view, swung a flat blow with her quarterstaff across the cave mouth, so hard and so level that Ilbei was certain she'd crushed one of the newcomer's windpipes even as Ilbei himself gasped for air. The other was barely nicked by her swing, but it caught his attention. He changed the course of his charge from Meggins to Mags, and if there was any relief to be had in that, it was that he held as a weapon a sledgehammer of the most common workman's variety. Ilbei hoped that whatever training Mags had gotten from the Sisters of Mercy was up to the man's combat abilities with that.

The hammer shot out, a low, punching-type strike. Mags leapt to her left, letting the hammer crash into the cave wall as she brought her staff down hard alongside his neck. Ilbei heard the crack of his collarbone at the same time he let out a yelp. Mags would be okay.

Kaige, like Ilbei had just done, blocked a blow that came

so hard it threw him back against the wall. He wasn't winded by the impact, though, and he, again like Ilbei, rushed back in to prevent the titanic human from getting any closer to their companions. That's when Ilbei was reminded of the fire burning there, just visible out of the corner of his eye. Maybe he could get the brute to stumble into it somehow. He needed something, some kind of advantage. They were running out of time.

"*Sorvanor maricopse veyn!*" Jasper shouted.

Ilbei had time to turn to look, his mind only beginning to shape a question about what that meant, when there came a thumping sensation down upon him, a soft thump like the quasi-solidification of air, a rush of it, all in an instant as if by a blow but not, a wave of pressure perhaps, soft and yet brutal, not so unlike the sort of blow that might come from a great club made of oak, if oak could be made of air. Then Ilbei saw the ground rushing up at him. At least, for a moment. And then he, like the rest, like Kaige, Mags, Meggins and the man he was grappling with, even the giant man and, sadly, Jasper, went off into the dark place called unconsciousness, leaving behind a whole cave full of motionless bodies. Even the forge fire went out.

Chapter 20

When Ilbei came to, he was lying on his back, staring up at the ceiling of the cave. Morning was just creeping inside, an angle of it slicing into the gloom like a blade of light. There were voices nearby, and he sat bolt upright, reaching for his pickaxe. It was not on his back, and for a dazed, post-concussion moment, he patted himself down seeking the weapon with his hands as his eyes looked around for the enemy.

He found them, several of them, five men trussed up like pot roasts, lying right where he'd left them, two more near the cave entrance, plus the great brute with the oak-limb clubs lying off to the left, nearly mummified in rope. He did not fight against the bonds, and Ilbei realized he was unconscious, just as Ilbei himself had been for apparently quite some time.

Ilbei looked for his companions and found them lying roughly in a row beside him to the right: Kaige immediately beside him, then Meggins, then Mags, then Jasper. He could see two lines in the dirt near Jasper's heels, drawn by the act of someone dragging him, and marking the path that someone had taken when they'd brought him from the cave entrance to where he was now. Ilbei noted that each of his companions breathed comfortably, a great relief, and all of them were asleep.

He stood and assessed himself, found that he was in fine health but for a headache, which was not much worse than those that follow a fine sort of evening, and discovered in a glance at the wall that his pickaxe was leaning there behind him. He took it up and looked about again, seeking the source of the voices that he heard.

Some came from the passage out of which the big brute and several others had emerged. Others came from outside.

Worried about those behind him in the cave, Ilbei entered the passage and crept down it, staying out of the little waterway running through it and following the curve until he'd gone beyond the last assistance of the dawn's light. He pressed forward into the darkness, squinting and hoping for some form of light to emerge. Then the dim flicker of firelight appeared from around the bend. He picked his way along until he came to where the passage branched left and right.

The light came from the right, so he peered around the bend and saw, to his surprise, Major Cavendis standing over Gad Pander. The counterfeiter's hands were bound behind him, his ankles tied together, and he sat upon a low rock with blood running from his mouth and nose.

Major Cavendis, still in his lordly attire, was shaking his head as he gazed down at the battered man, and Ilbei saw that he held an extinguished torch, the wrappings at its end dangling loose like a tangle of untied boot strings.

"Listen here, Pander," Cavendis was saying. "I really don't enjoy this sort of thing, but I'll stand here all day and all tomorrow if I have to until you tell me where they are."

Pander spat blood out into the dirt at the major's feet. "I already told you where they were. I've told you fifty times. Fifty-one will be the same."

The major smashed the torch down on Pander's knee. The

captive cried out, and Ilbei recognized it as the same sound that had woken him from unconsciousness. The bloody miner fell off the rock, his body rigid with the wave of anguish until the worst of it had passed. The major pulled him back up by one arm and resat him on the rock.

"Let's try the other one then," the major said, as casually as if they were discussing the results of a recent royal tournament. "What else have you seen?"

"I don't know. I don't know. Please, just tell me what you want me to have seen, and I'll say I saw it yesterday. Gods, I don't know what you want from me."

"You're a stubborn man, Pander. And braver than I'd have given you credit for." The major struck him twice across the face with the torch, once forehand and another back. One of Pander's teeth flew across the cave and bounced off the rocks. "The problem is," resumed the young lord, "that bravery here nets you nothing. So, let's start once again. Where are the molds?"

"In the packs," Pander gasped, his head drooping, chin to chest, blood running in a stream. He began to sob, barely more than a whimper, repeating over and over, "They're in the Mercy-loving packs like I've told you a hundred times."

Ilbei could tell the answer infuriated the major by the way he straightened, his face rising so that he might gaze up toward the ceiling, an exasperated prayer to the gods of patience, perhaps. "I've checked the wretched packs, Pander. You were sitting right there when I did it. So where are they in all of that, hmmm?" He pointed with the ragged end of the torch toward the wall just inside the opening, the wall behind which Ilbei hid, so Ilbei could not see what he was pointing at. Cavendis struck the man once more, a powerful blow to the ear, so hard it knocked him off the rock again. He left him there and spun to exit the room. At which point he saw Ilbei gawking at him.

"Spadebreaker!" he said. "Good. I see you are revived. I

trust you had a nice nap?" He grinned as pleasantly as if he and Ilbei were great old friends.

"Aye, sar. I suppose I did." Ilbei's gray brows wriggled unevenly on his forehead.

"Well, your timing is excellent. As you can see, we've found the animal that Pander here claims you took from him, and having gone through the packs, we can't seem to find a particular item that we came looking for."

Ilbei stepped into the chamber and looked where the major was once again pointing, toward that nearest wall. Sure enough, there were the two panniers Ilbei had gone through and then carefully repacked.

"What might ya be lookin fer, sar?"

Cavendis studied him for a long string of heartbeats, the same sort of look Ilbei had seen him employ when they'd sat together and played cards so briefly not so many nights ago. Ilbei's face remained exactly as it was. There was cheating at cards, and then there was the real game, where the façade mattered as much as the cards.

"We're looking for the other half of those." He directed Ilbei's gaze to a long table in an alcove opposite where Ilbei stood. He took another torch from a sconce mounted on the wall and led Ilbei to the table, where there were ten flat ceramic bricks. Each of them had perfectly circular impressions pressed into them, all depicting in relief a gryphon and its rider flying above the great Palace in Crown City. There were words written around the top and bottom edges along the rim, presumably backwards and in the language Ilbei couldn't read.

"Them's counterfeiters' molds," Ilbei said.

"Precisely, Sergeant. And as you can see, they are but half of what is needed to forge a proper gold crown of Kurr."

"So they are. And a two-tailed crown wouldn't buy a man a grope, even in the brothels of Murdoc Bay."

"No, Sergeant, it wouldn't. Which is why I know that

somewhere there exists the other half of this set. Our friend Pander here insists that you took possession of that other half when you relieved him of his horse."

It was once again Ilbei's turn to evaluate the major's hand. He had a bad feeling that the major, despite his youth, was the better liar between them, a man likely trained to it since birth. But Ilbei knew there was something missing still, despite having no evidence of it. He wondered if maybe it was simply because he didn't like the man, because he knew that Cavendis was a cheat. Cheats and liars were hardly better than animals in the end. But he was a major, even if he didn't bother to wear Her Majesty's colors most times—yet another thing about him that crawled under Ilbei's skin. But he had to answer something for it.

He glanced at the major, then at the molds, then across the room where Gad Pander lay. He nodded his head. "Yes, sar," he said. "He's told ya true about that—and seems a number of times he told ya too, what with ya havin beat him half to death so as to hear it over and over again."

"Well, where are they?" Relief was evident in the way the major's shoulders moved, lowering as tension left—relief where Ilbei had expected reproach or some abuse for what he'd just said and how he'd said it. "Then why didn't you say something before?"

Ilbei watched the major watching him back. "You was pretty quick to run me off last time we spoke, as you'll recall, and I near forgot all about it till we was on our way. I turned back to go tell ya, when we seen that feller ya been poundin on come skulkin out and run off into the woods. Seemed sinister how he done it, so we went off after, thinkin we'd find where he was perpetratin the counterfeits."

"Well, clearly you found it, Sergeant. But perhaps in doing so, you bit off more than you could chew." The major stood casually, relaxed, his smile marginally gloating.

"Right, sar, so it seems. We was in a spot, it's true, though

I expect the main trouble was our mage run off some kind of magic accident. We'd have done all right in the end otherwise."

"Yes, well, likely he did you all a favor, as there were several more men outside the cave, on their way in when we arrived."

"*We*, sar?"

"Yes, myself, Locke Verity, whom you met the other day, and a few others."

"Well then, it was right good timin ya come along."

"It was. Now, please, Sergeant, where are those other plates?"

"I sent em off to Hast with the corporal."

"You *what*?" The major's face flushed.

Even in the prejudiced light of the torch, Ilbei saw him reddening, but he pressed on. "I sent them tiles off to Hast with a note fer General Hanswicket hisself. Told him we'd get in touch with ya and see to the situation as best we could after, or send word fer reinforcements if'n we thought it was more than my boys, and yerself of course, could get done."

"You idiot!" the major spat. "By the gods, Spadebreaker!" He spun and stomped across the room, overcome with rage, profanity spewing forth like foul odors from a foundry. He went on so long Gad Pander actually began to laugh, though it was a choking, blood-soaked sort of sound.

Ilbei thought that was even odder than the major's tantrum, and would have remarked on it, but the major stomped over to the local man and kicked him so hard in the stomach he began to choke in earnest, and eventually to throw up, retching and gagging up blood and teeth along with his last meal.

"When did you send them to Hast? How long ago?"

Ilbei blinked and made a show of perplexity, clearly confounded as to why the major was so upset. He finished the display with an appropriate bit of stammering. "Why, I, uh, well, sar, seems it was ... it was five days before yesterday—no, make that six, given we done come back, went back, come back again, and then up here fer a night. So, countin that, that'd be eight if'n today is one, what's barely begun, otherwise seven not countin it."

The major glared at him, the heat of fury evident, his eyelids low. "Don't you shovel that stinking peat at me, Spadebreaker, you simpleton. Where are they?"

"I told ya, sar, they's at Hast by now." He pretended not to see the malevolence in the major's eyes. "If'n you're worried they didn't get there, just have old Jasper fix ya up with the general usin one of his fancy paper talkin spells. Ya can speak straight to the general yerself and verify he got em safe and sure by now."

"Why would you do that, Sergeant? Why?"

"Why what? Why put ya in touch with the general, sar? Seems to make the most sense, what with ya worried about them tiles and all. Jasper can do it right quick, just say the word." Ilbei had to concentrate to keep his eyes wide and innocent.

"No, idiot. Why would you send them away, the crown molds?"

"Oh. Beg yer pardon, sar. Yes, that. Well, it seemed like too much vital evidence fer us to pack around was all. Never know what might befall a feller out here, what with bandits, harpies and even ettins what supposedly used to be in this here cave." He glanced at Gad Pander lying nearby and raised one bushy gray eyebrow. That was an awful lot of violence lying there.

Anger burned behind the major's glare. So much so that Ilbei knew for certain that whatever facts were missing were big. But for all the rage brimming there, the major had no more to say. He simply spun and stormed out of the chamber, apparently too riled to speak. Ilbei watched him go, then shook his head, not sure what to make of the man. A good ruffs player wouldn't come so close to unraveling as all that.

He crossed the room to where Gad Pander lay and took him by the arm, pulling him back up onto the rock he'd been seated on. "Are ya hurt worse than ya look?" he asked. He looked him over in the dim light that remained. His face seemed hardly human, lumpy and swollen as it was. "Even the likes of you deserves better than what ya got."

"Piss off," Pander spat. Strands of bloody mucus flung out toward Ilbei, but snapped back elastically and stuck to Pander's chin, red webbing that glinted wet and sticky in the torchlight.

Ilbei shook his head again. "Fine," he said. "I'll take that to mean ya got no need fer me to help." Then he too turned and left.

Chapter 21

Ilbei exited the small chamber and took a moment to look down the passage opposite, where the water was coming from. There was a strong smell of lead coming from that way, so he followed it out of curiosity. The passage bent back and forth, and soon the light coming from the chamber he'd just exited no longer served. Just as he was about to give up on it, he noticed a soft blue glow tracing the outline of a curve ahead. He went straight to it and found himself in a low-ceilinged natural chamber where water trickled down from above. The water fell in twisting ropes, glinting like silver in the blue glow as they stirred the surface of a small pool. The light came from luminous fungal blooms that grew around the pool, some creeping up the wall and others around the edge. Illuminated by the fungus, but not luminous themselves, were other growths within the pool, identical in appearance but not glowing for some reason. All were bulbous and knotty, a few nearly as big as his head, and the smallest hardly as large as his thumb.

Ilbei's thirst was upon him the moment he saw the water, and given that there were several buckets and several tin cups set about, Ilbei dropped to his knees and stooped down toward the surface, intent on a drink. As he dipped his cupped hands into the water, he noticed gray foam floating around the edge of the pond. He pulled his hands out. He didn't need to smell it to know what it was. Gad Pander and his men used the pond to separate the lead. The foam floated all around the side of the pond opposite the glowing fungus, and beneath it, heavier sediments slicked the bottom. He went to where the stream ran out of the chamber and found metal plates placed there, meant to catch the slurry when Pander and his people worked back here. He was just beginning to wonder what kind of idiot would do such work at the head of the only water supply around, when he realized why the buckets and cups were there.

He rose and took one of the cups, holding it into a trickle of water falling from the roof. It smelled clean to his sensitive nostrils, and it tasted wonderful, like the very heart of Prosperion. He took a long draught and was refreshed. When he finished, he looked round for another way out and saw that there was none. He could see how an ettin would have found this cave a proper lair. Nothing to sneak in from behind, and water right on site, with little chance of flooding even in a wet year. Good place to set up a counterfeiting operation as well.

He went out with a bucket filled with fresh water and brought a few of the handiest cups along. He found Mags and Kaige both on their feet and for the most part looking none the worse for wear. Meggins and Jasper were still out, lying there like a pair of logs.

"What happened?" Kaige asked, gratefully taking the cup that Ilbei proffered.

"I think Jasper's spell backfired," Ilbei replied. "Then it seems Major and some locals come along."

"And why do you think that is?" Mags asked, dipping her cup into the bucket for a second round. "Did you get a look out there at the carnage they made coming in?"

Ilbei shook his head, indicating that he hadn't, then went

to the front of the cave for a look. The sun was well over the trees now, and Ilbei saw three men lying dead outside the cave, two with long, black-shafted arrows in their chests. Ilbei could hear the major speaking to someone around the edge of the cave mouth, but he thought it might be best if he didn't go bothering him just yet. He returned and crouched beside Jasper instead.

With a gentle shake, he called to him a few times. Shortly after, Jasper's eyes fluttered open and filled with surprise.

"Easy, son," Ilbei said, preempting the question. "You're fine. Everybody's fine."

Jasper blinked a few times more, and Ilbei helped him sit up. Mags brought him water, while Kaige tried to wake Meggins up. "What happened?" Jasper asked. "Did my spell fail?" He rubbed his temples, grimacing. "I think it must have."

"Yeah, I expect it didn't work like ya had it wrote down," Ilbei said. He even managed to laugh. "But it done well enough with some luck. Ya took that big bastard down, so that was all right, but ya got the rest of us too. The major come along before the wrong folks woke up, so it's all right in the end."

"I did?" Jasper perked up at that. "I got the big one?"

"Well, like I said, ya got everyone, but yeah, ya got him too."

Jasper looked up at Mags and grinned broadly. "Then it worked?"

Ilbei sighed in Mags' direction, tilting his head toward Jasper, indicating that Mags should tend to him. Then he went to where Kaige was hauling Meggins to his feet.

"A man ought to at least get the wine and the women the night before if he's going to have the hangover next day," Meggins said as Ilbei approached.

"Aye, he should," Ilbei answered, clapping Meggins on the shoulder. "I seen it the same when I come round."

With his people all on their feet and in relatively good shape, Ilbei braced himself for his next encounter with the major. There would be orders coming soon. He glanced to the cave entrance, then summoned his group together with a low sound.

"Now listen up, quick," he said. "I done told the major we sent them coin-makin tiles off to Hast with the corporal. And before ya go askin what fer or why, don't. Far as you're concerned, they went off just like I said. Got it?"

Nods from everyone.

"Right. Now, I'm gonna go see what's next. Kaige, come on out with me and see if'n ya can find that packhorse we had. Don't bother with the major, just look fer the horse and get on over to it. See if our gear is nearby. If it ain't, ya come on back inside casual like."

"What if it is out there?"

"Then get it and bring it in." Ilbei had to stifle a sigh.

They went together outside, Ilbei pausing long enough to survey the area. There were two more bodies he hadn't noticed before, down the slope a dozen paces and both pierced by the long black arrows. A glance to his left showed yet another man, impaled and stuck to a tree, the morning light glinting silver off the long shaft that pinned him there like a bug in a collector's box. Ilbei frowned and looked to the major. Cavendis was engaged in conversation with Locke Verity, who leaned casually upon his fancy black bow.

To the right and tied to a tree not far beyond the cave was the packhorse they'd been using since their first encounter with Gad Pander at Camp Chaparral. Ilbei saw that their gear was lying on the ground not far away, all of it open and rifled through. The chest in which Jasper kept his scrolls and enchanting implements had been dumped, and there were scrolls lying about and leaves of blank parchment everywhere. Many had been blown several spans away, whisked along the steppe or down into the trees. Ilbei frowned at that too, but pointed Kaige to it with a movement of his head. "Gather up Jasper's stuff and put it back in his box," he said. "Then get the rest."

Kaige moved off to comply, while Ilbei went to address the major and Locke Verity.

"Mornin, Master Verity," he said, adding a nod for courtesy. "I expect them black shafts are the work of you and that fine bow?" He tipped his head back toward the bodies lying about.

"They are. It seems we came along just in time," he said with a pleasant grin.

"It seems indeed," Ilbei agreed. "I must say, that's some fine shootin. And damn powerful too. Never seen a man pinned up like that one in the tree line there. That there weapon must have one mean pull."

"It does," Verity agreed. His smile was easy, and he wore an effortless sort of confidence.

Ilbei watched him for signs of duplicity, but detected nothing. Verity accepted the question and gave answer readily. Ilbei looked to the major, who was looking back, watching Ilbei with cat eyes as if the sergeant were a rat.

"So, Major, what now? We off to find the rest?"

"The rest of what?"

"Well, I don't see Ergo the Skewer lyin here, so I take it he got away."

The cat might have growled at the rat, the eyes narrowing even further for a flash of time. He glanced to Verity, who only maintained his pleasant smile, and then back to Ilbei. "What are you talking about, Spadebreaker?"

"Ergo, the Skewer. Ya know, that feller what done the thievin and brung us all out here. I'm seein he was here, but I don't see him lyin nowhere. Lest he run off and died somewhere down in the woods there." Ilbei only said the last to give the major an out. He didn't want to corner the animal lurking behind the predator's eyes.

The major stared down at Ilbei for a long while, then stared past him, surveying the prior night's battlefield. His eyes widened at one point, briefly, barely a flicker, but enough that Ilbei saw.

"He's not dead. He ran off."

"Mmm," Ilbei hummed, sounding disappointed but resigned to that bad bit of luck. He changed the subject some. "So how come nobody told us he was counterfeitin coins? We might have been on the lookout for em as we come through the camps. Maybe asked around."

"That's exactly why we didn't tell you. We had an operation underway to find them, which was why they sent me."

Confusion set Ilbei's eyebrows to contortions for a time. "I don't take yer meanin, sar."

"I came here to sample their coins, Spadebreaker. With ruffs. To find the counterfeits and the counterfeiters. It's why they sent me."

"Oh." Ilbei hadn't considered that before. He blinked a few times, then frowned, then twitched up one corner of his mouth, glancing to Locke Verity, who smiled a patient smile. Ilbei returned his attention to the major. "Well, ya might have said somethin, then. I could have served in like capacity."

"No, Spadebreaker, you couldn't. I played with you, remember?" The major's tone was dismissive and annoyed. "When I saw how your game was, well ... we didn't tell you because you didn't need to know."

Ilbei looked once more to Verity, who was cleaning his fingernails with the point of an arrow. "Hmmph," Ilbei relented. "So what now?"

The major drew a long breath, his jawline tight as he considered it. He didn't look happy about the decision at first, but then he visibly relaxed. He let go the breath. "Well, my primary mission is accomplished well enough for now. We've found our counterfeiter—with, I suppose, some small thanks to you—and the Skewer is on the run. He's wounded too, so he won't get far. Besides your man shooting him a few days ago, he got another arrow in him by our friend Verity just before sunrise. He's routed, and I have people on his tail. All that's left is to get those molds in there to Hast— as you already had the foresight to have done with the obverse halves."

"The what?"

"The front-half molds, you imbecile. The ones you sent to Hanswicket."

"Right, sar. Of course." Ilbei remained silent, waiting to see what the major would do. The major surprised him thoroughly.

"Go get those others, and load them on that horse you took from Pander. Then you and your people get them to Hast as fast as you can. I'll be taking Pander back to Twee with me."

Ilbei couldn't believe it. He looked to Verity to see if there was some indication of surprise, but Verity was still working on his hunter's manicure.

"Yes, sar," Ilbei said, unable to hide his surprise. He watched the major's eyes for a time longer, but the man merely stared back at him impatiently.

"Is there something else, Sergeant?" the major asked at length.

"No, sar. Sorry, sar. We'll be right on it, then."

"Good. Get moving."

With his mind awhirl, Ilbei turned back and went inside the cave. He wondered if maybe he'd been imagining things all the while. The only thing he knew for certain was that it had been a long time since he'd felt as foolish as he did just then.

Chapter 22

"But why?" Meggins asked as they marched along the stone wall of the steppe, heading northeast along it and following the trickling brook that ran out of the ettin cave. They were once more moving toward Harpy Creek and now several hours out of earshot of the major and Locke Verity, far enough for Ilbei to have told them what had transpired. "And," Meggins went on, "why would Major want to game real money to win fake coins? Her Majesty doesn't shine too kindly on fake money, and she'll hang a man for having it, even a nobleman."

"Well, that's what he said he done, and it weren't fer spendin hisself that he done it. He done it to flush it out. I reckon it makes sense to do it that way, as a man will get reckless tryin to reclaim what he's lost."

Meggins stepped over the brook, which had once again meandered in their direct line of travel, the others following suit. "I suppose that seems reasonable. Maybe that's how he got to be a major so young, and it does explain why the army sent a cheat up here."

"Did ya see him cheatin?" Ilbei asked. "Or are ya speculatin?" He hadn't wanted to suggest such a thing about a superior officer to his men, but he'd had the thoughts sure enough himself.

"No, I never saw him do it, but he was. He whipped us like we were wearing mirror-shined breastplates and he was seeing every card. Not to mention, nobody gets cards as bad as we did and as good as those two got every time. Nobody."

"I seen it the same," Ilbei said. "A man could love up Lady Luck and do it real nice, take her like Anvilwrath hisself, and never get so much of her favor in return." Meggins nodded that he agreed.

They continued along, working their way down the slope, following the angle of the rock as it gradually became less cliff face and more precipitous decline. The little brook turned and dropped down a declivity too narrow to follow, so they left it behind, staying with the upper steppe until eventually it turned them east and more directly downslope. Down and down they went, and as the sun grew hot and cumbersome in the sky, and the trees grew scarcer and stingier with their shade, the company found themselves once again winding through the low scrub and brushy dryness of the high foothills. Eventually, they caught sight of the little brook again, and followed it along until the occasional apple tree began to appear, indicating they were once more nearing Harpy Creek.

"Well," Ilbei asked of Mags when they finally found the creek, "ya sure ya want to go on back there alone?" They'd promised to escort her downstream to Camp Chaparral before they cut across the bottom edge of the Sandsea on their way back to Hast.

"I suppose so," she said. "With the bandits gone, maybe people will return. It's not much to look at as a town goes, but this country is beautiful. Maybe I'll get serious about my winemaking, maybe even enter it in the big apple festival they have every year in Hast. I've been meaning to do something like that anyway. Besides, I really don't have anywhere else to go."

"This country is hotter than the deepest places in a dragon's arse," Meggins said, wiping his forehead with his sleeve. "You couldn't pay me to live here. It's only ten degrees better than the desert, I bet."

She smiled. "It is hot in summer, I'll grant that, but the evenings are wonderful at the end of the day, and come springtime, there is no more spectacular place to be. It explodes with color."

"Oh, something explodes all right," Meggins said. "It's called the sun. No thanks."

"Home sets in on folks like that, Meggins," Ilbei said. "Don't matter where it is."

"What about the craze?" Meggins asked. "Won't that keep people away? Home isn't nearly as appealing when everyone's dying all the time."

She grimaced at that. "I don't know what to do about that. But there's nobody left to contract it from but me, so maybe it finally played itself out with poor Candalin."

"I'm tellin ya, that disease is in the water," Ilbei said. "I know ya got yer cask fixin up the water with whatever that alchemy is that feller taught ya fer them little demons and all, but who's to say folks don't drink straight outta the creek? I done as much at most creeks I come across all my life."

She sighed. "Yes, I am sure you are right. I suppose it is possible that I am the only one who didn't drink directly from it at some point. I admit I was more enamored with my big-city cask filtration system than anyone else."

"Well, if'n you're gonna stay out here, let's at least pull that nasty harpy outta the water before we part ways."

"I'd appreciate that," Mags said. "Cask or not, I'd rather not have to know it was in there every time I took a drink."

Everyone present agreed that was the best course of action, and in short order, they made their way the short distance up the creek that got them to the small opening out of which the creek emerged. The damp line of Meggins' rope was still dancing in the water where it came out, apparently untouched since he'd secured it previously.

"All right, you two," Ilbei said to Meggins and Jasper after they arrived. "Ya know what ya need to do. Get on up there and knock it loose. Holler when it's comin through, and me and Kaige will fish it out. We'll haul it down where it can't wash back into the creek, bury it and be done with all of this."

Neither Meggins nor Jasper appeared particularly happy about their part, but Kaige looked absolutely horrified. "You mean we're gonna touch it, Sarge?"

"No, son, I'm gonna read me one of Jasper's spells there so as I can levitate that carcass out with magic all by myself."

Kaige looked confused for a moment, then seemed as if he might laugh, except then clearly realized that he was back to his original problem. He made a face that might have accompanied a growl had he not been afraid it might stir Ilbei's anger, so he nodded meekly, waiting for the misery to begin.

Jasper rummaged through his satchel but could not find a levitation spell to help them get up the jumble of crumbling shale. He mumbled and muttered for some time before finally turning to Ilbei and pronouncing, "This is what happens when you let barbarians sort my scrolls."

"What's the problem?"

"I need to get the trunk down off the horse."

Ilbei looked to Kaige, who immediately set himself to it. After a few minutes working at the ropes—all the while Jasper bemoaning the onerous imposition of Her Majesty's mandatory service and the injustice of having been "sent to the bottom of the sweatiest pore in the rankest part of Prosperion's most unwashed armpit" where he'd been "cruelly bound to butchers, bumpkins and illiterates"—Kaige set the trunk full of spells on the ground. Jasper continued to mumble as he opened the trunk, but then he fell silent. His movements in the chest became more and more frantic, and the rustle of the scrolls grew louder and more conspicuous to the rest of the company.

"You've lost them, you great, mindless mastodon," Jasper said. "How could you be so reckless? You left most of them behind. Did you even bother to look around?"

Kaige splayed his hands out at his sides innocently. "I looked. I swear I did. I just did what Sarge said and picked up what I saw."

"Well, you didn't pick them all up. Half of them are gone. Look here, there isn't one speaking spell, and all the long sight spells are out. I had four major levitates and five minors, and now all I've got are two minor ones. I don't even have the one version of 'Rainbow's Beacon Spell' we had." He dug around some more. "All the fireballs are gone, and the lightning and ice lances as well. You've let them all be blown away." He tipped the trunk toward them to illustrate his point. "Look, it's all minor healing spells and a handful of fogs, oils and other garbage spells. What am I supposed to do in a fight?"

Lines rippled down Ilbei's forehead as he listened. He stepped closer to the chest and glanced in, but he didn't know how many were in it before.

"Well, I just don't know how the army can employ people if they have no value for expensive equipment like this. I certainly never—"

"Jasper, let off," Ilbei cut in. "He done as I told him, and ya seen yerself when we left that cave that there weren't none lyin around. I'd have got em myself if'n there had been. They been blown off, or the locals grabbed what they could. Like ya said, there's money in those."

Jasper continued to grumble. "Then why didn't they take any of the divining spells? I've got a dream-reading spell that they could have sold for three crowns and a handful of silver."

"They likely just reached in there and run off with whatever they come up with," Ilbei said. "So you're gonna have to get to it with what spells ya got. Ya can replace what's gone when we get back to Hast."

Jasper was not happy about that, but he found his levitation spell, which calmed him some. He drew in a long breath and looked back through the chest, taking a less emotional inventory this time. He found a few fireballs he'd missed and one lightning spell. He held two of them up, one in each hand, triumphantly. He stuffed the spells into his satchel along with a handful of others, and then spent a bit longer than Ilbei would have liked trying to reorder the rest in the chest. Eventually, however, he was ready to assist Meggins in getting up to where the water ejected itself from the rock face, and soon enough, both of them were inside.

Ilbei was helping Kaige tie Jasper's chest back atop the panniers on the packhorse when Meggins' call came. Ilbei left off with the packs and immediately waded into the creek, stooping and holding his arms out wide. He looked up and saw Kaige staring at him, unmoving and clearly reluctant, the big man's arm lying limply across the horse's rump where it had fallen at Meggins' call.

"Get yer fool self in here and help me, Kaige, or I'll tap yer gizzards with this here pick," Ilbei shouted. "I ain't keen to go chasin some rotten old harpy corpse halfway to Chaparral."

Kaige pouted, but he came down and waded into the creek beside Ilbei. Mags took a position on the shore beside them with her quarterstaff ready to help stop the harpy as it washed down the creek.

They waited, all of them watching the white spray where the creek spewed out.

There came a fluctuation in the flow of water, a thinning

sort of pulse, only for an instant, and then a dark shape flew out as if spit out by the mountain itself. It landed with a wet *thwap* on the rocks at the farthest edge of the spray, half in the water and half out. Mags ran up to it and pinned it with her quarterstaff as Ilbei and Kaige climbed out of the creek and joined her. Kaige could not have looked happier.

Ilbei took Mags' staff from her and used it to haul the harpy corpse up the draw a few paces, well out of the stream. In doing so, he rolled it over and saw something that gave him pause. "Would ya look at that," he said. He handed the staff back to Mags and drew the knife from his belt. He used it to push at one of the rotted wings, a skeletal thing, wrapped in a filmy slime of remnant skin, and most of the feathers gone. Something silver glinted underneath.

With his boot, he held the body in place and got a better bit of leverage with his knife. Peeling the wing back like a box lid, he reached underneath with his free hand and grasped the silver object. He had to wrench it back and forth a few times, but finally yanked it out. It was a long steel crossbow bolt, a full hand-width longer than the length of his arm.

He held it aloft for Kaige and Mags to see. "Look at that. And where have ya seen one of these before?"

They both recognized the bolt immediately. "The Skewer's skewer," Kaige said aloud, grinning for both having known the answer and his own cleverness in describing it.

"Damn right it is. And damn strange."

"Why strange?" the burly warrior asked. "A crossbow like the one he's got would have the range for shooting harpies easy enough."

"Better than most," Ilbei agreed. "But how does a man shoot a harpy and have it end up in that there hole?" He looked up and saw that Jasper was just beginning to let himself out of the opening. "Hold up there, Jasper," Ilbei called, shouting to be heard over the water rushing out.

Jasper looked back, and though what he said couldn't be heard, Ilbei was sure it was some sort of complaint.

Turning to Mags, Ilbei presented the crossbow bolt as if it were a prized bit of evidence. "Now what would make a man shoot down a harpy and then go to all the trouble of squeezin it up in there? Especially a big man like the Skewer, what couldn't get in there hisself any better than Kaige or I?"

"Maybe you're right about that disease," she said. "Maybe that was his plan, to run people off. If so, it worked."

"But why?" Kaige couldn't help but ask. He looked shaken by Mags' suggestion, as if he'd stumbled upon an astonishing new idea, a type of danger that had never occurred to him in a life growing up on a farm. "It ain't right to do such a thing."

"No, it ain't right," Ilbei agreed.

"But wouldn't he have known that it would wash out of there eventually?" Mags asked. "Or was it tied in place? And why not get your bolt back?" She hefted the one she held, weighing it in her hand. "These are expensive to make."

Ilbei nodded at that. "Good point." He raised his hand beside his mouth and shouted up at Jasper again. "Jasper, was this harpy tied to somethin in there or weighted down with rocks? Anythin to keep it in place?"

Jasper looked as irritated by the question as any human could possibly be, but he turned back and fought his way against the current again, crawling inside to consult with Meggins.

Ilbei sniffed the air, reaching for and taking the crossbow bolt back. He sniffed it. "I still smell vinegar."

Jasper poked his head out of the hole a few moments later, clinging to the rope and trying not to get flushed out like the harpy had. "No," he shouted down. "He said it was just stuck between two rocks."

"How far in does the creek go?" Ilbei called back. "Is there more cave upstream or only room for the water?" He couldn't hear the belabored sigh, but he could see the dramatic rolling of the wizard's eyes, as if Ilbei had just asked him to dig a tunnel through the entire world.

Jasper once more vanished into the hole. When he came back, he shouted down to Ilbei again. "He says it goes back too far to see."

Ilbei hummed deep in the back of his throat. It didn't make sense how a harpy got in that hole. Unless it crawled in there to die after being shot, which was an unexplored possibility. But if it had, why would a harpy put itself in range of Ergo the Skewer and his spectacular crossbow anyway? They were rumored to be a savage, filthy and awful sort of creature, but they weren't so dumb as that, and powerful as that crossbow was, harpies could fly awfully high. Everything he had ever heard about harpies said they were just as smart as humans—though that wasn't necessarily saying much.

He wondered if maybe the Skewer had come across the harpies that picked clean those two corpses downstream, the skeletons he and his men had found their first trip up the creek. If so, he might have shot others as well. He called to Jasper again. "Are there any others up there? Any more dead harpies farther in?"

The display of indignation that followed Ilbei's question was such that an outside observer might have thought he'd demanded Jasper cut out all his own organs and sacrifice them to the gods right there on the spot. Jasper was prudent enough to get himself back into the hole, however, lest Ilbei come and do it for him, and for a long time, there was no more sign of the soggy sorcerer—such a long time that Ilbei began to worry.

"Ya don't suppose they run into trouble in there, do ya?" he asked Mags. "Are there any other sorts of monsters or vile critters around here that ya know of?"

"There's the sand dragons hiding in the apple trees," Kaige said. "Don't forget about them."

Mags and Ilbei turned toward him as one, their faces scrunched up in the grip of bewilderment for a time until Ilbei recalled the source of that. He hated to be the one to ruin a good joke, but he had no choice this time. Impatience required that he explain. "They was funnin ya, son. There ain't no dragons hidin in apple trees on account of their privates or any other parts bein red. Meggins was havin a joke on ya was all."

Kaige looked as if he couldn't decide if he felt stupid or relieved.

The sound of the water spewing out changed for a moment, followed by another spurt of water. A second harpy body shot out with it, this one landing short of the first. It stuck for a moment to the rocks, but the resumption of the normal water flow pulled it back into the stream. It might have gone right on down, headed toward Camp Chaparral, had not Mags reacted as quickly as she did.

She ran along the creek bank, chasing it, hopping from rock to rock, as nimble as a mountain goat, until she was clear of the jumbled stones and shale that filled the head of the ravine. She leapt down into the dry grass and caught up to the harpy corpse, punching the butt of her staff into the body and pinning it to the opposite bank. She held it there until Kaige and Ilbei arrived. They realized immediately after they got it out of the creek that this harpy was different from the last. The difference drew a gasp from Mags.

"What happened to its wings?" Kaige asked.

Ilbei studied the boney stumps that jutted from the waterlogged harpy's back, each of them protruding two hand-widths from its spine where the wings had been. He judged from the smooth, flat angles at the end of each that they'd been sawed off, done by the tools and the labor of a man. The ends were burned, apparently having been cauterized.

That set Ilbei off, and with no more than a "that's the last twitch of it" to explain, he began barking orders. The orders ultimately led to getting him to where he could set himself to work at the edge of the hole, widening it with his pickaxe.

Perhaps it was curiosity that did it, or perhaps it was frustration, but Ilbei couldn't let it go. The sawed-off stumps of that harpy's wings got under his skin like a cocklebur in a cinch strap, and there wasn't any way he was going to stop until he got it out. So it was with grim determination that he set himself to widening the hole, making Jasper levitate him up to where the water emerged so he could work. Meggins had assured him that if he could widen it by a half hand for the first quarter span, he could fit through the rest, but nobody expected him to stay at it for three hours like he did.

About two hours into the work, as the sun drooped lower and lower toward the ridgeline high above—and after it occurred to Jasper that Ilbei had no intention of stopping his furious assault on the opening—Jasper offered to cast a spell on Ilbei's pickaxe to expedite the work. He did so mainly in hopes of seeing the work done, so that they could get back to civilization, but at least partly in sympathy for the massive efforts of the laborer himself.

With the aid of a spell called "Tooth of the Leviathan"—officially intended to preserve the sharpness of sword and axe blades during long battles—by the time darkness was full upon them, Ilbei had carved out enough room that both he and Kaige could squeeze through the narrow opening.

He came down to the fire Meggins had gotten going while he worked. Meggins was cooking a few quail he'd shot, which Ilbei noted appreciatively. He took the wineskin Mags offered him, and gulped at it for a while. The wine was cool and refreshing, as Mags had put it in the creek while Ilbei worked. "Get some torches, people," Ilbei said after, wiping his mouth with the back of his hand. "I mean to go on in there tonight."

"Tonight?" Meggins asked, as Jasper and Kaige looked on with equal incredulity. "Come on, Sarge. You've been at that hole all afternoon, and we've been walking since just after dawn. None of us had a decent night's sleep, either. Only reason we got any at all was because Jasper's damned magic knocked us out."

"You're awful young to be snivelin like that," Ilbei said. "The three of ya. And here I'm three times yer age, and Mags a woman what ain't been trained fer marchin at all." He winked at Mags as he said it, and she smiled. Kaige looked sheepish, then laughed, and eventually so did Meggins, though he made a show of busying himself with the quail suspended above the flames. Jasper, in usual form, managed not to share in the humor, but rather than complain, as Ilbei expected, the wizard went right into the issue that had set Ilbei's resolve to begin.

"It doesn't seem reasonable to assume that a wingless harpy could have gotten in there," Jasper said. "Unless the first one we found dragged the second in behind. But that seems unlikely, don't you think, given the diameter of the hole and the outflow of water as strong as it is? Not to mention carrying capacities. Given what we can see of the wingspan of the first one, it seems unlikely it could have lifted a second harpy's weight in addition to its own, particularly given that the first one was female and the second male. Like many species, the males are typically larger and stronger—other than the matriarchs of course. Harpies don't have magical buoyancy like dragons and gryphons do, so she would have relied completely on the lift provided by those wings."

"Plus, she was shot," Kaige pointed out.

"Right, she was." Jasper regarded Kaige across the

firelight, looking surprised and impressed. "So, given all of that, it doesn't seem probable that she could have dragged the other in after her."

"That's why we're goin in," Ilbei said. "Only way that one got in there was someone else stuffed em both up there together. That, or they came from the inside. And seein as how you and Meggins found that cut-winged harpy two hundred paces into the mountainside, and not in the water at all, I'm thinkin it's the second one."

Mags shifted uncomfortably. Ilbei couldn't tell if it was due to the rock she sat on or what she was about to say. "I'm not disagreeing with your premise, Sergeant, but I'm curious why you feel so strongly that it is necessary to go."

"Because somethin don't smell right around here, and I don't have to be shat on to know I'm downwind of the latrine."

She nodded, either appeased or unwilling to wade any further into Ilbei's reasoning. None of them were. For a time, they satisfied themselves with carving up the birds and serving them with slices of the sour apples that Mags had softened by baking them on the stones around the fire. The only one who spoke was Jasper, who came upon a realization as he ate. "How would being shat on tell you that you were downwind of a latrine?" he asked. "That doesn't make any sense."

The weariness and the tension broke immediately upon his inquiry, and all the rest of them began to grin, shaking their heads and marveling at how a fellow like Jasper came to be. Jasper saw it and, of course, had no idea why.

"What?" he said as he watched them. "I don't see how that's funny. Any number of flying creatures could fly over and move their bowels onto the sergeant. And their doing so wouldn't have anything to do with the direction of the wind or the location of a latrine. So it's neither funny nor an accurate analogy of anything."

Well, that was enough to bring roaring guffaws and pouring tears, and for a time all the others could do was clutch their ribs and bellies and exchange glances of raucous sympathy for their clueless companion. Eventually, after the tears were wiped away, Meggins wrapped a one-armed hug around the flustered and blustering Jasper's shoulders and declared him to be the "best traveling companion of all time." So much revived were they by their merriment, in fact, that Meggins was brave enough to take another crack at getting Ilbei to relent on going into the cave that night. He was actually still laughing as he said it, no less. "So, Sarge, I suppose now that, you know, all that frustration's worked out and we can think through it clear, can we be steady on it and call it a night? Head out in the morning?"

Fortunately for Meggins, Ilbei, too, was still laughing when he replied. "Nice try, son, but we're goin once these here quails is gone."

Chapter 23

Shortly after the meal was done, the company made their way by torchlight up into the hole where Harpy Creek emerged. Even with Ilbei's work, he and Kaige had to struggle to get through, and both of them were sputtering and choking as they did, their respective burliness combining with the bulky chest and the two panniers to nearly plug the stream as they crawled inside. Eventually, however, with patience and much profanity, they made it through—though getting inside and getting to where it was even marginally comfortable were two different things. Once through the opening, they still had to crawl on hands and knees for the first six spans until it widened enough that they could get to their feet. From there, they had to crouch and shuffle another ten spans before there was enough space to stand upright, though only barely so for Kaige.

Once Ilbei and Kaige had caught their breath, and Jasper had muttered and mumbled over his trunk of spells before verifying that at least the army did provide properly watertight boxes for the "precious things," Meggins was finally able to show Ilbei where the harpy corpses had been.

"Here is where the first harpy was," Meggins said, dipping

a torch down toward a jumble of rocks lying half in the stream and half out. "And up here is where the second harpy was." He took the light and moved up the passage, the floor widening enough to make smooth stone banks on either side of the waterway. The slope was gentle, and by the time Meggins got to where the second harpy had been, the cave was much wider than it was tall, by nearly three times. The water-polished bank was not steep, perhaps rising only a span over the course of it, but where he'd found the harpy was a good two and a half spans up the bank from the waterline, near where the cave wall began. "It was lying next to these rocks, like it might have been resting against them for a while before it died."

"Way up there?" Ilbei asked.

"Yeah. Like I said, nowhere near the stream."

"Well, come some parts of the year, this here might run pretty full."

Meggins nodded. Ilbei ordered Kaige to drag the two panniers up to where Meggins stood and stuff them behind the rocks along with Jasper's trunk. "Get what ya need, Jasper," he said as Kaige set to work.

They'd unloaded the packhorse and left it to its own devices, as there was no telling how long they might be in the cave or whether or not they'd exit the same way they came in. Ilbei simply didn't want to be slowed down with all that equipment for what he hoped would be a quick in-and-out search. With luck, he'd find his answers, and they would be right back, the horse still nearby for their return to Hast.

When they'd taken what they needed to explore the cave further, Ilbei nodded for Meggins to proceed. The younger soldier complied, moving up the passage with a torch held out before him.

For several hours they followed the stream along. Ilbei noted that the vinegar smell grew stronger, but other than that, there was little change in the scenery. The cave had turned slowly back in the direction of Fall Pools and stayed that way, or at least as near as Ilbei could tell, and he was certain enough to announce it to his men when they came across a small patch of glowing fungus, which Ilbei recognized as the same type he'd seen in the ettin cave.

"We're gonna undo all of this morning's march," Kaige said. "We're going the wrong way."

"We're goin the right way is what I expect."

"Right way for what?"

As if to stymie any answer Ilbei had, the next few steps brought them to where the cave split, a low-ceilinged branch leading left and a slightly narrower one leading right. The stream came from the left passage. The right one was completely dry, but it had not always been so, for it too was smooth and polished, obviously by the flow of water over the course of many centuries. How recently those centuries had come to an end was impossible to tell. Meggins stopped for a moment and peered into one passage, then the other, then back at Ilbei, his face traced in golden curves of torchlight. "Well, Sarge, you were saying?"

"Hmm," Ilbei hummed, the sound low and rumbling in his barrel chest. He waded up the stream to the left until he was at the edge of Meggins' torchlight. He sniffed the air, then listened in silence for a time. All he could hear was the running water.

He went back and entered the right-side tunnel, taking the torch from Meggins as he passed. He repeated the listening and sniffing thing.

"Well, I suppose we ought to go left, bein as I smell copper and lead that way," he said at length. "But the vinegar is comin from the other one."

"The vinegar might be something natural, something fermenting up there, maybe something leftover from before the water ran dry," Mags said. "This one might only run in wet years or when the snowmelt is on with the first heat."

Ilbei glanced over at Jasper, who appeared to agree, though he was mostly busy retying the knot in his robes, which he'd made to hold them up and prevent them, sort of, from getting wetter than they already were.

"All right," Ilbei said, "then left it is. I expect ya all ought to be ready fer whatever comes. Kaige, pull that shortsword ya wear; that long blade won't be nothin in here. Meggins, be ready with yer bow." He turned to Mags and Jasper behind him. "Mags, light another torch from the ones we put in that pack of yers, and come along behind with Jasper. Hold it fer him if'n he needs to read some kind of spell. Keep an eye out behind us too as we go along." When they were ready, he took the torch and the lead from Meggins, then headed up the stream.

The cave grew narrower as they progressed, making the stream deeper and with very little in the way of dry edges to serve as a bank for walking upon. In places, the passage narrowed so much that they had to get into the water and wade, above the knees for Ilbei, well below for Kaige, somewhere between for the rest. Ilbei's main concern was noise, splashing along as they were, and the shape of the tunnel amplified the sound of every step.

He followed the tunnel for some time, perhaps another hour, occasionally passing through sections where tiny patches of the glowing fungus grew, noting that it grew around cracks that blew cool air, suggesting they were near the surface or the face of the steppe somewhere.

At length, they came to a very small chamber, more of a bulbous expansion of the passage, really, and in the center of it, some three paces in, was a waterfall. It crossed the chamber in a shimmering sheet, spilling out from a long crack in the ceiling and splashing into a pool of its own making like a curtain. The veil of water was backlit by more of the glowing fungus, which grew around the edges of the pool more thickly than in other places along their way. The blue light seemed to dance with the golden glow of the torches, giving the waterfall a colorful, nearly prismatic effect. Ilbei noted that the smell of lead was strong, smelted lead, not just raw ore. It was a difference as obvious to him as would be the varied aromas of fine wines to a connoisseur. Stepping through the sheet of falling water, Ilbei discovered the far end of the chamber only a few paces away. This was the end of the passage, he realized, and the beginning of Harpy Creek.

Turning back to face his companions, he saw that there was a narrow ledge to his left, a shelf perhaps a half span wide. On the right, there was hardly anything of an edge at all, only the sloping angle of the cave wall as it bowed into the rock, the work of the waterfall eating away at it for countless spans of years. The fungus grew all around the water's edge, and he noted that a good deal grew at the bottom too. Unlike those in the little pool in the ettin cave, the clumps of fungi at the bottom of this pool glowed dimly, just like the ones that weren't submerged. He turned full circle, making sure he hadn't missed any dark openings or crawl spaces, but there were none. He did notice, however, that in one place the fungus grew in a straight line up the wall. He went to it and discovered a crack in the stone, wide enough he could get his fingernail in it. A cool breeze blew out of it, heavy with the smell of lead. He leaned closer and sniffed. Sure enough, that was the source of the scent, lead with a hint of copper. And with it came the voices of men.

He snuffed the torch in the water and motioned for the rest of them to stay back. Only Kaige had come through the curtain of water to join him, but the big man had the sense to lean back through and convey Ilbei's instructions that they stay put.

Ilbei pressed his ear against the damp stone. The cool air chilled his cheeks, the moist breath of a mountain stirring through his beard. He listened, but he couldn't make out what the voices said. They were men, but that was all he could tell. Frustrated, he returned to his companions beyond the waterfall.

"There's somebody down there, but damned if I can hear a thing. Jasper, ya got anythin in that bag of yers to lend a hand ... or an ear?"

Mags gasped at that, as if she were about to laugh and then changed her mind. Then she pitched forward and splashed into the pool right in front of Ilbei. The light of her torch extinguished as she fell, plunging them into darkness for the span of blinks it took for their eyes to adjust to the soft light of the fungus all around.

"Mags," Ilbei called out as he stooped and reached for her. He bumped heads with Meggins, who was doing the same, and his helmet clanked against Meggins' skull. Something hissed right above him, followed by a *thwick* noise from the sheet of water behind him and another, much louder sound like something huge had struck the stone. That loud strike was followed by a rainfall patter of small objects, like gravel landing in the pool.

"To the sides, to the sides," Ilbei hissed, pushing them all out of the line of the main passage. His eyes were beginning to work in the dim light, which was amplified a little by the waterfall. He risked a peek around the edge of the chamber, down the passage through which they'd come. The stone near his face erupted as he did, pieces of it embedding themselves in his cheek. A dark shadow passed in that same instant, long and skewing off sideways upon impact with the curve of the stone behind which Ilbei ducked. Something wooden clattered off the wall opposite him, followed by a splash.

He could just make out the dark island of Mags floating facedown in the water, nearly carried out of the chamber and down the stream. He hooked her backpack with his pickaxe and dragged her back, hauling her up onto his lap.

He rolled her over, pressing his face down near hers, leading with his cheek to feel her breath as he had the air coming through the crack only a few moments before. There was none.

"Assassins," Ilbei hissed. "They've killed her." Something cut his hand as he moved it over her body. It was the point of the shaft that had struck her down, shot all the way through and emerging several finger-widths through her chest. "The Skewer," he hissed. But when he felt the tip of it, it didn't feel right. The bolts that Ergo the Skewer's crossbow fired had narrow, three-pronged heads. This was a two-barbed arrowhead. He rolled Mags' body over enough to see the black arrow in her back, the shaft a dark line in the dim luminance, the bright green fletching glowing in the ghostly light of the fungus all around. "Verity!"

"That's right, Sergeant," came the reply. "And you're trapped like wintering bears in there. No sense making a fuss."

"Jasper, can ya do anythin fer her?" Ilbei pushed Mags toward the mage, whose teeth were chattering audibly. Ilbei could see the whites of his eyes glowing blue in the fungal luminance. Ilbei had to ask again. Jasper looked up at him, fighting with his fright.

"N-not if she's d-dead. Is she ... dead?"

"She might be. She ain't breathin. Can ya do anythin fer her?"

Meggins pulled her toward him, a little deeper in the chamber, and followed the same procedure Ilbei had. He pressed two fingers against her neck as well. He shook his head. "I think she's done," he said, but he pushed her toward Jasper and held her so the skinny mage could look.

"I'm n-not a n-necromancer," Jasper said.

"Just check and see what ya got in the bag," Ilbei hissed. "This is what we brung ya fer." He started to look away, but stopped, adding, "And quit that chatterin so as ya don't bungle it somehow."

"I think you people think I'm a doctor or something," he said, but he was rummaging through his satchel as he mumbled it.

Ilbei watched him and could tell by the way he moved, breaking off a piece of fungus and using it to look inside his bag of spells, that he didn't believe he was doing anything that would be of use. At least he'd found the will to get the chattering stopped.

"Verity, ya son of a basilisk," Ilbei spat. "Mags is dead."

"Of course she is," Verity called back. "As the rest of you will be. So let's not prolong this. I'd really like to be done before sunrise, or at least before dinnertime tomorrow if you people insist on dragging it out."

"Ya done shot a woman in the back!" Ilbei said. "What kind of sorry whoreson maggot does that?"

"She had a quarterstaff," Verity replied, "declaring her as a combatant, which you know perfectly well."

Ilbei glanced to where her quarterstaff had landed, half in the water, half nestled amongst a clump of the glowing fungi. "Well, she didn't declare no fight with ya that I seen. Fact, there weren't no declarations made at all, as last time we seen ya, we was all on the same side. But now ya gone and got me riled some, so this here is me declarin fer ya, honest like."

"Yes, yes, Sergeant, your bravery and pugilistic talents were well known long before the army brought you down from Leekant. But I have no intentions of getting close enough to witness them firsthand."

"Coward," Ilbei called back.

"I think *prudent* is a better word. We all have our own unique gifts, Sergeant."

"She never done ya one lick of harm," Ilbei said. He turned and regarded poor, limp Mags lying in Meggins' arms, Jasper muttering over her under his breath, reading from a scroll by the light of a busted fungal knot. She hadn't even gotten past her twenty-first year.

"Listen, if it's all the same to you," the hunter said, "I can see as well as you can that you're at a dead end. Which means, you're trapped. And since you really don't have any way of getting past me, wouldn't it be easiest if you just gave up and let me finish this?"

"There's four of us," Ilbei called back.

"Yes, three infantrymen, one of whom has a standard-issue shortbow, and a scroll-mage who sits there in the dark with you chattering like a chorus of yammering clams. Unless whatever he's muttering strikes me down soon—which seems unlikely given that the boys went through and pulled his offensive spells—I think the odds are grossly in my favor."

To punctuate that statement, a chunk of the wall where the passage narrowed exploded into bits of gravel, once more sandblasting Ilbei's face. The arrow ricocheted off the rock and hit the back wall with a dull wooden *thunk*. Ilbei scowled at it as it splashed into the pool.

He turned toward Mags and the muttering of the mage, but Jasper had just finished. He saw Ilbei looking at him and shrugged. "That's the best I can do for now. I don't even know exactly what it does. It just says 'Growth Heal – One.'"

"How in the nine hells do ya not know what it does? Don't ya have to know that stuff?"

"I do know them if I am the one who writes the enchantment. This is obviously a standard-issue spell down here in Hast because they gave me tons of them before we left. I have no idea who penned them." He held up the parchment, but it was blank, the words gone after the reading of the spell. "It's the same version as the one I read for Kaige's head. They gave me some other healing spells that are surely better, but they'll take several hours to read properly." He glanced around them, then down at his shaking hands. Ilbei could see the parchment corners vibrating in the light, and the tightness in Jasper's jaw suggested that he was trying very hard not to chatter.

Ilbei would have cussed, but there was nothing to be had for it just then. "Then dig a little deeper in that there sack and tell us what ya got that we can use." Ilbei kept his voice low, loud enough to be heard over the splashing waterfall but not beyond, or so he hoped. It was hard to say how far off Verity was. It was pitch black down the tunnel as far as he could see.

He glanced to Meggins and Kaige, the two of them having pulled Mags' body off of Jasper. They were in the process of getting her out of the water, up onto the shelf of stone. There was barely enough room to stuff her onto it, and even with that, her legs were going to stay wet. Not that it was going to matter much to her now, Ilbei thought.

He noticed the black wooden arrow bobbing in the pond, floating lightly on the surface, its green fletching glowing slightly bluer in the ambient light. "Kaige, get that fancy arrow he just shot. Use yer sword. Stay out of his line of sight." Ilbei hoped maybe there was some kind of magic in those black shafts that they could turn back on Verity.

Another arrow broke flecks of stone away.

Jasper leaned against the stone, head down, shoulders drooping. Ilbei took the wilting wizard by the shoulders. "Listen here, soldier. I understand you're cold and wet, and Mags lyin there like that done yer spirit an awful turn. But givin up ain't gonna get us out of here, I can tell ya that. Now straighten up, take a breath, and wake the man in ya. Think of Her Majesty's glory if'n ya need, or of that mum ya got back home, waitin on yer return, but find a way to snap to. We need yer brain workin fer somethin other than rattlin yer teeth. Now come on, son, think, what have ya got?" When Jasper merely looked up at him, his eyes blank, fear and cold smothering him, Ilbei slapped him hard across the face. "I said snap out of it, boy. We need ya with us."

Laughter echoed up the cave at them.

"A fine troop of men you've got there, Sergeant. Her Majesty's finest no less."

"You'll see it true when we get done pullin our steel out of ya."

Another spray of rocks peppered the side of Ilbei's face, the arrow splashing somewhere beyond the waterfall.

Jasper was at least blinking when Ilbei looked at him again.

"Come on, Jasper. Ya got to have somethin in that damned bag. Think, son."

Jasper's wits seemed to be returning.

"I can't get it, Sarge," Kaige said.

Ilbei turned to look, and saw the big man bent over, both hands wrapped around the black length of one of Verity's arrows as it floated in the blue glow of the pool. Kaige's broad back was bent and his tree-trunk thighs flexed as he strove to lift the arrow out of the water, straining and grunting as if it were an enormous thing and bolted in place.

"Won't budge," Kaige said after another try. "Like it's stuck on the water. Might as well be ten tons of stone."

Ilbei didn't risk trying to climb over Meggins and Jasper for fear of exposing the protuberance of his belly to Verity's brutal bow. And to what end, anyway? If the great strength of young Kaige couldn't lift that arrow from the surface of the pond, floating and bobbing as it was, as easily as a bit of cork might, well, then there wasn't likely much more Ilbei could do. Clearly, Verity's arrows were cursed. Or at least, cursed as far as Ilbei and his men were concerned.

Another arrow hit the wall, and more bits of stone stung him, biting into his skin like insects. "Gods damn ya, Verity!" he called.

He glanced at the line of the crack from which the voices

and the huffing air came. They were close to somewhere else, even if there wasn't a crawl space. If he tried to make one with his pickaxe, he'd expose himself like a damned gopher jumping out of its hole into the haymaker's blade. But there might be something Jasper could do, even though Ilbei hated the very thought of what he was about to ask.

"Jasper," he hissed low. "What about teleports? Have ya got one of those in that bag of yers?" He shuddered as he asked it. Few things made him shudder like the thought of teleporting did. For some it was spiders, others heights. For Ilbei, teleporting was everything unnatural in the world. But, short of blind, headlong assault, it was the only way out of here.

"I do have teleport scrolls," Jasper replied. "But they won't get us out of here."

"Why not? What the hell are they fer if'n not fer that?"

"They only gave me teleports with a fifty-pace range."

"They what? Fifty paces? What kinda— Well, that makes as much sense as sendin ya out joustin on a three-legged horse. Why on Prosperion would they give ya a gimped spell like that?"

"Too many first-year wizards would rather not be in combat," Jasper said. He sighed and looked as if something had struck him funny. "They told me that when I—" He paused, as did Ilbei, as another crushing arrow struck, blasting them with stone chips and bits of grit.

"I can chip away at that all day," Verity called. "I'm not going to run out of these."

Jasper continued where he'd left off. "They told me these spells were for getting up onto castle walls, or through them if I knew where to go on the other side."

"Well, can't ya do one of those seein spells them sight wizards always do? We're right above a place where some fellers is talkin down below, the ones I heard through that crack. Sure there weren't more'n fifty paces between here and there."

"If I had a seeing spell, I would have told you that I did." Jasper turned back toward Kaige for a moment and sighed again, the big man still trying to deadlift the bobbing arrow out of the pool. Jasper rolled his head back to face Ilbei again. "If *he* hadn't lost half my spells, I would have three seeing spells with me rather than five useless teleports."

"Verity said it was them what was at yer stores," Ilbei said. "And Kaige done what he could, so let off that like I already told ya." Ilbei watched Kaige still unable to budge the enchanted arrow. He was damned sure he didn't want anyone else getting hit with one of those.

"So what else ya got? I don't know how far off Verity is down there, so I can't say how much use fifty paces would be fer goin after him—not with the dark and him and that damned bow—but it might be our only shot."

"Besides the teleports, I have two oil spells," Jasper said, pushing the chunk of fungus around inside the satchel and keeping his voice low as he confirmed what he had in memory. "And there is the lightning bolt spell and two fireballs—obviously Verity's men didn't know what they were looking at—four healing spells, two like the one I just cast and two of the longer ones ... oh, wait, no, this one is just for headaches, and, well, here's another mend, but it's for armor and shields. The rest are food, water or laundry spells. That's it."

"Well, why don't ya hit him with that lightnin and let's be done with it? Sweet Mercy's smilin lips, ya could have done that five minutes ago."

"Well, if I had, we'd all be floating downstream, steaming like baked fish," Jasper said. "This one is M-ranked and not to be trifled with. And that pretends I knew where he was, which I do not, and therefore I couldn't have hit him anyway."

"Fire, then. Just send one of them big burnin bastards

right down the pipe. That'll do fer him. Fill the whole thing up with fire, and ya won't need to know where he is."

Jasper rummaged through the satchel again, reading ribbons wrapped around scrolls. They both flinched when another arrow pounded into the wall. "I should tell you boys, I waited seven days for a chimera to come out of her cave once," Verity called in its wake.

"No," said Jasper, ignoring Verity's comment. "These are fast to read, but small. The big ones, like what you're asking for—and they only gave me three to start, of which only one remained after the ... looting—are in the chest back where we came in."

"Ya mean ya had em?" Ilbei looked as if he wanted to hit something. "Why in Hestra's name would ya not bring somethin like that when ya had a choice? Ya might as well choose a cabbage over a cutlass fer yer next duel."

Jasper looked at Ilbei and ticked his tongue against his teeth. It was apparent that he thought both the question and the comment ridiculous. "First of all, I have no intention of dueling anyone. But, to answer your question, it is because those are for castle gates and leviathans, not cave explorations where space is limited and where heat and distance have an essential and necessary relationship for the caster ... and his allies."

"What if we'd found a dragon in here?"

"I'm not even going to dignify that with a response."

Ilbei's eyes narrowed, but he let it go. "How fast, then? And how big? And how far?"

"Fast. One is seven words, the other nineteen." He looked at the scrolls again and frowned. "The small one is the longer of the two, sadly—a poorly written E-class fireball, probably well under two hands in diameter. The other is K-class; the script is neat, so likely a full span. I didn't write that one either, but whoever did made a much better job of it."

"Well that's big enough," Ilbei said, ignoring the useless parts of Jasper's statement. "Go ahead and put that one down the hole."

"But I still don't know where he is."

"Can't ya shoot it straight down the middle and just let it go as far as it will? Ya said it's a full span. That's a boatload of fire."

"Yes, but he'll shoot me as soon as I step out there to cast."

"No, he won't. When ya get to that sixth word, I'll jump across, make him shoot at me. Ya can jump out behind me and let it go while he reloads. Jump back before he's got time to stick ya."

Jasper didn't look especially enthusiastic about that plan. His teeth were chattering again.

"You're too fat, Sarge," Meggins said, leaning in close. "That pregnant gut of yours will get you killed. I'll jump across."

"Fat enough to dot yer eyes closed, soldier," Ilbei said. "Besides, I got us into this mess. I'll be the one what jumps across."

"Sarge, you're also the one who can get us out of this," Meggins said. "I heard the stories about you when they transferred you to Hast. If even half of them are true, we need you. But you're no good to us with one of those black shafts through your head. You know I'm quicker, at least for something like this. I'll do it."

Ilbei would have snarled something back, but Meggins pointed at the black arrow that was floating past Ilbei's foot. Ilbei watched the current carry it out of the little chamber and down into the darkness. No wonder Verity knew he'd never run out of arrows: they were going to drift right back to him, and there was nothing Ilbei could do about it. Ilbei grunted, knowing Meggins was right. He looked back to Jasper. "Ya realize what we're goin to do, right?"

Jasper nodded.

"Ya can't hesitate. Ya got to get out there, say what ya got to say, and get back." Jasper's teeth had stopped chattering again, which Ilbei took as a hopeful sign.

"I will," Jasper promised.

Ilbei made a face and started to change his mind.

"He'll do it," Meggins said. "He'll be fine." He fixed Jasper with a long, steady look, smiling just a little bit. "I know he will."

What other choice did they have? So Ilbei agreed.

Jasper got out his scroll, and Ilbei held the piece of fungus so the wizard could read. They all counted six words, every one of them mouthing the numbers as Jasper spoke the unfamiliar sounds. On the sixth, Meggins threw himself across the chamber, and in that instant, the dark line of a green-tailed arrow streaked across the chamber like death's black rope. It had barely spit through the waterfall and blasted out a chunk of the back wall when Jasper stepped out and shouted the last word of his spell. The fireball erupted into existence and shot down the passage at meteoric speed. Jasper stood in its light and watched as if hypnotized by the need to see it fly.

Realizing Jasper wasn't moving, Ilbei tackled him and drove him across the space, the two of them crashing against the wall near Meggins. Something burned along the back of Ilbei's thighs as they slammed into the cold rock. Bits of gravel rained down into the pool right after. When he righted himself, he reached back and felt the line of the cuts that ran across the back of his legs, deep enough to bleed, but no worse than that.

The cave down which the fireball roared glowed orange for a short time, dimming with each passing heartbeat, and then it was gone. Darkness followed the glare for a moment as their eyes adjusted once more to the faint blue glow.

"Did you get him?" Kaige had to ask, anxiousness giving

volume to his voice.

Verity's laughter was his answer.

Chapter 24

"Gorgon's stone," Ilbei swore as Verity taunted them from the darkness downstream. Ilbei stared across the scant distance of the pool, Kaige staring back hopefully and Mags lying there with her legs dangling in the pool, stirred some by the movement of water. If she wasn't dead yet, she would be from hypothermia soon enough. They needed to get clear and to a dry place where Jasper could read the longer healing spell on her. She couldn't afford for them to let Verity keep them under siege.

"I saw him," Jasper whispered. "He's eighty spans down, against the right side, where the cave bends."

"I don't remember it bendin much," Ilbei said. "Not enough fer cover anyway. How'd the fireball miss?"

"I shot it down the middle, like you said. We should have done it along the floor. He dropped down and pressed against the wall. It went right over him."

"Well, can ya get him with the other one?"

"Not without targeting him directly, which means I need to get out there and actually see him before I cast. There's no other way. Anything else is guessing at last known location."

"Well, we can't do that. Might as well throw ya in a

direwolf den wearin a pair of bacon underpants," Ilbei said.

"Why would I be wearing underclothing made from bacon? That's hardly likely. I can't imagine anyone making such a thing, much less wearing it."

"It's just a saying, Jasper," Meggins said.

"Oh," Jasper replied. "Yes, I keep forgetting. The underclothing made from bacon is the humorous element *because* no one would do that, and therefore it would excite the direwolves terribly." He actually grinned.

"Ya picked a strange time to find a sense of humor," Ilbei observed. "Now both of ya, help me think."

"Come on, Spadebreaker," Verity called. "If that was the best you've got, then we all know how this is going to end. I really see no point in prolonging it. I'm not even in the water and my feet are cold. You all ought to be getting pretty uncomfortable in there."

Ilbei ignored him. He looked to Kaige, who sat watching him think, the big man's expression suggesting he had absolute confidence that Ilbei would think of something. Mags lying beside him troubled Ilbei, though. A trickle of blood had begun to run off the shelf, the droplets falling into the water and turning purple in the blue light. That was both promising and not.

That's when Ilbei realized the fungus was giving Verity the advantage over them. He cursed himself for being so slow to realize it. He reached down into the water, where his own wounds were dripping purplish whorls that stretched and flowed away, and pulled off a chunk of fungus. He broke it up into smaller pieces like crumbling bread and threw them into the water, where they bobbed and turned and slowly floated away. Ilbei grinned.

"Kaige, get yer cloak," he ordered, whispering. Kaige didn't hesitate or ask why. He was only a moment in getting it out of his pack, then held it up for Ilbei to see. Ilbei made a motion with his hands, indicating that Kaige should wad it up and throw it to him, which he did.

"Toss me that," Ilbei said then, pointing to Mags' staff. Kaige scooted around the water's edge and retrieved it, then threw it to Ilbei as well. He did appear curious as to what Ilbei was about, but he had sense enough not to ask.

Ilbei turned to Meggins and Jasper, whispering as low as he could to still be heard over the water splashing down. "I'm goin to make a curtain with these," he said. "It will be nearly wide enough to cover the entrance there. Meggins and Kaige can hold it up from either side, safe as can be. Then Jasper, you and me is gonna knock all this fungus loose and send it downstream. He can't shoot what he can't see."

Meggins' head bobbed up and down, realizing what Ilbei had planned. But Jasper didn't look pleased. "He can still shoot through it. And he'll see our feet in the water until it's all gone."

"We'll stay up along the edge here, and we'll use Kaige's sword to get the stuff at the bottom."

"Then what?"

"Then we wait fer it to float down there where he is. You watch it till it gets to him, and then ya blow his gods-be-damned head off with that last fireball of yers."

Meggins' teeth reflected blue light from the curve of his smile. "Genius, Sarge. The ruddy bastard will never know what hit him."

"I don't think we'll be able to scrape the whole pool clean, clinging to the edge and working it with the point of a sword," Jasper said. "He's still going to have something to shoot at. And I can't read the spell without seeing him the entire time to target him. And I also can't do it stooped over peeking through the crack in your curtain either. Targeting fireballs isn't like lobbing snowballs or dirt clods at your friends, you know?"

"When was the last time you were in a snowball fight?"

Meggins asked.

Both Jasper and Ilbei glared at him. "That's a right pointless thing to ask," Ilbei said.

"I just never saw Jasper as the snowball-fighting kind. And dirt clods, well, that's a whole different level of commitment. That's all I'm saying."

Ilbei was going to rebuke Meggins for it, but surprisingly, Jasper agreed. "You're correct. But I have observed both orders of conflict from afar, and often enough the children would glance out from behind trees or over snow fortifications, then duck back. Then, when they felt the timing was adequate, they'd expose themselves long enough to throw toward where their enemies were when last they looked. It's a well-established strategy for both types of combat, and I hardly think one needs to have participated in either to recognize the analogous suitability for our predicament."

Meggins, for once, appeared at a loss for words. Ilbei, however, stayed on point. "Fine," he said. "So if'n ya can't cast a fireball without watchin him the whole while, what can ya cast snowball like?"

"Nothing," Jasper said. "I already told you what spells I have. The lightning works just like the fireball for targeting, and we're lucky to even have it as an option, because most lightning works by touch, and only the very advanced sorts have range like this one has, albeit not a great range. And, excepting the teleports, which I've already said are also minimum range, I simply have nothing else that counts for ranged combat at all."

Ilbei stared into the water. He pushed a chunk of fungus off the wall with his boot heel and watched it float downstream. He knew the floating fungus idea was a good one, despite Jasper's objections, but it was worthless if they couldn't target Verity properly. He thought about having Jasper cast the fireball as an opening move to give Meggins a shot with his bow, but a shortbow wasn't much use at eighty spans, especially in a low-ceilinged cave. They needed a finishing move. Mags needed a finishing move. Soon.

"How far ya say that teleport will get me?" Ilbei asked, leaning in close and nearly whispering in his ear.

"Fifty spans," Jasper replied.

"Can ya cast that like throwin snowballs?"

"I suppose. But I have to know where you want to go."

"I want to go right there where I can put a pick blade in Verity's head."

"He's too far away. And he may have moved."

Ilbei stared into the water again.

"Well, we can float the fungus like I said, and ya can peek round after it till ya see where he is. Once it gets close, ya send me over there near as ya can, and I'll let him have it."

"What if he sees you first?"

"Wait till the fungus gets right up to him, then."

"I think that's a reckless plan," Jasper said. Meggins agreed with the mage.

"Have ya got a better one?" Ilbei asked. "Any of ya?"

Nobody did.

"Then let's get to it. That young lady there don't have all day fer us to be gassin on. Jasper, get that spell out, and if'n ya teleport me into the wall or lose me somehow in the demon realms, I swear to Mercy, my ghost will come back and haunt ya to fartin fer all yer days. Won't be a soul will sit with ya till you're dead and gone. Ya hear me?"

Jasper recoiled from Ilbei's threat, and he spent a moment working through all of its content, extracting what Ilbei meant from what was "just a saying."

Finally the grizzled old veteran put a hand on Jasper's forearm, sparing him having to parse it all. "Just don't botch the job, son. I'm not keen fer teleportin is all."

"Oh," Jasper said, obviously relieved. "Yes, of course. Many people are uncomfortable with it, actually. It's perfectly normal. Transportation Guild Services call what you are suffering Place Shift Anxiety. In the southern duchies, the TGS offices actually allow travelers to imbibe large quantities of intoxicants before teleporting; in South Mark, they use spiced rum in conjunction with a poppyseed extract from the eastern isle of—"

"I take it back," Ilbei cut in. "I'm fine. Just do what ya got to do. I'd rather die bein vaporized or put in a wall than suffocate from ya suckin all the air out of the cave. Find the spell. Have it ready and be quick when time comes." He turned to Meggins. "Squeeze on over past us, and get this here curtain made up so we can break out the fungus and get underway."

They switched places as carefully as they could, and Meggins went to work. He cut slits along one edge of Kaige's massive cloak and then threaded Mags' quarterstaff through them. When he was done, he turned to Ilbei and waited for the go-ahead.

Ilbei in turn looked to Jasper. "Soon as he drops that down, get to clearin off all these along this edge. Work quick, and start from the back. Stay out of the center. I'll cross and work on that side, then get the middle with Kaige's sword. Ya ready?"

Jasper looked as if he might throw up, but he nodded that he would do as he was told.

Ilbei gave Meggins the signal to drop the curtain across the opening to Kaige, who was ready to catch the other end. "Keep yer hands out of arrow shot as ya hold it," he told them. "Includin what he can shoot through the stone."

Meggins spread the cloak out along the length of the quarterstaff and swung it out to Kaige. Kaige caught it, and the two of them lifted it up. The cloak was long enough that the bottom lay in the water, and the current pulled it downstream a little, which created long, angular openings on either side.

"Shite, didn't foresee that," Ilbei said, and just as he said it, an arrow shot through the cloak, coming so quickly it barely moved the cloth. It made a *whisk* sound as it snipped through the heavy wool, a second as it nipped through the waterfall, and then it struck the back wall hard. The arrow and bits of rock fell into the pool.

"I don't think now's the time for modesty, Sergeant," Verity called out. "Or do you and your boys have plans for the dead girl that you don't want me to watch?"

"Only a twisted sort thinks to say a thing like that," Ilbei called back. "I look forward to yankin out yer tongue."

"Yes, I'm looking forward to that, too. Please get on with it. There's a nice meal planned up at Fall Pools tonight. I was hoping I'd make it, as I'm the one who shot the bear they're having. Have you ever had bear meat, Sergeant? It's fantastic. I often wonder why people don't eat it more often. It's the fat, you see, same as it is with pigs."

Another arrow came through the cloak, this one lower and at an angle. It plunged into the water only a half hand from where Jasper crouched.

"Pull it toward ya," Ilbei hissed at Meggins. "So it touches the wall."

"That other side will be open even worse," Meggins said.

"We'll do this side first."

Another arrow cut through, splitting the difference between the flight path of the last one and the first.

Ilbei motioned with his head for Jasper to get started breaking off fungus along the edge.

The two of them worked furiously. Ilbei scraped the wall beneath the surface with his boot, then used the head of his pickaxe to clear the walls above and the few that grew overhead.

He tried to step around Jasper to get to the back of the

chamber, but the stone was slick where the fungus had been stripped away. He slipped and fell in.

An arrow cut across the side of his neck, though not deep; a cat might have done worse with its claw. Still too close. Ilbei rolled heavily in the water, got his feet under him and dove headlong toward the shelf upon which Mags lay.

Another arrow thudded into the rock at the back of the pool, taking a chunk of Ilbei's left boot heel as it passed.

He landed heavily on Mags. Her body absorbed the shock some, but he bounced on her and began to roll off, back into the water and the line of sight afforded by the gap in the curtain. Kaige reached out and caught him, the muscles of his long arm and broad shoulders bulging as he hauled Ilbei one-handed onto the sloping edge of the pool beside him.

"Tidalwrath's teeth, that was slicin it thin," Ilbei said. "Fine reflexes ya got there, son."

Kaige grinned as he straightened his half of the curtain. "Don't need you full of holes, Sarge."

When Ilbei was back on balance, he noticed Jasper gaping across the pool, aware of what had almost happened and, therefore, again paralyzed with fear. "Jasper," Ilbei said, sharply enough to get the wizard's eyes blinking again. "Get on with it!" He pointed into the water at the glowing fungus.

Looking downstream, Ilbei was relieved to see a slick of the luminous fungal chunks shaping up, big pieces and little bits that whirled in the current like floating dust. Through the gap in the curtain, he could see it moving down the cave, its soft glow gently coloring the walls.

"It's workin," he hissed. "Keep on."

He reached for the giant sword on Kaige's back, and the soldier bent down, angling his shoulders so that Ilbei could slide it free. Ilbei drew it out and cleared the edge of the pool around them, then worked toward the back. He reached across as far as he dared, clearing toward Jasper's half of the pool. He didn't want to expose his hands to Verity through the curtain gap, though he got very close.

He discovered this by the fact that Verity's next shot put a hole through the flat of Kaige's blade, a short, loud clank, as if it had been struck with hammer and punch. He stared at the hole for a moment and cringed. "Ya'd be better off with an ogre kick to the face than to take one of them arrows to anythin." Kaige and Meggins readily agreed.

Ilbei waited until Jasper had cleared off as much of the fungus as he could on his side, then had him slide back over to the safety of the curve where Meggins was. Then he instructed Meggins and Kaige to pull the curtain over to the near side of the hole where he was, and he set to it again with the sword.

Two more arrows came through, one high and one low, the second striking the sword beneath the water. The water slowed it enough that it didn't punch through, but the shock rattled up the sword so violently that Ilbei dropped it into the pool.

Ilbei groped around in the near dark for it. Their progress clearing out the fungus had dimmed the little chamber down significantly. He found the weapon, and with a few more scrapes, he broke loose the last big chunks of fungus, making darkness almost complete. Only little bits here and there remained, crumbs whose light shone in tiny spots like submerged starlight. Ilbei scraped most of those away with his boot. Soon after, it was dark enough that Ilbei dared to wade back across the pond. No arrow came through.

"You think he left?" Meggins asked.

"No. He ain't the sort to leave," Ilbei said.

He leaned out to where he could see through the gap in the makeshift curtain and looked downstream. Verity crouched against the wall on the left side, opposite where Jasper had said he was, but at the same distance. He only knew it was Verity and not some round feature of the rock by the way the green feather on the arrow glowed, the arrow he had nocked and ready to let fly.

There came a hiss right after Ilbei saw it. The curtain moved, and there was a splash in the water. Ilbei jerked back behind cover, but realized as he did that the shot had been nowhere near him.

"Doesn't change anything, Spadebreaker," Verity called. "I'm as comfortable in the dark as you are. Likely a lot more so than your mage."

Ilbei turned to Jasper. "Get the spell out. Let's go."

He couldn't see Jasper's expression until the satchel was open and the small bit of fungus Jasper had kept illuminated his face as he searched.

"Keep that light back if ya can," Ilbei said.

"I still think this is a terrible idea," Jasper said.

"Just do it. Let's go before the light is all washed away." He crossed the pool and gave Kaige back his sword.

Ilbei chanced a glance out through the opening. He could see the last of the fungus they'd broken loose was perhaps twenty paces upstream of Verity. He noticed as he looked that Verity had moved back to the right side of the cave again.

Another arrow whistled past, this one through the opening at the curtain's edge. It missed Ilbei by less than half a hand.

Jasper looked up from his glowing satchel, unfurling a scroll as he did. "Are you ready?"

"Go," Ilbei said.

Jasper began to read as Ilbei pulled his pickaxe over his shoulder and gripped it in both hands. The trailing edge of the glowing fungus floated even with Verity.

Jasper continued to read.

The blue glow moved past Verity and began to fade around the gentle bend.

Jasper read.

"Son of a hydra," Ilbei muttered. Then he was in water halfway to his knees. He heard the hiss of an arrow, felt it by the wind on his face. He ran forward, his feet splashing loudly for three long steps. He knew he was giving himself away, even in the pitch black of the cave. As soon as he thought it, he dove and rolled.

Chunks of shattered stone hit him in the back of the neck. Some went down inside his armor as the sound of the arrow rattled on the stone. He jumped up and ran downstream three more paces, then dove right, rolling up against the side of the cave wall where he hoped the curve began. He used the gurgling of the running water to help him navigate what he hoped was straight.

He heard another arrow strike the stone on the other side of the stream.

He was up again, running around the bend. He saw in silhouette the figure of Verity drawing back his bow, pressing himself against the edge of the cave another twenty paces down, the hunter backlit by the floating fungus washing gently away. Ilbei dove again, and this time the arrow cut through his chainmail at the shoulder, driving several links into his flesh and spinning him all the way around. His pickaxe hit the wall and splashed into the stream.

He made a move to go for it, then leapt across the water, leaving it behind. An arrow plunged into the water where he would have been. He jumped back, grabbed his weapon, then jumped forward again, intentionally splashing the water with his feet. He stepped across quietly and went low, this time creeping silently along the edge, staying out of the water. He could see Verity as a black shape, but growing less and less distinct as the fungus drifted farther and farther away. He wouldn't be able to see him at all very soon. But he knew Verity couldn't see him at all now. It was now or never.

He sprinted forward, holding his pickaxe high. Five steps, six. He knew they were audible. He jumped across the flow of the water, using the dimming light like a guiding star. He saw Verity's elbow move, the barest of movements, an angle of shadow. Ilbei pitched himself forward, headlong into the stream, sliding down the smooth slope of its bed as the arrow whizzed over him. He was on his feet the instant after and saw the shadowy movements of Verity drawing yet another arrow from the quiver on his back. Ilbei flung his pickaxe, end over haft, sprinting forward right after it.

He heard the crack of bone as he approached, the dull, woody splintering of something hollow breaking open. By the time he'd finished the distance between them, Verity had tipped over onto his side and lay pouring out the contents of his head. Soon after, the glowing fungus washed out of range, leaving Ilbei and the body in the dark. He called back to the rest, "That's done it, boys. Nice work."

Chapter 25

With the wan light from Jasper's bit of fungus, he, Meggins and Kaige made their way downstream to Ilbei, Mags cradled in the big man's arms. When they got to Ilbei, Meggins pulled one of their two remaining torches and lit it. It was wet, like the rest of their gear, but with the help of one of Jasper's oil spells, he got it to burn. Doing so brought a gasp from Jasper, for the light illuminated the wreckage of Locke Verity's head, gray bits of brain clumped like curd, spilling into the waterway, an oily residue clouding the water and drifting from his broken skull like seeds from a busted melon, at which point the wizard turned away and retched.

"Hey, do that downstream," Meggins said, though his attention was stolen right after by what he saw. It was not the seeping brain matter that transfixed him. It was Verity's black bow.

Ilbei raised his hand, shielding his eyes as Meggins approached with the torch. He saw immediately where the warrior's eyes had gone. He nodded and kicked the dead hunter over, raising the quiver filled with arrows out of the water for him to see as well. "Too bad these things are so heavy ya can't shoot em," he said. "But the bow is yers if ya can do anythin with it." He turned back to Kaige, who was standing upstream from Jasper still holding Mags in his arms. "Get what you're gonna get, and let's get downstream where we can lay her out long enough fer Jasper to do his fancier spell."

He took the torch from Meggins and went to check on Mags. He leaned down and listened for breath again. The water running past was still too loud, but there was warmth blowing against his face. Not quite willing to be excited by it, he pulled back and stuffed two fingers against her neck, digging in deep enough to feel her pulse. His fingers were too wet and cold, and he couldn't feel anything. He blew on them and then tried a different angle, pressing into her neck again. Still nothing. He tried twice more. Her flesh was wet and clammy, but he told himself it was the water she'd been lying in. Finally he felt it, the barest pulse.

"Her heart's a-thumpin, boys. By the light of sweet Mercy, she might come through yet. Get that stuff gathered up, Meggins." He turned to look at the man, but the soldier already had the bow in his hand and an arrow nocked.

"See there, Sarge. You just got to have the quiver on, or maybe just close." He drew the arrow back as far as he could, then relaxed, not firing. "Draws back easy too. Could have pulled this back when I was twelve."

"Well, ya can brag on yer new prize later," Ilbei said. "Just watch it fer now. Jasper, ya got any of them magic seein spells what can get out ahead of us? Be our luck to finish off Verity here just in time to amble right into the Skewer."

"Oh dear," gasped Jasper, and a long, whining sound issued from his stomach as his intestines churned. "But I don't. I've already told you what I have."

"Well, we need light the way on up ahead, otherwise, we're targets just the same as we were back there."

"I can use my last fireball," Jasper said. "But it will be

gone pretty fast, like the other one."

"How about the oil?" Meggins said. "Like the stuff you used on the torch. That burned, wet and all."

"I'm not sure how that will help," Jasper said.

"Same as the floating fungus did. Can't you light something and float it down the creek?"

"Technically, the oil will float down the creek," Jasper said. "And I suppose it might work." He looked down at the water running by. "I think it will still be moving too fast."

"Not if we run," Ilbei said. "We only need to get her back to the fork where it's dry."

"But that's a long way," Jasper protested. "Do you have any idea how far that is?"

"Yeah, it's an hour. Maybe more. If'n they'd put ya through boot camp proper instead of in the pillory half the time, ya wouldn't be worried none."

"Well, that's just too far." Jasper's voice was high and whining like his guts had been. "We didn't even get a good night's rest."

"I been on three-day drinkin binges what used more energy than what we done so far," Ilbei said. "Mags needs ya to man up, son." He looked past Jasper to Kaige. "Can ya keep up while carryin her?"

"I can keep up," the big man said. "And drag Jasper along too, if I have to."

"Good lad," Ilbei said. "Ya tell me if'n ya need me to spell ya some runnin her."

"I will."

"All right, let's get movin. Go on, Jasper, read yer oil magic."

Jasper studied all three of his upright companions in turn, an expression of horror growing upon his face as he realized they were serious. He would have protested again, but he saw the way that Ilbei began to broaden about the chest and shoulders, preparing for a tirade or perhaps worse.

Jasper wisely let out the breath he'd drawn for his complaint. "Fine," he said. "But if I die of exhaustion or heart failure, you'll have both deaths on your hands."

"I can live with that," Ilbei said. "Now cast."

Shortly after, a tacky patch of flame drifted downstream, spreading and contracting as it went, sometimes stretched very thin and long, other times seeming to pile up against the narrow strip of stone serving as creek bank. Jasper assured them it wouldn't stick to the rock because he hadn't read the spell with the inflection for adhesion but rather with one for a congealing property to keep it from breaking apart. It was an explanation that everyone else ignored as they waited for Ilbei to gauge that the flames were far enough downstream for them to follow at a trot. The command came soon after, and they were off: Meggins in front with the bow ready, Ilbei right after, Kaige and Jasper doing their best to keep up.

Running as they were, they arrived at the branch in the tunnel in a little under an hour, each of them in various stages of breathlessness. At one end of the weariness spectrum was Jasper, wheezing and sounding as if he might collapse and die, and at the other Meggins, who looked as if he'd hardly done more than cross a road.

"Meggins," Ilbei said, as he waited for his wind to return, "follow them flames down another three hundred paces and set yerself on watch. Kaige, go on over there where it's dry and get Jasper goin on Mags. Then grub up and rest a spell."

"But I ain't tired, Sarge."

"Right, and I aim to keep it that way. Ya can take a couple of hours while Jasper works, and then the rest of us will if'n Jasper ain't done yet. I expect he'll need to rest after, likely more than the rest of us, so get to it, boy."

Not long after, Meggins was off, hidden in the darkness downstream, and Kaige was snoring at the edge of the flickering shadows of their single torch, whose illumination was augmented some by the bit of phosphorescent fungus Jasper had.

Propping the torch near the wall, where its golden light reflected dully off the smooth stone, Jasper set himself to work. He pulled out the healing scroll, unfurled it partially and weighted the top portion down upon Mags' ribs with two rocks so that it wouldn't roll back up on itself. They'd had to prop her on her side with her pack still on to accommodate the length of arrow that ran in through it, through her and out through her chest. Jasper was patient enough to watch the stones for a moment to make sure they wouldn't roll off with the movements of Mags' breathing.

Satisfied, he scanned the document carefully, unfurling the spell the rest of the way and discovering the scroll was nearly as long as his tinder-thin arm. Ilbei, watching over his shoulder, not only marveled at its length, he once again marveled how anyone could possibly write so small—much less read such minuscule script in the near dark with only the light of a flickering torch and a scrap of fungus.

Jasper looked up at him and ran a finger across a portion of the scroll about a quarter way down its length. "It says here that an embedded object—that will be the arrow there—will begin to glow. And here, it reads specifically, 'Your assistant must take hold of the object and draw it out before the glow abates.' That, of course, will be for you to do."

"All right," Ilbei said. "But do ya mean the very moment it starts to glow, or is there some kind of sign that it's done glowed bright enough?"

Jasper's mouth opened, a reflexive inclination to talk down to him, no doubt, but he appeared to realize that Ilbei's question was a fair one. He turned back and reread the passage. "No, it just said it will begin to glow. So, if we assume that whoever wrote this scroll employed careful language, then the choice of the word 'begin' was purposeful."

"Well, you're the expert, so assumin is exactly what I'll be doin. When it glows, the first second of it, I'll pull it out." He glanced at the arrow protruding from Mags' chest, then leaned over and studied the feathered back end. "I'll break that off now to make it easier." He reached down and gripped the shaft in his powerful hands and made to snap the last half-hand's length off before Jasper could say anything, but his efforts were to no avail. He'd have had as much success trying to snap an oak tree in two. "I guess we need Meggins back here with that quiver to make it normal like."

"We don't need him. It will come out anyway," Jasper said, clearly annoyed as he held the two rocks in place. "Can you please just do as I ask, and leave the rest to me?"

Ilbei fixed Jasper with a crooked look, digging deep into the wizard's unflinching eyes. The wizard seemed confident, at least in this. "Fine," he said. "Go on, then. I'll wait till that there lights up."

"Good. Be patient. This is going to take a while."

"I heard ya the first time ya said it."

Jasper shrugged. Then, after one more scan down the spell, he began to read, his voice low and level, steady as a song.

Two hours passed before the arrow began to glow, and Ilbei was fighting to keep his eyes open when he realized the light had come. It startled him to full consciousness, and with guilty fear that he'd be too late, he gripped the glowing arrow in one hand, braced the other just below her ribs and drew it out. The effort he thought he'd need was not needed at all, and such was the force of his initial draw that he nearly snapped his arm back and elbowed Jasper in the nose. He caught himself, however, then caught one of the rocks before it could roll off of Mags and set the scroll curling up on itself. But yank he did, and out the arrow came, straight through her body as if it were a thing made of light.

He half expected it to solidify again and drop like a twenty-ton brick, but it didn't. Instead, it hissed and crackled like dried pine needles in a fire, then vanished in a puff of smoke. Ilbei would have praised the young magician on a fine bit of magic, but Jasper was still reading aloud. Which he continued to do for the next four hours.

By the time the spell was cast and Mags was breathing easily, Kaige was up and had relieved Meggins on watch down the tunnel. Ilbei, Jasper and Meggins took a few bites from their stores to refresh themselves, then fell in beside her and took some sorely needed rest.

When he woke, Ilbei guessed it was late morning or early afternoon of the day following their entrance into the cave. They'd been in longer than he'd expected, but at least everyone was healthy and alive. He woke the rest of them, and shortly after, all were on their feet, refreshed to greater or lesser degrees. Mags complained that her chest hurt and that she had a backache. Jasper complained that his back surely hurt worse than hers did, as he hadn't been healed after having to sleep on solid rock, which he continued to moan about for the next few hours as they made their way downstream. He only stopped complaining because, finally, they could see the entrance to the cave, the bright daylight beyond shining like a beacon of all things warm and dry.

"I'll never complain about the heat again," Jasper promised, which of course set Meggins and Kaige to speculating on how long those odds would be. In truth, the sight of the sunlight raised everyone's spirits more than a notch.

Unfortunately, however, upon drawing near the exit, and upon Ilbei's having sent Meggins to check outside in case Verity had stationed any of his crew out there, they had their spirits put right back down where they had been. Lower, really. Sent there by the metallic clatter of a pace-long crossbow bolt that came clattering off the stone, the vicious tip of it only missing Meggins' forehead by the length of an eyelash standing on its end.

He jerked sideways to avoid it, as if by spasm, and he had to fight his way against the current to get back out of the line of fire. He was sputtering and swearing all the while as he scrambled and splashed away from the opening, and as he did, another of the long steel bolts ricocheted off the edge of it and glanced off the hard leather of his armor. It flew up the tunnel and skittered to a stop ten spans beyond the rest of the company. Kaige went and got it as it began rolling down toward the water. He brought it back to Ilbei, who took it from him and shook his head.

"The gods-be-damned Skewer. I knew that bastard was gonna be out there. I knew it like a burnin rash."

Chapter 26

"So what's the Skewer doing out there?" Kaige asked. "Didn't the major say he run off?" The man's brawn and the strong line of his jaw sometimes belied his youth and farm-grown naivety.

"Aye, lad, he did. So either the Skewer come round this way on account of our bad luck, or the major is as low and slimy as a snail's arse."

"I think it might be the second one," Meggins said.

"As do I." Ilbei stroked his beard, and bits of sand and gravel fell out, bouncing off the bulbous projection of his belly, the larger pieces ticking first off his chainmail and again when they fell to the ground. "Ya happen to get a count of em out there?"

"I didn't," Meggins confessed. "I only just saw the movement when the Skewer raised his crossbow. It was all I could do to duck back in time. I think I saw someone else with him, but I got nothing like a count of who all might be out there. Could be no one, could be fifty of them."

"He only had two men with him when we run him off, Sarge," Kaige offered helpfully.

"Right, he did. But no tellin how many he's got now. Major surely gave him reinforcements when he sent him down here with Verity."

"What?" That came from both Kaige and Jasper.

Ilbei shared a look with Meggins, who simply shrugged. Meggins had at least twenty years on the other two, and likely a lot more living in those decades than Jasper or Kaige would have by the same count.

A third long, silvery shaft careened off the edge of the tunnel entrance and cut through the air. It whipped between Ilbei and Meggins and actually puffed Mags' hair, slicing off a few strands just below her ear. They heard it land several spans beyond, followed by the metallic hiss of it sliding deeper into the darkness.

"Back upstream, let's go, let's go," Ilbei said. He put one hand on Meggins' back and the other on Mags', shepherding them both along. When they were out of range, Ilbei shook his head. "By the gods, we're pinned down again. Never seen two archers so mean."

"But they've got damn fine weapons, you have to admit," Meggins said, holding his newly acquired bow out and twisting it in the torchlight. The flames reflected dully off its black surface. It had a thin green line running through one of its composite layers, but Meggins, for all his experience with bows, could not muster a guess at what it might be. It matched the fletching on the arrows though, suggesting the feathers might be treated with something, or not be feathers at all.

"Yes, they do," Ilbei said. "Too fine. Strikes me squirrely to find two weapons what can shoot the moon right outta the sky, and both of em here in a backwoods like Three Tents."

Meggins nodded.

"Perhaps it really is because of the harpies," Jasper said. "As you suggested before."

Ilbei started to scold him for going on about harpies again, but stopped. "What makes ya say that?"

"Well, what else would require such weapons? I've never actually killed one, but I can't imagine you need a thing like that to hunt deer. I've known lots of hunters, and none of them used anything like either of those."

Ilbei scratched his beard again, dislodging more bits of stone in the doing. "You're right, son. He wouldn't. And a man who has resigned hisself to makin his livin off a handful of dirt-poor miners hasn't got no reason to have such a weapon neither. He'd make a fine bit more with that thing workin fer Her Majesty, or fer any of the nobility, whether huntin or mercenary work."

"Well, I did see him leaving the barracks back when I shipped in," Meggins reminded him. "So he was military for a time."

"Right," said Ilbei. "And now he's out here spearin grouse and peahens for copper coins. And right friendly with the major too."

"Maybe they sent him out here to help flush out the counterfeit coins," Mags said. "He's been up at Fall Pools often enough over the last year or so."

"Did he come down to Camp Chaparral much?"

"On occasion. There weren't enough of us to feed, so he didn't come by often. But I saw him a few times. We bought a boar from him for Candalin's last birthday. She turned one hundred and sixty-five."

"Not bad fer a commoner and a blank," Ilbei said. "Especially livin out here with no casters healin folks."

"Too bad it turned out to be her last," Mags observed.

"Aye." Ilbei looked down for a moment. He regarded the panniers sitting next to Jasper's trunk, all of which they'd retrieved before their attempt to exit the cave. He jerked his head right back up. "Speakin of that, and just so as it matters to ya all, and in the event I get one of them steel spits between my eyes, them other coin molds ain't gone to Hast like I told the major back there. I put em in with poor old

Candalin. The dirt was fresh dug, so I buried em down a half span."

"You mean you lied to Major?" Kaige said. He looked disappointed and surprised.

"Aye, Kaige, that I did. But only as he's been lyin to us since day one. And I figured if'n things worked out right, we'd make what I told him true enough in time."

Kaige thought about that for a while and seemed mollified. Mainly. It was obvious to all who observed that his particular notion of reality was being shifted sideways considerably.

The metallic scrape of another crossbow bolt sliding across the stone sounded a few paces downstream.

"Well, we can't stand here all day. We need to figure a way out of here." He nodded to the trunk filled with Jasper's scrolls. "Jasper, ya got all yer spells back now, what do ya have that can get us out of here? Can ya teleport me, Meggins and Kaige behind them fellers out there so as we can sneak up on em and clear a path?"

"Not without getting much closer to the entrance," Jasper said.

"Well, I'll stand in front of ya while ya cast. I can use that trunk of yers to shield us some."

"I still only have fifty spans, you know. And we are twenty spans up the wall. How far away was the Skewer from there?" Jasper looked at Meggins as he spoke.

"Maybe twenty or so down from where the creek turns down the hill," Meggins replied.

"Well, if he doesn't have any more men down there, I think it might work."

"Can't ya look first? Don't ya have them seein spells?"

"I do!" Jasper went to the trunk and started looking through it, using his bit of fungus to light the inside. He muttered what served him as epithets, cursing Kaige for shuffling them all around, but eventually he pulled a proper seeing spell out. "All right, let's go have a look." He actually seemed giddy about casting it.

They waited in silence as Jasper read the spell, his eyes seeming to stare at the words and at nothing simultaneously. After several long minutes of this, he stopped chanting and blinked. "Well, they certainly spare *every* expense with these things. I'm beginning to think the only spells of any value in that whole box are the ones I wrote myself."

"What did ya see?" Ilbei asked.

"There are six of them out there. The Skewer is where Meggins said he would be, and there's another man with a crossbow as well, although not like that one the Skewer has. The rest are down where the shale gives way, not far from the second harpy corpse. And before you ask, no, I can't get you behind them."

"How about above? Can ya get us up top?"

"I didn't look up top. But I think it's too high. And these seeing spells are terrible. I don't think the seer was ranked higher than a G. No wonder the outlands here are in chaos. If this is all the army cares to spend when it sends out a patrol, it's hardly a surprise."

Ilbei did not hide his impatience. "Well, you're gonna look anyway."

Jasper was clearly irritated as he went back into the chest to pull out another seeing scroll. He found one, and once again went to work. When he was done, he came back to the group with a look of triumph on his face. "You see, I told you. It's too high. I couldn't teleport you to the top with these shoddily written scrolls if I jumped before casting them. I should like to place a formal complaint about it, and as you are my immediate superior, I will register it with you. The slapdash workmanship is simply inexcusable."

"Noted," Ilbei said, in part to silence the complaint but, to a degree, in agreement with him as well. While there were some advantages to having a scroll mage along—technically giving Ilbei and anyone fighting alongside Jasper the benefit of access to spells from all eight magical schools, like having an Eight, really–the disadvantage was that the range and power of the magic available seemed to be all over the place, and mainly on the short side. His mustache twitched for a time as he thought about Jasper's report. "I reckon that don't help us much."

"You said you heard voices back there where Verity had us pinned down," Meggins offered. "Must be something close enough around. Now that we got Jasper's trunk with us, we could go back."

"Aye, we could. But I got a nasty feelin that it's the major and his boys in that cave."

"How do you figure that?"

"Well, Mags here says there is only three places where there's water along the steppe. Given we gone about as far up that cave as we come down along the rock face earlier; and given that crack I was listenin to run down into the pool; and given that the pool in the ettin cave done filled itself through the roof and was ringed with the same glowin stuff as we cleared out, it seems likely enough that that there pool we was waylaid in is the source of the one below."

Mags was nodding even before Meggins did. "So we know where we are at least," he said.

"Aye, we're havin to choose which bunch of Major's crooks we want to fight our way through. And that's assumin Jasper there can sight us through the rocks and get us through with that infernal teleport." He shuddered thinking about it. Bad enough to have it done to him once already.

"We could look up the other tunnel," Mags suggested. "There must be an opening. Water ran through it at some point, so it had to come from somewhere."

"Well, we don't know that's the case no more," Ilbei said. "All this could have been cut out a thousand years ago or more, and that one might a' gone dry by collapse any time since."

"Yes, but that vinegar smell you're talking about means there's something rotting up there. That didn't happen a thousand years ago, or it would be gone by now. And even if I am wrong on that, there's still a chance it might run us up closer to the surface. Even a thousand years ago, the water still had to come from somewhere, and the odds are decent the source is snowmelt and rain from above. If we're lucky, it might even bend nearer to the northern face of the mountains, where they look out toward the Sandsea. If we take enough water with us before we go out, we could make it to Hast by skimming along the desert's southern edge."

"Well, I'll take my chances with the heat over the major and whatever tricks he's got up his nobleman's cuffs, that's sure," Ilbei said. "It's worth a look."

They gathered their equipment, loading poor Kaige like a pack mule, and headed once again deeper into the mountainside. Meggins trailed behind, keeping watch for pursuit, and Ilbei led the way, the torch held out and seeming to drive the darkness before them, the black spot of it retreating steadily down the tunnel like a cork being drawn out of a bottle that might never end. They reached the fork in the passage, and Ilbei wasted no time moving up the right-hand branch. He turned back long enough to see what Kaige was cussing about and discovered the big man was forced to stoop now, making carrying Jasper's trunk and one of the panniers more difficult.

Kaige saw Ilbei looking and said he was fine. His eyes sparkled in the dancing light of the torch in a way that told Ilbei he meant it, despite the profanity. Ilbei nodded and looked beyond him. "You still with us back there, Meggins?" Ilbei called.

"I am, Sarge," came the reply.

Onward they went. The slope was barely perceptible for some time, and after an hour and a half, Ilbei thought Mags might have been too optimistic when she suggested this passage would lead them to the top of the steppe, or even just near enough for Jasper to get them teleported out. But, gradually, and before he decided to voice his skepticism, the incline grew steeper and more promising again, so steep that, for nearly a quarter measure, it became slick and precipitous. They scrabbled and clawed their way up, Ilbei having to pull Kaige along in places, with Mags shoving him from behind. Even with their cooperation, it was all they could do not to slide right back down again. But finally the stony slide gave way to a slope so gradual it seemed nearly level again, and Ilbei wondered if they'd climbed high enough to be close to the surface yet. Hoping that they had, he asked Jasper to try another one of the seeing scrolls to have a look around.

Not only were they not at the surface, they were somewhere deep enough in the mountain that Jasper couldn't even run his magically enhanced vision out into anything. "It's all black," the sorcerer reported when he was finished with the spell. "Solid stone everywhere except up ahead. At least for as far as I can see." This was followed by another long diatribe about the low quality of the standard-issue army scrolls, which Ilbei didn't bother to silence and rather just waved everyone along, onward up the passageway.

Eventually the cave bent in a direction Ilbei believed was taking them southwest, deeper into the mountain rather than toward the north and the desert beyond. He was about to call a halt when, just like that, the cave ended in an oblong chamber not unlike the space Verity had trapped them in at the end of the other passage, though larger by half again. This one, however, had no small pool and no glowing fungus. Nor was there any fermenting anything to explain the vinegar smell that filled the air. It was strong enough now that everyone could smell it, and Meggins, upon finally catching up to them, came into the chamber making a lemon-eater's face. "A damn fine place you led us to, Sarge. Smells worse than those heaps of rotting grape skins out back of Gallenwood wineries."

"Well, I expect them didn't smell quite like this here. Whatever it is, it's worse than some rottin grape skins or vinegar. This here is somethin else." Ilbei held the torch out and examined the wall all around. All told, the chamber wasn't more than five paces across, and it wasn't tall enough to allow poor Kaige to stretch himself. Jasper, next in height amongst them, could only stand upright in places, and those with his hair brushing the rock.

Ilbei went round the chamber twice, looking for where water might once have come in, but he couldn't find any obvious cracks or openings.

He handed the torch to Mags and closed his eyes, trying to smell his way to where the source of the vinegar stench came through, but it was so strong that he couldn't find any place stronger than all the rest.

Mags followed him around the room as he sniffed, the torchlight casting a long shadow of him up the wall.

"Well that don't make no sense," Ilbei said at length. "It ain't comin from nowhere."

"I'll tell you what doesn't make sense," Jasper said. "Look at this over here." He was leaning close to the rock and shining his bit of blue fungus up and down. "Mags, bring the torch, if you please. The blue light may be illuminating something."

Mags brought it to him. He took it, stepped away from the stone and held the torch out near where he'd been. He squinted at the wall, then moved the torch to the left, once again squinting and scrutinizing something there. He went back and forth, then brought the torch near where he'd started. He raised it upward, then around, then down, until at length he'd described a roughly egg-shaped patch.

"Look here," he said. "Come feel how rough this is." Mags

did as he asked, as did Meggins, who was standing closest by. "Now feel over here." He brushed his fingers down the cavern wall near where the cave came in, a long swipe like a prolonged caress. Mags and Meggins did likewise. "Feel the difference?" He went to the opposite side of the chamber, where Ilbei stood. Again he swept his fingers down the wall. "It's the same here. Smooth as can be. But not over there." He went back to where he'd started, rubbed the stone and shook his head. "Definitely not the same."

Ilbei touched the wall near where Jasper had been only moments before. It felt exactly like what he'd expected it would: cool, hard stone, slightly undulating but polished smooth by the passage of water and time. He went to the place where Jasper was leaning down close with the torch. Jasper looked up at his approach and pointed. "There, try it there."

Ilbei did. It felt rougher than the other spot. More like brick than polished stone.

"Now how do you suppose that should happen?" Jasper asked.

"A cave ooze would do it," Ilbei guessed. "I've seen small ones creepin around in mines and caverns before. They do somethin like that. They leach minerals out fer food—when they ain't droppin on a man and suckin his juices dry."

"I too am familiar with oozes. When I was thirteen, I wrote a paper on them and submitted it to the *Royal Journal of Mining* in Crown. It was rejected, of course, because I haven't got a noble name, but the work was thorough as can be."

"So with all of that there wind, are ya sayin we got oozes to worry about?"

"No, that's precisely what I'm *not* saying."

"Jasper, if Ilbei doesn't come squeeze it out of you, I'll do it myself," Meggins said. "By the gods, just tell us what you mean."

"This is a plug." Jasper turned as he made the announcement and tried to cross his arms over his chest triumphantly, but holding the torch made it impossible, which he realized belatedly. An awkward moment followed, but he adjusted himself, turned sideways and assumed a haughty stance instead.

"Jasper," Ilbei threatened, "get on with the rest of it, or I'll let Meggins have at ya."

"Oh, fine. You're all perfectly fine running off into the darkness throwing pickaxes through people's skulls or lurking around rearguard in the pitch black all alone with fancy magic bows, but when I do something of value, it becomes simply, 'Go on, Jasper, just say what you mean.'"

"That's right, son, it does. So, please, I'm even askin nice. What kind of plug do ya mean?"

Jasper was appeased by Ilbei's "please," so he went on as if nothing had occurred between his original statement and his next. "This is melded stone, and not done very well, I'll tell you. A second-year student at the transmuter's academy could have done a better job with only a rank of E."

Ilbei hummed, low in his chest. "So the plug is where someone sealed up the hole where the water come through?"

Jasper rolled his eyes, but he said, "Yes."

"Which side were they on when they done it?"

Jasper's eyebrows rode high upon his forehead, and he stood tall, proudly erect, as he was finally being appreciated for his expertise. He bumped his head against the ceiling with a thud, which forced him to stoop again. Worse, after thinking on the question for a moment, he had to admit he didn't know. He looked wounded when he said it.

"Well, how about ya go on and have a look through on the other side," Ilbei said. "Ya got more of them seein spells, don't ya?"

The young sorcerer's pride was resuscitated by Ilbei's continued need of him, and he went to his chest of scrolls, sifting through them for a seeing spell. He appeared to find one, but kept looking through the collection for a time after. "Oh dear, we've only got two left," he announced.

"Well, get to it with one of em," Ilbei said. "We need to get out of here while there's still time." He turned to Meggins. "Go on back a ways and keep an eye out fer that brigand with the spear-throwin crossbow."

Meggins vanished into the darkness.

Jasper set himself to work reading his magical sight spell, and the rest of them waited impatiently. Mags closed the lid on Jasper's chest of magic and sat on it, resting her head in her hands. Ilbei felt bad for her and knew she was likely still in considerable pain. A healing spell that reversed the type of damage she'd had likely didn't set her body fully right in a single day, much less a day of tramping around in caves. Ilbei had been seen often enough by gifted army healers to know that even the best spells still required rest if the injuries were severe enough.

Jasper's voice began to elevate as he read through the spell. At first none of them paid any attention to it, assuming it was normal, but soon it was clear that something was agitating the scrawny wizard, as his breathing became increasingly rapid with each passing word. It was as if they were watching him having a nightmare.

"Should I wake him up, Sarge?" Kaige asked, reaching out with a giant hand, ready to do it.

"No," Ilbei snapped. "Ya might scramble his brains worse than they already are."

Kaige jerked his hand away, his face drawn back as if someone were pulling hard at the back of his scalp. "Sorry, Jasper," he whispered. He clapped his hand over his own mouth for fear of waking him with even that.

Shortly after, Jasper gasped and turned wide eyes around the room. "There's a light," he said. "And a creek falling down into a widening cavern. And I think there are lots of harpies in there. I couldn't get this sad excuse of a three-copper seeing spell to carry me down far enough to confirm it, and there wasn't quite enough light, but I'm sure I saw several lying on ledges along the walls."

"Well, if'n ya couldn't confirm it, what makes ya think it's harpies lyin there?"

"Because there are two dead ones on the other side of that wall."

Chapter 27

The stone Jasper discovered sealing the end of the tunnel turned out to be porous and easily broken through, or at least, easily when assaulted with the brute force and practiced hand of Ilbei Spadebreaker and his miner's pick. Both were long acquainted with that kind of work. Once again Jasper enchanted Ilbei's pickaxe blades with the Tooth of the Leviathan spell, the original cast having long faded away—the recognition of which had, of course, set Jasper off on another long, rambling soliloquy about the poor quality of army-issue scrolls and how one day he would show Ilbei what a proper version ought to look like.

Despite Jasper's discontent, it was only a matter of two short hours before Ilbei had beaten through the transmuted patch of stone and knocked enough out that he could squeeze through. He did not go in right away, however, for the vinegar stench was something awful on the other side, and added to it was the reek of another kind, the foul odor that none of them had experienced before, some combination of rotting flesh and raw sewage and filth of an inexplicable description. Before opening the wall, they'd only had a hint of it, mixing with the vinegar in a vague sort of way that ought to have forewarned them. But once Ilbei bashed out the last bit of separation with his pick, the odor was upon them in full. They fell away together, as if on command, all of them gasping and waving their hands before their faces in futile attempts to abate the acridity of the stench.

"By the gods," Ilbei choked, fumbling for a handkerchief that he kept stuffed in a pouch on his belt. He pressed it against his face, his eyes watering, the putrescence filling the chamber with a palpable humidity like sweat when there are too many bodies in a hot room. "What can it be?"

"I already told you," Jasper said. "There are dead harpies in there. How else did you think it was going to smell? And if there are dead ones, there are likely live ones nearby. And since we've already determined that none of you are fond of reading, you may not know that harpies nest in their own excrement, layer upon layer. The whole thing is porous, with each layer drying out and creating a sponge-like foundation for the next. Fluids run through to the bottom, and the whole thing compresses under the weight of the layer above in perpetuity, the outflow of effluence eroding the lowest layers but the uppermost layers replacing what is lost. That is why the odor is constant and fresh. It's actually a very ingenious strategy, exemplifying great efficiency and conservation of resources, though I understand that the small bones of the creatures they eat are everywhere in the nest, and they tend not to pick them out, so they lie in them, which causes sores that often fester and add to the odious smell."

Ilbei might have complained or cut the didactic mage off on that, but he hadn't read any of it, and figured it might not hurt to know. "All right, so it stinks. Is it gonna make us sick? I ain't keen on us dyin of some disease halfway across the Sandsea with no help to come. Ya said before ya ain't got nothin in that there box of yers fer no harpy disease."

"Well, if you'll recall, I told you that I believe I can stave off any harpy diseases if we don't let them set in." Jasper made the ticking sound he sometimes issued when he was weary of inferior intelligence. His confidence had risen—and his abiding wariness of harpies inexplicably dissolved—in the pleasure of having been allowed to speak as an expert once again. "At very least, I believe I can hold off symptoms with what I have long enough to get us back to Hast. You really should pay attention more closely when I explain these things the first time."

Meggins laughed as he watched Ilbei's left eye begin to twitch. "Jasper, you got anything to stave off a pickaxe to the head?" he asked. Jasper glanced to Meggins, then back to the sergeant, and he realized that he'd let his mouth get ahead of his mind for a moment. Fortunately, Ilbei had moved on to other things.

Satisfied that disease was not an immediate problem, Ilbei set down his pick and went to the hole he'd made, the handkerchief firmly mashed against his nose. He wriggled into the hole and pulled himself through it far enough so that he could see what was beyond. It was just as Jasper had described: a distant light ahead and slightly to his right, the stream off to his left pouring over the ledge of an escarpment, and below the opening, at the bottom of the escarpment, lay two harpies, dead as an old pair of boots. But Ilbei didn't think the foul odor was coming from them. With his head inside, and despite the overwhelming smell of vinegar, the other odor, the putrescent one, was worse, far worse, and well beyond the simple stench of death. His eyes watered, and it was all he could do not to throw up. He gagged a few times anyway.

He put the handkerchief away, as it did nothing to help, and forced himself to suffer it as best he could. He steeled himself and took a look around. To his immediate left, a waterway not much bigger than the one they'd been wading through the day before emerged through an opening in the stone and shot out over an abrupt drop. The drop was obviously man-made, which came as a mild surprise. It didn't take a man of Ilbei's groundbreaking experience to recognize that the stream had once bent round toward the hole he'd just unplugged, which was clearly the original, and natural, course for its flow. Someone had come and cut through the mountain and diverted the water away.

The hole Ilbei had widened allowed him to crawl along that upper edge to where the water plunged down. From that vantage, he looked out over the escarpment at a long, narrow cavern that someone had gone to great lengths to cut. It bent right, then left, ultimately moving off toward the dim source of illumination that seemed very far away. The stream itself jetted out from the opening near him, then bounced over and down a series of unnatural outcroppings, jagged ledges and crumbling stone heaps, all angling down, all of them forming a steep declivity that wouldn't have occurred naturally and, therefore, had to be remnants of excavation. Whoever had cut the channel had been more concerned with speed and utility than symmetry or easy access to the water source. Despite that, the work had been considerable all the same.

The stream splashed loudly and steadily down the ragged slope as it fell away, its sound mixing with a faint but distinctive clang of metal on stone in the distance, the symphony of at least a hundred picks, shovels and hammers pounding against rock somewhere ahead, a song Ilbei was well familiar with. The water flowed toward the sound, dropping twenty spans vertically over the course of sixty horizontal spans before it flowed out of sight, dropping over a ledge and traveling off toward the faint light and the sound of excavation work.

Looking down the stream toward the dim glow, Ilbei saw a bright flare of golden firelight illuminating the farthest wall, the source somewhere around the bend. It came on suddenly and remained that way for several minutes, flickering but brilliant, like the breathing of a dragon in the distance. Whatever and wherever the source was, it had to be big and very hot. But then it was gone, leaving in its place the fainter but constant glow from before, the sort of glow that made Ilbei think of a distant town, though he knew it to be unlikely given where he was, so deep in the mountain. He watched for a while with that in mind, but seeing that nobody came around the bend, Ilbei turned back and motioned for Meggins to hand him his pickaxe. He crawled back along the ledge and looked through the hole to his companions. "Come on, people; I'm guessin this here is the way out."

One by one, he helped pull the rest of the group up and through the hole. Once everyone was through, they began the treacherous descent, slipping over the edge of one blocky, black ledge to the next, stumbling down short slopes of loose rock, each drop made dangerous by the slicking mist that the falling water set upon everything.

As they climbed down, Ilbei noticed a gray layer along the ledges across the wall, a coating that lay upon the flat surfaces like ash. In the moments during which the brightest light flared and flashed, he thought he saw man-shapes on some of them, lying flat as if sleeping there. "I think there's harpies over there," he said. "A couple of em way up on that far wall."

"Of course there are," Jasper said. "I already told you I saw them there. Don't you see the bed of excrement on the ledges? Don't you ever listen to me? Someday you're going to miss something important, and that will be the day when—"

"Pipe down, mage, or you'll have the lot on us." Ilbei growled the words, low and through gritted teeth.

"Jasper, you sure got over your fear of harpies fast enough," Meggins observed. "You know, when we first got here, the mention of one of them nearly set you to wetting yourself."

"I did not wet myself," Jasper protested. "And even if I had, it would certainly be understandable. Harpies are vicious, human-eating creatures riddled with disease and vermin, which also carry disease. Anyone in their right mind is afraid of harpies if they are alone in the wilderness, away from proper medical care."

"Well, you had medical spells in your bag all along. So why did you suddenly find your spine now?"

"My spine was never missing, but if you must know, I find them much less intimidating without their wings."

"Without their wings? You mean those harpies up there haven't got any wings?"

"No, they don't, at least not that I could see. Neither do these two, in case you didn't notice." He pointed to the two harpy corpses he'd spotted when casting the seeing spell. The company had descended far enough that they could see the bodies more closely. Meggins cocked an eyebrow, and his upper lip curled as he gazed upon the corpses, both with hacked-off wings and one with enough flesh rotted away that the remnants of its face sneered up at them. Jasper appeared burdened by having had to point them out.

Ilbei looked away from the ledge where he'd been contemplating the man-shapes and gazed upon the two corpses lying only a few paces away. Sure enough, they had no wings, like one of the two they'd found at first. Unlike that one, however, each of these appeared to have died with a sledgehammer in its hand. Ilbei jumped down and pushed the nearer of the two over, revealing a long steel crossbow bolt in its skull, the silvery shaft having been hidden beneath a film of dust. Searching the other revealed it also had one, a shot through its ribs that had penetrated deep enough to pierce both lungs. "The Skewer's been in here," he said unnecessarily. "I wish I knew what in the nine hells is goin on."

"Well, Sarge," said Meggins, "I have a feeling we'll find out when we see what's over there in the light."

Ilbei was half-tempted to turn back, but he didn't. The hope of something better ahead, even in the unknown, was preferable to the certainty of something nasty where they had already been. So down they went.

Soon enough, they made it to the rough-cut bottom of the man-made cavern, which grew in size as they moved along until it was clear that they'd come into the upper reaches of a natural cavern instead. The former had clearly been added to the latter through the labor of men bent on getting to the stream—an advanced bit of planning and engineering, Ilbei noted silently.

Moving on, they approached the bend around which the light came, treading cautiously and waiting until the latest bright flare of light dimmed down. Ilbei peered first around it to see what was beyond.

The floor of the natural cavern they had come into fell away abruptly, dropping another seventy spans, this time straight down. The stream plunged over it and fell in a long white ribbon where it crashed to the floor below. As it flowed away from the base of the rock face, it painted a black stripe across the bottom of the now very large cavern, which was at least a half measure long and a quarter measure wide. The stream vanished around another leftward bend and disappeared.

The walls of the cavern were riddled with mine shafts, angled into the rock and clearly abandoned, given there were no ladders or long flumes anywhere nearby. Ilbei knew exploratory excavations when he saw them, and oh, what a scale this exploration had been on. How could he possibly never have heard of this work? Jasper's expression showed that he was thinking the same thing, clearly having never read anything of it in his mining journals or books. Ilbei knew that if he had, the pedantic wizard would be babbling on about it just then. Which meant, it had to be a secret. And no small one. And what's more, it damned sure wasn't an operation bent on copper or lead.

"What is it, Sarge?" Kaige asked. Having grown up on a farm, he had no experience with mining, but it was apparent in the way both Ilbei and Jasper stared out into the open space that something was unusual. Meggins' expression suggested he was interested to hear what answer came.

"If'n that there ain't a gold mine of the most modern make, then I'm the royal assassin and Jasper here is the Queen."

"It might be silver," Jasper said. "The royal silver mines in southern Great Forest are equally vast. Unfortunately, given that that sad D-class seeing spell wouldn't allow me to get this far, much less any farther, I couldn't tell you which, making either guess as likely as the other."

"Ya might be right, Jasper," Ilbei said, "but—" He cut himself off when a wave of people, small in the distance, moved together out from behind the bend at the far end, hustling in a tight group into the center of the cavern, looking like a foamy wave washing up a beach. The wave stopped halfway across and did not rush back right away. Right after came the bright flare of fire from around the bend. The little figures waited together, motionless, as the bright light filled the cavern. When it was gone, the wave of them returned to the sea of their unseen origins, running out of view as one. Something hissed briefly a short time after, and once more the air was filled with the sound of metal on stone.

"Well, one thing is sure," Meggins said. "Whoever they are, if they all got in here, there's a way for them to get out."

"So we can too," Kaige added.

"Aye, lad, we can," Ilbei agreed. "But first we got to get down this here cliff. That's quite a drop down there."

He lay on his stomach and crawled to the edge, where he

peeked over and looked for an easy way down. A little past halfway was a narrow ledge that ran twelve or so paces along the cliff face. He drew back and got to his feet again.

"There's a ledge breakin it up," he said. "I got my rope, and Kaige still has his. We ain't used Jasper's yet either, so we'll still have one when we're done."

"Why don't Jasper send us with his teleport spell?" Kaige asked, appearing very happy to have had such a clever idea.

Ilbei had to force himself not to snap at him, realizing there was nothing wrong with the suggestion—other than Ilbei's hatred of teleporting. It was one thing to teleport out of real danger, but letting himself be dissolved and reappeared to avoid a simple thing like climbing was too unsettling for thought. If his life was going to be at stake, he'd rather trust himself to hammer his own stake into a rock face and climb down like a man. But the basilisk was already out of the bag, so to speak, so he waited to see what Jasper had to say.

It seemed that the sweet goddess Mercy shined her love down on Ilbei, for Jasper sadly pronounced, "I've got four more. Not enough to get everyone down all the way, and only enough to get four down to that first ledge." It was all Ilbei could do not to shout for joy.

"Well, that's just hard luck on us, boys and girls," he said, so as not to let his relief be known. "Now let's get to it. That wall ain't gonna climb itself."

Jasper frowned and seemed to wonder how that made any sense, while Meggins secured Kaige's rope to an outcropping of stone, and Ilbei put his weapons and gear in order. Ilbei looped his own rope around his shoulders and tucked several pitons and a hammer into his belt. He tied the rope Meggins handed him around his waist, then nodded for Kaige and Meggins to lower him down. Soon he was inching down the wall like a four-legged spider in chainmail and a steel hat.

He came down gently on the ledge and saw as he did that there was an opening in the cliff a few paces from where he stood. The ledge was just wide enough that he could make his way to it. He inched toward it, quietly, his back pressed to the rock. When he was at the opening, he peered around the edge, but the entry gave way only to blackness. Blackness and the reek of harpy filth. He suddenly knew what the indescribable odor was. He didn't have to ask anyone, he didn't even have to see a harpy. He'd caught enough of a whiff from the dead ones to know what it was. And now he knew what it smelled like in concentrate. He'd never forget it either. Olfactory stains like that don't erase from memory.

He pulled back, mainly to catch his breath, but also intent on waiting for the next flare of fire so he could see farther inside. But from inside the darkness came a low, throaty rasp that made him reconsider.

Ilbei looked back up the cliff at his companions as he drew his pickaxe. Kaige was just preparing to start down, but Ilbei gave him the signal to wait. He gripped the weapon firmly and laid his arm across his chest, prepared for a vicious backhanded strike if anything untoward should poke its head out of the cave.

Nothing did, however, and after several heart-pounding moments, the rasp was gone. The light at the far end of the cavern flared again. Ilbei watched in its brilliance as once again the cluster of small figures ran out into the open and stood together patiently. He contemplated them for a few moments, then decided to risk another look into the opening. He couldn't bring his people down until he knew what was in there making that noise.

He inched back to the edge of the opening and, before the bright light went out, he chanced another look.

She dove at him with her claws out, human hands, but long-fingered and taloned at the end where slender fingernails ought to have been. She rushed out in a wind of wings, a flurry of feathers that might once have been gray but were mainly brown and black with filth. The hissing rasp was the same as it had been before, but louder, and she was upon him with gaping mouth and gnashing teeth.

He was too close to swing his pickaxe properly and only managed an elbow strike. It struck her in the chest, soft tissue and bone beneath, the bared breasts of a woman, though grimy and caked with filth. She shrieked but came on anyway, the force of her leap and the power of her wings driving her forward. She grappled him as she dove, clawing at his face and wrapping her powerful legs around him, pulling him into her, as her teeth strove for his throat. His helmet tumbled down, bouncing once with a clang against the cliff.

Her momentum swung them out from the side of the rock face together, Ilbei still tethered to the ledge above. They flew out over the cavern floor some forty spans down. He thrust his hand between his throat and her face, his palm against her chin, and snapped her mouth shut, pushing her head back. His pickaxe fell away right after, chasing his helmet. He had to let it go in order to catch her wrist and tear away a clawed hand that was digging deep gouges into the back of his neck. Her breath was hot and moist against the side of his face, reeking foul with carrion and decay.

"By the gods," he spat. "Get off me, demon!" He let go her wrist and punched her twice in the side of the head, shaking loose a cloud of dust and a smattering of lice, some of which wriggled beneath the shirt he wore underneath his mail. She hissed again, trying to straighten her head for another bite, but Ilbei clutched her in his powerful grip, squeezing her jaw, pressing her cheeks in between her teeth as he bent her head back all the more, so much so that he could see the lump in her throat and the tendons at her neck drawing taut beneath the soft, filthy skin.

"I'll break yer head right off," he snarled at her. "By the

gods, I will. Lay off, or I'll open ya up like a stein."

Her free hand struck out, a downward swat, and her nails cut down the side of his face, narrowly missing his eye. She coughed twice and spat something warm and gray into the air. The motion of their swinging carried Ilbei right through the spray. Whatever it was she spat arced up, thick and heavy, gray like a dead mouse, and landed in his hair.

She gripped his throat with the hand that had raked his face, her taloned fingers nearly long enough to wrap all the way around his neck, and he had to let go of her head to pull that grip away. She slammed her forehead into his, so hard they were both dazed. He shook the dimness off just before she did, and was about to grab her by the tangled mass of her long black hair when they hit the cliff face hard. They spun on impact, and the stone ground against his back, catching on the tools he'd tucked in his belt, which in turn sent him and his harpy attacker spinning, rolling together against the stone as the rope swung them along it, bouncing and scraping like cheese on a grater.

But they were moving up. He realized that Kaige and Meggins were reeling him in, bringing the fight to where they could lend a hand. Thank the gods!

Inspired by the knowledge that help was on the way, or at least that he was on the way to help, he tried again to grab her by the hair. But she was coming to her senses as well, and once again the claw raked down the side of his face, the same side, the ripping strike crossing the first set of tears and splitting part of his ear. She spat into his eyes, blinding him, and she made the choking cough sound again, something wet in her throat, then sent another wet mouse-mass at him, this time straight into his face.

Blindly, he groped for her hair and yanked her head back. Better the claws than whatever the hell that was she was spitting. Or at least he hoped.

He heard Meggins say, "Keep hold, I'll get her." Then

came a dull thump, two blunt sounds like a rock on muscle and bone, but muffled some. The harpy shrieked, and Ilbei felt strong hands grip his arm. Another, smaller pair of hands grabbed him on the other side. Then he was being dragged up and over the cliff's edge.

Her legs around his waist released, and a great wind blew on him right after. Dust and sand and bits of gravel pelted him. The harpy shrieked. Meggins shouted and cursed. "Evil bitch," he snarled. Mags shouted something as well. The harpy shrieked again, but the sound of it, loud at first, rapidly diminished, as with distance. Ilbei wiped at his eyes, blinking through the haze of filth, and saw the blurry wingspan of the harpy as it soared out over the cavern below.

"By the gods," Ilbei said.

"No shite, by the gods," Meggins agreed.

"Quick, quick," Jasper said, his face looming suddenly at Ilbei from one side. "Open your eyes." He began dumping water in Ilbei's face. For a moment Ilbei sputtered and moved to fight him off, but realized immediately what Jasper was about. He held still and let himself be ministered to. "Hold them open," Jasper ordered. "Stop closing them."

Ilbei hadn't realized he had been. "Sorry, then," he said, but Jasper pried one of Ilbei's eyes open with his fingers, roughly, and dumped more water in it.

"Now the other," the wizard said. He repeated the process with Ilbei's other eye. He dumped more water into the sputtering sergeant's face, wiping at the cuts with a cloth. From there, the mage treated the cuts on Ilbei's neck and arms, each meticulously and in turn. He didn't stop until he was satisfied by whatever measure was operating in him. When that was done, he sought one of the quicker healing scrolls from his satchel and read it in Ilbei's cause.

The reading took several long minutes, all the while Meggins pacing back and forth along the edge of the cliff, his newly acquired bow ready to shoot anything that flew near. But the reading was fairly short as healing went, and it wasn't too long before the cuts on Ilbei's face, neck and arms closed, though they remained puffy and red.

When Jasper was done, he set himself to rolling up the spent scroll without so much as a second look. Ilbei watched him and couldn't help but grin. "Thank ya, son," he said.

"I'm not done," Jasper replied, stuffing the rolled parchment into his satchel. He asked Meggins for his waterskin. After receiving it, he poured that over Ilbei's head. He then combed through the sergeant's thinning gray hair roughly with his fingers for a while. "Is that all the water we have?"

"No, here's mine," Mags said, handing over hers. "But that's the last of it."

Ilbei was doused and roughly cleaned some more, but just when he thought Jasper's ministrations were through, Jasper leaned down and looked him square in the eye. "Did you swallow any of that?"

"Of what? The water or what she spat?"

"Either."

"I don't know." He couldn't recall. It seemed likely that he had, but he wasn't sure of it. He didn't remember opening his mouth.

"Then vomit."

"What?"

"Vomit. Use your fingers. If they aren't long enough, use this." He knelt and rummaged through his cast-off pack, pulling out a piece of steer jerky that was a few fingers wide and twice as long as his hand, standard-issue field rations. He folded it in half lengthwise and stuffed it into Ilbei's hand. "Don't eat it. Jam it down your throat until you throw up."

"But, I ...," Ilbei started.

"Sergeant, do you have any idea what harpy disease can

do?"

"Ya said ya have scrolls. And ya just read one."

"I do, and I did. That one I just read was basic growth healing. The other will need an onset disease to have anything targetable, and that assumes it even works for this. We've already been over this twice. Do you really want to wait for symptoms, or would you rather try to prevent them?"

Ilbei growled and set his worst frown on the bossy young wizard, but he took the jerky and went off for a bit of privacy in the dark. He kept at plunging the jerky down his throat, sliding it around the bend at the back of his tongue until his stomach cramped and his intestines convulsed. He kept doing it until his abdominal muscles hurt. Finally, when it was done and his eyes ran with the tears of the stomach spasms he'd given himself, he returned to Jasper and asked if he was satisfied.

"I am," Jasper said. "Now, as long as your tongue doesn't swell and your skin doesn't start turning green in the next few days, you'll likely be fine."

"I thought ya said ya weren't a doctor."

"I'm not. But I do read, as I have mentioned before. They put all sorts of useful information in books. You people should try one some time."

Ilbei ignored the jab. Jasper was clearly upset, and the stress, now that the immediate danger had passed, was making him snippy. Ilbei had been at the soldiering game long enough to understand, but he also wasn't too keen on swollen tongues and turning green. "Can't ya just read the spell on me now?"

"You don't have the disease now, so it's not *onset*. Surely even you know what that means."

Ilbei wanted to argue that point, but he suspected he had no real ground to stand on for his protest. He wasn't sure if he thought Jasper might be wrong medically or magically, but he supposed it didn't matter either way in the end. The only thing he knew for certain was that he didn't know. So with nothing to be done for it, he let it go. Besides, they still had a cliff to climb.

He straightened himself and checked his gear. He'd have to get his helmet and pickaxe back anyway. "Let's go, people," he said. "And just what ya can carry on yer backs. Keep it light, as we might be needin Kaige fer somethin other than a packhorse."

"But what about my trunk?" Jasper asked. "Is Kaige going to carry it? I certainly can't."

"No, he ain't. So load up yer satchel, and let's go."

At which point, of course, Jasper began to protest. Ilbei, however, was already lowering himself down the cliff.

Chapter 28

Meggins stood protectively at the edge of the cliff with his newly acquired bow, guarding the descent as Ilbei made his way down. Kaige came right after, with Ilbei waiting on the ledge, trying not to make any sound lest he draw another attack from any harpies that might still be inside the cave.

Kaige got down quickly enough, and Mags lowered a torch to them, already lit. Ilbei, armed with Kaige's shortsword, took the torch, and Kaige drew his massive broadsword off his back. Together they scooted along the ledge and leapt inside, darting across and planting their backs against the far wall two spans in.

The torchlight revealed a man-made cave cut twenty paces deep, an exploratory mine shaft, as Ilbei had surmised. There didn't appear to be any more harpies inside, but the stench coming from its depths was so cloying both of their stomachs convulsed, which made Ilbei grunt for having worked his stomach mightily only a few minutes before.

"What's that back there?" Kaige asked, pointing with his sword. "Looks like a nest."

"A silver piece says that's exactly what it is." Ilbei crept forward with the torch, which flared occasionally, its flame expanding in a huff of blue as if it encountered puffs of gas. Sure enough, when they got to the end of the cave, there was a nest, much like Jasper had said there might be: a great mound of grayish-white powder, dried excrement, heaped up at the back of the cave and with a hollow in the center like a bowl. Small bones poked out of it like thorns, and more than a few that were not so small. In the very center of it sat two eggs. They nestled together like a pair of brown jars, swaddled in filthy bits of rag and old, molted feathers. The smell this far in was so bad it made the men's eyes water, and tears ran down their cheeks as if they mourned the death of their very own mothers.

"By the gods, I can't take it no more," Ilbei said. "We seen what we seen. There's no danger back here."

Kaige gagged and coughed as he backed away. "Won't ever complain about backfilling latrines again," he said. "I swear it. I won't."

"Aye, lad. I'll second that."

They returned to the mouth of the cave, which by odiferous comparison was like moving from a sewer to a coffeehouse. Ilbei leaned out and waved for Meggins to lower Mags down.

"Let's get this other rope set and get out of here," he said as Mags was getting underway. He found a suitable crack in the rock and pounded a piton into it with a few sure strikes. He placed a second a span farther up for safety, and then tied his rope through the rings. By the time Mags had joined them, the rope was set.

Mags held Meggins' old bow and quiver, which she handed to Kaige when she came in. "I can't draw it back," she said. "But Meggins wants you to cover him and Jasper on the way down, in case that harpy comes back."

Kaige took it, but shook his head. "I ain't no archer. Give me a javelin or spear. Bows is for sissies."

"He told me you'd say that, and he made me promise to

say, and I quote, 'Just shut your hole and do it, and don't break it when you pull it back.'"

"That sounds like you, Sarge," Kaige said. "Sounds funny coming out of a girl's mouth."

She smiled and turned to Ilbei. She was about to say something, but her eyes widened as she looked beyond him out into the cavern. "She's coming back."

"Who?" Ilbei said, but figured out what Mags meant immediately after. He leaned out of the cave entrance far enough to see that Jasper was only a quarter of the way down.

"Kaige, get over here with that bow. And don't break it, like he said."

Kaige stepped-to right away, all traces of humor gone, his mouth as straight a line as the arrow he pulled from the quiver. He drew it back carefully and waited for the harpy to come in range. They all saw immediately that she was flying straight for the cave. Meggins was likely the only one of them that was safe.

Kaige let fly the arrow, which went high and wide. He drew another, and got it off as the harpy swooped in, sending them all diving for the floor lest they be swept off their feet by her extended wings. The arrow punched through her wing but did nothing to slow her down.

Her momentum carried her past them, deeper into the cave, and they all leapt nearly as one to their feet.

"Get farther inside, stay away from the ledge," Ilbei ordered. "Do it now!" He led by example, crouching and picking up the torch before moving deeper into the cave. He advanced slowly on the harpy, Kaige's shortsword in one hand, the torch in the other, ready to strike with either or with both.

The harpy spun back and crouched, her wings swept out on either side, the long vulture talons that served as her feet curling into the layer of dried fecal dust and grit on the floor, prepared for a leap.

Blood ran down her forehead where she'd struck Ilbei with her head, and her dark eyes flashed black in the light of his torch. He moved toward her with his sword pointed at her heart. Kaige moved in with him, his sword gripped in two hands, raised for the long, sweeping strike that would cleave her in two, its gleaming blade angled over his shoulder and ready to come down the moment she was in range. Mags went between them, quarterstaff gripped tightly in hands with knuckles gone white again.

"Listen here, you," Ilbei said. "We don't mean you and yer unhatched brood back there no trouble, but we do need this here ledge to climb down. So why don't ya just go on back there and tend to them eggs, and we'll be off fast as ya can spit."

She hissed at him, a rasp from the back of her throat, just as the fire blast at the far end of the cavern flared, casting her in bright light. She flinched, turning sideways as she shielded her eyes with a long, pale forearm, revealing as she did the feathered side of one thigh, where, midway down, human muscle gave way and became the limb of a bird, a vulture's limb, for it could be nothing else.

"I'm tellin ya true, we mean no troubles fer you or yer nest. So go on back. We'll back off if'n ya do." To prove that he wasn't lying, even though he had no idea if she could understand what he said, he backed up a step, indicating that Mags and Kaige should do likewise. "Give her room. Let her know we mean it."

They stepped back, and Ilbei watched her warily in the temporary light of the flare behind them. She studied him, her eyes narrowed, intelligent and watching, her expression fierce. He thought she had rather fine features for such an awful bird, delicate even, almost beautiful. The layers of sweat and oil, the filth that clung to it as it lay upon her skin and hair, the bits of bone and flakes of white excrement in her hair, somehow couldn't hide the intelligence or symmetry. But the feral growl that came from her throat suggested otherwise. There was no beauty in that hatred, nor, apparently, any comprehension. Still, she did not advance on them.

"That's a good lass," Ilbei said. "Weren't no cause fer violence. That last we had, you and me, that was a misunderstandin. No sense ya gettin all carved up on account of nothin, and them stinkin babes you're makin back there will need tendin I expect."

The fire at the far end of the cavern died down, and once more she was shrouded in shadows, made worse by the effect of the sudden darkness on their eyes.

"Jasper, fer the teeth of Tidalwrath, are ya down yet?"

"I am, Sergeant," Jasper said, just then entering the cave. He saw the harpy and, in his reflex to retreat, stepped back, nearly over the ledge. He would have fallen had Mags not lunged for him and caught him by the collar of his robes.

The harpy hissed and shuffled forward, menacing in her predatory crouch.

"Mags, do ya think ya can lower Jasper down that rope I set there?" Ilbei asked.

She looked at Jasper, then at the rope. "Yes, I think I can."

"You *think*?" Jasper said. His eyes, already round and white around his irises for having just seen a hissing harpy and nearly fallen off a cliff, managed to widen even further. "I don't think *thinking* is adequate for something like this."

"Well, then ya have to do some of the work yerself, son. But get movin."

"Well, why should I have to go first?"

"Jasper!" That was all Ilbei said, a volcanic blast that set the frail figure in motion, his face an odd mixture of insult—for having been deemed both weakest and least valuable in the fight—and relief at being able to remove himself from the harpy cave. Apparently it was one thing to be brave in the face of a harpy disease and another to be in combat proximity to the harpy itself.

He secured the rope around his waist, and Mags checked the knots. She braced her foot against the first piton Ilbei had sunk, pulling the rope toward her through the second until there was no slack between her, it and Jasper. "Go on," she said. "Between us, we'll be fine."

Jasper frowned and started to say something, but Ilbei blasted him with a string of profanity so wroth and violent that it set both him and the harpy in motion, Jasper moving down and the harpy back a step.

"Sorry there, lass," Ilbei soothed. "That weren't meant fer you."

"Meggins," Ilbei shouted out. "You down?"

"Half, Sarge. A minute."

Ilbei turned back to the harpy again, watching her watching him back. They remained that way until Meggins called that he was down. "Should I come in, or will that just piss her off?"

"No, stay out there fer now. Keep an eye out in case there's another. There might be, given we got eggs back here in the nest."

A few more minutes passed, and Mags announced, "Jasper's on the ground. Want me to let myself down?"

"Can ya, lass?"

"I can," she said.

"All right, go on, then. Be careful now."

Mags lay on her stomach and folded her legs over the cliff. She let herself the rest of the way over, gripping the rope and moving down, hand over hand. A glimpse behind him showed Ilbei that she'd gone. To the harpy he said, "All right, so there's two of us already away. Now I got another one outside what needs onto that there rope as well. I don't expect ya understand me so much as I hope ya can hear it in my voice, but he don't mean ya no harm neither." He watched her but couldn't tell if the slit eyes she glared at him with were slit in hostility or wariness.

"All right, Meggins, once Mags is down, ya come on over nice and easy and get on down that rope."

"Aye, Sarge."

Several more long minutes passed. The harpy began once more the raspy growl Ilbei had heard right before she'd attacked him the first time.

"Meggins, she almost down? I don't think Lady Buzzard here figures we're gettin done quick enough."

"She is, Sarge. Give her a minute more."

The harpy shifted her weight to her other foot, the movement flashing her nakedness fully and unashamed, stem to stern, as Ilbei remarked. He glanced to Kaige, hoping he'd not be distracted. The big man was grinning, holding his position, but with a dull vacancy upon him, his mouth open and his jaw slack.

"Kaige, fer lovin's sake, quit yer gawkin. That there'll send ya home with root rot they ain't even got names fer. Weren't that water nymph half drownin ya a few days back lesson enough?"

Kaige blinked and nodded fearfully, getting a better grip on his sword. "Right, Sarge. Sorry, Sarge. Just, a man can't help his eyes. They just take hold sometimes."

"She's down," called Meggins. "I'm coming in."

At this, the harpy's rasp grew loud and menacing. She looked sideways at Ilbei, and he knew she'd understood.

"Ya know exactly what we're sayin, don't ya?" he said. Her gaze moved to the edge of the cave entrance. She saw Meggins come into view, his black bow in hand, a black arrow ready if need be. Apparently that was the last of her patience. She lunged, her wings out, her weight pitched forward, her strong legs driving her.

Kaige swung his sword, intending to halve her at the breast, but she dove under it, gliding beneath, only a finger's breadth off the ground. The strong bones at the leading edge of her wings struck them both at the ankles, knocking their feet out from under them as if by truncheon blows. They landed in near unison, *thud, thud,* face first in the dust. Meggins saw it in time to get off a shot, but it was barely a knick given the quickness of her dive. A few feathers flew, and the enchanted arrow blasted out a fist-sized crater in the floor.

She angled her glide upward enough to get her feet and hands beneath her again, and she charged straight at him, arms wide, intent on carrying him off the edge, just as Ilbei had predicted she might do. Meggins, fleet fellow that he was, dove for the rope as she came at him. He caught it with one hand as she veered and struck him despite the dodge. He kept his grip, but his bow flung out into the air, a black arc turning slowly as it spun away from him and fell.

He too spun, and he slammed against the rock, barely holding on. He grabbed for the rope with his other hand as he started to slide, his knuckles grinding against stone. He squeezed the rope with both hands, braking with all his might. The friction burned into his flesh, but he managed to prevent his descent from being free fall, and eventually stopped himself. He wound a stretch of rope around his foot and leg and grimaced at his hands before continuing down.

"Keep goin," Ilbei called, already at the cliff's edge and peering over anxiously. Relief washed over him as he saw Meggins working his way toward the ground. "Go, go, go." Kaige appeared at his side and added his encouragement to Ilbei's.

Meggins let himself down as quickly as he could, the pain in his hands making him wince and grunt with each new grip.

The harpy wheeled round in the air above the cavern floor, her shrieks echoing loudly from the ceiling. Ilbei watched beyond her, certain that the scores of little figures in the distance would come running around the bend and attack them, ending the escape well short of Hast. But they did not. In fact, the fire blast was flaring up again, and all the little people seemed bent on watching the flames and nothing more. He couldn't tell for sure, but it seemed that only a few even turned to see her soaring there. If they had turned to watch, they looked away again right after. He supposed they were long used to her by now, though he couldn't fathom why they tolerated her at all. That had to be their bones in that nest, at least someone they'd known.

She flew toward them again at terrific speed, this time coming across at an angle that would bring her parallel with the cliff, a pass across the ledge. She dove down and made a grab for Kaige with her taloned feet, causing both Ilbei and the big man to dive back into the cave.

They rolled right back to their feet when she'd passed, and they rushed to the edge again. She was already banking steeply and coming back for another try. She angled lower, and Ilbei realized immediately that she was going for Meggins this time. "Meggins!" he shouted, pointing at the harpy diving down.

Meggins looked up, saw Ilbei, then turned and saw her. He waited until the moment before she was about to strike, and when it came, released his grip, just enough to let himself free fall for a bit. The sound he made upon catching himself, upon sliding to a stop, made Ilbei and Kaige both wince, the pain he suffered made obvious by the ferocity of the sound he held back between clenched teeth. The harpy swooped out and began a long turn again, gaining no altitude and clearly bent on trying for Meggins again. Ilbei ran back into the cave at full speed. He clambered up onto the harpy nest, dust flying all around him in a rancid cloud. He snatched one of the eggs, finding it heavier than he'd expected, and then had to roll out of the nest, unable to climb out as its sponginess gave way beneath his boots like snow—dry snow, but in places slick with a creamy wetness that had a reek so foul it burned his eyes and turned his throat against itself.

He waded out of the last of it and ran back, gagging and choking, just as the harpy made another pass. Meggins slid down as far as he could, but the pain got to be too much, and he lost his grip, plunging the last four spans to the ground. He landed hard, but he managed to get his feet under him and roll as he hit.

The harpy swung round and came again, bent to set herself on him anyway.

"Here, here!" Ilbei shouted at her. "Look what I've got, ya reekin old witch. I've got yer nasty get right here in my hands!"

She looked up at him as she glided toward Meggins, Jasper and Mags, barely a man's height off the ground. He saw her eyes grow large, the narrow black spots suddenly like orbs of onyx glaring hate at him.

"That's right, ya ornery cow. Now get off of my people, and this here won't get broke." She pulled up, banking sharply and climbing with long beats of her filthy wings. She flew right by him, up from below, skimming so near to the cliff it hardly seemed possible. She grasped for her egg with long, viciously taloned toes.

Ilbei snatched it away. "Not bloody likely, you," he snarled. "Now go on and leave us be." He turned to Kaige. "Get down the rope, son. Be quick about it."

Kaige set himself straight to the task. He grunted as he lay flat and pushed himself over the ledge, the starting of the descent the hardest part. He went down hand over hand, his long arms devouring the rope a span at a time and his movements effortless. Ilbei kept his eye on the harpy as she circled on high, all the while holding her egg above his head, ready to dash it on the ground if he had to. She circled around and around, watching, the sound of her outrage a shrieking, hissing rasp of absolute contempt that rained down on him like acid. He listened to it less than he listened to the sound of Kaige's descent, the big man's boots buzzing against the rope as he slid quickly down.

Ilbei chanced a glance down when the sound stopped, and he saw that Kaige was at the bottom at last. This final bit was going to be tricky, getting himself down. "Ya all need to cover me," he called as he looked up at the harpy again. She was still circling. A second glance below revealed Kaige holding Meggins' old bow and Mags wrapping Meggins' hands. That was not reassuring. "I'll do my best, Sarge," Kaige called up.

The harpy sounded something that might have been a laugh, a sound that was part cackle and part shriek. She swung around, still watching Ilbei, her eyes glaring black like poisoned darts.

"I'm settin it down right here," Ilbei called up at her, as he squatted and placed the egg on the ledge. "I didn't do it no harm, nor the other inside. No sense we can't do this peaceably."

Again came the cackling shriek, and he knew she was daring him to climb down. But there wasn't much for it at that point. He had to get down. With another glimpse down the cliff, at which Kaige raised up the old bow reassuringly— or so he intended anyway—Ilbei set himself to the descent.

No sooner was he over the cliff than she began her dive. Ilbei had seen Meggins do it, and he was ready enough to let himself go sliding painfully down as well. He let himself down another span, then stopped, waiting for her. He knew he had to time it right. He gritted his teeth and prepared to drop. She was almost on him. A blinding flash crackled, and a line of lightning split the air. A hot blast of moist air hit him, and all his hair stood on end, his beard puffing like a blowfish. He had to blink to clear his vision, and when he did, he saw the harpy spinning toward the ground like a wounded dove, wings limp and partway folded, her cries silent.

He shook his head and blinked a few more times, squinting down to the cave floor. His ears rang something fierce. Jasper was waving a scroll at him. "Lightning," he called up. "I told you I had one."

With a grin that was half relief and half pleasant surprise, he let himself down the rest of the way, taking his time given that the jolt he'd gotten made it hard to close his hands properly.

When he was down, he looked off to the left. In the shadows near the cavern wall, he could see the dim gray shape of the harpy where she had crashed into the rocks. He wondered if she was dead. If it wouldn't have required the work of scaling a steep jumble of broken stone to get to her, he might have gone and seen to it that she was, but she wasn't moving, so he let it go.

"Meggins, how are yer hands?" he asked.

"They're fine, Sarge. I'll be okay till we buy some space and time for one of Jasper's jiffy scrolls."

Ilbei turned to face Jasper square. "Nice work, Jasper. Fer a feller what near washed out of caster boot camp, ya done good. That lightnin spell worked fine."

"Well of course it did. Why wouldn't it have?" Jasper said. "I already informed you that the only limitation of the lightning spell was one regarding visibility. There's enough light coming from all that over there to meet the visual requirements of the spell, even to the ceiling. To be honest, my only concern was whether or not there would be an issue with grounding, because, as you know, lightning can—"

"Son," Ilbei injected, "ya done good. But we don't need ya to write the book about it as we stand here listenin. Let's get on our way, and hope some of them folks up yonder will direct us to the door."

"Well, I wasn't writing anything," Jasper said. "I was talking. And I really don't think there is going to be anything as simple as a door." But he fell silent after, looking completely put out. After depositing the blank parchment of the spent lightning spell in his satchel, he did, however, fall in line with the rest. None of them, not even Jasper, was willing to protest a command for them to get out of that cave and into the light of day.

Chapter 29

With the noise they'd made, and the fact that they were now on the ground level of the cavern, Ilbei didn't want to linger longer than they had to. They retrieved Ilbei's helmet and pickaxe, found Meggins' bow and then set out immediately for the bend around which they'd seen the little crowd run out when the fiery light flared. Using the relative shadows along the base of the cavern wall, they crept along as silently as possible, Ilbei with his weapon out but the others with theirs put away. The sight of a man with a pickaxe ought not to seem out of keeping with the situation, but a war party would arouse suspicion for sure. Ilbei suspected he and his people would do that anyway, but it was at least worth a try to avoid trouble if possible.

The pounding of many picks, hammers and iron bars beating on stone grew louder and louder as they approached. Ilbei held up a hand, signaling a halt as they were nearly to the corner. He crept closer, intending to peek around, when came the abrupt cessation of the clatter. The pounding of picks and mashing of hammers stopped and was followed immediately by the thumping of feet. Right after, the wave of figures they'd seen from the far end of the cavern passed by, close now and perhaps a hundred of them, though Ilbei didn't try to count. All of them were as naked as could be—naked but for the feathered portions of their legs and the dangling bits of feathers at their backs, which were stained and filthy, hanging from the sawed-off stumps of what had once been wings. The whole lot of the "people" they'd observed from afar were harpies, or what remained of harpies.

The two harpies nearest Ilbei looked over as the bright light flared, which was accompanied at this proximity by a furnace-fire roar, loud and thunderous. The nearest of these maimed creatures, a male, saw Ilbei standing there. For a moment Ilbei feared the harpy would call out and bring the whole flock of them upon his little band, a swarm of bashing picks, shovels, rakes and bars. But the harpy did not call out. He simply stared at Ilbei with a hollow look in his black eyes, the skin beneath them sallow and lined. The whole of him was shrunken, with barely enough flesh to cover his bones, the lines and angles of which were visible beneath, though none so visible as those two protrusions where his wings had been cut off and the stumps cauterized.

The harpy saw Ilbei, seemed to be aware that someone was looking at him, and then turned back and waited for the bright flames to die down. When they did, he ran with the rest back beyond the bend.

Ilbei turned to his companions, bewilderment apparent. He shuffled forward a few moments after and tilted himself so he could look around the bend.

There came a loud hiss as he did, and he saw that men, human men up on railed platforms, had been lowered down through openings high above. They held long, flexible tubes that dropped down out of the holes from which the platforms had descended. The men directed spouts of clear liquid down onto a heaping pile of broken rock on the cavern floor. The stone, glowing red in places, hissed and spat when the liquid splashed upon it and cooled it rapidly, so rapidly that some of the larger pieces split open on contact. For a moment Ilbei assumed it was water they used to cool the pile, but only for a moment, for right after, the smell of vinegar assaulted him in a hot, humid wave.

He jerked back behind the cover of the wall, pulling in clean air, or at least better air, and then tipped back out to look again, holding his breath this time.

The stump-winged harpies fell upon the heap like a pack of wolves on a fresh kill, and once again the chamber was filled with the sound of iron on stone. Some of the harpies beat upon the jumble of rocks while others raked down the pile, dragging the crushed ore to a long sluice that had been made in the creek, which ran along the far wall. More harpies worked the sluices themselves, and Ilbei could see them pulling out gold, which glinted in the light of the lamps that hung everywhere up and down the walls. The harpies working the troughs were a line of constant motion, bending and raking with short rakes, plucking out chunks of gold, then turning to toss them into baskets before turning back and raking again. They never straightened. They just worked and worked, like machines made of skin and bone.

Ilbei looked up to where the men who'd sprayed the vinegar down were drawing the long tubes back onto the platforms, piling them in great coils. As he watched, movement at the end of the cavern caught his eye. Small tunnels cut into the rock face now yawned out lines of more wingless harpies, all of them running two at a time to the open mouth of a tunnel and dumping ore down onto the pile by the basketful. Thin gold veins like threads sparkled as the pieces fell, and much more of it flashed as chunks rolled down the pile after some harpy's hammer smote apart the bigger rocks. Gold was everywhere.

Ilbei pulled back a few steps and turned to his companions. "It's a gold mine all right, fertile as a womb. And them harpies is slaves to it, weren't no doubt. They all been butchered like that one we seen back in the creek, and now put to the slaver's whip."

"But, we're north of South Mark by a hundred measures still," Meggins said. "There's no way we turned down that far south. Not in the two days since we came into the mountain. It's not possible."

"You're right about that," Ilbei agreed.

"So, Her Majesty would never tolerate such a thing. Not even harpies. At least I don't think she would." His voice trailed off a little at the end. He glanced at Kaige, then back to Ilbei, adding, "Would she?"

"She damned sure wouldn't," Ilbei said. "This here operation is somebody's secret, sure as kissin a colonel's wife."

"Well, then we're not likely to be given directions to the front door," Mags said.

"No, I don't reckon we will. All the same, that poor devil what seen me didn't seem to give two coppers I was here, so I expect we can make fer an exit if'n we find one without them harpies standin in our way." He crept forward again and once more surveyed the scene around the bend. There were no openings at ground level in the opposite wall, and none on the far end beyond where the fires were other than the low, narrow passage through which the water ran out. He noticed as he looked that a basketful of ore was thrown right down onto one of the harpies working the heap, knocking him flat, face forward into the pile. Steam began to rise around him. Ilbei shook his head.

He glanced up to see if any of the people, the humans, up on the railed platforms were watching, but none were turned his way, so he risked a look down the near wall, right around the bend, hoping for a way out. Again there was no sign of an exit or passageway. That left only the stream.

He took a second look at where it exited. It ran out

through a narrow opening that had clearly been cut into the wall for it, just as the shafts above it had been. It wasn't very large, and it obviously would lead them farther down.

He turned back, shaking his head. "Well, folks, we got ourselves into a bit of a fuss. Only way out and up I see is them platforms what come through the roof. Otherwise, we'll be goin down again, either followin the creek we don't know or goin back to the one we do and takin our chances bein spitted by the Skewer."

Meggins stepped past him and peered around to see. He spent several long moments looking up and down, then came back and nodded that he agreed with Ilbei's assessment. "Any chance one of those caves up that far wall leads out?"

"No. Look at how they're all straight angled. You can see by the slant of the roofs. They're all cut in by hand."

Meggins went back and looked. After a few moments, his head jerked, as if he'd gotten a jolt of some kind, and for a long time after, he watched, shaking his head. When he came back, his voice was filled with awe. "You should see how much gold they just threw into baskets out there. Some pieces big as my head."

Ilbei was nearly trampled by Kaige as he went to look, Jasper and Mags right behind.

Sure enough, Meggins had been on the mark, and they watched as the last chunks and shovelfuls of gold gravel from the bottom of the flumes were piled in two very large and very sturdy-looking baskets. The baskets were dragged beneath another opening in the ceiling, where they were then attached to a pair of hooks at the end of a rope that had been lowered down. When the baskets were secure, they were raised up into the darkness by someone unseen above. No sooner had the baskets vanished, both the platforms were hauled up into their respective shafts as well.

"Well that's the damnedest thing I ever seen...," Ilbei began to say, but he let it die off as all the harpies turned and ran back toward them again.

Just as before, all in a wave, the harpy slaves rushed out of the area where the pile of broken rocks lay, all but one harpy anyway, the one upon whose head the stones had fallen. He remained motionless but for the wisps of steam rising from him. The rest ran past the corner, again unconcerned by the fact that anyone looked on—even the harpy that had seen Ilbei earlier did not bother to look back again. They stood together, staring expectantly, and their scrutiny prompted Ilbei and the rest to follow the line of their collective focus up to the ceiling. Ilbei realized there was a large hole up there that hadn't had a platform lowered from it, not quite so large as the others, and closer to the back wall. In the time it took him to make the assessment, a gush of flame blew out of the opening, straight down in a rush, as if the bottom of a barrel full of dragon's fire had broken loose.

The blazing column of fire, at least thirty paces thick, burned and burned, roaring almost deafeningly, the heat blasting them as they observed, just far enough away to be at the edge of bearing it. Even at that distance, beads of sweat broke out on all their faces, only to be instantly evaporated. Kaige and Jasper wiped at the salty dryness upon their brows as Mags dabbed unconsciously at her upper lip with the back of her hand.

They watched and waited until the fiery deluge stopped, three minutes or so, Ilbei gauged, and then as abruptly as it began, it was gone, the roar, like the flames, retracting up into the hole from whence it had come. The heap of ore glowed bright red, pulsing as if it were the molten heart of this strange place. A heart of gold, in the most literal sense, and Ilbei suspected an evil one. Ilbei shook his head.

The harpy wave, caught in the tidal beat of that heaping glow, rushed back as the platforms were lowered again. The men upon them once more pushed out the lengths of tubing until the nozzles were clear of the platforms, which hung like dangling balconies over the nightmarish scene. One by one, the tubes jerked, then spewed streams of pungent white vinegar. The men washed the pile down systematically, the hot rocks hissing steam, spitting and crackling, ejecting splinters of stone while many pieces cracked and fell apart. Clumps of gold fell away sometimes when the rocks broke open, as if separated by invisible hands, and rolled down the pile.

When the hissing steam stopped and the red-hot glow was gone, the harpies once again clambered up the jumble and set themselves to crushing the rest with their hammers and picks. Shortly after, the other harpies up in the caves along the back wall once more emerged and began throwing down ore. Somehow most of it managed not to hit anyone below, and Ilbei wondered if that was intentional or simply luck. He thought as he watched that, were he one of those maimed wretches out there beating on that pile of rocks, the kindest thing that could have been done to him would be for one of those harpies above to simply cave in his skull with a load of rocks. He thought the harpy that had been struck down before the last fire blast was likely the luckiest one of the lot. A glance proved that particular harpy was no longer in evidence, his corpse vaporized by the column of flame. Ilbei harrumphed, disgusted. He'd seen a lot of mining in his day, but never anything like that.

He pulled his people back and pressed himself into the shadows with them. "We've got to get news of this to Hast," he said. "We need to get word of it to Her Majesty. This here is intolerable."

All were nodding as Kaige asked, "So how do we get out of here, Sarge? We gonna climb up on one of those hanging things?"

"We do that, we're like to end up with that fire comin right down on our heads while we try. Even if it don't, I don't expect them fellers is gonna sit idly by and let us up neither, so I figure our best bet is to keep on like we have been and follow the water. Seein as this here cavern ain't filled up yet, that water is gettin out somewhere. Eventually." He couldn't keep the discontent from his voice. He didn't fancy the idea of having to go down into the mountain, but there wasn't much to be done about it now.

"There's a lot of open ground between here and there," Meggins pointed out. "They'll see us if we run across."

"They take a little time after the fire to come back down out of the hole," Mags said. "But I'm not sure I can run fast enough to cover the distance between here and that opening."

"Well, I certainly can't," Jasper said.

"Why doesn't Jasper use one of those fog spells?" Meggins said. "I've seen that used before."

Jasper scowled at the suggestion and rolled his eyes. "Jasper doesn't have one," Jasper said. "Jasper had to leave his trunk up on the cliff because Jasper can't climb cliffs with a huge box of magic on his back, and none of Jasper's cohorts could be bothered to assist after Jasper's sergeant insisted Jasper 'travel light and with only what he could carry on his back.'"

"Ya don't need no fog," Ilbei said. "Besides, how'd that look down here? And we don't need nobody to run fast neither." He pointed with a motion of his chin, his beard directing their gaze. "Didn't ya see how them harpies pay us no mind? We'll just go easy as ya please out there amongst em when they come near again. Walk straight across. Kaige, you'll need to bend down some so ya don't look the lone redwood in the walnut grove. We'll sidle on through to the far side, and when the fire dies and they all run in, we'll just run right on down the stream and into that there tunnel."

"You're sure giving those harpies a lot of credit for playing along," Meggins said. "It may be they haven't done anything to us because they haven't all noticed us yet. Maybe the one that looked at you hasn't got the sharpest beak in the flock, so to speak."

"Well, I won't make none of ya do it until I try it first, because there is a risk, I'll grant. But I don't see how it's much worse than goin back and tryin to jump through one of them lances that bastard Skewer is shootin."

On that they were all in agreement, so the plan was confirmed. They waited for the cycle to repeat itself, and soon enough, the fire shaft blew down its hot column just after all the harpies ran away. All together, the five of them slipped in among the harpies, Kaige doing as instructed and trying to hunker down. The reality was, he couldn't hunker down enough, for the harpies were to a man, or to a bird, all slight by comparison—by natural stature, certainly, but also by privation. They were to the last among them all shorter than everyone but Ilbei, and built hardly more powerfully than Jasper was. But there were so many of them. And oh, how they reeked.

Sweat ran in rivulets through the mire that caked their flesh, and it brought to life the stench of the older sweat that had been layering there for who knew how many months or years. Some smelled like death itself, and there were more than a few whose wing stumps seeped pus and gore. These looked the sorriest. Though they were all bent and nearly broken with the toil of what must have been endless-seeming days, the wretches with the oozing wing bones were feverish and teetered on the verge of collapse. They looked out through rheumy, pink-rimmed eyes, the tracks of their endlessly flowing tears black against their gray flesh, streaks that shimmered in the firelight.

Not one harpy, not a single bird-man or bird-woman in the group, gave them more than the barest movement of their eyes, as if the simple act of looking up might cost them the last of their strength. Ilbei didn't know why they didn't

327

all break for it through the tunnel to which he and his company were bound. Which, of course, gave him pause. He certainly hoped there wasn't some very, very good reason for that.

The fire died away, the absence of its bright glare darkening the chamber by a large degree, and in the shifting light, Ilbei led his people out of the harpy mass and to the far wall, wading across the creek to get there.

Once they were clear of the harpies, they crept along the stream, as quickly as possible, pressed against the wall and hoping to pass unnoticed by any of the men that were surely on their way back down by now. As they passed beneath the opening, they could hear the pulleys from somewhere high above, the squeaks and creaks echoing down and sending the intruders scampering like a line of rabbits toward the only exit available to them. The heat coming off the pile of just-heated ore struck them like a blow, and they all gasped as they ran past.

Ilbei glanced down into the flume as he ran and saw that it glittered almost solid with gold despite having just been cleared, the dust apparently too inconsequential to be bothered with for all the larger golden stones. There was an unbelievable amount of wealth in that alone. It was all he could do not to stop and grab up pockets full. But he didn't, nor did the rest, and soon after they were once again in the dark and narrow confines of a subterranean waterway.

"This is my last torch," Mags said as she pulled it from her pack.

"Well," said Ilbei, "then let's hope this here cave is short."

Chapter 30

Once they had a torch lit, Ilbei took the lead again, taking them away from the noise and glare of the chamber where so many harpies labored on that glowing heap of ore. The passage was narrow enough in places that Ilbei and Kaige had to turn sideways, and it was low enough in others that they all had to crawl for a time. Ilbei thought the passage had been made hastily, but he noted that it had been braced with thick wooden beams, set properly at even intervals. It was not the work of inexperience.

The tunnel cut fairly straight through the stone, the slope consistent, and it was only a matter of half an hour before they saw light at the other end. They could hear the water falling into a pool or lake beyond and a rough, dull churning, like wheels of wood, the sort of sound one associates with a mill.

Ilbei crept up to the edge to investigate. Below, no more than Kaige's height at most, was indeed a rather large pool of water, filling up the bottom of another cavern. It appeared to have at one time been a high, narrow natural crack, but someone had come in and widened it since its natural beginnings. Three long wooden forms, built in the style of wine barrels—but each of a length like forty barrels stacked one atop the next—angled up from the water and disappeared into a wide, low cave that spread like an arcade halfway up the cavern wall. Each end of the wooden constructs was open, like great wooden pipes, and it was from the lower part, where they dipped into the pool, that the milling sound issued. At the base of each, where the open end of the barrel dipped into the water, a ring of stairs was mounted, looking rather like a waterwheel mounted onto the end of a very fat, hollow axle. Upon each of these wheeled staircases trod a pair of harpies, one following the next, the two of them stumping up the stairs as the ring rotated in perpetuity.

Mags and Meggins had crawled up next to Ilbei by then, and they spent a moment watching the six harpies walking in place on their endless stairwells, stair wheels, climbing to nowhere but tedium and misery. Mags gasped.

"What are those things they're walking on?" Meggins asked a few moments later. "I've never seen anything like them."

"Them there is Kordiak screws," Ilbei said. "Newfangled water machines, like ya see in the royal mines up north. Like ya *only* see in the royal mines. But I ain't never seen one what wasn't equipped with sheet sails and enchanted wind magic blowin em round. That there is right primitive."

"And cruel," Mags observed. Ilbei nodded.

"What do they do?" Meggins asked.

"They're pumpin water out." He pointed up to the arcade in the wall above.

"Then that's a good sign. There must be an exit somewhere up that way."

"Aye. As long as we can fit through it, we're on our way. Come on now, let's get up them long-barrels quick. Be ready in case these steppin wretches ain't as friendly as that other flock behind us."

But the harpies on the stair wheels gave them as little heed as had the harpies with the picks and hammers in the fire-filled room. Perhaps less, if such a thing were possible. And so they ran to the screws unimpaired, and, with a boost from Kaige, they were all pushed up on the nearest of the three wooden shafts and ready to climb. Mags and Ilbei pulled Kaige up behind them with a grunt, and shortly after, the five of them were in the arcade.

It turned out that the arcade was another pond chamber, much like the last, though this one was more geometric in shape and entirely man-made. It, like the previous, had three vertical screws pumping water up another ten vertical spans, once again disappearing into a low, wide opening.

Again they ignored the harpies on the stair wheels and again the harpies ignored them, the whole experience as strange as anything Ilbei had ever been party to. The chamber above was identical to the one they'd just left. So was the next. And the next. And for a period of an hour they repeated the climbing exercise, one three-screwed chamber after another, ten vertical spans at a stretch.

It wasn't until they heard voices that they knew the screw they were climbing might likely be the last.

Ilbei crawled to the top of it and peered over the edge, looking into the chamber beyond, expecting to see another set of pumps. He did not. The water fell out and formed a gently flowing stream again, one that ran through a small caged-in space and then out across the floor of a low-ceilinged cavern roughly a hundred spans long and forty wide. This chamber, like the first cavern they'd climbed down into, where the harpy tides washed back and forth in the flaring light of the fire column from above, was producing gold in much the same way: harpy slaves working to extract gold. There were fewer of them here, and they were hacking directly into the far wall rather than into heaps tossed down from shafts dug into the rock face, but other than a few procedural differences, the ultimate circumstances were the same. The voices they'd heard as they climbed up came from two men who were standing near where the screw spurted its water out, kept separate from the harpies by a barrier of bars that were hardly any different from those of a prison cell. Ilbei lay flat and listened.

"... that's what he said. Just laying there."

"What did she do, try to kill herself?"

"No. They don't do that. At least, not that one. I don't think they can."

"So what?"

"I don't know what. He just said to pay attention. Said it looked like lightning."

"Gangue?"

"Of course it wasn't Gangue. Why would he do it?"

"I don't know. All I know is I didn't sign up to fight wizards. That was the whole point. What am I going to do, throw harpy shite at them?"

"Calm down. There might only be one."

"How many does there have to be? You been here long enough to know better than that, and ours ain't even that spectacular as they go. What if it's one of the royal ones? The Queen has Fours and Fives, and Ys and Zs."

"It's not. So just keep your eyes open. Listen for the birds to fuss. They said she was screeching her whore face off before, so they'll likely warn you if you keep your head straight and your ears on."

"And if they do, then what?"

"Call out."

Ilbei could hear the sound of one pair of boots walking away, the voice that was closest to him calling after, "How can I call out if I get a lightning bolt up my arse? Hmm? Anyone mention that up there while they were jawing it over?" The other man never answered, however, so the man who remained muttered to himself as he paced back and forth, mainly a string of profanities.

Ilbei carefully backed down the barrel of the Kordiak screw to where the others were. "I reckon they know we're here," he said. "Them two up there got word of Jasper's lightnin bolt, so someone found the harpy that he killed."

"I never said I killed her," Jasper said. "I never said that." He looked alarmed, even horrified.

"Well you shot her with lightning," Meggins said. "What did you think was going to happen?"

"I already told you—or I tried to tell you—that she wasn't grounded properly. You people never listen to me."

"Well, whatever all that is, we don't have time fer it now," Ilbei cut in. "So listen up. Seems them fellers are afright with the prospects of wizards runnin around down here, which is a fine piece of luck we're finally gettin. If'n they weren't fixated on the magic, they'd damned sure know right where we are, what with us only havin the one way out back there. But the situation now is this: we need to get movin and get movin fast, before they turn out whoever they got lookin fer us in earnest. Sooner or later they're goin to figure out where we went."

Meggins, Mags and Jasper all agreed with his assessment, and Kaige was, of course, happy to go along.

"I'm goin to get back up," Ilbei said, "and see if I can't knock that feller agreeable real quick. Then ya all come in after. Maybe we can get him to show us the shortest way out." He set his eyes on Jasper most seriously. "Now, Jasper, ya need to remember that you're the big, scary mage of this here company, so when ya come up, don't be shakin and quiverin and askin fool questions. We got one good card to play, and it's that this here feller thinks you're gonna burn him down with lightnin, so make sure ya put on yer best scary-wizard face."

"But I don't have any scary-wizard faces," Jasper said. "Much less a best one. Why would I cultivate such a thing? I hardly like being scared, so I certainly don't like scaring anyone else. I don't even like being startled, if it must be known. I recognize that some people derive amusement from it, but I—"

"Jasper, I think yer mother needed to clench another month before lettin ya flop out into the world. Yer head wouldn't be so soft and undercooked if'n she had."

Confusion contorted Jasper's face, but before he could ask Ilbei to clarify, Meggins came to the rescue, or at least he tried. "Jasper, it's easy to play mean," he said, leaning closer to the wizard and speaking as if he meant for Ilbei not to hear. "Just make like you're Sarge there. Pretend you've got a bad rash or something, then put on one of those growly faces Sarge wears all the time. You can't get a much scarier model to imitate." He winked at Ilbei, who rolled his eyes but nodded after seeing that Jasper was actually considering that seriously.

"Whatever gets it done," he said. "Now let's get on it. Kaige, you're with me. Come up right after I go in. The rest of ya wait till I give ya the sign."

He and Kaige crawled up the barrel of the screw, and once again Ilbei peered over the edge. The man who'd been mumbling to himself had moved across the caged space beyond the opening and was watching through the iron bars as harpies dumped oil on a long heap of firewood. The wood had been stacked against the wall in the time Ilbei had been discussing his strategy, suggesting a long-practiced efficiency. Most of the harpy slaves were standing back near the creek by flumes similar to those Ilbei and company had seen in the first gold-harvesting cavern. When those pouring on the oil were done and had fallen back with the others, the man inside the cage went to the rock wall near where the bars began and threw the lock on a large wooden gear, using a crank handle jutting out from it. He stepped back and let the gear spin. Shortly after, there came a dull thud along with the clinking of chain in the distance. The oil-soaked wood burst into flames right after, and the man immediately began winding the crank handle on the gear as the light flared. The chain that had fallen into the woodpile was drawn back up, and Ilbei saw that it had a firebrand attached to it. Not as high end a process as the larger chamber with its column of flames, but it was effective enough, for soon the whole far wall was one giant sheet of flames. The man locked the wheel in place, then watched the fire burn, his posture that of someone who has seen a thing a thousand times before.

Ilbei glanced over his shoulder at Kaige, nodded, then grabbed the edge of the screw barrel and pulled himself up and over it. In two quick strides he was upon the man, his powerful arms around the man's neck and choking him like a vice before he'd had time to turn halfway around at the sound of footsteps.

"Now here's the situation, friend," Ilbei said. "I have need to know some things, and you got need of breathin. So, bein as we both have somethin to trade, what say ya play nice and don't make trouble fer anyone. That gonna happen, or is this gonna be yer last day down here mindin the fires, and with only a horde of harpies to see ya off to the afterlife ... assumin Mercy sees fit to send ya along to it?"

The fellow's eyes grew like boils in his head, and he nodded fervently that he would cooperate, even before he realized there was another giant of a man now standing before him wearing a sword nearly as long as he was tall.

Ilbei relaxed his grip and nodded for Kaige to signal the rest of them to come up. "So, here's how ya save dyin," he said. "First you're gonna tell me how I get out of this here complex. No mammoth-sized heaps of dung neither. Tell me true. And next you're gonna tell me who's takin all this gold. The truth of that too."

The man again nodded that he would comply, a rapid up-and-down movement, or at least as much as he could muster given how securely wedged he was in the crook of Ilbei's elbow.

"So go on then, speak up. Not too loud now."

"Up that way, behind us," Ilbei's captive said. "Go up to the original drift tunnel, go right and stay with it until it starts to bend. You'll come to an intersection. Go left up the next passage where all the stacked baskets are. You'll hear the river as you go up. Follow that out, half a measure."

"Any guards out there? Patrols?"

"No patrols, but there are two guards at the entrance where the river runs out." He stammered a little and added, "Well, there usually are two. They'll have archers out if they think harpies are around."

"From what I've seen, there's always harpies around, or what's left of em. Don't be funnin me, son, this ain't the time fer it."

"No. Not these. Wild ones. They come back sometimes."

"That seems a fool thing to do, given what ya got goin on here."

"You asked me. I'm telling you."

"That's fine. You're doin good. Might actually survive. So now, who's doin all this? It sure ain't Her Majesty." He noticed that the fire was dying down as he looked up, the motion of Meggins climbing over the ledge of the screw having drawn his eye for a moment.

His captive nodded that it was true. "It's not the Queen, but I can't say whose mine it is."

"Oh, you're gonna say." Ilbei flexed his bicep, which in turn pressed vice-like into the man's tender throat.

"No," he gasped, his face transformed by panic. "They never said who. Nobody ever said." His eyes bulged as he groped uselessly at Ilbei's forearms with his hands. He might as well have tried to claw through iron with kitten paws.

"Listen here, you," Ilbei said. "Ya don't really think I'm dumb as all that, do ya? I might take insult to it if'n ya do."

He began to squeeze harder, not enough to hurt the man, but enough to scare him quite a lot. The rock of his bicep swelled and drove into the side of the gasping man's throat, crimping down on his windpipe.

"I swear, I don't know; I don't know. They never said. They never told me." He could hardly get it out.

"Quiet now, not so loud." Ilbei let the pressure off just a bit. "No man works fer nobody, and since this here ain't yer cache, then there is somebody else. So who is payin ya? Who divvies up yer cut?"

"The overseer does. He's the one who pays us. He pays us all. Keeps everyone in line."

"And who's he work fer?"

"I don't know. I've only been here eight months. They don't tell me anything."

Ilbei flexed a bit harder. "What they never told ya ain't much use to me, is it? So tell me what ya heard from other folks what do talk about such things, even ones what are guessin. Men get to speculatin about such things in their off hours, 'specially as nights in a place like this get short fer conversation and long fer wine and mead. So go on and spill me the rumors and gossip as ya come to find."

"I ...," the man started, but stopped. So Ilbei squeezed a good deal harder than before, causing the poor man's eyes to swell, nearly right out of his head. He continued to squeeze until the fellow gagged.

"I've had a long day," Ilbei said. "I'd rather not have to kill a poor sod like you on top of it, mainly on account of me knowin you're nothin but cheese in the buffet of whatever is goin on here. It might make me stay up nights feelin bad fer yer old mum and dad somewhere, grievin yer sorry loss." He relaxed enough that the man could speak again.

"I don't know," the man gasped. "I don't know."

Ilbei swore and released him, letting him slump to his knees. He knew the slaver was lying, but he wasn't going to kill a man for that. But he wasn't opposed to scaring him some more.

"Jasper, come on over here," he said. "I need ya to hit this feller with a bit of lightnin. Gentle at first, nothin to boil his brains, but, ya know, enough to make his bladder steam and his pecker whistle."

Jasper looked mortified at the suggestion and opened his mouth to protest, and perhaps even to explain the nature of lightning magic in general ... again ... but he realized his mistake before it cost him a berating—or worse. He paused, closed his mouth, and gave his head a little shake as he straightened himself. He even wiped down his robes with a smoothing sweep of his hands. He put on his most regal and theatrical façade and approached the figure quivering on the ground before him.

"No, please," the trembling man said. "Don't burn me down. Please. Swear to Anvilwrath, I never meant anything by it. Please. I can't take more lightning. I swear I don't know anything."

"Well, swearing won't help you now, you ... you villain," Jasper began in his most menacing tones—Ilbei and Meggins both suppressed groans. "For I am not unwilling to smite you with the most injurious of magicks: the very hammer of Anvilwrath's fifth hand will strike down upon you, and the energies of storms gathering, a terrible static charge ... a static charge that will ... it will ...." He looked at the man, who was cringing, writhing before him on the ground, obsequious as a fresh-beaten harpy slave at his feet. The craven captive pressed his forehead against the ground and pleaded. Jasper turned to Ilbei and made a "what comes next?" face, but Ilbei waved him on. Meggins snorted, trying very hard not to laugh. "And so," Jasper began again, leaving off the static-charged dead end, "I will do it too, because I can. In fact, I derive great joy from killing people. I do it all the time by my various methodologies. And you will, too, by my smiting. Die, I mean, not enjoy it or derive anything, obviously. Well, except death. Death you will derive terribly!" He cringed and made an obvious effort *not* to look at Ilbei that time. "That is, if you don't tell us what we want to know."

Meggins looked as if he might burst, the pressure of such restraint squeezing tears from the corners of his eyes. Ilbei grimaced and shook his head. His sigh was loud enough for everyone to hear, but he stepped forward and raised their captive up by the back of his jerkin, committed to the show. "So there ya have it. Ya can have all that static and smitin there from our most heinous mage," he turned briefly back to Jasper and scowled, "or ya can tell us what sort ya are workin fer, honest like. Last chance to be out with it, or I let ole Jasper go at ya as he is so inclined."

"No, please. I just don't know anything. I swear I don't. I can't take any more. You have to believe I don't know."

"Well, ya ain't even had it yet, but that's yer choice. Ya got to three, then it's comin." He began the countdown, slowly, drawing each number out. The man shook and pleaded on his knees, drooling into the stone, crawling to Jasper and hugging him around his ankles, begging him for mercy and to not bolt his brains right out of his skull. Jasper looked absolutely mortified by the display.

"Time's up," Ilbei said. "What's it gonna be?"

"I don't know," stammered the man, the living embodiment of a personal temblor. He was far more desperate than could be faked. Urine ran freely on the ground around him.

"That's it, then. Go ahead and do him, Jasper. We'll get the next one to tell us."

"But I—" Jasper began, but Ilbei silenced him with an upraised index finger.

"Do him, Jasper. Fill him with the power of Anvilwrath and ... the static energy of all the gods and so on. Go to it, son." He made a zapping sound through his teeth. "Zzzzzt!"

The man simply collapsed and shook in abject terror, his body quaking as if Jasper had actually cast a lightning spell. He reminded Ilbei of the dogs some men kept, dogs who'd been kicked too often and developed a curling reflex in their spines. Someone had been on this sad bastard sorely, and many times before.

"Why ya so afeared of wizards?" Ilbei asked. "I ain't never seen nobody cower so."

The man remained where he was, folded over his knees, his arms out and his hands still lying atop Jasper's soggy shoes. Ilbei had to go and pull him up physically, gripping him by the front of his jerkin. He hung limply in Ilbei's grasp, knees too weak to support him, as Ilbei stared down into his face.

"I said, why ya so afeared of wizards?"

"Gangue," he said.

Mags groaned.

"Who?" Ilbei asked.

"Gangue," he repeated. "Ivan Gangue."

Ilbei looked at Mags. "Ya know him?" It did sound familiar, but he couldn't recall where he'd heard it before.

She nodded. "It's, well, you know who."

Ilbei frowned as he resumed his questioning. "Who is he? Is this here his mine?"

"No, he's the overseer. The one I told you about. Pays us and keeps everyone in line."

Ilbei let go a strangled gasp. They were going in circles now. "So who's he answer to?"

"I don't know."

"Then how do ya know it ain't his mine?"

"I just know."

"How?"

"By the way he sneaks around sometimes, like he's hiding something."

"So why has he been roughin ya up so much that he's got ya quiverin like a shovelful of puke?"

"Men get tempted to take gold sometimes," he said. "It's only natural. You know? And then, when the weights are off, he knows. Somehow, he knows. And then he puts you on the grill and calls lightning on you. Even if he only thinks you did. Same for anyone who tries to run off on their contracts. Straight to the grill."

"The grill?"

"Yeah, the grill." His eyes narrowed as he spoke, and for the first time Ilbei caught a glimpse of something other than terror there. Nascent embers of outrage. "A table, made out of the same as these." He pointed to the bars that kept him separated from the harpies outside, all of whom had formed a bucket brigade and were at work throwing liquid on the wall now that the fire had burned down. "Nobody crosses him twice."

"So why stay? Just leave."

"It's not as easy as that," he said. "Nobody that works down here gets to leave, not for visiting, not for supplies. It's all part of the contract. There's a man they send for anything we need, and that's it. You need something, it goes through Gangue, and he arranges to have it brought back. Only place we go is here and, if we're lucky, Fall Pools on our eighth-days. That's it."

"Sounds like a rotten way to live. Why'd you get on a deal like that?"

"It won't be so bad once we get the prize. They pay us enough copper coins to live on, and the promise is a stone's weight in gold crowns when the lode is all out." The anger that had glinted in his eyes faded, exchanged for the sparkle of greed.

"How long's that supposed to be? Seems a lot of rock been dug out around here. The whole mountain is full of holes as I seen, and a lot more mountain to go. Could be a while before ya see that pile."

"It is a lot of digging, but it's close now. The vein is played out. There's seven drift chambers like this one that have been working all year, plus the big one down below. This one is almost done. Another two or three spans and it's spent, and word is most aren't much farther from it than that. The big one will go for a while longer. But they say even that one will be cleaned out before Harvest Festival next year." He looked around him then, suddenly wary that someone might come down the passage that led up and out. "Gangue will kill me if he finds out I told you all of this." He turned back to Ilbei, and it was as if he saw the crimson sergeant's stripes for the first time. "You heard all this from me, so now you have to get me out. He'll kill me instantly. If not him, someone above him will."

"Well, if'n ya keep yer fool mouth shut, nobody has to know."

"They'll divine it. They'll find a way."

"That Gangue feller a diviner too? How many schools he got? Any chance ya know his ranks?" That would be a valuable piece of reconnaissance.

"No. He can call lightning is all I know."

Ilbei watched him carefully and gauged that he was being candid now. He was too far in to try lying.

"Tie him up," he told Kaige. "Make it somethin he can work loose in a few hours if'n he needs to."

"No! You can't leave me here now."

"Listen, I can't trust ya leadin us out, as you'll just run off. And I can't have ya followin along like some nippy little pup. You'll turn on us the second it's convenient, and until that time, you're nothin but a liability. So just go back to what they expect ya to be doin and play yer hand man-like until I can get us out of here. You give me a name, and I'll make sure the army goes lenient on ya when they get in here and shut it down. Lenient as possible, all given, of course."

"You mean the army doesn't already know it's here?"

"Ya think Her Majesty would let all this go on if'n they did?" He pointed out through the bars with a flick of his eyes.

"Well, you're here. I thought ...." He let go a low moan.

"Yeah, well, us bein here ain't so much by design as ya might expect. But we'll be fer fixin that straight away."

The man's eyes filled with a frantic sort of terror, the expression of a man who's just realized the ice has given way beneath his feet, the instant before the plunge into the lake. He bent his gaze toward Jasper, suddenly welcoming the sight of him. "Can't he just tell someone? You know, with his mind? Telepathically?" He looked at Jasper and gave a shudder, then back to Ilbei. "You've got to get them underway now."

"We ...." Ilbei slid his jaw around, unwilling to tell this man anything about Jasper's singular school of magic, and which one it happened to be. Ilbei had already given more information than he liked. "We have reason to delay our report a bit longer yet," he said. "So ya do as I told ya and get back to it, regular like, once ya work out them knots. Keep yer head here in the short term and, well, maybe you'll keep it long term after."

Gauging by the way he moaned, the man might as well have been being electrified right there. But he nodded.

Ilbei pulled him close, so their faces were nearly nose to nose. He stared into the slaver's eyes and fixed him with an earnest glare. "If'n I hear ya call out the alarm like that feller what was in here before told ya to, I'll come back and push this here pickaxe straight through yer eye, ya hear? I don't need no lightnin fer that."

Despite the threat, the man's trembling abated some. He seemed resigned. "Please don't forget me. Promise you won't."

343

"I won't. Give me yer name, and I'll make sure they know."

He said his name was Sett, and Ilbei made sure that the others heard it, in case something untoward should befall the burly sergeant before they got out. That seemed to mollify the man, though he still collapsed on the floor moaning when Ilbei finally let him go. Kaige bound him as Ilbei had instructed, and then they left him there. They made for the tunnel leading out of the caged-in area, Meggins mumbling that there was no chance Sett wasn't going to run to the overseer the moment he got loose.

Ilbei didn't argue because there was a large part of him that agreed. But right was right. Which prompted him to turn back into the room just before heading up the steep incline. "One more thing," he said. Sett raised his mournful eyes, hopeful perhaps that Ilbei would invite him along. "Go easy on them bird-folks in there. Mercy's watchin, and there may still be a chance to redeem yer rotten soul when this is done. Doubtful, but maybe." The man nodded and dropped his eyes, pressing his forehead to the floor. Ilbei thought it was good that he at least had sense enough to be ashamed.

Chapter 31

Ilbei led his companions up the sloping passage and out of the metal cage where he'd interrogated Sett. Meggins continued to complain several minutes after, certain that the slaver was going to call the whole place down on them the instant they were far enough away. Ilbei figured there was more than a fifty percent chance of it, but there was little he could do about it. He had no desire to drag a prisoner around, and killing him in cold blood was not an acceptable alternative. He would have to trust in the man's fear and leave the rest to fate.

They followed Sett's directions for finding the way out of the mines. Eventually the narrow, sloping passages opened onto a long horizontal tunnel. It was a wide passage, three paces across and nearly as high, cut out of the rock and braced every five paces with thick wooden beams from which hung small, oil-burning lamps. The air was heavy and warm, rich with mineral smells. There was movement in the lamp flames that revealed a consistent flow of air, evidence of a system to move it put in place by whoever had built the mine, someone who had known what they were doing. Seeing it, recognizing that the tunnel complex was as sophisticated as it was, got Ilbei to thinking about those harpies walking the stair wheels on the Kordiak screws. That was no doing of the monarchy. It was clear when he'd first seen them, and it was even clearer after talking to that fellow in the cage. Her Majesty didn't abide torture generally—not unless it was dire convenient, he supposed— but surely not for a mine. And she definitely didn't have harpy slaves in any operations that he had seen, which were numerous. And while it was true that the men who worked the royal mines weren't paid near as well as they ought to be, they were free to come and go when the workday was done, and they were free to quit the job if they were so inclined. A man can't grub in the dark bowels of the world without a respite, some time with his family come evening. And the work would be unbearable if a man thought he could never simply walk away. So, since such slavery and torture were not the way of Her Majesty, and yet the mine itself was clearly an enterprise on a scale beyond any but the nobility, Ilbei didn't have to work very hard to figure out who had to have a hand in it somehow. It had to be Cavendis.

However, easy as it was to suspect Cavendis, it was harder to figure why he would be involved in such a nasty enterprise. He was a son of the House of South Mark, which meant he had all the gold he could possibly ever need, at least personally, so why risk association with such goings-on as were taking place beneath this mountain? That liability, the risk of losing the peerage for his family, much less of losing his life, suggested he couldn't and wouldn't have anything to do with it. But what a coincidence, then, that he would have been sent out here to gamble in the attempt to gather clues about a counterfeiting operation. Certainly such a thing flouted Her Majesty's laws and mucked up the economy—and there certainly was counterfeiting going on, as he'd seen it himself. Because of that, Ilbei might have been willing to entertain the coincidence of Cavendis' arrival as legitimate had it not been for the obvious problem of Locke Verity and that infernal Ergo the Skewer. Cavendis was obviously confederates with both of them, which put great big black-shafted, green-feathered, steel-bolted holes in the likelihood of Cavendis' innocence. Therefore, Ilbei came to the only conclusions he could make: Cavendis of South Mark was pulling gold from the Valenride side of the Gallspire Mountains; he was willing to kill anyone to prevent the word from getting out; and he was in a hurry to get it done. In fact, he was in such a hurry that he'd resorted to enslaving a wild's worth of harpies and allowed the torture of Her Majesty's subjects as part of enforcing the "contract" Sett mentioned.

So why the hurry? Who was he hiding from? Her Majesty or his mother, the Marchioness of South Mark? As far as Ilbei was concerned, that was the only real question left. Was it Cavendis' operation or his mother's? The ramifications of that were huge. But, they were also above his pay grade and therefore something he could leave to the general back at Hast. Let the high folk squabble over whose mountain of gold it was in the end. He just needed to get his people out alive.

Exactly as Sett had said, they came to an intersection where the main passage began to bend ahead. Near one wall several large, stoutly made baskets were stacked, each easily big enough for Kaige to recline inside comfortably had he wanted to. Peering up that passage to the left, Ilbei could hear the distinct sound of running water, the rush of a river. To the right, as he crossed over and listened down that way, he could hear the creak of heavy ropes, the clunk and rattle of wooden gears, and the distinctive squeak of a block and tackle at work. Ilbei had been in enough mines to know the sound of a whim mechanism when he heard one. There were voices coming from that way as well. Ilbei was tempted to go confirm it, to see if the whim was the one winding up the baskets of gold from far below, but light began expanding on the wall ahead where the passage curved away out of sight. Someone was coming toward them with a lamp.

He glanced at the baskets and considered ordering everyone to hide in them, but extinguishing the torch would take too long and leave smoke behind. "Go on," he said, his voice low and urgent. "All of ya, up, up." He practically shoved Jasper and Kaige into the left passageway, driving them behind Meggins and Mags, who'd responded more quickly to Ilbei's commands. "Go, go, go!"

Meggins led the way up the sloping tunnel, and for several minutes they climbed, Ilbei lighting the way from behind. He pulled his pickaxe off his back, ready to fight whoever came up from behind as they ran, and he heard more than he saw Meggins slide his axe and dagger free. Ilbei wished he hadn't left Kaige's shortsword back at the cave with the harpy's nest, for the big man wouldn't get much use out of that giant sword of his in these tight confines. For that matter, nor would Mags get much use out of her quarterstaff. Still, Kaige in a brawl could do more damage with his fists than many men could with clubs and war hammers.

The sound of the rushing river ahead grew louder as they ran. So did Jasper's panting. Though the incline was not precipitous, it was steady and the corridor was long. It seemed to Ilbei's ears a contest to see which would grow loudest in the end, the river or Jasper's gasps.

By the time they found the top of the passage, the wizard could hardly go on, and Ilbei was short of breath himself. Fortunately, the huge cavern through which the river flowed was vacant, a great black expanse, yawning left and right, empty as far as they could see, though the darkness easily swallowed the paltry light of their lone torch.

They bent over, hands on their knees, regaining their breath, all except for Jasper, who collapsed to the ground.

Meggins recovered quickly enough, however, and with an unspoken exchange, Ilbei sent him back down the tunnel, just far enough for him to see if there was anyone behind. Meggins returned minutes later and indicated that there was not.

"Good," Ilbei said. "Then let's be on with it." With a glimpse down into the water to be sure of the direction of the current, Ilbei made to follow it out, but then came a scream of anguish such as he'd never heard, echoing up at them from behind.

"By the gods," Ilbei said. "What was that?"

Whatever it was, it was frightening enough to get Jasper to his feet with an effort nearly like a leap. Once again Ilbei could see the white all the way around the wizard's eyes. Poor Jasper had gotten himself a fearful dose of reality on his first foray out into the field these last few days.

The scream came again, a piercing shriek, someone in unfettered agony.

"We have to go," Jasper said. His face had gone ghostly pale, visible even in the light of the single torch. "We have to go now. Let's go." He took Ilbei by the arm, pulling him downstream. He even reached for the torch, willing to lead. "Come on," he pleaded.

Once more the scream sounded, rising up through the passage they'd climbed, a long and labored wail of excruciating pain.

"By the heavens." A shudder ran down Ilbei's spine.

"Sergeant, please," Jasper said, yanking on Ilbei's arm, leaning back and hauling with the weight of his body behind it.

"I ain't never heard anythin like that," Ilbei said, unmoved by Jasper's attempts to drag him along. "And I'm afeared to even speak what it sounds."

"I'll speak it," Meggins said. "I got a silver piece says that's that Gangue character working at the grill."

"You don't suppose they found Sett already?" Mags asked. Her expression was one of horror and of guilt.

"Or he did like I said he would and ran straight to his boss, hoping a confession would spare him the misery." Meggins looked smug. "I told you. And look what it got him."

"Damn the tides, I knew it," Ilbei spat.

The shriek came again, high and miserable. Whatever they were doing to him had him screeching with such energy it might have been a woman's wail, which had Ilbei grumbling profanities. "Well, damn it, we can't just leave him like that." He cursed himself for his own sloppiness. He should have just broken the man's neck.

Mags and Meggins were nodding that they agreed. Jasper gaped in horror at them. He put his whole body once more into the work of tugging Ilbei toward the promised exit. "We just came up here. We can't go back now. We have to go."

"Jasper, if'n that was you down there sizzlin on that rack, some conjurin bastard fillin ya with lightnin, how'd ya feel if'n ya knew we was here but done run off and left ya to it?" A quick upward jerk of his arm yanked Jasper upright. Ilbei stared the slender mage down, burrowing into him with the ferocity of his truth. Jasper didn't reply right away, so Ilbei asked again. "I asked ya a question, son. How would ya feel if'n that was you?"

"Well, I'd be ... well ...." The mage tried to maintain eye contact, but he couldn't. He struggled to find the right words to get out of what he already knew was an impossible dilemma. But that still didn't mean he wanted to go down, made evident by the way he began to pout.

"Stay up here if'n ya'd rather, but we're takin the light," Ilbei said. With that, the rest of them turned back and went down again. Jasper managed to wait until the glow of the torch had completely disappeared before imagined terrors sent him running after them, willing to face audible ones in the company of his companions and the light.

Back down at the intersection where the baskets were, they waited for the screams to resume. They didn't have to wait long, and again the awful cries echoed throughout the tunnels. Determining that the sound came from directly ahead, they passed by the baskets and crept warily onward. When the cries died down, there followed a brief silence, heavy and absolute, as if the ropes they'd heard earlier dared not creak and the block and tackle dared not squeak for fear of being treated the same.

The passage led to a door made of heavy iron, which stood ajar, swung halfway into a wide, low-ceilinged chamber. The chamber was roughly circular and well lit by lamps mounted on its curving walls and placed, here and there, upon long tables. The lamplight glittered and gleamed all around, for the tables were heaped with gold. Mounds and mounds of it. At the center of the room was a large hole, three spans across and looking rather like a well, cut right into the floor. Above it was a pair of whim mechanisms, the hoists that Ilbei had heard before. Unlike the traditional varieties he'd seen before, however, these were counterbalanced boom cranes, each with a short boom end that reached out over the hole and a long, weighted end that stretched all the way to the arced walls several paces away. The shorter end of each had block and tackle affixed, through which ran ropes as thick as Ilbei's wrists. One end of each rope dropped like a plumb line into the hole, while the other ran back along the arm to the center post, over an angled pulley and down to a large cylinder that turned by the workings of wooden gears and a crank. From the longer end of the arm, near the walls, short platforms dangled, held in place by chains. Upon these platforms, and arrayed around them, on and under a nearby table, were iron cylinders of varying size, some as small as the tip of Ilbei's thumb, some as large as an ale keg. There were numerals cast into the sides of the larger ones, and likely the smaller ones as well, though Ilbei couldn't verify that from a distance. He didn't have time to contemplate it much, the whole of it taken in at a glance, but it seemed obvious to him that both whims also served as giant scales.

And there was a lot to weigh. Around each of the center posts were baskets filled with gold. Basket upon basket upon basket of it. The more Ilbei looked, the more he saw, and while he couldn't see the left side of the room, he supposed, given how many baskets were lined up along the far wall, there were more out of his sight. A king's ransom to be sure, gathered and stored in baskets like picked fruit, with still more baskets sitting empty and waiting to be filled.

Ilbei also saw that the chamber was occupied. He could see six men working inside, four at the nearest of the cranes and two at the one across the hole, the lot of them hauling up gold in an obviously long-practiced routine. Two of the closer men had just cranked up a basket of gold, and another man, standing near the center post, threw a lever that allowed him to swing the short arm of the boom over the edge of the floor with surprising ease. A fourth worker disconnected the hooks as the two fellows from the crank joined him, and together they dragged the basket out of sight somewhere left of the door. The man at the center post went to help his two comrades on the other crane. They had also just cranked up a basket full of gold. The three that had hauled away the first basket reappeared, and two of them went to help with the other load, while the third set himself to attaching an empty basket to the hooks, preparing it to be swung out over the hole again.

It was a busy and rapid sequence, the men's movements quick and sure. They worked in rhythm with one another, grunting occasionally but otherwise at their ease in the way of draft horses drawing a loaded wagon along a good road.

They must have been at it a long time, for they were all huge, each of them shirtless, revealing heavily muscled frames that gleamed golden with sweat in the lamplight, the play of light and shadow emphasizing the brawn acquired by lifting baskets of heavy metal, day after day. Brawny as Ilbei was, even as Kaige was, neither soldier could claim the nearly inhuman bulk of those six men.

Once again, a shriek of agony issued forth, and it came from inside the room, to the left, somewhere behind the open door and out of sight. None of the laborers looked up as they heard it, which Ilbei saw as evidence of their long conditioning in this chamber. Despite the racket, they simply worked together in perfect unison, as if the screams were but wind in the trees or the crackle of a hearth fire.

Ilbei shook his head. There wasn't going to be any way to deal with those screams that didn't take them straight through those brutes inside. Everyone with him saw it the same. He set his jaw and nodded to Meggins and Kaige. To Mags and Jasper he said, "Stay back. These boys ain't fer ya, not unless ya got somethin ya can spell fer us, Jasper." Both nodded that they understood.

Whoever it was being tortured continued to wail; it went on until breath failed and silence came at the end of misery's fading rasp. It occurred to Ilbei once more that it sounded like a woman in there.

"Come on, then," he said in low tones. "Let's have at it."

Meggins nocked an arrow and put another in his teeth. Kaige drew his sword off his back, and Ilbei was glad that at least the big man would have room to wield it. He kicked the door open the rest of the way, and together they ran in.

There were eight of the big fellows, not six. Two more were sitting in chairs near a closed iron door, apparently taking a breather while the other six worked. It was the seated pair that spotted them first, and one of them called out, "Oy, who's that lot?"

"Stand aside," Ilbei said. "Ya don't have to die."

One of the six near the baskets lobbed a chunk of gold at Meggins the size of a Winterfest ham. Meggins, ever agile, leaned sideways enough to avoid being smashed by the glimmering meteor, which instead slammed into the wall several paces behind him. Meggins' bowstring thrummed right after, and his missile did much the same, though it passed first through the big fellow's head and then hammered into the stone wall beyond, creating a scatter of gravel, which clattered to the floor. Meggins grinned as he snatched his next arrow from his teeth.

The other five near the hole reacted less quickly than their comrade, and they watched his throw and subsequent death with surprise. Surprise turned to rage, and plucking up their own hunks of gold, together they charged at Meggins, two of them hurling theirs and the other three simply intent on pulping him directly. Meggins had to dart to his right to avoid the flung gold and couldn't get off his shot. Kaige ran forward to intercept them before they could get to his friend. Ilbei might have as well, but the two that had been seated took up their chairs, wielding them as weapons, and lumbered toward Ilbei, their footsteps heavy and thudding upon the floor.

The nearest to Ilbei flung his chair when he was barely two steps across the room. Ilbei ducked and rolled sideways. There came another crash as a hunk of gold smashed into the wall behind Meggins. Right after, Ilbei heard the hiss of Meggins' second arrow whizzing overhead. Another of the men who'd been working the baskets went down. Meggins' bow clattered to the floor, tossed aside for now. Ilbei heard his companion's axe and dagger sliding free as the soldier drew them and ran to Kaige, ready for close-quarters combat beside his friend.

Back on his feet, Ilbei had to raise the torch, using it to block a gold-fisted punch directed at his head by one of the men who'd apparently been discouraged by Kaige's enormous sword. The torch burst into splinters, but it wasn't enough to stop the blow, leaving Ilbei to deal with the remaining energy, of which there was a lot. It spun him all the way around, forcing him to scramble to keep his feet, which in turn nearly sent him into the hole. He teetered at the edge of it, swinging his pickaxe backward, using its weight to hold his balance. Even so, he was only prevented from falling in by the fact that the man with the other chair hit him. The blow struck him in the ribs as he tipped into the opening, painfully but also hard enough to give him lateral momentum, which he used to dance around the rim of the hole like a tightrope walker. Three steps, and then he was out of it on the other side. He couldn't help noting as he skirted the rim how small the tiny spot of light was down at the bottom of that hole—such a fall would have lasted a long time, long enough to think about the nature of it on the way down. He shuddered even as he dove clear and rolled toward the far wall. He was just about to regain his feet when all three men were on him. The nearest of them leapt upon him and pinned him to the floor with a knee to his chest that landed like a hammer blow, and the one that had thrown his chair kicked him.

Another hammer blow, this time in the form of a huge hunk of gold, plunged toward his face, courtesy of the man pinning Ilbei to the floor. Ilbei raised his pickaxe to ward it off, just as the man with the chair brought his makeshift weapon down. He managed to stave off both attacks, through luck, mainly, but bad luck followed right after as the chair broke over the head of his weapon and nearly cost him his grip. He had to catch at it, and in doing so, he lowered it. The remnants of the chair were brought to bear against him in that opening, and had he not rolled his head to the side, the point of a broken spindle would have impaled him straight through the mouth and out the back of his neck. A kick to his ribs from the third attacker knocked his breath out, and the big man on top of him held his chunk of gold in two hands, raised on high to finish Ilbei off. Ilbei was done for this time, he knew.

He heard the *thwack* of wood on bone. He thought it was one of his ribs being kicked in, but it wasn't. Mags had swung her quarterstaff full and flat, and nearly caved in the skull of the brute wielding the chair. His eyes rolled up into his head, and he pitched face forward, stiff as a felled tree. The remnants of the chair clattered and broke apart, rolling on the stone around Ilbei's head. Ilbei managed to get his pickaxe up to block the two-handed smash that would have brained him, but his attacker let go of the gold with one hand and used it to grab Ilbei's wrist. The man's strength was astonishing, and he applied it well, moving his grip up enough to force Ilbei's hand backwards, clearly intent on breaking his wrist or, at very least, making him drop his pickaxe.

With his free hand, Ilbei punched him in the chest, then twice in the stomach, all three blows in rapid fire. He might as well have punched the wall. The brute tried to smash Ilbei again with the gold in his other hand. Ilbei twisted enough to avoid it. Twice more he narrowly rolled his head aside from similar blows. When the man tried a fourth smash, Ilbei blocked it with his forearm, rolled his wrist over and on top of his assailant's, and then drove the man's hand down hard, using the energy of the swing to slam both the hunk of gold and the man's fingers against the stone floor. Ilbei's attacker yelped. The gold rolled away, but the brute punched Ilbei in the side of the head anyway. Ilbei tried to turn away from the mammoth-sized fist plummeting toward him, but no such luck this time. He took the shot full, the power of it driving the opposite side of his face hard against the unrelenting stone—which finally made Ilbei mad.

He twisted his right arm, still holding his pickaxe, against the force of the man's left hand, in particular against his thumb. Strong as his attacker was, he couldn't prevent Ilbei from getting his hand, and his weapon, free. Ilbei swung it sidewise right after, a rotation of the wrist, and pounded two quick hammer strikes against the man's temple, stunning him just enough for Ilbei to shove him off and clamber to his feet.

He scrambled back, getting his bearings, and felt the hot spray of blood splash against the side of his face, a lot of it, wet and warm. He blinked it out of his eyes, looking through the haze, dreading that it might be Mags paying the price for saving him. It wasn't. Kaige had just cleaved the man he'd been fighting in two. The upper portion of the body, cut clean through just below the ribs, had fallen into a basket. It landed at an angle that allowed the still-beating heart to jet blood in a long arc that spurted across the hole and, by random chance, hit Ilbei in the face.

Ilbei saw, however, that Mags was busy. Her intervention had drawn off the man who'd been kicking Ilbei in the ribs, and he was onto her in earnest now. It was all she could do to hold off the pounding onslaught of his attacks, but she worked that quarterstaff better than Ilbei would have thought—the Sisters of Mercy clearly were not the pacifists he'd always assumed they were if they'd taught her all that. The ends of her staff blurred as she *whack-whacked* at her attacker with furious speed. The hardwood rapped the tempo of her fury as it struck the bones of the man's forearms, raised up as they were in his own defense. Ilbei might not have worried about her if she weren't steadily backing away. Despite her efforts, the brute pressed her methodically, moving like a trained pugilist. When he got her backed up to the wall, she was going to be in trouble. He didn't think she could hit him hard enough to knock him out without a full, flat swing like she'd gotten earlier. He hoped he was wrong. But he couldn't get to her to help her yet, for he still had his own adversary to contend with. The man he'd stunned was already back on his feet and reclaiming his chunk of gold.

A glance Jasper's way showed that the wizard had fumbled a scroll out of his satchel, which gave Ilbei some hope. But he couldn't watch, as his opponent was moving in on him, the gold in his hand gripped firmly and ready to smash Ilbei's head.

A lightning bolt flashed, and for an instant Ilbei was filled with relief, thinking Jasper had finally gotten the spell off and struck down an enemy. But when his vision recovered from the flash, he saw that quite the opposite had occurred, for Jasper now lay on the ground, the brown length of his scroll limply rolling itself back up on the floor where it had fallen from his hands.

But Jasper's spell hadn't backfired. Another magician had come into the room, through the iron door near where the two burly fellows had been on their break. The magician was a well-groomed man in a long gray tunic. He wore a close-cut beard that was nearly as black and lustrous as his belt and high boots. Though Ilbei didn't recognize him from two nights before in the tavern at Fall Pools, he knew instinctively that the spell caster had to be the honorless rogue Ivan Gangue. Right behind Gangue, stepping around him to join the fight with his silver-hilted sword already sliding from its sheath, came the man who called himself Major Cavendis. Ilbei might have cursed him for the liar he was, but he barely had time to call out, "Watch out behind!" before he was back to fending off a furious rain of blows from his more immediate, gold-wielding adversary.

Fortunately, Kaige had seen the two new entrants to the melee in his peripheral vision, Cavendis already darting across the room toward Meggins' unguarded back. Kaige feinted with his sword at the man he'd been engaged with since cutting the last in half. He slid to his left, trying to get position between the newcomers and his friend. His opponent tried to dodge the feint, a sideways step that left him with one foot half over the edge of the hole. Kaige saw the opportunity, roared and pretended to lunge at him, which the man took to be a tackling move. In trying to leap back along the edge of the hole, away from Kaige's feint, he slipped and fell in instead. This allowed Kaige time to knock aside Cavendis' sword before it ran through Meggins' kidney from behind. Kaige blocked that thrust and the next, drawing the major's ferocity onto himself, but then it seemed as if he finally realized who he was fighting with. As Cavendis turned on him in full, the big soldier fell back, barely able to defend himself from the onslaught. Kaige parried two more blows, continuing to backpedal, more out of surprise than by the force of the attack. "But, Major, why?" he asked, parrying more thrusts and cuts as he retreated yet another step. Ilbei heard it all, and he knew Kaige was suffering for his innocence again. There just hadn't been a place in his farm-boy experience for betrayal like that.

Meggins heard it too. "That's no major," he called to Kaige. He'd just blocked a punch with his knife, the blade slicing a neat cut clean to the bone and causing his attacker to drop his hunk of gold. In the instant after, the brute was gaping down at the opening Meggins had cut into him, just beneath his upraised arm, the war hatchet planted deep, its blade driven between two ribs. He howled as Meggins shoved the axe handle down like a lever and spread those ribs apart, snapping both and dropping the man to his knees, where pain knocked him out. Meggins kicked him into the hole and ran to help Kaige, who was still retreating under Cavendis' onslaught. Meggins repeated what he said. "He's no major, Kaige. He's a fake. Cut him down."

Kaige seemed to grab hold of this idea slowly, but the

addition of a second adversary was enough to halt the young lord's advance. Meggins brought a flurry of blows at him, the axe and the knife darting in rapidly, sparks striking off the blades as Cavendis struggled to bat them all away. Kaige caught on a few moments after, and then he too brought his sword to bear more aggressively. The two of them were able to drive the man they'd called major back, his defenses nowhere near up to the task of warding off both of them, and against such diverse weaponry. They pushed the nobleman back until he struck a table near one wall, knocking a stack of gold to the floor. He tried to hop up on it, but slipped. He barely swatted Meggins' axe aside. Kaige thrust straight for his heart. And then Cavendis vanished.

Kaige's thrust hit nothing, spearing through empty space and striking the wall, sending a jolt back up its length into Kaige's shoulder. Meggins' axe whizzed through the air as well, striking the wooden table and biting off a wedge of wood. Together they spun around, Kaige right, Meggins left, searching. They found him again, on the other side of the room now, the man in the gray tunic beside him. Cavendis stooped and picked up Meggins' bow, beginning to grin, but then, looking about, realized he had no arrows to go along.

"Missing something there, Major?" Meggins said, and ran toward him again. Kaige made to follow suit, but Ilbei, seeing it, called him off.

"Get Mags," Ilbei shouted. "Kaige, go on and cut her free."

Kaige realized immediately the predicament Mags was in. The burly pugilist that had just backed her up against the wall realized his trouble only in the half heartbeat it took for Kaige to heave his sword at him like a spear, an underhanded, scooping sort of throw, that drove the blade straight through the man's body, staggering him sideways, where he struck the wall and then fell to the ground, limp and dead.

Kaige ran to him right after and, with a boot braced on his hip, worked his weapon free, flashing a smile at Mags, who looked relieved. She ran immediately to help Ilbei. With another long, flat swing, she brought her quarterstaff around and against the side of the man's head, the thud resounding like she'd struck an empty casket. The brutalized man staggered left, then right, then left again, careening off the wall, spinning and tumbling backwards into the hole to join his two companions who'd gone before.

Lightning flashed again, and Ilbei turned in time to see Meggins crumple like a scarecrow fallen off its post. Ilbei ran full tilt for him, hurling his pickaxe at the wizard, who'd now struck both Meggins and Jasper down. The weapon sounded a low *whoosh-whoosh* as it turned thrice, end over end. The last rotation spun it to where the sharp tooth of its blade would bite right through Gangue's head, but Cavendis knocked it aside with the black bow. The pickaxe struck hard enough to knock the bow from Cavendis' grip, but the nobleman had spared the wizard certain death. Cavendis drew his sword and stepped between Ilbei and his pickaxe.

Grimacing, Ilbei drew his dagger from his sheath just as Mags came up beside him, her stance a practiced one, her weight distributed well and evenly upon the balls of her feet.

The magician laughed when he saw her. "I should have beaten more sense into you."

"Your mistake," she said. She and Ilbei advanced, spreading apart a little as they went, Ilbei intent on getting to Cavendis, and Mags seemingly intent on having some revenge.

The magician was chanting again.

"Better make it quick," Cavendis said. "Or her old beau is going to have one of you down like your other two friends. Isn't lightning fun?"

Ilbei tried to maneuver around to Cavendis' right,

wanting to move him away from the wall—and Ilbei's pickaxe. But this wasn't the South Mark lord's first fight. Cavendis lunged, first a feint, then a real strike, a long stab that nearly got Ilbei through the wrist. Ilbei pulled back in time to receive only a cut, a neat slice at the tip of his middle finger, which dangled now, open like a cap.

"Hah, close, Spadebreaker," Cavendis taunted. "You're quicker than your fat frame suggests."

"And you're a sorrier excuse fer a man than yer noble blood suggests."

"Touché." He lunged at Ilbei again, but the steady old soldier batted it away with the flat of his knife.

Lightning arced again, a long white line of it blindingly drawn in the air before Ilbei's eyes. It hit the blade of his knife, and for an instant he thought some invisible giant had tried to yank his arm out of the socket in one great tug. Spots swam before his eyes, and he was dimly aware of Cavendis lunging for his heart with his longsword. Ilbei crumpled, his mind turned to hazy gauze. He heard wood strike steel through the buzzing in his head, a sharp, single note as he fell, then the clank and clack of it in a rapid *rata-tat-tat* as he lay on the floor. He couldn't figure out which way was up, or he'd have gotten up to help.

Someone was mumbling then, singing maybe. And something else very heavy crashed against the wall, followed right after by another one, like someone throwing rocks. Then something else hit someone really hard, a dull thud, followed by a sword clattering to the ground. Kaige laughed. Then someone else screamed as the room grew bright. The screaming got louder, and there was a fluttering of cloth. Ilbei fought to clear his head.

He got himself up to his knees. His ears were ringing. Something was burning a few paces away, where the magician had been, where the screaming was coming from. This screaming definitely sounded male. Dull wooden *thwack*ing sounds also came from where the fire burned, and a shadowy figure stood over the flames. Blinking a few more times, Ilbei realized it was Mags whaling away at what had to be the wizard, who was lying on the ground, burning.

Slowly, Ilbei got to his feet, his vision still blurry and a tone in his ears so loud it made him squint. Careful to teeter toward the wall and not into the hole, he made his way to Mags, who continued to bash upon the burning Ivan Gangue, who continued to scream. Blinking a few more times, he saw that the lump he had to step over was Cavendis, the young lord out cold on the floor. Ilbei stopped, squinting as he peered down at the man. Gauging by the way his shoulder and arm lay, most of the bones at the joint were crushed. There was a hunk of gold the size of a cantaloupe lying just beyond the disabled lord. He glanced over at Kaige, who saw him looking and grinned. "Busted him up good, Sarge. It's what he gets for impersonating an officer."

Ilbei smiled back, though doing so made his head throb. "It is, son. That it is." His balance still precarious but his mind mainly working again, he gently stepped between Mags and the mage and caught her wrists in one hand and the quarterstaff in the other. Despite his superior strength, the effort, and the sharp pain in the end of his finger, set him off balance, staggering him backward, where he nearly tripped over the prostrate form of Cavendis. Cavendis began to moan. Mags, still in Ilbei's grip, moved with him a step, then leaned her weight against his fall, steadying him. He thanked her, and together they collected their scattered thoughts.

They locked eyes for a moment, and he peered into hers to see if she was okay, knowing well that combat was a traumatic experience all by itself, much less with the sort of man as was Ivan Gangue. She looked frightened, but she mustered a smile and a shrug. "It's what he gets," she said.

"That's my girl," Ilbei said. "We'll make a soldier out of

ya yet."

He turned and saw that Kaige was putting out the last of the flames in the magician's long tunic, the work made easier without Mags' quarterstaff beating all about. Meggins was crawling to his hands and knees right behind them. From the way he was groaning, Ilbei knew exactly what he was going through. But at least he was up.

He went to check on Jasper next, but the young magician was already coming his way, fishing through his satchel of scrolls as he did. "It's a good thing that man can't be more than a D- or E-class conjurer," he said as he approached. "And he's not a very smart one at that. Everyone knows an ice lance is a better choice for lower-ranked combat conjuring. I would never have cast a D- or E-class electrical spell in a situation like that. You might as well just throw the scroll itself." He laughed a sniffy sort of laugh, enjoying his own joke.

Ilbei straightened and shook his ringing head, unable to share Jasper's assessment of the usefulness of the lightning spell, but he did not give the thought voice. Instead, he let the young sorcerer enjoy having amused himself as he sifted through his satchel looking for what Ilbei hoped were healing spells.

Jasper saw the look on Ilbei's face, however, and realized that Ilbei didn't understand, clearly mistaking that to mean he cared to be enlightened. "Well, I'm sure it wasn't pleasant to be on the receiving end of that lightning," he explained. "But look how much good it did. That's my point, and that's why I wouldn't have cast it. As a matter of comparison, the small fireball I just read on him was only an E-class spell as well. And as you can see, it only barely did its job. Clearly he couldn't have done worse than lightning, as my fire was only a marginally better choice, and it was the only one I had. Anyone who's ever read a book, much less a conjurer himself, would know that an E-class conjurer can't generate enough power to evaporate a hogshead in one bolt. At very least, a touch lightning spell is the only proper method for a rank that low. A bolt at that level is pure pride.

"Finnius Addenpore—who did his best work under Tytamon at Calico Castle, despite what people say about Finnius' having killed himself—observed that a spell bolt that can't turn a hogshead of water to steam will be nonlethal over eighty-one percent of the time. He dubbed that the 'hogshead quotient for lightning'—or HQL for short—and proved lightning at the rank of E was much less desirable than an ice lance of the same level, which has greater range and no lethality limitations beyond the armor an opponent wears. He even suggested that—"

Ilbei didn't have the heart to tell him to shut up, given that he'd performed so well when it mattered most, so he interrupted gently, saying, "You're a fine lad, son. And a fine mage too. Don't let nobody say otherwise." He gave the wizard a kindly smile, but was unable to help himself adding, "Not that ya'd hear em fer all the talkin ya do."

Jasper took no insult from the last, as the compliment had caught him off guard. He was soon glowing at the praise. Ilbei gave him a firm pat on the shoulder, and the rise of the young wizard's elation brought forth a whole new round of happy didacticisms, which, of course, Ilbei ignored.

Leaving Jasper to go on about ice lances and lightning bolts, Ilbei went to help Kaige, who had begun binding the two men they'd captured, hands and feet. He cut a strip of unburnt cloth from one of the sorcerer's wide sleeves, which he used to wrap the end of his finger, and then set to work.

When Cavendis and Gangue were bound, Ilbei straightened once more and rubbed his jaw. He was sure his head was going to hurt for a week. He looked down upon the pair of prisoners and shook his head. "Meggins, if you're up to it, see if ya can find somethin to gag this one with beyond just a stretch of cloth. I don't want him castin magic around it somehow." Ilbei gestured toward the wizard as he spoke. "And Kaige, until then, if he even starts talkin, bash his head in. Don't wait for a second word, hear?"

"Yes, Sarge."

Gangue glared at him and was rewarded by one of Kaige's farm-boy grins.

"Meggins, are ya all right?" Ilbei said, seeing Meggins hesitate.

Meggins waved him away, nodding and still blinking. "Yeah, yeah, Sarge. I got it. Just give me a second to clear my head."

Satisfied, Ilbei went to the door through which they had entered and peered down the corridor, listening. He didn't hear anything, nor did he see light approaching. Maybe no one had heard. Even if they hadn't, he figured someone would see the three bodies lying at the bottom of the hole, and if not that, they'd certainly notice the baskets weren't coming down anymore. Someone would notice something, he knew. He just didn't know how long it would take.

He shut the door and barred it, then turned and looked across the room at the door from which the tortured screams had to have come. That had to be dealt with. He retrieved his pickaxe and drew in a long, deep breath. He let it go slowly, steeling himself for what he figured he was about to see and hoping he wasn't too late to help. "Come on, Mags," Ilbei said. "Jasper, you too. Let's find out what all that screamin was about."

Chapter 32

The three of them entered the room cautiously, Ilbei with pickaxe in hand and ready to strike. Jasper held a scroll with an oil spell on it, having instructed Mags to throw the lamp she carried at whomever he might have cause to cast the magic on; it was the most offensive magic he had left. But there was no need for it, not for pickaxe or flaming oil spells, for the room's only occupant was a captive harpy. Ilbei recognized her as the one they'd fought in the cave high above the cavern floor, evidenced by the cut on her forehead and the large hole burned through her left wing—Jasper's lightning had done that, or so Ilbei surmised. There were so many burns on her now he couldn't be sure.

She was bound to a set of bars, the grill just as Sett had described, an ironwork three spans high and not quite so wide. Her head hung limply, chin to chest, snarls of her long black hair dangling like matted horse tails. Gangue, or Cavendis—or both—had clamped the harpy's wrists and ankles to the frame with iron manacles, and another iron band was locked tight around her throat. Blood trickled from all five localities, little rivulets drawing lines that wavered over her grimy flesh, graphing the jolts and contortions of her recent agonies. Her wings were fanned out to either side of her, lashed in places along the top of the frame and again at the sides where they angled down. They were too long for the width of the grill by a span or more, and the last three hand-widths of the left wing were bent at an angle, suggesting the wing had been broken recently. Ilbei wondered if it had been the fall that had done it when Jasper's lightning hit her or the torture she'd received after.

Mags and Jasper gasped together, Jasper actually backing out of the room. "Oh no," he muttered.

"You're damned right, 'Oh no,'" Ilbei said.

The room had a powerful reek of burnt flesh, feathers and hair. Were it not for the burn marks in the most sensitive areas of the harpy's body, the smell alone would have given evidence that most of her injuries were more recent than Jasper's spell. Black spots distinctly marked where she'd been burned directly on the bottom of her taloned vulture feet, both at the very bottom and at the tip of the centermost claw.

More burns like those were visible on her fingertips, her earlobes and places that a man ought to have been too ashamed to violate, and Ilbei turned round and stormed out, pacing straight across the room. He delivered three quick kicks to the side of the magician's head, and had Cavendis been lucid, he would have done likewise to him, lord or no. He didn't bother explaining it to either of his men, as both of them stared at him with mouths agape.

He went back into the chamber and saw Jasper digging through his satchel for a spell, as usual mumbling under his breath. All Ilbei caught was "not a healer" and "wasted on a thing like that."

"What's he lookin fer?" Ilbei asked Mags. He wasn't in the mood for foolishness.

"I told him to heal her," Mags said. "We can't leave her like that."

"Is she even breathin?" Ilbei asked.

"She is. I checked. It sounded okay too, though I can't be too sure how human they are on the inside."

As if she'd heard them, the harpy's head lolled from side to side. She raised it with obvious effort and looked up at them through the gaps in her tangled hair. The low rasp she'd sounded while defending her nest rattled weakly from her mouth.

"Easy there, sister, we ain't come to do ya no harm," Ilbei said. "And we done fer them fellers what has." He moved to the side and pointed through the door, where both Lord Cavendis and Ivan Gangue were visible, tied up on the floor.

The harpy's eyes narrowed upon seeing them, the tone of the growl changing, then fading to silence again. She watched them for a time, then regarded Jasper when the rustle of his scroll drew her eye.

"Listen," Ilbei said. "Jasper there is disposed to mend ya some, if'n you'll tolerate such things. I'm not sure whether ya understand a word I'm sayin, but seems polite to ask all the same."

She growled again, reminding Ilbei of a feral cat.

"Well, it don't hurt to try," he said, shrugging. "But I expect that solves it fer whether we cut her down straight off. Jasper, ya go on about it, and we'll set her loose once she's on the mend. Be quick about it, though. We'll have them other fellers knockin soon."

"I still don't think we should be using army scrolls for this," Jasper complained. "When they entrusted me with these," he held up the scroll and shook it as if Ilbei somehow hadn't seen, "they expected I would use them responsibly. I tried to explain how costly these are, but–"

"Just cast the spell, Jasper," Ilbei said. "Let me know when you're done." With that, he went out to rejoin Meggins and Kaige. They'd pulled Meggins' leather armor off, and Kaige was winding a strip of cloth around a burn on Meggins' shoulder where the lightning had split the leather pauldron and, to a lesser degree, the flesh.

Ilbei studied the work in progress and shook his head. "Wait up a few, and Jasper will get ya with one of them healin spells. Her Majesty spendin all that money on em, might as well use some of em on her men, eh? Besides, readin it will keep him quiet fer a while."

"I'm okay, Sarge," Meggins replied. "We'll be fine."

Ilbei glanced down at Meggins' hands, wrapped up after he'd slid down the rope so fast. "I know ya will, son, but ya look like one of them mummified fellers the ancients made, ya know, the ones what they dig out of the desert sometimes. Wrap ya up much more, and you'll have half the priests on Kurr chasin ya around wantin to set ya on fire and send yer demon soul back where it come from."

Meggins laughed. Kaige looked confused, and Ilbei went to regard his captives again. Cavendis was still incoherent and in pain. Ilbei would take his time issuing the order for Jasper to read a scroll on that one. As far as the wizard went, he'd just as soon cut his throat and push him into the hole. He might have done it if there weren't witnesses. There were some people the world was better off without, and that mage was one of them. He didn't do it, though, and he also resisted the temptation to kick the man again.

He turned around and studied the room. It took him a few moments to appreciate the monstrous wealth around them. Besides the four long tables they'd seen before rushing in, there were two more to the left of the door, beyond which Jasper and Mags were helping the harpy with her wounds. Those tables, like the others, were heaped with baskets and with gold, piles upon piles of gold, in every conceivable size, from dust to nuggets to chunks that he thought might be too big for even Kaige to lift, and there were more baskets stacked and stuffed underneath.

Upon one of the tables was a set of scales like those he'd seen often enough in big city banks. He'd turned in enough of his own dust and dug-up nuggets in his youth—not to mention the occasional score during his leaves over the years—to recognize the type. In addition to that one, and the very large scales that the cross arms of the whims represented, there was another scale, something of an in-between, near the wall to the right of the table holding the standard one. Three sets of scales, all in the same room: small, medium and large. That struck him as being odd.

He went to the tables and started looking them over more closely, contemplating the huge quantities of gold that lay upon each and guessing at the total worth. He pulled off the baskets to count what was beneath and behind, and he relied on his experienced eye to get it at least nearly right. He valued the first table at some fifty thousand crowns. He thought the second might have twice that, and the third maybe a quarter more still. The fourth table was another eighty thousand at least, and even the table with the scales upon it had some ten to fifteen thousand heaped there.

Beneath that one, hidden behind baskets that were stuffed under it, he found several crates stacked three high, each of them roughly three hands square. They were just like the ones he'd seen back in the ettin cave. He reached under to slide one of them out and found he couldn't budge it. He pushed the rest of the baskets out from under the table to give him room, revealing a few more stacks of the same type of crates and one large chest made of heavy oak, bound in steel bands and locked with a heavy steel padlock.

With room and better leverage, he tried again to slide a crate off the top of one stack, but still he could not. He broke the leather-strap handle instead, the release of which sent him rolling backward so suddenly, he nearly fell right down through the hole. He came to a rest with his head and neck projecting over the edge. He turned and looked down into it, grimacing. Wide eyed, he lifted his gaze and saw Kaige and Meggins staring at him, both with expressions transforming from an instant's horror to the recognition that it was now appropriate to be amused.

"That wasn't quite agile, Sarge," Meggins said with a crooked grin. "I thought we'd lost you for a second."

"I thought I'd lost me too," Ilbei agreed, rolling to his stomach and sliding away from the edge. He got onto his knees and settled back on his heels, letting his heartbeat return to normal speed. "A fine way to end this escapade, me flat as a stepped-in prairie pile down there, a load of harpies trampin on me like a rug."

Meggins and Kaige laughed, their relief as evident as Ilbei's was.

"Kaige, come on over here and help me with this," Ilbei said. "I can't even drag one of em out."

Kaige tied off the wrapping on Meggins' shoulder and left the nimble warrior to pull his armor back on alone. They knelt together at the table under which Ilbei had found the crates and considered the task.

"If'n I make my guess, they're all full of gold in there," Ilbei said. "But I'd like to peek. So get hold of the top one there on yer side. Reach around back and get yer fingers in, like this." He showed him what he meant. "I'll yank it on my side, and we'll just tip it all down."

"But it might break open if there's gold in there," Kaige said. "Won't it?"

"Aye, lad, it might. But I don't see no other way without unloadin this whole damn table and movin it. We ain't got time, and I'd like to know fer my report. Come on, now. Give a pull."

They each took a side, and on the count of three, both powerful men gave a mighty yank. Just as Kaige had predicted, the boxes, after reluctantly giving way, crashed to the floor, and the top one broke open, spilling out gold coins in a glimmering splash. They bounced and spun everywhere, several rolling across the room and dropping out of sight through the hole, others traveling to the walls, the scales, the whims and the door. One of them even made it all the way across the room to Meggins.

He'd just gotten his armor over his head when it rolled up and tapped against his boot. He stooped, picked it up, studied it for a moment, then sent it spinning into the air. "Don't mind if I do," he said, smiling as he savored the hushed metallic ring it made as it spun. He caught it and dropped it into a small pouch on his belt.

"That ain't yers," Ilbei said, "and we ain't looters. We start with that, and there won't be no difference between us and them."

"I can live with that," Meggins said to himself as Ilbei turned back to study the coins that had spilled all around his boots.

"Kaige, ya reckon them big fellers could lift a box full of these? They was somethin bigger even than you."

Kaige shook his head immediately. "Not easy, they couldn't. That was at least forty stone."

Ilbei agreed. "So what's a man gonna do with crates of coins too heavy to lift? And where's he gettin em?" His gaze went to the locked chest he'd uncovered as he twisted up his lips and began chewing on the ends of a few unruly and overlong mustache hairs. "Especially a big one like that?"

He stooped and reached under the table and gave the lock a tug, mainly intent on seeing if the chest was as heavy as he expected it would be. It was not. It came away so easily, he almost tipped it over.

He slid it out and studied the shiny steel lock, then drew his pickaxe and gripped it in both hands. With a wink at Kaige, he raised it on high and then brought it down with a neat and perfectly placed swing. The lock banged heavily against the chest, but did not break.

"By the gods, that's a good one," Ilbei said, looking a little embarrassed as he glanced back at Kaige. "But I had a bad angle on it." He moved to get a more convenient angle and raised his pickaxe again, just as Jasper came out.

The young mage saw the lock, and the chest, and said, quite calmly, "That's a terrible idea."

Ilbei paused, his pick still on high, and swiveled his head. "And why's that?"

"Well, I'm assuming that noise I just heard was you striking that lock a moment ago." He pointed to the steel padlock. "And yet there it is."

"Yeah, I struck it all right. And yer point?"

"My point is that padlock is a Fist of Duador. It's made from West Daggerspine steel by the locksmiths Goorier and Morst of Sansafrax, brothers who learned the secret from their father's father, who learned it on Duador in the last years before the dwarven demise. I read a book about them, but I can tell by the way you are glaring at me right now that you aren't interested in the important details, so I'll just tell you that a Fist of Duador costs fourteen crowns and, depending on who sold it, some portion of silver too."

Ilbei's face wrinkled all the more. He knew that somewhere in all of that, Jasper had some kind of point, despite his being incapable of getting to it, but Ilbei didn't have time or patience to try to shake it out. "Well, as ya can see, these folks aren't short on funds, so I reckon it's no surprise they got themselves a fancy lock." Then he swelled with breath and once more prepared to hit it.

"The only people who spend that kind of money on locks are banks, nobles and magicians with something to hide," Jasper said. Apparently having not been made to "stop his gob" or "quit his yammerin" constituted encouragement for him to carry on. "Being that we aren't in a bank, that leaves nobles and magicians. A magician would trap that lock, and anyone opening it without first canceling the spell would be either killed or somehow subdued. A noble, whether magician or not, would pay to have it enchanted if they'd gone to the expense of buying one as well."

Ilbei paused once again, the angles of his arms flattening at the elbows some, causing the pickaxe blades to tip toward the floor. "Magic lock trap, ya say?"

"Yes. I do say. And I would suppose it would be something lethal for the purposes of efficacy, as anything less makes little sense. A lock like that is a commitment. I can't prove it, however, and I suppose there is some tiny likelihood that it might only be D- or E-class lightning of the variety you've already experienced. So if you insist on hammering at it, just let me get out of the way." He backed into the doorway leading into the room where Mags and the harpy were, stopping just inside and leaning out far enough to peek, one eye peering around the doorframe.

Ilbei stepped away from the chest, glaring at it as if it were a rabid wolverine. "Fine. So how far off do ya expect I should be?"

"At least halfway across the room," Jasper said. "All the way would be safer. Although, if it's a blast-wave type of fire spell, it could pick up these gold coins and send them flying everywhere, which could be just as deadly as the magic in the end, if less spectacular."

Ilbei took another step back. He'd already seen enough gold being thrown around for one day. "So how do ya suppose we open it? Ya got a scroll in there fer that?" He pointed with his chin at Jasper's satchel, which swung from the magician's neck as he peered around the doorway. "Speaking of which, how'd that harpy turn out?"

"She'll be all right given time. It's not a proper healing spell, as you know. But we did get the wing straightened and the burns closed. Some of them will leave scars if she doesn't get a better spell soon, and I'm not too sure about that hole in her wing. It didn't close up much at all."

"Well, is she done sufferin?"

"She is. Or at least, her pain is gone as far as I can tell.

But, as I continue to try to explain to you, I am not a healer, so I really can't be called upon for that kind of expertise. I simply happen to be able to read—"

"So, the lock, how about the lock?"

"You know, that's very rude," Jasper said. "You really ought to let me finish at least one idea before you go on to—"

"Ya see these here?" Ilbei said, pointing to the crimson stripes on his tabard. "These say I got Her Majesty's permission to be as rude as I want, at least to the likes of you. So ya don't need to fret my manners none." Meggins snorted but fell silent when Ilbei swung a ferocious glare at him. Back to Jasper, Ilbei said, "Now, the lock. Fer the love of sweet Mercy, how do we get through that infernal lock?"

"Well, I should think you'd try the key," Jasper said. He said it as if it were the most obvious thing in the world. And because it was, Meggins snorted again, this time at Ilbei's expense. It was even funnier a moment later as Ilbei spun, preparing to unleash a full barrage of profanity at the man whose chuckling went on too long, and discovered Meggins fishing through Ivan Gangue's tunic pockets. Right after, Meggins drew out a small steel key, which he dangled toward Ilbei, grinning. The chuckling was barely contained laughter at that point, and Ilbei scowled for a moment, but then realized it was pretty well justified. It came upon him slowly, like wine filling up a large glass, and before long, all of them were laughing. All but, alas, poor Jasper, who just never seemed to get the best jokes, even when they were by his own design.

Jasper's poor humor, however, turned out a blessing in the end, for when Meggins tossed the key to Ilbei, the sergeant went immediately to set it into the lock.

"I still wouldn't do that," Jasper said, which, of course, made Ilbei stop yet again to roll his eyes and glare at him.

"Dragon's teeth, Jasper, what now?"

"Did you check to see if there are spell-cancelling runes

on it?"

"Ya know I didn't. Ya was standin right there."

"Well, you should check, you know. Because if it doesn't have them, and there is a magical trap, it will still go off."

"Then why didn't ya say that when ya said I should try a key?"

"I didn't say try *a* key. I said to try *the* key, meaning that you find it and confirm it is correct by checking that it has runes on it that might dispel a magic lock."

"Well, why didn't ya say all that the first time?"

"I was trying not to bore you with the details. I know how you hate them."

"Jasper, I swear, you're goin to be the one what drives me straight into the daft house where the burnt-out mages and the broke-minded blank folks go." He once again backed away from the chest, this time approaching Jasper with the key.

"Well, I don't think that's how mental disorders work," Jasper said, but he took the key and fell silent while he looked at it. "Yes, that's exactly what it does. I was right, by the way: it was a more powerful spell. It's still lightning, but much better. I don't think you would have survived."

"So what do I do?"

Jasper stepped past him and casually opened the lock, turning back when he was done and presenting both lock and key to Ilbei. "Just open it."

Meggins and Kaige were both smart enough to keep their laughter to themselves.

Still cautious, Ilbei borrowed Kaige's sword. He slipped it into the latch, then threw the chest open. Everyone, even Jasper, made a point of cowering in advance of any explosion that might be on the way. Nothing blew up. The lid swung open easily, and Ilbei leaned forward, too distrusting of magic now to risk looking directly inside. He frowned at what he could see: two squat clay jars with wide mouths corked by broad, flat stoppers the size of lily pads. Feeling less intimidated, he crept forward and looked in earnest. Inside, lying in a space made for it in the bottom of the chest, was a steel rod, thick as a piton and twice as long. On the left was a strange sort of rack made of copper, a miniature version of the grill, but this one had small, flat loops projecting from it like little shelves, five loops across, five rows each. There were places where the copper glimmered gold. Last was a short length of copper wire, no thicker gauge than the links in Ilbei's chainmail. And that was it.

Ilbei leaned over the chest and studied the contents for a while, his bushy eyebrows low over his eyes and a harrumph sounding in his chest. He straightened and turned back to the rest of them, all eagerly awaiting the news of what he'd found. He shrugged. "Some kind of contraption. Ain't much to look at, to tell it true. Whole lot of fuss fer nothin."

Jasper didn't appear satisfied with that answer. "It *is* too much fuss for nothing," he said, and came to have a look of his own. He also harrumphed, though his had a much different sound than Ilbei's had. He bent down and removed one of the wide, flat-topped corks. He wiggled the jar, which was difficult as it was set into a slot made to secure it well. He leaned closer and took a whiff. He replaced the cork and opened the other one, glancing in it and taking a whiff as he had the first. He jerked away quickly, his face contorting as if by bitter medicine, his eyelids fluttering. He recorked the jar and turned a satisfied expression to Ilbei.

Ilbei waited for him to say it, but he didn't, so he had to ask. "So what is it, son? Don't just stand there like the dog what finally ate the cat. Speak up, boy."

"Someone is counterfeiting coins."

"In here?"

"Yes, in here. That contraption, as you called it, is for electroplating. And unless I miss my guess, that first jar contains gold salts."

"Gold salts? I ain't never heard of such a thing. What kinda fool would eat somethin like that, and what's it got to do with fakin coins?"

"Well, you say you can smell metal with that finely tuned nose of yours, why don't you come verify it?" Jasper turned back to the chest and uncorked the first jar again. Ilbei moved beside him and leaned down, peering inside. It was filled half-full with a dark fluid, almost black but with a touch of color like cognac or red wine. He sniffed the air tentatively.

"Hard to say if'n I'm smellin what's in the jar or the gold all around."

"Get closer, then. I really would like to know."

"I would too," came a voice from across the room. It was Cavendis, who was sitting up despite looking very pale.

Ilbei bent lower and sniffed close to the top of the jar. Sure enough, there was gold in the liquid somehow. "Well, that's the strangest thing I ever heard of. Gold water?"

Jasper's was the face of smugness. "In a manner of speaking, yes. I told you. It's a technique called electroplating. The Conjurers Guild wrote a piece about it in their almanac several years back. A few of them were trying to figure out how to bond one metal to another, and they wanted it to be permanent, as if it were meant to be that way. It's yet another idea taken from those poor, long-lost dwarves, although they say the dwarves somehow did it with fruit juice, as I recall. That was what had the conjurers confused. They ultimately gave the process up as lost—or rumor—as they simply couldn't find the right combinations of fruit juice, and they couldn't get powerful enough lightning bolts to work. They even had a Z-ranked conjurer blasting at it for a time, but nothing ever came of it, even with power of that magnitude working on it."

"What happened to him, the Z?" Ilbei couldn't help but ask. "That thing kill him?"

"Her. And no, she died of old age. She was four hundred and seven years old. Her passing was why they wrote the article."

Ilbei rumbled some in his throat, regretting having been sucked into a worthless bit of history from his long-winded wizard. And besides, he didn't understand much of what Jasper was telling him anyway. He couldn't see the sense in talking about fruit juice and conjuring experiments just then. The one thing he did recognize, however, was that there was no need for counterfeiting in a place such as the one they were in.

"There weren't no reason fer makin fake gold what with all this real gold lyin about like sand on a beach," he said. "A man would do better to just pocket some of it if'n he were inclined to thievin. A thief don't get half the penalty a counterfeiter does, so there weren't no reason to risk it." He noticed that Cavendis was glaring at the unconscious wizard lying bound and gagged at his side. It didn't take the wily old veteran long to figure out what the look was for. "What's the matter, Cavendis, yer man there somehow cheatin ya? Skimmin off the top? Has yer counterfeiter been right there under yer noble nose all along?"

"Spadebreaker, you have no idea what kind of trouble you've dug up down here. If there's anyone you love out there in the whole wide world, you'll never hide them well enough to protect them from what you've done."

"Horrible as all that sounds, Milord, I reckon you're in it deeper'n I am. I only run aground of ya. Fer yer part, you're gonna have to take it up with Her Majesty herself, or with yer high Lady Mum back in South Mark if'n it turns out it's her ya been crossin. Maybe you'll get both of em havin at ya, you and that piece of villainy lyin there next to ya. None of them splinters is under my nails."

"You better kill me, Sergeant. You won't get better from the Queen. You're in way over your station now." The steadiness of his gaze, the certitude, made Ilbei think there might be more to the threat than he wanted to believe.

"I'm just a grunt doin my job. I was to come dig out what's been plaguin these folks around here, find the Skewer and make things right. But turns out the plague is less about the Skewer than it is about you. I reckon I'll trust my luck on Her Majesty's justice landin fair when it all shakes out. If the gods is watchin, there ain't no way a cheat like yerself comes out when it's done, noble or no."

"That depends upon which gods are watching, doesn't it? But the truth is you won't even get me out of here, Sergeant. Much less brought before the Queen."

Ilbei ignored him. "Let's get these lot ready to haul out of here," Ilbei said, turning to his men. "Meggins, get His Lordship on his feet. Watch him, though. He'll kick sideways like a mule. Kaige, you get that other one up and goin too. I didn't kick him that hard; he'll wake up." Seeing them in motion, Ilbei went back into the small room where Mags lingered with the harpy.

"Mags," he said as he entered, but silenced himself, seeing that she was trying to speak to the creature still strapped to Gangue's grill. He smiled and let go some tension with his next breath. It was that kind of goodness that made facing the danger he'd been through worthwhile. People like Mags. Talking to a harpy. Sweet, silly, hopeful girl.

The harpy recoiled at his approach. The chains that bound her clanked against the ironwork grill as her body stiffened.

"Her name is Miasma," Mags said.

"Whose? Hers?" One eyebrow lifted as he indicated the harpy with a thrust of his tatty beard. "Ya went and named her, a mean and nasty critter as that? That's like namin an animal ya might have to eat one day."

"No, I didn't name her. It's her name. She told me. She's been here for seventeen hundred years. She's their queen, and this was the first harpy wild on Kurr—well, not here but the steppes above Fall Pools, obviously."

"She told ya all that, did she?" His eyes glimmered with the indulgence. He was polite enough not to laugh.

"Sergeant, I'm serious. That's what she said."

Ilbei saw the solemn look upon Mags' face, so he continued to indulge her, scanning the harpy with a long, careful gaze. Nothing in the harpy's countenance softened, no part of it shifting toward civility or an inclination for a chat. Ilbei turned skeptical eyes back to Mags. "I expect she's pullin yer chain with that. She can't be a lick over thirty-five, fer one, unless them human parts of hers don't respond to the pull of time. Even a highborn sorcerer shows more years than that by eighty-five, and noble ladies, even bird ones, don't spend no time in slaver caves, much less gettin tortured on lightnin racks."

"Well, she's telling the truth."

"Oh, she is, is she? And how can ya tell?"

"I could see it in her eyes."

"Mags, she's spinnin stories what will get ya to cut her loose. Like as much, she'll claw yer throat open the moment ya do. She's even got reason to, if'n ya think on it."

Mags shook her head. "No. She won't. She just wants to go home."

"Home? Ya mean down there where all them sawed-off harpies are? That home?"

"Yes, that one. It's all the home she has now. And they're her children."

"By Hestra, now there's a story fer ya."

"It is, and it's a terrible one. She told me some of it. Oh, Sergeant, it's awful. We have to do something. We can't leave them all like this."

"Well, I'm inclined to agree with ya on that. Them sorry creatures down there is gonna be top of my report when we get back. No tellin what they'll do about it, but I'll wager some of them feel-good city folks will put up a preserve or somethin fer em somewhere, stuff em in and then all paw theirselves, cluckin and botherin to each other how kind and wonderful they are fer bein benefactors."

"We can't leave them and wait for that. Not now. Not if we're taking ... Ivan and your major out."

"Why not? They been here this long. They'll make it till I put in my report."

Mags glanced to the harpy, Miasma as she claimed her name to be, and smiled, a patient thing, as if trying to convince the harpy not to give up on her. "If they, if Ivan is the keeper of order around here, what will happen in his absence? There are many other men here, and it's at least four days back to Hast from here. Even healed, she can't protect them all."

A low hum issued from Ilbei's throat as he considered that. He reckoned if the men did figure out Gangue was gone, and Cavendis—assuming they even knew the young lord was there, given that Ilbei didn't get the impression he came around much—most of them would go straight to grabbing as much gold as they could carry and get out. The way piss-soaked Sett had told it, fear was the only thing holding them there, fear and the promise of a stone's weight in gold. Near as Ilbei could figure, if the enforcement broke down, the miners would get off with well more than a stone's weight each, making their contracts worth about as much as all the gold blowing in the wind. Which he remarked on.

"They most likely would run off with the gold," he said.

"Most would," Mags allowed. "But not all. Some of them do terrible things to her children, simply because they can. The gold has drawn only the worst kinds of men out here." Her eyes seemed to glaze, but Ilbei saw that she was looking past him to where Gangue was being slapped awake by Kaige.

Ilbei grew irritated then. He couldn't solve everything. He was only one man. "Listen up, Mags. Best we can do is get on out of here quick, before them others figure out Gangue is gone. Sooner we do, sooner we'll get help back here to clear the rest of these fellers out. There ain't no other way, and there ain't no perfect solutions. The more we dawdle talkin, the worse off it might get. We get caught, nothin gets fixed at all."

"We have to get them out," she insisted.

"Mags, we ain't gettin nobody out but us and them two villains. That's the end of it."

Mags clearly wanted to argue, but she saw in Ilbei's eyes that that was the end of it. He was a man long used to having final authority, unpopular authority, and he was perfectly comfortable having people mad at him. She acquiesced quietly on the point. "Well, I am going to let her go," she said. "We can't leave her here like this."

Ilbei grimaced, but agreed. He'd known it too. He called out loudly into the other room. "On yer guard out there. We're lettin this here harpy loose. Don't fuss with her if'n she goes out quiet like."

When they'd all answered back affirmatively, he stepped to the left side of the iron grating and regarded the harpy with a sigh. "Listen here, you," he began, but Mags' expression made him stop.

"Her name is Miasma," Mags told him again.

"I heard what ya said." He tried to read the harpy's expression, but she was staring up at the ceiling. He could tell by the rapidity of her breathing she was anxious. He hoped it wasn't in preparation of ripping his face apart again. "Let's go on and cut her free."

They worked together to undo the bindings, starting at her ankles, then her wings, then her wrists. Her whole body tensed as her limbs were freed, her powerful legs bending, her talons gripping the grill.

"All right, ya harp—Miasma, I'm gonna take this last collar off of ya, and I expect ya to play nice just like Mags says ya will. I'd sure hate to regret this here action all the rest of my days."

The familiar low, rasping growl issued from her throat. He shook his head, sending a resigned look Mags' way. "See?" But he unlatched the neck clamp anyway.

The harpy leapt away, then spun back and crouched low, just as she had when Ilbei first fought with her. He knew right then that she was going to jump on him again. But she did not. She glared at him, her rattling hiss low and menacing, before she whirled and pinned her wings back. In one great leap, she sprang through the door and down into the hole.

Ilbei, not in position to see that she'd gone down the hole, rushed out after her, intending to help his men fend her off. But she was gone. He went to the edge of the opening and looked down, seeing her in silhouette as she hurtled toward the light of the cavern far below. "Hope she's got enough room to pull out of that dive," he said, as Mags joined him. Together, they watched as Miasma neared the bottom of the long shaft, her wings opening like the spring-loaded blades of an assassin's folding knife. She spiraled the last fifty spans or so, then shot out the bottom, though they could hardly see her for how small she'd become. The long, screeching cry of her triumphant return was the evidence she'd survived.

Ilbei turned back to his men, and his captives. "All right, folks, let's get these two sorry bastards to Hast and the justice of the War Queen."

Chapter 33

With torches made from broken table legs and aided by Jasper's oil spell, they headed back out into the tunnels beyond the gold-filled room. Ilbei led the procession with Mags behind, followed by Meggins, who pulled the two prisoners along. In breaking apart the table, Ilbei had also pulled up one of its long planks and fashioned a crude yoke for the captives. He'd carved shallow arcs into each end of the plank and widened the nail holes with his pick, wide enough to accommodate loops of rope, which were put around his prisoners' necks. Cavendis was lashed into the lead end of the yoke and Gangue to the back. Jasper followed behind them, having been instructed to keep an eye on Gangue for "anything magical," and Kaige was tasked with rear guard.

They moved quickly, but carefully, up the passage and soon found themselves at the intersection where so many of the extra baskets were stacked. Ilbei peeked around the corners, dreading to see scores of men sneaking toward them with weapons drawn. The crossing was clear.

"Quick, let's go," he said. He ran across, with Mags right on his heels. Meggins hauled on the lead rope that was bound to Cavendis' wrists. The noble prisoner tried to resist, but Kaige saw it and put one big hand in Gangue's back and the other against the back of the magician's head. Then he gave a mighty shove. Gangue gagged as he stumbled forward, his throat driven against the board, which then clunked into the back of Cavendis' neck, causing a whiplash effect that got the young lord moving again.

Meggins tugged him along, and soon they found themselves nearing the top of the steep passageway where the rush of the river grew loud. Ilbei motioned for them to stop, still several paces from the top. He handed Meggins the torch, then finished the distance. He stooped low and looked out, again dreading to discover the approach of many men. This time, there were torches and lanterns moving his way, coming from both sides. Whoever carried them was in a hurry, if the wild movements of the lights in the blackness were any indication. They weren't sneaking, that was sure. The nearer they got, the clearer came the sound of their voices, even over the river's noise.

Ilbei ran down again. "Back, back, back," he said, as loud as he dared. "They're comin fast."

The passage was too narrow to turn the prisoners around, so they had to run backward down the steep passage as Meggins pushed and Kaige pulled. Cavendis was fit and agile enough to manage it, if more by reflex than choice, but Gangue tripped and fell, dragging Cavendis down with him.

Kaige and Meggins tried to get them up, but Cavendis lay there laughing through his gag, his legs limp like a child throwing a tantrum and refusing to get up.

"Kaige" was all Ilbei had to say as he stepped around Meggins and just past Cavendis lying there. Kaige saw Ilbei's intent and nodded back. The two of them took up the weight of the prisoners between them, Ilbei gripping the plank just behind Cavendis, and Kaige grabbing Gangue by the hair. Together, they dragged the prisoners easily enough as they resumed their hasty descent. Downhill made the going easy enough, even so encumbered, and Jasper had sense enough to get out ahead and stop at the intersection to look and see if the way was clear. He came back with frightened eyes and carping mouth. "Someone's coming," he said. "Voices. I heard voices."

"Which way?"

"Both."

Ilbei looked behind and saw light moving down from where they'd just come. Again. It seemed they were never destined to get out that way.

"Gaze of the gorgon, we've got to move," Ilbei said. "Back in where we were. Go, go. Get in and lock that damned door."

"Then what?" Jasper had the nerve to ask.

"Go, boy. Go!"

Kaige gave him a shove as hard as the one he'd given Gangue, not out of malice but out of urgency. It had the same effect, however, and Jasper went sprawling forward and slid down into the intersection. Nobody was laughing at him this time.

He was up quickly and down the passage past the baskets. He held the door open as the rest of them rushed back into the room, careful not to dash right into the hole in their haste. Jasper slammed it shut and dropped the lock. He turned back, panting, looking to Ilbei. "Now what?"

Kaige pointed to the tables. "We can block the door with them. Weight them down with gold and crates of coins."

"Good thinking, big man!" Meggins said. Ilbei agreed.

"Get it done quick," Ilbei said. "Jasper, keep an eye on these two criminals." He ignored Jasper's "what am I supposed to do with them?" expression and moved with Kaige to the table nearest the door. Heaving together, they tried to move it. Nothing. Mags ran over to add her weight and strength to the effort as well. It was still too much.

"Scrape off the gold," she said, pushing off chunks as fast as she could. Soon after, they were pushing hunks of gold onto the floor, the dense masses thudding dully to the stone in a rich and heavy rain.

"Try again," Ilbei said when the table was half-cleared. This time they were able to move it, if barely, and got it pressed up against the door, lengthwise. They began loading it up with gold again, the sound of their breathing heavy as they worked.

Soon the table was piled high with gold again, a great mound stacked up and sloped against the door as high as they could get it. Ilbei and Kaige then pushed over the table with the scales to get at the crates below. They threw off the top two crates on one stack. Both broke open and more golden coins spilled out, rolling everywhere. The bottom crate, still intact, they dragged away from the wall. They grunted and groaned, heaving at it as they pulled it toward the door. When it was far enough from the wall, Meggins got in behind and gave a shove. Finally they had it pushed against the bottom of the door. They ran for another one, once again pushing the top two crates over and letting them smash. Black coins spilled out everywhere this time, slugs made of lead. It was as obvious to Ilbei's trained eye as it was to his sense of smell. Once again they dragged the bottommost crate, unbroken, against the door.

They could hear voices coming down the corridor.

"We've got to get out of here, Sarge," Meggins said. "Fortifying is only going to work so long. They'll just break it down."

"Where, then?" Ilbei asked, but even as he said it, he looked at the hole in the middle of the room down which the harpy, Miasma, had gone. They all did.

Jasper saw them and stepped away. "No," he said, but Ilbei was already heading for one of the big baskets dangling near the edge of the hole.

"Get that other one hooked up," Ilbei called as he worked. Mags ran for a basket and dragged it to the hole near the second whim, setting it beneath the hook as Kaige lifted it out of the way for her.

"Kaige, you're gonna take Meggins, Jasper and Cavendis down," Ilbei said. "I'll get the rest. Meggins, give Jasper yer knife. And Jasper, I swear to ya, if'n Cavendis makes even one odd squeak, ya stick him in the guts. And I mean it, now. Ya stick him, and stick him good. This ain't no time fer the mouse in ya, hear?"

Jasper turned very pale as Meggins handed over his knife, a big, cheerful grin on his face. "It's easy," Meggins said. "The belly is all soft anyway, especially if you get them here on the side. Slides right in." He poked a knuckle into Jasper's side playfully, but the scrawny enchanter was not amused.

Kaige tried to set the hook into the ring woven into the basket handle, but the hook had an odd, spring-loaded contraption on it. It snapped against his thumb as he fumbled with it, which caused him to lose his grip. The hook fell away and swung out over the hole.

"That's right, Kaige. Make sure that's on good and tight," Meggins said, teasing the big man. "It's a long fall. I'll have time to cuss you five times over by the time we hit if that thing slips off on the way down."

Kaige thought that was very funny, and the two of them made falling jokes the whole time Kaige worked to set the hook, which, of course, horrified Jasper all the more.

"Kick the lock on that windlass, Mags," Ilbei ordered, not sharing in the humor. He was focused like a spike on getting his people out of there. "Meggins, help her haul that rope off of there and throw the slack down. We can't wind ourselves down with them levers, as them ain't made to be cranked from down the hole."

Meggins frowned, as did Mags and Kaige, but Ilbei

demonstrated his intent on his side of the hole, unlocking the gears and yanking out span after span of rope, throwing it down the hole. Soon after, they followed suit.

"Here's how we're goin to do this," Ilbei said, once he'd thrown out enough rope to get them to the bottom. "We'll go together, baskets side by side, hand over hand. We go slow and easy, but quick enough as we have to. Won't be fun, but me and Kaige can do it if'n we keep our wits, and the rest of ya keep these two from spoilin it somehow." He glared at Jasper to make that point, then took hold of the plank that ran between the prisoners and moved them violently into position. "Let's go, you two."

Cavendis tried to resist, but Ilbei simply lifted him up by his neck with the yoke and set him in the basket. The young nobleman gasped at the pain the lift caused in his shoulder and went limp for a time. Kaige moved around Ilbei and lifted Gangue, more gently but just as easily, and placed him in the basket that would be Ilbei's. The plank that yoked them together bridged the gap in a sobering sort of way.

Someone tried to open the door. First a knock, then the rattle of someone trying to come in, then a loud bang.

All eyes flashed to the door, then back to Ilbei. Ilbei was calm. "Get in, Kaige. Jasper, get in there with him, careful not to hurt nobody with that knife. Kaige, haul yerself up off the ground. Then Meggins will swing the boom around. Mags, you'll swing our boom around same time he does. Then both of ya get in yer baskets. Meggins, help Kaige with the rope if'n he needs, since you boys have an extra man. Mags, take my knife here and be ready to stick that old acquaintance of yers through the guts if'n he moves so much as a twitch."

"Gladly," she said.

"I got to tell you, Sarge," Meggins said. "I'm not too keen on hauling any more rope."

Noting the bandages on his hands, Ilbei fully understood.

"Well, if'n ya think you're not up to it, we can have Jasper pullin with Kaige, leavin ya fer keepin that knife in Cavendis' ribs."

Meggins grimaced. "Right. I'll get the rope."

The door thundered as something hit it, dust falling from the doorframe and even the ceiling right around.

"They'll get through quick enough," Ilbei pronounced as he stepped into his basket. "These folks are lousy with diggin tools. A few heaps of gold and some lead boxes ain't no obstacle." He glanced right to Mags, who was still studying the boom apparatus, figuring out how it worked. He looked left to Meggins, doing the same. "You two ready?"

Mags got the rope off the crank handle and, after a frantic search, found the small iron pin that locked the boom itself in place. She called out to Meggins, showing him where the pin was. "Right!" he called. "Got it. Ready."

"Ready," Mags said.

"Go on, Kaige," Ilbei said as he pulled down on the rope and hauled his own basket a half hand into the air. "Swing us out over."

Mags reached up, nearly on tiptoe, and pushed on the long, weighted arm that reached across the room. She grunted and stretched, and Ilbei thought she might not be able to move it, but at last she did. He and his basket companion, Ivan Gangue, swung out over the hole. He couldn't help but look down over the rim. A shudder ran down his spine.

"Get in, let's go. It's a long way down hopin that door will hold the while."

Mags looked over the short distance between the edge of the hole and the basket. "It's too high," she said. "I can't get in. Go down a little."

Ilbei lowered the basket, hand over hand, until the basket's edge was nearly level with the floor. Mags still looked tentative. "I'm going to have to jump," she said.

"I'm ready," Ilbei replied. He braced himself, teeth grinding together, and waited for her to land. She did so gracefully, and he was relieved that the weight was not too much. He heard, more than he saw, when Meggins jumped into the other one, Kaige's grunt audible.

"All right, let's stay as even as we can. Let's go."

And so they went, down and down and down. Ilbei worried about their weight as they went, but he realized that neither the ropes nor the pulleys made a sound. He actually managed a laugh. "How about that? First time I wasn't too stout fer the furniture."

That got a chortle or two from Kaige and Meggins. Were it not for the drumming racket of the men pounding on the door above, anyone listening might have thought they were at the descent for fun.

They'd gotten perhaps midway down when a loud crash sounded, followed by the metallic clatter of falling coins, several of which tumbled down the hole. One landed in the bottom of Ilbei's basket, just missing his boot. Another thudded loudly on the plank connecting Cavendis to Gangue. Meggins cursed as one bounced off his armor, right above the split where he'd been burned, and a fourth one struck Cavendis in the head. He grunted, and Jasper, taking his orders and Ilbei's threats seriously, did just as he'd been instructed and stabbed Cavendis in the side.

Cavendis gasped, a muffled sound, and pitched forward, nearly knocking Meggins out of the basket. Kaige caught him, but in doing so, the basket slid down nearly a full span before he miraculously, brutally, stopped it with just one hand. That drop, however, jerked Gangue forward and over the edge of his basket, which nearly tore Mags out as well. She caught herself and, with a desperate reach, managed to catch Gangue by the elbow as he tumbled out.

The whole escapade had them swinging back and forth, and for a time at least, the ropes actually did protest, though not nearly so loud as Gangue did. The sounds of his terror chilled them all.

"I can't hold him," Mags said.

"I can't hold him either," Kaige said. In addition to those in his basket, he was now holding up the bulk of Gangue's weight as the man dangled at the end of the yoke opposite Cavendis. Cavendis, in turn, barely held on, kept from falling out only by the fact that Meggins had recovered enough to grab him around the waist.

"Cut him loose, Jasper," Meggins said. "Use my knife. Cut the yoke off, quick." He sounded nearly as worried as Gangue.

"I can't." Jasper's voice was high and meek.

"Why not? In the name of plunging death, Jasper, cut it."

"It's still in him." Jasper was staring at the spreading red stain of Cavendis' blood, which had begun to drip into the bottom of the basket near his feet.

"Well, pull it out. Cut the rope at his neck."

"Just push them both out," Kaige said. "I can't hold us all day."

"Mags," said Ilbei. "Can ya pull him back? Can ya try?"

She tried, but in doing so, she tipped the basket toward him, making it worse. She had to stop. "I can't," she said. "I really can't."

Gangue's eyes were huge, and the frenzy of his pleas was setting everyone on edge.

"Can ya get to his hands?" Ilbei asked, doing his best to keep his voice calm.

"What do you mean?"

"Can ya cut the ropes on his hands? He can pull hisself back in."

She glanced up at Ilbei, frantic. He tried to nod encouragingly, not knowing that all she could see was the white of his beard moving in the near dark. It was enough.

She looked back down, looked into Gangue's eyes. So full

of fear, so dependent on her goodwill. She glowered back at him. "I should just let them cut you loose," she said. But she leaned into the basket and fished around for the knife where it had dropped when she'd nearly fallen out. She found it and then dared to reach out far enough that she could, by pulling Gangue closer and reaching precariously down, saw at the bindings around his wrists.

The moment the ropes were severed, his wrists came apart, sending his left arm, the one that Mags held, swinging up toward her and the rest of him dropping away the length of his reach. She fell backward with the temporary release, but then his weight hit the end of his outstretched arm, and she was nearly dragged back out of the basket again. She held onto him only by his sleeve.

"Come on, you guys," Kaige said. His voice was strained. His basket dropped another half hand with the motion of that change in positioning. "Sarge, I'm going to have Meggins push him out. I'm sorry, but I can't hold it no more."

"Mags?" Ilbei asked, the question deadly urgent. Time to decide.

Gangue was reaching for her with his other hand, but his back was to her now, the arm she held nearly twisted out of joint. His terror was palpable.

"I can't get him," she said. "I really can't."

"Cut him loose, Meggins," Ilbei said. "Do it now."

Gangue's eyes flew as wide as dinner plates, and his mouth opened dark spaces above and below the line of his gag. "I'm sorry," Mags said. "I'm so sorry." Then, his brows lowered a little, his eyes a little less wide, and he looked away from her. He looked up, saw Meggins pull the bloody knife out of Cavendis and move it to the rope around the nobleman's neck.

"Be ready to let him go soon as this cuts loose, Mags," Meggins warned. "Do you hear? Say you will."

"I will."

"Here he goes."

She looked back down at Gangue. He was looking down the hole. He looked back up at her. And smiled. He reached up and pulled off the gag. His weight against the yoke rope was half strangling him, but he began to chant.

"He's casting something," she shouted.

"Three ... two ...," Meggins said, his voice wavering with the motions of his knife. He paused. "If I didn't have to worry about cutting this bastard's throat ...," he said, shifting the knife and sawing madly. "Okay, three ... two ... one ...." Gangue vanished just as Meggins said, "Let go."

The plank fell away as soon as Meggins cut the rope, tumbling down, bouncing off of the smooth sides of the shaft and sending wooden echoes up at them as it fell, until finally it was lost in the glare of the light below. But it didn't matter anymore.

Though the cutting of the rope had cut him as well, and the coarse rope had gouged him beneath Gangue's weight, Cavendis still managed to laugh as he watched the empty yoke fall away. He mumbled something incoherent from behind his gag. By the tone and cadence of it, it was derisive and full of ridicule.

Chapter 34

The descent through the shaft became a race, a race to get the baskets to the bottom before the men above broke into the room and hauled Ilbei and company up, or worse, cut the ropes. Despite the great strength of both Ilbei and Kaige, there was also the matter of fatigue. Everyone present understood the possibility of failing strength, and the entire company fell silent and let the two men work. All that could be heard was the sound of their breathing, the measured huffs of exhalation here and there, as the two brawny soldiers went hand under hand under hand.

Here and there along the descent, Cavendis made some snide remark, tossed aloft some insult rendered inarticulate due to the gag in his mouth, but likely enough on the subject of lowborn men, low stations and lower intellect. No one cared. The work was at the center of everything. Everyone in the baskets, Cavendis included, strained to hear the last crash as the door barricade failed, which would be followed by voices shouting down the hole.

And of course, those voices did come, and too soon, for the baskets were still some forty spans from the cavern floor when men began shouting down. Fortunately, the distance was great enough, and the dark was dark enough, that the men at the top could not make out who it was going down. Not a gaggle of geniuses by any means, they actually—despite having had to step over the corpses of several of their dead comrades—called down to inquire, "Gangue, is that you?"

"Uh, yes, it is," Meggins shouted back. "Give me a moment, boys. I'm on the heels of a burglary."

A pronounced silence ensued. Ilbei, whose work had him looking up the whole time anyway, saw the silhouetted shapes of the men around the opening turn toward one another as they discussed the possibilities. In the interim, Ilbei and Kaige managed five spans more.

"You ain't Gangue," one of them called down. And right after, an arrow whistled past. It struck the stone wall near Kaige's basket, sounding like a tossed stick as it hit, but it flew harmlessly by. Then came another, and three more after that, plus a few coins someone kicked in, likely on accident. Only one arrow found a mark, grazing Mags down the side of her calf. She made no noise, and Ilbei only knew she'd been hit by the way her eyes narrowed and her breathing changed. They'd descended another five spans.

Two more arrows came down, one so close to Ilbei's arm that the fletching bristled across his elbow like a soft brush. A third thudded into the bottom of the basket between his feet.

Jasper cried out and fell to the bottom of his basket screaming that he'd been hit. "Oh, oh, oh," he screamed, so loud it unnerved everyone and set all their hearts pounding even faster than they already were.

Ilbei somehow found strength to quicken the pace, his aching arms and cramping hands revived by his concern for Jasper. "Meggins," he called. "He all right? Where's he hit?"

Meggins leaned down to look at Jasper. "Straight through his wrist, back to front," he reported.

"He gonna bleed out?"

Meggins was a moment in responding, not wanting to lose pace in handling the rope, adding his strength beneath the work of the mighty Kaige. If Kaige let go or slipped, Meggins wanted to at least serve as a brake. Seven spans lower and two more arrows down—one of which ricocheted off the hard leather of Meggins' pauldron while the other glanced off Kaige's breastplate with a clank—Meggins was able to reply. "I think not, Sarge. It's plugged itself for now." By the volume of the screams that Jasper let out, Ilbei would have thought poor Jasper was on fire. But he supposed the young man had little experience with pain, having come to the army after living a sheltered life.

There came the familiar *tink* of an arrow striking a metal plate straight on, and nearly in the same instant, Kaige let out an *"Argh!"* His basket dropped two full spans, and Meggins grunted right after, but brought it to a halt. It hung there for less than five heartbeats, then began descending again. Ilbei could hear Kaige's teeth grinding, and a quick glance across the intervening space revealed an arrow sticking straight up out of the man's giant bicep like a feathered weed.

Ilbei gritted his own teeth and tried to increase speed even more. Mags gasped, and he looked to her. She was holding her head. She pulled her hand away, and it was red with blood. "Bad?" he asked her.

"No," she said. "I'm fine."

An arrow clanked off the head of Ilbei's pick, and another gold coin spun down, emitting in its revolutions a tinny whine.

He glanced over the edge. Less than ten spans.

Five spans.

"Shite!" Kaige rasped, and his basket dropped precipitously, fast enough Ilbei lost sight of it below the edge of his own. It landed with a thud and four gasps, the impact silencing Jasper's cries.

Ilbei let his basket drop the last span, and it too landed with a thud. "Get out, get out. Out of the line of fire!" He and Mags leapt out of the basket and rolled away. He got to his feet straight off and turned to where Kaige's basket lay. Kaige and Meggins were dragging Jasper out of the line of fire. Cavendis had seen to himself and was running for the creek that ran along the wall, headed for the exit Ilbei and his party had used.

"That's not gonna happen," Ilbei shouted. He ran after the fleeing nobleman, his short, bowed legs eating up the ground between.

"The fire!" Mags called. "Sergeant, the fire!"

Ilbei heard her and glanced back over his shoulder. He saw all the harpies in the distance behind her, all the way past the bend in the cavern wall, waiting in their lonely crowd. He got to the creek just in time to dive in. It was shallow, too shallow, particularly given the bulbous nature of his belly, which raised his backside out as he tried to hunker down. He looked up and saw Cavendis only thirty paces from the exit through which the creek ran. Ilbei was another twenty behind Cavendis. The flare of the fire ignited, and the heat came at him in a wave. He rolled away from it, to the farthest side of the creek. By the gods, it was hot.

He fished and wriggled forward, found a slightly deeper trough, and began to roll in it as if he were on a spit.

The fire roared for what seemed a century, and even with his rolling and splashing, and with the water running by cool as it was, he still thought he must be cooking something fierce. But at last the flames went away.

He lay there for a moment panting, the air in the vicinity having thinned dramatically, but realized right away he wasn't cooked to death. He jumped up, intent on chasing Cavendis into the narrow cave. With his hands bound and a stab wound in his side, the young lord wasn't likely to outrun Ilbei. But then Ilbei saw he would have little need of pursuit, for Cavendis had fallen not ten steps from the exit. He lay facedown on the cavern floor, his clothes blackened and smoking. Ilbei feared that he was dead. He really wanted that man to go back and face what he had coming to him.

When he got to the downed nobleman, he rolled him over and saw, to his great relief, that he was still alive. He was struggling to breathe, however, and the pain of the deep, seeping burns on his back hurt all the more for having been rolled onto them. Ilbei did him the mercy of pulling the gag out of his mouth.

"I see ya ain't laughin no more, Your Lordship," he said. "But I'm glad ya ain't dead as yet." Cavendis was too anguished to reply, which was fine with Ilbei, and the stout old sergeant hooked him under his elbow and hauled him to his feet, causing him to groan and teeter on the brink of unconsciousness. "We get out of here far enough, I'll see that Jasper there reads a spell of healin on ya." The promise of that kind of relief put the motion into Cavendis' feet that Ilbei had hoped it would, and soon the two of them were moving through the wave of returning harpy slaves toward the rest of Ilbei's company.

Jasper looked haggard, clearly in misery, the arrow through his wrist making a cross of his forearm. Kaige had already pulled the arrow out of his own arm and was looking at the cut on Mags' head. "It ain't too bad," he was telling her as Ilbei arrived. "But head cuts bleed bad. Mine did the other day, remember?"

Mags nodded that she did and smiled gratefully up at him. "It doesn't hurt too bad, so then I guess it's good news for now."

"Come on," Meggins said. "Let's get out of here. They're going to know where we are, and near as I can tell, there's only two ways out of here that don't require Jasper turning us all into fish."

"Well, we're not goin back downstream," Ilbei said. "Much as I'd like to think we could get around em and go on out that main passage along the river, seems the gods went out of their way to keep us from gettin more than a step down that trail. So, back out we go the way we came in. Come on."

Meggins was already heading that way, Kaige and Mags right behind. "Let's go, Jasper," Ilbei said. "You'll be all right. We'll get clear of this here, and ya can read one of them spells on yerself and then another on this here bit of blue-blooded dung."

Ilbei had seen wet laundry that didn't droop so bad as poor Jasper did. The forlorn mage looked at his wrist and back at Ilbei, his jaw quivering. Had it been anyone else, Ilbei probably would have shouted at him, or challenged his masculinity, but such things wouldn't lift the spirits of a lad like Jasper.

"I know it hurts, son, but it ain't gonna kill ya like them what's chasin us will if they catch us. So ya just have to eat the misery fer a bit. Come on, now. I know ya can do it. Sooner ya get movin, sooner it will be done."

Reason and kindness worked as he'd hoped, and soon after, Jasper was moving in the direction of the wall down which they'd first come. Kaige, despite his punctured bicep—much less the long and very recent descent—was already hauling himself up the lowest rope. Ilbei shook his head admiringly as he watched. That was one tough son of the goddess there.

By the time Ilbei and his captive arrived at the base of the cliff, Kaige had reached the ledge and was hauling Mags up after him. She held tightly to the rope and used her feet to expedite the climb. Ilbei took the time to look behind them, trying to reclaim some strength and breath. He saw Ergo the Skewer coming around the bend. Ergo and at least a dozen of the mining men.

"All five hands of Anvilwrath are turned against us, folks," he called out. "Meggins, get that bow of yers."

Meggins turned back, saw the problem, and went immediately to work. He hadn't had time to test the range of the black bow yet, but his first shot showed that its range was marvelous. "Sweet soarin long shots," Ilbei muttered, noticing the range as well. "That's the thing fer it! Hold em off, son."

Meggins fired several shots in rapid succession. He missed the first, but the second and third found targets despite being over a hundred spans away. Ergo the Skewer, nearly skewered by Meggins' first shot, dropped to a knee behind a boulder near the shadowed wall. Right after, the metallic clank of one of his long steel bolts sparked off the cliff face near Ilbei's head.

He jerked reflexively, though it would have been too late had the shot angled left a half hand more. He shuddered as he looked down at the long bolt lying nearby. "Well, there ain't no luck fer the straight player round here, is there? That damned ballista of his has got more range than a trebuchet."

"More power too," Meggins muttered between measured breaths. He let go another arrow and sent a man who'd been trying to advance flying back against a pile of rocks. "But I have better arrows." He laughed, if only one note of it, and then continued with his work. Ilbei glanced at Meggins' quiver and saw that he couldn't have more than twenty arrows left.

He craned his neck around and saw that Jasper was already halfway to the ledge that fronted the cave where the harpy's nest was. The moments that followed were an agony of waiting. Finally, Jasper was up, and Kaige threw the rope back down. Sparks flew near Ilbei's head again as he tied it to the bindings at Cavendis' wrists. "Like as not, this won't be comfortable," he said, "but I expect you'll live." He waved for Kaige to pull their captive up.

Meggins shot one of the Skewer's compatriots in the chest, the impact hurling him backward several spans. Meggins laughed. "Gods, but I love this thing." Ilbei ducked behind a rock that only half covered him at best, and he watched impatiently as Kaige dragged Cavendis up the wall. He knew that to speed this along, he was going to have to go up next, on his own, so that Kaige could get to the top.

"Don't let that bastard shoot me in the back while I go up," he said, leaning down to Meggins. "And save a few shots fer coverin yerself while I drag ya up after. This ain't gonna be pretty." Meggins nodded as the arrow he'd just fired punched a hole as big as his fist through another miner's head, a perfect eighty-span shot. He hardly had to give it any arc at that range.

Cavendis was up, and Kaige dropped the rope to Ilbei. Ilbei called up that Kaige should get to the top, which the big man immediately set himself to. Ilbei took the end of the rope and turned back to Meggins. "One sec. Raise up yer arms." Meggins did, leaving off shooting for the time. He jerked his head aside as a steel bolt came whistling by.

Ilbei tied the rope around Meggins' chest, then made another loop, which he dropped down between the archer's legs. "Don't get no ideas," Ilbei said as he reached down after it and pushed the rope through.

"Aw, come on, Sarge. You don't even buy me flowers first?" He tried to shoot another of the approaching men, but Ilbei working with the rope behind him ruined his aim. Still, the shot managed to drive the man to cover behind a boulder.

"I'll kiss ya sweet if'n we both get out of this alive," Ilbei said. "Just keep shootin, and try to save enough of them arrows to cover yerself goin up. And keep that bastard Skewer pinned down so he don't nail me to that wall up there like some fat tapestry."

"I will, but hurry up."

Ilbei once again set himself to a rope, and with the help of his feet this time, he made quick work of it. Only twice did the long, wicked steel of Ergo the Skewer get close, but neither so much as to give Ilbei pause. By the time he was up to the harpy's ledge, Kaige was pulling Jasper up to the top. Mags was warily menacing Cavendis with her quarterstaff as the two of them waited beneath the rope. She could lever him off the ledge if he tried anything, but he looked too beleaguered to do much beyond keeping his feet.

Ilbei leaned out over the edge. "All right, Meggins, here comes the hard part."

"Just get it done, Sarge," Meggins called back.

Ilbei began the work, drawing the rope taut, which prompted Meggins to stand up in clear view of the Skewer and that infernal crossbow. Ilbei waited until Meggins fired another shot, which sent the Skewer ducking behind his rock, then Ilbei started pulling him up. His arms and shoulders and hands were tired from the excruciating descent down the long vertical shaft, and though he pulled mightily and there was only one person's weight to lift, he could only pull him up so fast. He kept at it, cursing the fate that had let him think coming down this cliff had been hard not so long ago. The chore was a nasty encore in reverse.

Meggins tried to fire a few shots, but it was hopeless. Ilbei tugging on the rope made it difficult. Meggins' armor, the rope and his gear snagging on the rough surface of the cliff made it impossible. He bounced along as he went up, turned a quarter turn this way one moment, a half turn the other way the next. Aim was impossible, though he did his best. His next two shots went wide, far wide, the arrows spent uselessly.

Sparks erupted between Meggins' legs. He cringed.

"Sarge, that kiss you promised me might be on the cold lips of a dead man if you don't get a move on."

Ilbei pulled harder, but there was still so much farther to go. The other men were running full tilt toward the cliff now, and several of them had ranged weaponry that they could bring to bear from closer range. Two dropped to their knees and aimed crossbows as two more ran up even closer with shortbows in hand.

"Shite. Meggins, swing!" Ilbei called. "Don't just hang there, move." He kept dragging up the rope, hand over hand.

He could hear the clatter of all the bolts and arrows sent Meggins' way even as the rope twisted in his hands, the movement proving Meggins had begun to swing. He didn't think he had his man even halfway up yet.

Fear for Meggins began creeping in, threatening to distract him from the work, but he breathed deep and kept pulling. He looked around as he did, seeking inspiration, praying to Mercy for it.

It occurred to him that while his arms were tired and slow, his legs were not. "Hang on," he shouted. He gripped the rope tight, then ran, sidestepping across the ledge until it widened enough that he could square his hips and run full on. The moment he came even with the harpy cave, he darted in, sprinting for its depths and dragging the rope up behind him. The rope buzzed as it slid over the lip of stone, and Meggins came up and over so quickly that he rolled twice before coming to a stop. Ilbei, his piston legs still driving, was not ready for the change in drag, and he shot forward, plunging headlong into the dusty puff of the dried-out dung nest. He crashed into it, raising a putrid cloud of gray powder, and with it, the furious screech of the harpy, Miasma.

She leapt upon him with the reflexes of a beast, and her long, taloned hands wrapped around his throat so fast he had no time to react. He couldn't see her for the choking dust cloud and only knew it was her for the terrible shriek, the flapping sounds of her wings and the stench. He blinked and gasped and groped behind his back trying to reach for her, but she beat down upon him with her wings, the bones in them like cudgels battering his arms and ribs. The wind she stirred threw up more of the cloying powder, further blinding him, and he sucked it in with each gasping breath, choking on it. The power of her grip was incredible, and soon he wouldn't be able to do even that.

"Back off, harpy," Meggins snarled from behind Ilbei. His bow creaked as he drew it back. "Let him go, or I peg you to the wall." He advanced slowly, with balanced, measured strides, and the tip of that black arrow pointed right between her eyes.

She recoiled at the sight, whether of Meggins or of the bow, they'd never know, but she scrambled back and crouched defensively in front of her eggs, her arms out, her wings spread to hide them.

"Get up, Sarge, let's go." Meggins' voice was calm, but the urgency was apparent.

Ilbei crawled out of the crumbled heap of dung as quickly as he could. It gave way like dry rot beneath his knees, worse than crawling in sand. But he got out. He stumbled to his feet, still half-blind, his whole body coated with the stuff. Choking, he stumbled past Meggins, who backed away after him.

The harpy jumped from her nest, and just as she had before, she approached them in a low crouch, ready to plunge at them, ready to sweep them over the edge with those wide, powerful wings.

"Now what, Sarge?" Meggins asked. "Do I shoot her?"

Ilbei glanced back; they were only twenty steps from the edge, fifteen or so from being visible to the Skewer and the other men with their bows. He faced the harpy again. "Listen here, you. I'm fresh out of time to do all this over again." He took a half step forward and made to hold his ground. Resisting the temptation to draw his pickaxe, he put his hands on his hips instead. "Infernal creature, I'm not yer enemy."

She paused, crouching lower, her eyes narrowing. Ilbei couldn't decide which would be worse: choked to death by a harpy, shot in the back by a criminal or falling to his death off a cliff.

"Damn you!" he roared, and strode forward, reaching back for his pickaxe. "Get on back there, so I don't have to cut ya down. I don't mean ya no damn harm, ya surly, stinkin thing."

She shuffled back, growling that low, raspy growl.

"Now stay back there," Ilbei said, giving ground again, though just a step. "Just get back to tendin them eggs, while I figure out how to get my people out of here." He turned halfway around, then paused, looking back. "And if ya got half the brain Mags says ya do, you'll do likewise and get yerself and yer brood out too. This here is no place fer nobody, not even the likes of you."

She shifted her weight, and Ilbei leaned forward, his hand rising again toward the pickaxe on his back. "I swear ...," he said, but let it trail off. He backed up another step.

So did she.

"That's a smart lass," he said, giving a little more ground. Her wings lowered some and the growling stopped.

"So what now, Sarge? We're still up get-bent creek without a raft."

"Aye, we are. And I'm full bust fer ideas."

Ilbei pressed himself against the right-side wall, stooped low and crept toward the mouth of the cave. When he was close enough that standing upright would grant him a view down below, he popped up and risked a glance. Two arrows and a steel bolt whistled in, two *thwaks* and a *clank* against the stone in the instant after, as Ilbei ducked and rolled to the side.

"Well, our duck is plucked and near sizzlin," he said, regaining his feet.

"Well, Kaige will have them all up top by now. We could send him and the rest along to Hast, while you and I try to hold out until help arrives. Be a long wait, but it beats going out there and dying for sure."

"We ain't got the water fer a siege that long. And there's no tellin what they'd come up with down there in the meantime. Start throwin fireballs or somethin in here. Not to say what this cranky old bird back here would do if'n she seen us squattin in her cave."

"Sergeant," came a call from above. It was Jasper. "You'll want to make this quick."

"Don't rush me, son," Ilbei shouted back. "I'm workin it out now." Imagine Jasper having the gall to rush him. Jasper wasn't the one down here, pinned down by a horde of archers at one end and a snarling harpy at his back.

"No, Sergeant, I mean you'll want to hurry up here before it wears off. I don't think it's going to last very long. It's too warm down there, and whoever wrote this spell was only marginally competent."

Ilbei and Meggins exchanged glances, both confused.

"Jasper, what are ya talkin about?"

"Sarge," yelled down Kaige. "He casted some cover for you. Come on up. Hurry now."

Ilbei frowned at Meggins, who shrugged in reply. Together they crept toward the edge, stooping as Ilbei had done moments before, then, like tandem gophers, popped up to peer over the edge.

The cavern was filled with fog, a low blanket of it some ten spans deep and reaching nearly halfway to the bend. Looking down on it was like viewing clouds from the back of a gryphon. The mist was thick enough to conceal their movements, for no arrows flew up at them as they observed.

"By the gasses of Gore, would ya look at that. We're saved."

"Hurry," Mags called down.

Ilbei wasted no time and put his hand on Meggins' back. "Get on it, son. Let's go."

Meggins went out, cautious at first, still expecting missiles to zip out of the cloud beneath him, but soon he was on the rope, climbing hand over hand, his feet on the wall and Kaige drawing him upward with long, rhythmic pulls. The rope creaked, and his boots knocked pebbles loose, which soon brought arrows whizzing up at him. They clattered woodenly against the rock, but none struck so close to him that he lost his nerve. They were shooting blind down there.

The moment he was up, the rope dropped down again. Ilbei started for it, then stopped, turning back. "I'm serious what I said," he called back into the cave. "Get yer people out. We'll leave the ropes here. Since, well ... since yer kin can't fly no more."

He got no reply, which he expected, and then he started up the rope just as Meggins had. And just like Meggins, he was fired upon by the men below. Again the arrows—and two steel bolts—bounced all around him, one close enough to make him suck in a startled breath, but nothing worse.

Soon, Ilbei had rejoined his companions and his prisoner at the top of the cliff. He told Jasper to grab whatever important spells—healing, in particular—that he needed out of his trunk before they once again left it behind. Jasper didn't complain this time. He did as instructed, and then the lot of them hustled up the treacherous slope toward the hole in the cave wall. Cavendis screamed as they pushed him through the hole, the scraping and prodding aggravating his burns terribly, but Ilbei felt no sympathy. He glanced down at the two dead harpies lying at the base of the escarpment and figured those rotting bodies weren't remotely avenged in a bit of misery. No, Cavendis had made a bet and lost, and he'd incurred a debt far bigger than could be paid with that.

Once Cavendis was clear, Ilbei was the last to climb through. Now all they had to do was make it to the opening where the creek came out before their one torch, the remaining table leg, gave out. Ilbei thought that might be a stretch, and he really didn't want to stumble along in the dark.

Chapter 35

Ilbei didn't let them run down the tunnel, though he wished they could. They were too banged up for it, and Cavendis could never keep up that kind of pace. The young lord could barely stumble along, and he only did so because the pain of being helped, much less dragged or carried, was worse than carrying himself. His only relief came in those moments when they arrived at the intersection where the two caves merged, at which point he laid himself down in the creek and moaned.

Everyone gasped and panted as they took the time to rest, the lot of them sounding like a roomful of old bellows. Cavendis started to shake, a whole-bodied shivering that rendered him helpless, lying in the waterway. Ilbei cursed the luck and ordered Kaige to drag him out. "Read one of them short healin spells on him, Jasper. Make it quick. We're gonna be in the dark here pretty soon."

Jasper, tired and weakened by his own wound, didn't argue. He opened the satchel, pulled out a scroll and read it by the light of the torch, which Kaige held for him. Ilbei took the time to go back up the tunnel far enough to be out of the light, and he peered down into the blackness, looking for signs of pursuit. He was just beginning to think their luck had finally turned for the better, when the first speck of light appeared, then a second, and then two more, tiny and far away, like watching fireflies across a pond. The lights were coming steadily closer, but didn't move up and down in a way that suggested whoever carried them was running. Ilbei jogged back to where Jasper was still reading the spell, and huffed. He couldn't wait much longer before he'd have to interrupt.

"They're after us," he said to the rest of them. "And they're gonna see our light here pretty soon, and that will set them to runnin, like we can't."

They waited several more minutes, and still Jasper read. Ilbei ran back up the tunnel. It was only a minute before he could make out the lights. He ran back.

"One minute, that's all he gets." Ilbei waited, counting in his head.

Jasper finished the spell with barely ten seconds to spare. Cavendis actually thanked the wizard in his way, saying, "I won't have you killed with the rest of them."

Ilbei once more hurried them along, and after what had been barely ten minutes of rest, they were once again plunging downstream.

The cave was cool and water abundant, and despite such a brief rest, Ilbei thought they might make it without losing their light, which was right when it had its last sputter and went out.

He looked back into the darkness. He still couldn't see the lights carried by their pursuers. He didn't know if it was due to distance or some gentle bend. "Hands," he said. "Join hands, and keep goin. Meggins, you're up front. I'll come behind and drag our friend along." He took Cavendis by the rope that bound his wrist and locked his other hand with Jasper's, causing the mage to cry out. "I'm sorry, son. I know that hurts. We'll get to it quick as we can."

Cavendis laughed, then called out at the top of his lungs,

"Come on down, boys. They're all worn out. Put the spurs to it and—" Ilbei hit him so hard that he fell into the water with a splash.

Ilbei stood over him in the darkness, leaning down close enough to hear him breathe. "I got more'n enough left in me to drag yer carcass all the way back to Hast. You're gonna get there, one way or the other, I promise ya that. So how ya go is up to you."

Cavendis was too woozy to laugh, or perhaps he might have, but he offered no response at all. Ilbei didn't wait for the man's head to clear. He dragged him out of the water and reached for Jasper again, this time feeling for his robe and grabbing him by the belt. "That'll hurt less," he said, to which Jasper agreed.

It was a long string of hours in the darkness. Cavendis called out twice more to the men that were following them. Both times, Ilbei busted him in the head, and both times bought them a degree of silence for a time.

Cavendis was just beginning to murmur again, the blood filling his mouth giving his voice a liquid quality, when Meggins called back that he saw the opening. "There," he said. "Finally, the ever-loving daylight."

"Praise the goddess, there it is," Ilbei said. Like drooping blooms resurrected by a sunrise, the weary party found their energy again. Their pace quickened—all but Cavendis, who tried to lean back against Ilbei's hold on the ropes. For raw power, Cavendis was but a child beside Ilbei, and Ilbei yanked him forward so hard he landed face first in the shallows of the stream. Ilbei jerked him to his feet and tugged him along again, roughly when he had to, and soon they had reached the nearly blinding patch of daylight.

They hunkered down against the wall, and Ilbei considered how best to approach the hole. If some of the Skewer's men were still out there—or even the Skewer himself, perhaps sent back by that teleporting Ivan Gangue—

then they were trapped, caught between the proverbial dragon and the manticore. He didn't want to ask any of his men to be first to look out, so he handed Cavendis off to Kaige.

"Go ahead and bust him to sleep if he calls out again," Ilbei said. "I was only bein nice on account of us havin to run along in the dark."

"Sure thing, Sarge." Kaige gave Cavendis a great big grin and sat watching him hopefully.

Cavendis shook his head. His face was a bloody mess, and his lower lip was split wide open. "You're a few days from the headsman's axe, Spadebreaker, so enjoy your time while it lasts." His words were slurred by the blood and swelling.

"That count, Sarge?" Kaige asked.

"No."

Ilbei crawled up the hole, careful not to get into the water until he had to. He knew from having been outside that being in the water changed the flow, which would announce that he was there. He craned his neck, bobbed back and forth, looking out as far as he could see, which wasn't much, and crawled into the narrow opening.

The water backed up behind him, his broad frame filling the narrow passage fairly tight. He wondered if maybe it wouldn't have been smarter to send Meggins after all. But he was committed to it, so he kept on. The water rose up to his ribs as he squeezed toward the opening, splashing and whirling all around. It wasn't quite enough pressure to wash him out as it had Meggins the first time he came in, but it was enough to make Ilbei work to brace himself. If someone was taking aim at that hole when he stuck his head out, he was going to be the apple in the pig's mouth for the time it took to fight his way back in.

As he came to the edge, the heat of a hot summer day blasted him like opening an oven. He might have welcomed it after having been underground so long, but the anticipation of an arrow to the face takes those sorts of satisfactions away. With no other way to go about it, he drew in a breath and put his head outside.

There were Hams, Corporal Trapfast and the two new recruits, the sisters Decia and Auria. Sitting on the ground not far from the corporal were two other men, their feet and wrists bound and both of them looking miserable.

"Hams, by the gods, look at ya sittin there like sweet salvation on a hot rock!"

Hams swung round and saw Ilbei poking out of the turbulent spew. He waved, a big, welcoming smile on his face. "Well, you took too damned long in getting back, so we come looking for you. We tracked you this far and found these two. Me and Decia here was just arguing over who ought to go in there after you."

"Well, we're comin out. And we got a few fools behind meanin us no good. Like as not, there's others on the way from up the hill, so get all yer gear packed. We need to get movin quick." Hams waved in a way that confirmed he'd get right to it, and Ilbei went back to share the good news.

Once they'd gotten everyone out of the cave, they decided not to waste any more time than it took for Jasper to read healing spells for himself and Kaige. Mags insisted she was fine, and Ilbei did likewise, regaining strength mainly from a long draught off of Hams' wineskin.

Ilbei decided to cut a straight line for Hast, determined to keep clear of the trees and use the open country for speed. "They'll expect us to head fer the Desertborn," he said. "So let's just hightail it direct along the desert's edge like we planned."

It was agreed upon, and they loaded up as much water as they could carry—and no help to be had from the packhorse, which had wandered off beyond any range they cared to pursue. Soon enough, they were on their way to Hast, moving with all due haste. Ilbei wanted to gain the remainder of the day on those who were in pursuit.

By the time the cruel sun was slipping down behind the far end of the world, Ilbei and his company were exhausted. Grateful for the pleasant evening temperatures, they were able to sleep under the stars and spared the effort of pitching tents. Hams and his people volunteered to take all the night's watches, and for the first time in what felt like an eternity, they slept. Ilbei snored so loud the crickets wouldn't chirp for a quarter measure round.

When he woke the next morning and discovered that no one had come near in the night, he dared to think they might be on the brink of a genuine getaway, though he knew the day ahead would be a tough one. Cutting across the bottom fringes of the Sandsea would be rough. The heat would be terrible, if yesterday's temperatures were any indication, but after, they'd have an easy way of it and could make Hast two evenings hence if they wasted no time.

After a quick meal of snake-belly bacon, as Hams called it, and boiled apples, they were underway again, the party's spirits high—and kept that way for Cavendis' having been gagged again. He trundled along behind the group, tied to the other two prisoners like mules in a pack train. The nobleman looked absurd in one of the makeshift hats Hams had made for him and the other two. It was a wide, floppy thing, woven from deer grass, and Cavendis had sneered at it when Hams approached him with it. But the seasoned old cook had patted it down on his head anyway. "You can knock it off if you'd like," Hams had said. "But I won't pick it up again. If you die of heatstroke out here, I got no reason to mourn you." He glanced briefly about and added, "Doesn't seem like any of these others do either."

"I know I don't," Meggins said. "For all I care, he can lie out here until the vultures come pick his eyes out."

"Or the harpies do," Jasper said, feeling much better now

that his wrist was healed and they were on their way back to something approaching civilization. "They eat carrion as well, and they are, as you are aware, known to frequent the area." He made his odd breathy laugh and looked to Meggins for approval at his having entered the taunting fray.

Meggins rewarded him with a grin, saying, "Not much on delivery, Jasper, but the material was good." Jasper was more than satisfied with the assessment, and unfortunately for the rest, in its aftermath he felt suddenly quite companionable. This amicability resulted in a half-day monologue on the health and social benefits of humor, in particular in a hospital setting, which was, of course, derived from an extensive study he'd read only a few months ago in the Healers Guild publication *The Crown City Journal on Health*.

During the first part of Jasper's dissertation, the travelers were too eager to get home to interrupt, and by the time the morning was growing short and the sun had scaled the summit of the sky, they were too hot to expend any energy in cutting him off. And so he rambled on and on, the rest ignoring him and conserving their energy and water as they went along.

And then a long, silvery shaft of metal streaked by Meggins' head and plunged into the sand not far from Auria, who was walking alongside him being regaled by his stories and manifest charms. She stopped when she heard the *tick* of it sliding into the sand, then stooped and pulled it free. She studied it, twisting it so the light glinted down its length, her brows down low, having never seen such a thing. "What in the Queen's name is this?"

"Ain't the Queen, missy, that there is the Skewer." Ilbei had already spun round, scanning the shimmering sands behind them, his hand an extension of his helmet brim. "Can't see a damned thing," he said. "Glare is terrible. We need to get movin."

"There!" Mags called out. "East."

Ilbei turned and squinted that way. Sure enough, he could see riders coming through the blur of the heat rising off the sand. He counted eighteen.

"Tidalwrath's teeth! That's damn near a score of them bastards, and mounted."

"I didn't think there were that many horses up there," Meggins said. "Where were they hiding them?"

"Who knows? But we're in fer it now."

Another steel crossbow bolt flew in. It landed only inches from the corporal's feet. The corporal pulled his bow off his back. Meggins and Decia readied theirs right after. Auria pulled a boomerang from her belt, at which Ilbei shook his head. But it didn't much matter what they used; those bows, that boomerang, none of them had the range to compete with the Skewer's mighty crossbow but one. Only Meggins' could, and Ilbei saw straight away he only had six of the enchanted black arrows left.

"Make yer shots count, people."

Hams moved up to stand beside Ilbei, carrying a javelin in each hand. "You want one?" he asked.

Ilbei shook his head. "I'm worse with them things than I am at tavern darts."

"I'm not," Kaige said. Hams tossed him one. Kaige hefted it in a way that assured Ilbei the man had thrown a lot of them, and that gave him cause to hope. Maybe they could get clear of this fight too. He couldn't say he hadn't expected something like this, but he had allowed himself hope that they would have a bit longer stretch of luck. He should have known better, what with them having a teleporter on hand.

The sun hit the incoming shaft on the way in, and Meggins stepped out of its way just in time. It would have cut straight through his heart. "Why's he picking on me?" he said. "What did I ever do?"

"I expect it's that bow of yers," Ilbei said. "Though I'm

surprised he can even make out which one of us ya are from there. Never seen anythin shoot that far."

"Well, he's still out of my range," Meggins said. "But not for long."

Soon after, the exchange began. They did have the advantage of the sunlight lighting up streaks of the Skewer's bolts for a time, at least so long as he was relying on the arc. But it wasn't long before he was able to level the weapon and fire straight on.

Meggins sent an arrow at him when he was just outside of a hundred spans. The Skewer dodged sideways, leaning in his saddle, and the arrow blasted the rider behind him off his horse. Meggins cheered. "I'll take luck over skill any day! Seventeen to go." Then he swore and staggered back, one of the long crossbow bolts through his side, in through the left side of his stomach and protruding three full hands out the back.

"Meggins!" Kaige cried, and both he and Mags rushed to the man.

"Jasper, can ya get us another one of them fog spells?" Ilbei asked. No reply followed, and Ilbei spun left, then right, afraid that he would find Jasper lying dead with one of those wicked steel shafts in him. But Jasper merely gaped into the distance, his pale flesh whiter than usual, transfixed by fear, seemingly unwilling to believe they were in combat again. "By the gods, man! Jasper, snap to."

Jasper turned, blinking as if just awakened from a dream.

"Fog, son. Can ya do the fog trick again?"

Jasper looked as if he were trying to recall something from the most distant past, but slowly began to shake his head. One of the Skewer's arrows whistled past, right over his shoulder, and buried itself a half-span deep in the sand less than a pace away. Fortunately, the addled wizard didn't realize what it was. "I can, but the heat will burn it off too fast." He turned numbly toward the oncoming charge. "I don't think I can get it read in time."

"Well, we're in the jaws of it, then. Here they come."

Another steel shaft shot straight through Jasper's satchel as he fumbled in it, looking for anything he might use. The force of the impact drove through the thrown-back flap, the front cover, the interior divider, and the back cover, all of them. And despite the layers of leather shielding, it managed to pierce the skin of the slender wizard's hip, though hardly deeper than the first joint of his little finger. Still, one might have thought he'd been decapitated and thrown in burning oil for how he screamed, falling to the sand and writhing about in agony.

The horsemen were within forty spans, and that was close enough for Ilbei. He drew his pickaxe and charged. "Ain't waitin fer another one," he said, and ran through the sand as fast as his bowlegged strides would carry him, angling side to side as randomly as he could, intent on making himself at least marginally hard to shoot. He saw the shadow pass just as he prepared to heave his pickaxe at the Skewer, and there came across the line of riders a streak of black and gray. Miasma!

The harpy swooped across the riders, unleashing an awful shriek. She tore the Skewer out of his saddle and dashed him against the man riding at his side. Then she loosed a wet spray of urine and foul excrement as she passed over, a yellow, spewing mist with flecks of black and gray. Ilbei could smell it immediately, and he was still twenty spans away. It was so foul it gagged him and stopped him in his tracks. His eyes burned with its acridity, and he staggered, choking, to his knees. He thought he might stop the gagging by force of will, but he couldn't, and for a moment he simply knelt there, his hands driven wrist deep into the hot sand, precariously balanced in the place between vomiting and not.

The horses were screaming, the terrified neigh such

creatures normally save for pain, though none of them had been physically hurt. They reared and jumped and kicked out their hind legs, leaping and spinning, their eyes as wide as hens' eggs, bucking and snorting as they scattered every which way. Their riders, had they been able to even think about trying to stay in their saddles, were not up to it, and they fell to the sand and rolled about, palming at their eyes and gagging as if befouled by some choking gas. They arced and writhed and vomited, a terrible sound.

Kaige, Hams, Corporal Trapfast and the sisters all ran up toward Ilbei, but they staggered to a halt a few steps short of him, as if they'd run into a wall. They may as well have, for how unbearable it was. Ilbei could hear them choking, just as he still was.

Kaige bore through it anyway and, holding his breath, ran forward three more steps and launched the javelin Hams had given him. The long, iron-tipped spear flew in a graceful arc, a black streak on the clear blue sky, then plummeted down again, pinning one man to the sand and ending his choking misery. Decia backed off a few steps from where she'd stopped and took a knee. She too went to work on their enemy with her bow, taking careful aim and striking down two of them in her first three shots.

The harpy, that foul and wonderful Miasma, swung back and let the thrashing horsemen have another blast of ... of that indescribable spew. She loosed the foul contents of her body on them as she loosed a cry of the most frightful sound. Ilbei looked up, his stomach in his throat, and watched her soar up after and begin to fly away. He thought she might have looked back at him, but soon she was lost to sight, climbing her way up toward the sun, driving for altitude with long, graceful strokes of her wings.

Around the tumor of bile that grew in his throat, he called out for his companions to finish the enemy quick. Once that fetid cloud was gone, the advantage would be lost.

Kaige called for Hams' other javelin, as the old man was still trying to force himself deeper into the edge of that invisible, noxious cloud. Hams could not match Kaige for range, not by forty spans at least. Arrows flew from Decia and the corporal's bows, and Kaige's second shot was true.

The men that remained were crawling away. Crawling like broken, impotent scorpions across the scalding sand, painting stripes of vomit like wakes behind.

Ilbei got to his feet and tried to move up to where Kaige was, but his eyes burned as if he'd stuffed his face into a forge. "All nine hells!" he muttered, and, coughing, he fell back again.

He saw the Skewer stagger to his feet and lumber drunkenly away, his monstrous crossbow gripped uselessly by one steel arc, its butt dragging in the sand. Ilbei wanted desperately to give chase, but he didn't want to overplay his hand. The harpy queen had given them the victory: best to take the pot they'd won.

So he did. He turned and saw that Mags had gotten Jasper to quiet down. She was just beginning to get him to his feet. Meggins was worse off by far. Ilbei grimaced, seeing that. He had to get his weary people back to Hast. And he had to get Cavendis to the justice he was due. All of this was his fault, a lying lord, a nobleman slaver and a cheat. He would pay for all of this. And if Ilbei's testimony amounted to anything, Cavendis would pay for it with his life.

Chapter 36

Ilbei's testimony did not amount to anything.

Traveling to Hast took them two and a half days after the encounter with the Skewer, and by the time they arrived, Cavendis had already been pardoned. A full pardon, waiting for him and broadly allowing for anything he might have done. He'd been pardoned before he'd been charged. Ilbei discovered it almost the first moment he and his company entered the garrison.

General Hanswicket was actually waiting for him on the front steps of the squat stone command building when Ilbei brought his prisoner in. Ilbei had delayed only long enough to see that Meggins, stabilized by Jasper's magic but in desperate need of a real healer for his terrible wound, was delivered into the proper hands. Then he dragged Cavendis by his bindings straight to the general. And despite his haste and urgency, it was already too late.

"This here is the worst snake what ever slid under a rock," he told the general as he approached. "He's a murderin, slavin, thievin, officer-impersonatin cheat what fouls the pool of his own noble blood fer every lyin breath he takes. He's done got—"

"Sergeant," the general said, cutting Ilbei off with a raised, gauntleted hand. "We've been made aware of Lord Cavendis' ... excesses, and Lady South Mark has come to see to his discipline personally." As he said it, an angular form stepped out from the shadowy interior of the command building, a tall, slender woman, regally dressed, her coiffeur on high and her icy gaze peering down at Ilbei from altitudes loftier than any that could be measured by a count of stairs.

"But General," Ilbei said. "All other laws buried and ignored, he was impersonatin an officer in *Her Majesty's* army, and I'm half-sure he was doin some kind of counterfeitin of *Her Majesty's* currencies too, though I can't make out how exactly all that worked. Surely, all that can't be ignored, even if the rest don't matter to nobody what's got the noble blood. Her Majesty has got to be informed. This here villainy didn't take place in South Mark."

"Sergeant!" This was pronounced with the strike of a thunderclap. "You will know your station or know the lash."

"But General," Ilbei pressed. "It's the law. The Queen must be notified of crimes perpetrated in her name."

"She's been notified, Sergeant. And she'll see to it by and by."

"By and by, sar?"

"By her authority, Sergeant, and if you utter another word, I'll tie you to the whipping post myself."

Ilbei glared up at him, his eyes stark lines, as straight and narrow as his lips. His teeth ground together, and for the second time in recent days, he found himself trying not to choke on something vile. But the general's countenance was a mask of discipline, and Ilbei saw something in the way his eyebrows moved that suggested Ilbei ought to let it go.

He turned his gaze on the great lady, the Marchioness of South Mark herself, and she matched his scrutiny and the slatted contempt in his eyes with hauteur that he could never manage, even if he should somehow live a thousand years. But she spoke in a level, measured voice. "Release my son, Sergeant. Do it now." Her gaze flicked briefly to Lord Cavendis like the tips of a forked tongue, and Ilbei thought she was not pleased with him.

Cavendis smirked when Ilbei took out his knife to cut the ropes. "Maybe next time, eh, Spadebreaker? If you live that long. I'm coming for you, you know." He said it low enough that it confirmed Ilbei's suspicions about Cavendis having incurred his mother's wrath.

"Go on with it, Your Lordship, if'n ya think you're man enough," Ilbei whispered back. "Soon as yer mum there is done paddlin yer behind." He cut the ropes and gave Cavendis a shove toward the general on the steps. "There he is, sar. A feller what butchers and slaves harpies, steals Her Majesty's gold right out under the royal nose, and does it wearin that same uniform you and I both got on and swore to honor. Yes, sar, I'm turnin the prisoner over as commanded, sar. Will that be all, sar."

The general's face narrowed, a storm rustling in the wrinkles above his dark brows. Ilbei knew he'd pushed the line far beyond what an intelligent man would have, but it was all he could do not to finish Cavendis right there, much less hold back the fire burning in his guts.

The general looked to the marchioness, who whisked at the air with a long, nearly skeletal hand, waving Ilbei away. She turned away from the gesture herself, as if having Ilbei in her sight was an irritation—although there was part of him that wondered if some of that might be for her son. Either way, with that, he knew he was clear of it for now.

He turned and went away, rejoining the rest of his companions, shaking his head and staring at the dirt.

"What is it?" Mags asked upon seeing dejection so apparent.

"They're not gonna do nothin to him. He's off of it

already, as if all he'd done was loosed a fart in church. That marchioness is gonna frown at him until the general's gone, and after, like as much, nothin. Nothin at all."

"What?" Kaige looked as if Ilbei had just told him that the Queen had rabies and sprouted antlers from her behind. "But, Sarge, he ...." He couldn't conjure the words to encompass it all.

"Aye, lad," Ilbei agreed. "He did."

"Well, that doesn't make any sense," Mags said. "Can't we do something? Can't we petition the Queen?"

"She already knows. General says she'll be seein to it on her own time. With all that gold up there, I expect it will be soon enough."

"But what about Cavendis? That's preposterous!"

"It's the way of things," Ilbei grumbled. "Them high folks will do as they please, and that's just how it works. Ya can go on and poke about, try to dredge up some kind of somethin, but I don't know what it is ya expect you're gonna find or who you're gonna find it from. The world's been workin the same way all along. High folks tend to high business, and low folks try not to draw no notice to theirselves. Leastways, the smart ones do. The squirrel don't fight the dragon if'n he's got more'n a nut fer brains."

"But it's not right," Mags said again. She turned to Jasper, Hams and Kaige standing near her. "It's not. We have to do something!" The big man and the old cook nodded that they agreed, but the wizard simply shrugged.

"Actually, Sergeant Spadebreaker is correct on that point," Jasper said. "It is a long-standing truth that the nobility, by right, by birth, by simple wealth, do as they please. It's perfectly legal. Anyone who's ever read a book of history can tell you that. Why, I once read that Korgon the—"

"Jasper, please." Ilbei's interruption was enough to cut Jasper off, despite how uncharacteristically weary the tone of it was. He looked them each in the eyes, gratefully. "You're good people," he said. "Get some rest. Right now, that's the right thing to do. We'll see about doin somethin else when our minds are fresh."

"Well, I know what we should do," Mags said. "If we can't do anything about Cavendis, there is something else. Something more important, anyway."

"What's that?"

"We should go back and see to those harpies."

"We should what?" That came from everyone but Ilbei, who was too tired for surprise, and perhaps not surprised at all.

"We should go back and help them."

"How?"

"We should get them out. Before Her Majesty sends her own people in. You know what will happen to them."

"Her Majesty won't keep slaves. That's against the law," Kaige said.

"It's not illegal in South Mark," Jasper put in. "At least, not exactly." He started to explain the complicated details of the Unification charters, but realized by the eleventh word that no one was looking at him and the conversation had already moved on.

"She won't keep them as slaves," Mags was saying as Jasper's words died upon his lips. "But will the troops she sends spare them? Will an army of men sent to take possession of the mines for the crown be any different than the men who are already there?"

Ilbei started to answer that, but stopped. He'd known a lot of soldiers in his time. And a lot of huntsmen. Animal trainers. Miners. Men of all types. Not all of them saw life or heard their consciences the same. He'd never met anyone besides Mags who thought of a harpy as anything other than an animal. Until two or three days ago, he'd been no different.

431

"No," he said. "I expect they won't. A whole lot of harpies is all they'll see. Worse than orcs, when it comes to it."

"Technically," Jasper said, "they aren't. Orcs are fundamentally more aggressive than harpies, and while both species have been known to kill and eat humans, orcs have ritualized the practice, although not all bother with ritual, and certainly depending on which clan. I read that the northern clans are ...." He let his voice trail off again, realizing that everyone had walked away—all but Mags, who remained, waiting for him to finish what he was going to say, or at least until he realized they'd all gone but for her.

She smiled and put a gentle hand on his arm. "Sergeant says he's going to clean up and head into town. He promised to buy us all a drink."

"But I don't want a drink. I want to know what he's going to do about the harpies. What if he decides to go back and makes us all go with him? What if he makes me go with him? I can't possibly relax until I know what he intends to do."

She smiled, a patient thing. "Jasper, what do you think he's going to do?"

Jasper thought about that for a moment. "Oh dear," he said.

Mags nodded, her smile widening. She gave his arm a squeeze and tugged it gently in the direction the others had gone. "Maybe now you'll want that drink."

The End

432

For more information about the author, his
other novels and his works in progress, please visit
DaultonBooks.com.

If you would like to be notified when
new releases are made available, sign up for the
Daulton Books newsletter.

CPSIA information can be obtained at www.ICGtesting.com
Printed in the USA
LVOW10s1141080615

441602LV00003B/388/P

9 780989 478724